Oliver Sta   As a
teenager,   nade
his first at   say,
this never reached publication.

After trying a wide variety of jobs, from working in a bookies to
managing   went
on to stud   ook in
Oliver's cr   Levene. His
debut novel, *American Devil*, was published in 2010. Oliver lives in
London with his wife and children.

Praise for *American Devil*:

'Impressive . . . written with pace and a delicate feel for the darker
shadows of the American psyche . . . Stark is an exceptional new
British talent' *Daily Mail*

'A remarkable debut by a British writer who captures the mood and
setting of New York brilliantly . . . Powerful and thrilling' *Peterborough
Evening Telegraph*

'Tightly plotted, intricately planned, not a loose end or an unexplained
action or clue anywhere, great characters, great pace, twists and turns
aplenty . . . and an exciting and thrilling climax which had me on the
end of my seat' Elaine Simpson-Long, *Random Jottings*

'Well written, paced steadily with a climactic finish and chock full of
thoughtfully crafted characters . . . Stark delivers an aptly stark
portrayal of the modern-day psychopath' *The Truth About Books*

'Stark holds his own in a debut that focuses on characterization and
has a villain certainly creepy enough to keep the pages turning . . . [His]
confidence and careful attention to the internal lives of his characters
add another layer to the hunt for this killer . . . Solid and scary'
bookgeeks.co.uk

'An assured debut, suggesting that Oliver Stark is a name we will hear
a great deal more from' *Material Witness*

By Oliver Stark and available from Headline

American Devil
88 Killer

Oliver
Stark

88 KILLER

headline

First published in 2011 by
HEADLINE PUBLISHING GROUP

1

Cataloguing in Publication Data is available from the British Library

ISBN 978 0 7553 7014 6

Typeset in Palatino by Avon DataSet Ltd,
Bidford-on-Avon, Warwickshire

Printed and bound in Great Britain by
Clays Ltd, St Ives plc

To my family

Hate isn't only a feeling. Sometimes it's an inheritance.

'Certainly there is no hunting like the hunting of man, and those who have hunted armed men long enough and liked it, never really care for anything else thereafter.'

Ernest Hemingway, April 1936

Prologue

Forest Park, Queens, New York
February 26, 5.14 p.m.

Abigail Goldenberg crossed Park Lane South as the delivery truck pulled out of a side street. The truck hit the brakes. Abby heard the loud squeal of tyres and jerked herself to a halt halfway across the street. She looked up at the driver, grimaced an apology and then felt her pulse start to hammer in her chest like an aftershock.

Inside the cab, two guys with long hair and baseball caps cursed and gesticulated. Some crude joke passed between them. Abby watched as their anger turned to lewd laughter. Then the window rolled down. 'If you want to be laid on your back, just climb on board, baby.'

Abby was sixteen and beautiful. She'd learned to deal with unwanted attention both politely and assertively. Smiling sweetly, she raised a middle finger and told them to swivel.

Abby then ran across the rest of the street and headed down towards Forest Park. She glanced behind her. These guys sometimes came back around for a second bite. She saw the truck disappear into the distance and was reassured.

She walked fast, scanning the edge of the woods, and soon spotted the broken wire fence. She had done most of the damage herself ever since she'd found the short cut. She jumped over the wire and pulled herself up the bank, holding on to a young sapling.

Abby could have walked the long way round to the bus stop on Myrtle Avenue. Reason told her that it was the right thing to do. It

1

was getting late, the light was fading and there were rain clouds overhead. Sure, she should have stuck to the sidewalks, surrounded by passing traffic in the safe orange glow of the street lights, but since when did Abby follow reason? Reason was something to be kept for when you were older and bored with life's experiences.

The clincher, though, was that the long route added twenty minutes on to her journey, and twenty minutes was way too long for an impatient girl trying to go see her favorite band in Manhattan and get home before her daddy found out.

Abby's secret trip to Manhattan had required subterfuge. It helped that her father, an academic who could tell whether you'd stolen a line in your essay from some Internet article on the causes of the Second World War at a hundred paces, still couldn't use a cell phone without help.

Sitting in her bedroom, she had called the house phone from her cell. She ran to answer it herself, down in the living room, right next to where Daddy was sitting.

There was no one on the line, of course, and Abby loved to act the whole conversation from beginning to end. She had held the phone close to her ear and listened for a moment. 'Hi, Suse, babe, how's things?'

Abby spoke, paused and spoke again, all the time watching her daddy's reaction. She played out a whole urgent scenario within his hearing. Suse had a test, was desperate for help, the only person in the world who could help her was Abby and the only person who could let Abby out was Daddy, so the fate of Suse all rested on his shoulders. Abby then stared across the living room wide-eyed, sweet and smiling.

Daddy had said yes. Of course.

Abby headed into the woods until the traffic was just a distant hum, and it was so dark that the uninitiated would have had trouble finding their way out again. She didn't care about that, though. She'd tramped the short cut so often that she could've done it blindfolded and backwards.

Abby was a free spirit like her mother, who had been living in New Jersey for the past twelve years with a succession of rich men.

It wasn't a quality her father admired but it was one he knew he had to live with. Abby ran wild at times, but she wasn't entirely stupid – she always carried what she called her 'Brooklyn dating kit': a charged cell, a rape alarm and a canister of pepper spray.

She pushed on until she reached a small clearing by a hollow tree. She checked her messages, took off her school bag that she'd packed with revision textbooks, and pushed it inside the tree trunk. Her jumper came off next, in one swift movement, to reveal a faded black T-shirt emblazoned with a grainy image of The Cramps. Next, she kicked off her shoes, pulled off her old jeans and rolled down a short red tartan skirt that she'd hidden from her father by twisting it up above her hips.

She placed her school clothes inside a plastic bag, put on a pair of old pink sneakers, let down her ponytail and ruffled her hair. Now she was ready for the gig and anything else life was going to throw in her path. If it wasn't an adventure, what was the point?

The rain started as she was trying to apply dark lines of kohl around each eye, which was never easy in the dark. She had hoped she'd have made it to the tunnel on Myrtle before the deluge. No such luck. A clap of thunder was followed by a sudden cloudburst.

She put her make-up back in her small canvas shoulder bag and started to run for the bus. The dense green canopy held back the worst of the rain, but the drops that got through hit her bare arms and legs.

After a few yards of running, she ran out of steam and slowed her pace. The woods were dark in every direction and she was alone, creeping through the undergrowth. She looked up towards the path ahead. Something flickered in the dark and she paused momentarily. There was something in the woods – a light, a flashlight or something. She felt very alert all of a sudden, with every nerve and muscle taut. Her eyes watched the light. It moved left and right and then started to move towards her, like a Cyclops's eye.

Abby darted behind a tree. When she looked ahead again, the light had gone, but her skin was covered in goose bumps.

She listened out. There was nothing but the sound of water

dripping from the high leaves. Her breathing was shallow and her body was tingling with adrenalin. She looked at her cell phone. Should she call someone? Who would she call? What would she say? She couldn't call her father. She couldn't call anyone. Maybe she should just turn back.

She stood still as the cold air and rain started to make her shake. No, she was too far into the woods and she was only five minutes from Myrtle. Maybe the light was just a car turning on the road. Yes, that must be it. She let her mind be reassured.

Abby walked with a slight shiver, her head jerking about in every direction. She felt underdressed. She took ten quick steps, and then heard a noise off to her right. She stopped, panting but trying to make no sound. What was it? An animal? Her mind started to grow fears. Suddenly everything seemed alien and frightening and able to swallow her up. She shouldn't have left the sidewalk. She wanted to whimper like a lost child, but told herself to be strong.

'It's nothing, Abby,' she said aloud to herself. 'You're a hundred yards from the street.' She started to walk again. Could someone have followed her into the woods from Park Lane South? Could someone be stalking the woods? To her right, about ten meters ahead, a twig snapped. It was a definite noise, not some figment of her imagination. Abby crouched down and listened.

She remembered her father's protective hand on her shoulder as she left the house. 'Promise me you'll be back by eleven.'

'Shouldn't even be that long,' Abby had said.

'You always say that and you're never home by twelve. Eleven, all right, honey? I mean it. I love you, Abby.'

She turned around again, trying to see into the darkness, opening her eyes wide as though that might help. She felt as if someone was watching her. Maybe it was the two guys from the truck? The thought made her panic. Maybe they had turned and parked up, tracked her and now were waiting ahead of her. She was so far from help. If she screamed, no one would hear. She edged towards a tree. Her hand reached into her canvas bag. She pulled out her pepper spray and flipped back the lid. With the other hand, she held her rape alarm.

She couldn't hear much outside the beating of her pulse loud in her ear. A sound again, somewhere behind her now. Circling? Was it a man, two men, more?

A high wind brushed through the leaves and Abby thought she heard a voice. It seemed to say her name. Was it just the wind? She stood again, pepper spray ready.

She was finding it hard to concentrate properly. Then a voice cried out, 'Abby!' high in the trees. Was she losing her mind? Was it her father? Had he started to look for her for some unknown reason? It was possible, wasn't it?

'Daddy!' she shouted. 'Daddy!'

She heard bushes move to her left, then to her right came another sound. No one replied. *Please. Please let it be Daddy.*

She remained still for what seemed like several minutes, but nothing happened and she started to think she had made the whole thing up. The voices had stopped. She tried to pull herself together. Reasoned it out. 'Nothing's happened, Abby. Nothing. You've just frightened yourself half to death.' She smiled as best she could. 'Come on. It's animals and the wind, nothing more.'

She stepped out on to the path, telling herself, 'Just keep walking.' Shadows from the canopy above flickered dark under the moon, making the path ahead appear to shift. 'It's just the wind and the moon. Guilt – that's what it is. This is your punishment for deceiving Daddy.'

She walked a little faster, and then up ahead saw the street lights of Myrtle Avenue appear through the trees.

'Thank you!' she said, lifting her head to the heavens. 'Thank you.'

She almost ran towards the gate ahead, pushing the cap closed on her pepper spray and ramming her rape alarm back into her bag. As she approached the last row of trees, beyond them she could see the wooden posts that marked the exit. She'd never been so delighted to hear the rumble of traffic.

Two trees ahead, a flashlight appeared from nowhere and danced in her eyes. She froze and called out, 'Who's there?'

Suddenly, the world seemed to tighten around her. A large

shadow loomed behind the beam of the flashlight. The light darted across her face then down over her body and on to her legs. 'Daddy.' It was a prayer, not a question.

'Abby,' said a low, deep voice, closer now. A hand reached out and unfamiliar skin touched her shoulder.

She screamed and turned, and in a moment, she was running back into the woods, twisting through thick undergrowth. She ran until she fell and lay, cut, bruised and sobbing on the wet earth. Beside her was a thicket. She crawled into the center of it, her arms and face scratched and bleeding. She picked out her cell with shaking hands. It fumbled out of her fingers into the dirt. She felt around in the dark and found it. She was panting and sniffing and shaking. The phone lit up. It was so bright in the darkness. She looked up, afraid, and tried to hide her phone while attempting to make a call. But she couldn't find the right keys. She tried again.

A beam from a flashlight swept across the bushes and crossed her legs. She shrank away as if from physical pain. The light came back across and hit her again, right through the thicket and into her eyes. It remained trained on her face.

She couldn't see what it was, but she could hear something pushing through the bushes. She retreated further into the thicket.

She felt a hand on her leg. It grabbed and tightened around her ankle. She screamed, held on to a branch as her body was dragged out. She kicked at his hand, but he jerked hard and her hands slipped off the branch, her body sliding over wet leaves and sharp twigs. She was crying out but her voice no longer made any noise.

He dragged her to her feet. She felt his palms circle her neck, his two thumbs hard on her throat. He was strong and not even breathing heavily. Her eyes remained open. She didn't fight him; instead she was fumbling in her canvas bag. Her hand found the pepper spray and flipped back the lip. She tried to see his face. She wanted to have something to tell the cops.

Her right hand rose out of the darkness and she sprayed the pepper directly at his face. The hiss of the spray was followed by an angry cry of pain. He yelled and let her go momentarily, but he lashed out hard with his arm, catching her full on the cheek.

6

She crumpled to the ground and the pepper spray flew from her hand. She tried to get to her feet to run, but he grabbed her and held her. He coughed and spluttered to his knees, but he didn't let go of her. He let himself recover with her body beneath his.

He finally stopped coughing and his hands returned to her neck and tightened. The blood beat hard in her temples. The pressure just kept building. Then her mind went white, her eyes misted over and she faded out of consciousness. The last thing she remembered was his cologne. There was something about it. It smelled familiar.

PART ONE

Chapter One

Jules Gym, Lower Manhattan
March 6, 8.12 p.m.

A tattooed arm swung in fast from the right and connected with a thud of leather. The guy in the red shorts took the full force of the blow on the point of his chin; his head jerked up and he staggered three steps backwards on to the ropes, then tucked his head between his gloves. The attacker strode across and started to pummel his body repeatedly.

In the faded ring, the boxers had been going two rounds, fighting toe-to-toe, trading uppercuts, right and left hooks, and body blows. Under their head guards, each guy's face was bubbling up with bright red bruises.

The audience whooped at every big punch that landed. It was not difficult to imagine that the head guards didn't so much protect as prolong the time in which each man was getting his brain pounded. But it was a precinct grudge match, honor was at stake and neither boxer was going to stand down. The big crowd roared their approval, jumping, shouting, spitting and drinking like a bunch of out-of-control rioters.

The NYPD's fight night was in full swing and it was brutal.

Through the double doors into the locker rooms, the narrow, airless corridor was tiled in blue and black. Inside the third locker room the next fighter prepared, listening to the excited bloodlust of the crowd. The air was coarse with the smell of sweat, and the striplight above, twenty years' deep with dead insects and dust, shed a clouded yellowing light on the fighter below.

Detective Tom Harper of the NYPD's Homicide Division tried to focus. He caught the image of the majestic peregrine falcon in his mind's eye. He'd spotted the raptor earlier in the day, perched imperiously on one of the pylons of the Brooklyn Bridge. The peregrine was a skilled hunter. It flew way up high and watched the world below, unnoticed and unseen until it sighted its prey.

The fight was ten minutes away. On the white clock-face ahead, the seconds ticked past, but Harper could only see the raptor.

There was a great roar from the gym; it rattled the doors, which hung loose on their hinges. Someone had gone down. The crowd loved a knockout – they loved to see someone hit so hard that the brain would momentarily lose motor control and the body twist and sink like a bag of cement.

The roar faded and Harper was left with the silence, the bare red brick of the locker room and the ingrained smell of male sweat. He shifted on the bench. He needed to feel ready for the fight, was waiting for the trigger – anger or a sense of injustice – but all he felt was the cold air, the hard bench and the fear trickling slowly through his veins.

He tried to imagine his glove landing on his opponent's jaw, tried to imagine hitting someone into submission, but the image faded as fast as it appeared. If you couldn't imagine beating someone, then how the hell could you go out and do it?

There was a loud smacking sound as Dylan, the all-in-one corner man, manager and trainer, chewed his gum. Harper looked down at the man taping up his fists. 'Can't you cut that out?' he said.

Dylan looked up, his unshaven face pockmarked. 'The champ feeling a little tetchy tonight?'

'Just trying to focus here,' said Harper. He exhaled slowly. Ahead of him, a boxer in red satins stared out from a torn poster, his shining gloves held high, his body tense and ready. Harper tapped his booted feet on the floor. 'Let's just get this done.'

Three years ago, Harper had made NYPD Cruiserweight Champion. He'd beaten an opponent who was bigger and heavier.

Harper had had reserves that night, and he'd wanted it bad. Now he didn't know what he was doing here. Rusty and tired even before he stepped into the ring. Maybe that was the problem – three years of rust was making his muscles feel dull and heavy.

From somewhere beyond the small room, both men heard another roar echoing down the corridor. Harper's muscles twitched. He imagined the referee lifting the winner's arm, the loser standing beaten. Avoiding failure used to be Harper's main motivation. It'd been three months since the end of his last big case. A tough case. And three months since he'd seen Denise Levene. And that hurt too.

Guilt still kept him from sleeping. He'd brought Levene on to the case – she'd impressed him, she was smart and eager. She knew things about criminal behavior that no one else seemed to understand. They'd worked well together. Then it all went wrong. The killer targeted Denise Levene and kept her for two terrible days. For three months since, Harper had been unable to put the monster to rest inside his own head and Denise Levene wouldn't speak to him or see him. And without forgiveness you can't go forward, you can only keep punishing yourself.

Out at ringside, the first bout was cleared. The ring was mopped of sweat and blood as more cops poured in from the street for the main event. They were there to see the ex-champ Harper take on the new boy Castiglione. Harper had retired as champ, had never been beaten and word was, he wanted his title back. People of all ages, from the old vets to the fresh-faced rookies, began opening beers and jostling for space on the battered wooden benches.

In the locker room, Harper thought about the weeks of preparation and training. He'd pushed himself hard, working long shifts at North Manhattan Homicide and then carrying on with lengthy sessions at the gym.

Cops weren't supposed to be affected by what happened to them, they were supposed to move on to the next case, the next body. The reality was different. The cops Harper knew hid their weaknesses. The hardening of the heart was the price you paid for being in the game, but every cop knew that underneath, every damn thing stuck in deep and clawed away at you. Awake, you could control your fears, but asleep, there was nothing at all between you and the abyss.

Harper stood up, his gloves on and laced. He was in good physical shape – six two with broad shoulders and toned muscles. His age showed only in the gray flecks in his hair.

Pushing his mouth guard in, he gritted his teeth and let himself be led out of the room into the darkness beyond. They walked slowly up the narrow corridor as the noise of the crowd grew louder and louder, the heavy beat of stamping feet rising to meet them.

The door to the gym opened up, the noise doubled in a moment and hit them like a wave. There was no fancy music, no fancy name. Just Tom Harper who had demons to face and had decided he'd try to face them in the place he knew he could fight best. The ring.

He looked across at Marco Castiglione pacing his territory. He was a short, bullish patrol cop with a mean and hungry look in his eye, who was out to prove himself. Once upon a time, Harper had been that guy.

As Harper walked towards the ring, the cops started shouting his name, rising from their seats and patting his back as he passed. He pushed the top rope high and stepped through on to the canvas, standing opposite the young Italian, who was shadow boxing in his corner.

The referee walked up and stood between the two men. The fighters came together. Harper held up his gloves, but stared right through Marco Castiglione's direct gaze. Denise Levene was still in his head, back in the dungeon, the face of the killer behind her. Fragments of his nightmares kept breaking in.

From ringside, Harper's partner Eddie Kasper slurped on a beer and leaned back, his arm curling around the shoulder of the cop next to him. 'My man is going to slay this guy,' Eddie boasted. 'It's going to be brutal. I've got a hundred dollars here that says so.'

In the ring, Tom Harper felt a wall of fear rise up like never before. It was like a sudden freeze, turning his muscles to waste and leaving his mind in flashes of white-frosted panic.

But time had run out. The bell rang three times and, from across the ring, Castiglione approached like a beast from the shadows.

Chapter Two

He sat in his car opposite the building, waiting. He had been watching for three hours, his focus on the door of the club. His hands were cold now. He held them out in front of his face and looked at them closely. Thin and elegant, like a pianist's, his nails were cut and filed. He liked all aspects of his life to be neat, ordered and clean.

He was a hunter. He was supreme. He could wait and wait. Sometimes for days, until the opportunity was right. The point was to be on duty at all times. Always vigilant. The hunt he could control. Not like everything else in his life.

Love hadn't worked out for him at all. For six months she'd made him happy, then she had cut herself free. She had rejected him and what he believed in.

He had never really understood her problem and he didn't believe she did either. She was part of the world – the world that was corrupt and out of order. He had to put it all back into shape. Frighten when necessary, hurt when necessary, and kill when necessary. But it had to start changing.

The man stared across at the black railings and stone steps that led down to a red basement door. He knew they were inside: him and her. He had planned this for a long time, had lived it in his mind and waited patiently for the right time. He had his kit on the seat beside him: the barbed wire, duct tape, knife, gloves, flashlight, pistol, needle and ink. There was going to be pain first, then resolution, and then freedom.

Orders were orders, whatever you thought about them and however you played it. People had to understand – there was no morality, no absolute, in battle and war. God's will was self-assertion and evolution – the drive to secure the future for your own kind. He'd read more than he could remember about it. The science was unmistakable. People were just a genetic code seeking its own silent future. They were just incubators for God's code. Bodies were nothing. But people had forgotten what God's chosen code was and what the inferior code was doing to the world.

His purpose had been sharpened over the years. He understood who he was now; finally understood that it was possible to be alive in both the present and the past. When he had absorbed that simple truth, the whole of his life fell into place. Time was not linear, time was all-present. It didn't matter if you weren't part of the original purpose, you were part of the eternal struggle which happened outside time and space. And anyone you killed was killed throughout eternity.

The man knew he wasn't really an individual; he was part of a hive, a single cell in a larger mind. He didn't need to understand the whole, only his work, his duty, his small piece of the city that needed cleansing.

Tonight was special. The order was to kill again. He would follow them slowly. He would make them cry out for death. Then, he would help them.

Outside the club, his watch chimed at fifteen-minute intervals. He checked the time visually before going through his other checks. The first was his weapons check. He pulled out the small pistol, examined the magazine, removed it, took the bullet out of the breech, clicked the trigger twice, replaced the magazine, levered the bullet back into the breech. Then he took out his army combat knife, a small four-inch holed blade. He unsheathed it, felt the blade, sheathed it and put it away. Next he took out his flashlight. It was combat standard, strong and simple to use. He flicked on the beam and picked out the shadows opposite, then quickly switched it off and replaced it in his pocket. He took out the gloves. They were industrial gloves, so that he could handle the barbed wire. He was ready. He opened the window a couple of inches and pulled out a cigarette. A match flamed in the darkness; he dragged deeply and felt the rush of nicotine in his blood.

Soon, it would be time. He held the anger in and felt it spread throughout him, the rage forming in each muscle in turn, mingling with the nicotine. He didn't just hate. Hate was for part-timers. He *was* hate. It was his DNA, his purpose, his sole trajectory.

Hate was a bloodline. It had grown in his cells like anything else: blue eyes, brown hair, muscularity – and hate. Hate was his inheritance, his birthright – and his duty.

He stared across, blew smoke out of the window and repeated the eighty-eight words softly to himself.

Chapter Three

Salsa Club, Upper East Side
March 6, 11.50 p.m.

Inside the basement salsa club, the dance floor was heaving with bodies, the walls running with condensation under dark red lights. The series of small rooms reverberated with the high-pitched hoot of the trumpets and the rhythm of the bongos. A barely audible singer led the song in Spanish.

David Capske was twenty-seven, engaged to be married and very pleased with how life had changed for him. He put his arm around Lucy, pulled her in tight, sipped his fifth Corona and stared at her. She was so perfect. Lucy's eyes followed the dancers; David, too, turned to watch.

The couple on the dance floor were breathtaking. The woman twirled in a tiny silver dress, flicking her long legs around on high heels, her elegant arms draped across the shoulders of her chisel-jawed partner. He was tall and taut in every movement – like a fixed bar against her fluidity.

The dancers moved quickly, their legs and hips lifting and falling to the rapid thump of the beat. David stared transfixed. Then he felt something on his thigh. He looked down and saw Lucy's hand slowly moving across it.

'You want to dance?' he shouted over the noise.

'I see you like to watch her dance,' she teased. 'You getting excited?'

David grinned. 'I was admiring her technique. She's got great upper-body isolation.'

'That's why you were staring so hard at her upper body region?'

'What's to look at? She's not half as beautiful as you and she's not even got the moves you've got.' He reached out and tried to kiss her. 'Now *your* upper-body isolation is second to none.'

She pulled away and smiled. 'I need proof.'

David leaned closer. 'That's not a problem.'

'How are you going to prove it to me?'

'By taking the most beautiful woman in this place home and showing you,' he said.

'Flatterer! Anyway, that might be second-hand excitement. You might be thinking of anyone. I want better proof than that.'

They stared at each other. This was happiness, David Capske thought. Whatever more was to come, couldn't compete with the feeling he had when they were together.

'My family have disowned me, is that not proof enough?'

Lucy laughed and stood up. 'They just want you to meet a nice Jewish girl and not some—'

'Talented and brilliant young writer.' He gazed into her blue eyes. He meant it. She was the one. True, Lucy Steller was not what his family had in mind for their firstborn. They were part of the wealthy establishment and she was still working in a supermarket.

'Let's go home then.' She took his hands and dragged him to his feet. David kissed her.

They stood outside in the cold night air. They were both sweaty from the heat of the club, and the cold air stung. Lucy had goose bumps. David put his arm around her and rubbed her bare arm briskly to try to warm her up. The road was quiet – just a line of dark shop windows and a row of parked cars under gloomy street lights.

'I love being with you,' he said.

In one of the parked cars across the way, a light suddenly flared in the driver's seat: a face illuminated for a second seemed to be staring directly across at him.

Lucy felt David's body tense. 'What's up?'

'Nothing,' he said. The light went out in the car and smoke drifted from the half-open window. 'Someone just lit a cigarette.'

'We should get going,' she said, and took his arm.

'He was staring right at me,' said David. 'Not a nice look, either.'

'Don't start with the paranoia,' she said, and drew him close. As they began to walk up the street, David turned and looked again over his shoulder at the parked car, but all he could see was a trail of smoke from the window.

Chapter Four

Apartment, Lower Manhattan
March 7, 7.04 a.m.

Denise Levene lay alone in her bed, staring up at the ceiling. Everything about her had changed. She used to leave her clothes all over the room, for one, but now her whole apartment was obsessively neat; even her shoes stood in an orderly line in the closet and there wasn't so much as a sock on the floor.

It suggested an ordered mind. And that's how she wanted it to look.

She felt just like a dam wall trying to stop the waters from breaking through. She knew she could neither fight nor outrun the panic attacks. The best she could do was to try to distract herself. But she could feel fears looming – the black thoughts that had started to seep through from her dreams into the new day.

She held the memories at bay for several minutes. Then a half-thought appeared. *His face in the shadows*. And suddenly she was in the dungeon again and the whole fragile world seemed in danger of splitting open.

Denise threw back the duvet and stood up. Movement helped. She rushed through to the utility room, took her sweat-pants from the basket and pulled them on, then an old tank top. She put on a hoodie and her old sneakers and ran out of the apartment, slamming the door, heading fast down the eight flights of stairs.

Then she was out in the street gulping air. The sense of terror was intense; she felt a momentary release, but she had only avoided it for a moment – the panic was still chasing her down. She felt the thoughts hiding somewhere in her mind, just behind her eyes, waiting.

Denise sprinted up the street, avoiding the look of anonymous faces, hearing only the rumble of the city and feeling only the morning chill. Her feet pounded with long strides and her heart raced. She turned south and headed across the Brooklyn Bridge, out to the projects – the destitute parts of Brooklyn where she had grown up.

On the street her head continued to swarm with dark thoughts. The fears returned, but so did the image of Tom Harper, the man she'd once admired. She could no longer deal with him in the aftermath – and as much as he tried to contact her and talk, she just flat out refused. Tom Harper had been cut off. Daniel, her boyfriend, was another casualty. He'd stayed around long enough to know she had changed, then he took the dog and moved someplace else. Denise didn't feel much about it.

She hit the ground hard, pushing her muscles as far as she could, and kept it going, thirty seconds, forty seconds, a minute . . . her heart rate soaring, her mind blank. It was working. She kept it up for another minute and then slowed her pace and settled into a rhythm, feeling the sweat start to form around her hairline and down her back.

Her therapist called it 'acting out'. To escape the panic, she had to put herself in danger out there on the streets. Because the danger made sense, and the fear of the outside world didn't seem as bad as the terror inside. The pain of burning muscles was nothing to the memories that left her choking on her own silence.

She knew the theory. As a psychologist herself, she had trained and taught at Columbia, then re-trained as a police therapist for the NYPD. She knew far too much about radical trauma and its manifestations. In medical terms, she knew what she was. In layman's terms, she was a basket case, running away from fear, losing touch with everything and everyone.

She ran for an hour then arrived back exhausted but calmed. She stopped across the street and stared at a car outside her building. It wasn't one she'd noticed before. She saw the window ajar and smoke twirling from inside and felt a stab of panic.

'You're being a freak, Denise. Stop it. It's just a car.' She tried to move but her limbs refused to obey. She looked around, feeling self-conscious as she stood paralyzed on the sidewalk, the sweat beginning to roll off her.

Two long minutes passed. Denise could make out two forms in the car. Two men, possibly. She twisted her fingers together as she looked at the door to her building. The car was parked illegally. She could see the two men looking around. They were waiting for somebody. She had to do something about this debilitating fear. After the abduction, Harper had given her the name of a specialist – a guy called Mac who he said could help her. She'd dismissed it at the time, but she'd always kept his number. Denise pulled out her cell phone and dialed. There was just an answerphone message giving the times of the classes and the address.

Denise had wanted to speak to a person. She needed help. She'd done so much herself and come a long way, but she needed to walk around without fear. She finally talked herself into crossing the street. She planned to keep her head straight, keep tight to the building and make her way inside immediately.

As soon as she started to walk past the car, the two doors opened. They must have been checking their mirrors. Denise jerked to a halt. She wanted to react well, to appear normal, but it sent a shiver right through her and her eyes shifted about for an escape route.

The two people were out of the car quickly, both medium height, purposeful, tidily dressed. Their quick eyes and languid movements told her that these were cops or gangsters, but most likely cops.

'Miss Levene,' said one of them.

Denise didn't speak, she just nodded slightly.

The first cop held out his shield. He had obviously sensed her apprehension.

'Sorry to jump out like that. Detective Munroe, Missing Persons.'

Denise looked at the second officer. She'd been wrong. It wasn't a man, but a tall athletic woman with broad shoulders.

'Detective Gauge,' she said, smiling.

Denise was standing and sweating, aware that she looked like a car-crash victim.

'What do you want?' she said firmly.

'You're hard to get hold of, Miss Levene.'

'Am I?'

Detective Sarah Gauge had warm brown eyes and a way of holding people's attention. She stepped forward, her gestures open and non-aggressive. 'I failed, if the truth be told, Miss Levene. I tried calling you, but you never pick up. I came round here three times, you never answer your buzzer.'

Denise Levene stared at them both. Still distrustful. 'I wondered who was calling,' she said. 'Most people stopped trying a month back. I don't socialize much.'

'We need to talk to you,' said Detective Munroe. 'If that's possible.'

'About what? I'm not a missing person, I'm just not very good company.'

Detective Munroe opened his hands, showed both palms. 'We just need your help. Can we come inside, Miss Levene? It'd be good to talk to you.'

'It's Dr Levene, for the record.'

'We're aware of your academic qualifications, Doctor. My apologies.'

'You must be desperate to look me up. Someone at the NYPD send you?'

Munroe shook his head. 'We can tell you more inside.'

Denise tried to imagine why they were there. 'You're both from Missing Persons?'

'Right.'

Denise looked up. The city was concrete gray under a pale blue sky. The traffic was rushing by in a frenzied continuous strain. The sweat was turning cold on her skin. She turned back to Sarah Gauge. 'So, who's missing?'

Gauge glanced at Munroe then cleared her throat. 'You heard of Abby Goldenberg? The missing schoolgirl, Abby?'

'No,' said Denise. 'Should I have?'

'It's been on the news. She went missing a week ago.'

'I don't watch much TV.' Denise hadn't heard of Abby, but the name Goldenberg rang a bell somewhere in her memory.

'Kind of cut yourself off,' said Munroe. He pushed a finger in one ear and scratched. 'It's not a solution.'

'You'd know this?' said Denise. 'Because you're a psychiatrist, right? Forgive me, I didn't realize.'

Munroe's lips formed a half-smile. 'No, lady, I'm no shrink. It's common sense. No one learned to ride again by hiding from a horse.'

'Yeah, well, what I do is up to me, right?' said Denise.

'Sure, but—'

She held up her hand, cutting him off. She walked past both detectives and opened the heavy glass door of her building. Munroe and Gauge followed her in. 'I apologize for being so persistent,' said Munroe, 'but a girl's life is at stake here. We need your help.'

'I'm on the eighth floor. You can take the elevator. I'll meet you there.' Denise went towards the stairs.

'You're taking the stairs eight floors?' said Gauge. 'You on some fitness program?'

'I don't take elevators,' said Denise. The door to the stairway closed behind her. She was sheeted in sweat. The brief conversation had not been easy for her. The two cops looked at each other and Munroe pressed for the elevator. 'What's with her?' said Gauge.

'The killer held her underground for two days,' said Munroe. 'Only way in or out of her prison was an elevator shaft.'

Chapter Five

Diner, East Harlem
March 7, 8.07 a.m.

He sat in the diner in East Harlem, five minutes from the murder scene, eating a bacon and egg bagel. He was alone on a table for four but the diner was only half full at that time of day. An old lady to his right sat staring ahead, her head slightly crooked on her shoulders, wearing a pompous and refined air as if she was better than the rest, but beneath the table, she had no shoes and her bare feet were cut and rancid.

There were two cops sitting in the corner booth. He stared at them as they ate and joked. Jimmy Headless and Johnny Neckless. Every day, he imagined that this was how they started their shift – sign in, drive two blocks up from the precinct, park up and take free coffee and bagels from Enrico.

He took out a cell phone. Prepaid, untraceable. He had used it to call David Capske the night before, just after midnight. He'd told David that he had photographs of him taking cocaine. Threatened the palpitating young man that he was going to embarrass the hell out of the Capske clan and lose David his job.

David asked what he wanted. 'Easy,' he'd said. 'One thousand dollars delivered tonight to a trash can on East 112th Street.'

He took the cell-phone battery from his pocket, put it back into the phone and waited for the software to load up and the satellite connection to show. He sipped some hot coffee as he logged on to a new Hotmail account and laboriously typed in the email addresses of all the networks and newspapers. Then he composed a short but important message.

He looked across to Jimmy and Johnny. Arch-morons of the modern world. Keeping up the illusion that we were all safe. He smiled at the waitress and nodded as she held up the coffee pot. He pressed send.

He sat and waited, the murder weapon still in his pocket like a memento of the kill. He remembered the feeling. He wanted to have that high again. But he couldn't, not yet. He knew that he must remain hidden. His task was not to bathe in glory but to conquer the inferior. His task was to carry out orders.

He let the emails sail through space and time, hunting out their electronic destinations, and watched as they disappeared from the outbox.

He waited a good fifteen minutes, and then he put the phone to his ear and called 911. The tone clicked. The voice seemed small and distant. Not what you want in an emergency.

'911, which service please?' said the wheezy voice.

'Police.'

'What seems to be the problem, sir?'

'There's a dead body on East 112th Street, in an alleyway at Jenson House.' He hung up, took the battery out of the cell phone and tossed it on to the floor. The phone would be wiped clean, smashed and deposited in a trash can on his walk to work.

He looked at his stopwatch and smiled at the number. His victim had taken seventy-nine minutes to die. There had been a lot of pain. That's what he enjoyed. Pain.

He walked out past Jimmy and Johnny. 'Hi there, fellas,' he said, his right hand wrapped around the plastic grip of his gun, feeling the dirty excitement of flaunting it. They both looked up and nodded.

As he left, he guessed that the police dispatch would be chirping on the police radio for some squad car to go take a look. He waited in the street and, sure enough, the nearest cop car belonged to Jimmy and Johnny. They ambled out of the diner, fat and stupid, in no hurry whatsoever, and already about five hours too late.

28

He wanted to follow the dumb cops to observe them as they came across the corpse, to see their reaction to what he had done. He would've liked to have gone back to see the corpse and to take some pictures. But that was foolish. The cops would scan the scene. He couldn't afford to be noticed.

He felt restless as he walked up the street, almost as if he'd set up a party that he wasn't allowed to attend himself. Most of all he felt hungry for more blood. He only just realized what it was, the sudden feeling, almost unrecognized because it was unexpected.

He stared across the street. People were walking to work or to school. Then he felt it again. He thought it might have been some leftover excitement from the murder. Maybe the remembering, the sending of death messages, maybe all of the paraphernalia of the morning-after was tripping him up.

He was standing still, wearing a leather coat, a little unshaven, already late for work, his stomach warm from coffee, the blood of the dead man smeared across his chest and left to dry. He repeated the eighty-eight words as if a prayer.

If anyone wanted to know, if anyone asked now, who had killed that guy at Jensen House, he'd fucking scream from the rooftops: *'I did, you fuckers! I did.'*

He smiled at a woman approaching. He felt invulnerable, like a man on something. A blood-high, he called it, the freedom that comes from a kill.

He decided that what he was feeling could be called happiness. He hadn't been happy his whole life long, but now . . . yes, that's what it was, wasn't it? That buzz of self-confidence, a sense of freedom, of optimism, of potency, of shamelessness – that was happiness, right there, sitting right there in his own heart and mind.

It was 8.22 a.m. on the streets of New York, the morning after the murder, and it came to him that he already wanted to kill again.

At first it was months before the intoxicating need filled his head, then weeks . . . now just a day. There was a feeling in his head like a ticking. Sometimes it went on for hours, like a roulette wheel slowed down. And when it stopped, then the order came.

It was ticking again.

He saw the world like never before, as if he was the central figure in his own movie and that movie had meaning. And its meaning was right there – blood on the streets, happiness, the urge to kill and a man nearly dancing with delight.

Chapter Six

Apartment, Lower Manhattan
March 7, 8.28 a.m.

Inside her apartment, Denise seated the two Missing Persons detectives in the living room. She left them for a moment and came back in clean sweatpants and a fresh top. She noticed the way Munroe stared at her. What was it? A chance to gawp or was he suspicious in some way? Difficult to tell.

Denise moved to the kitchen and poured a glass of orange juice. She didn't offer the two detectives a drink and she didn't sit down, either. She stood in the center of the room and looked at one then the other. She felt her nerves rising and falling, but tried to keep it hidden.

'Nice place,' said Sarah Gauge. 'I like your things. All sleek and modern. I like a modern style.' She gestured at the Italian sofa and then two angular aluminum candlesticks.

'Can you get to the point?' said Denise.

The two detectives sat on the sofa and Denise watched them, then leaned against the wall. Munroe took a white envelope out of his pocket and pulled out a photograph.

'This is Abby,' he said. 'This is the most recent shot we've got of her. Red highlights included, although she was brunette when she disappeared.'

Denise stared across at Abby. She was a striking-looking girl. 'What is she? Tenth or eleventh grade?'

'Senior,' said Munroe. 'She's just turned sixteen. She's a Queens girl – Forest Park area. Parents divorced. Lives alone with her father. Mother lives in New Jersey with a new family.'

'The girl is Jewish?'

'Yeah, she's Jewish. Her father's keen on his Jewish heritage, if you know what I mean.'

'Before you jump in with your locker-room anti-Semitism, you do know I'm also Jewish?' said Denise. She glared down hard at Munroe.

'I didn't mean anything wrong by it,' said Munroe. 'It's just that he's a specialist. An academic. He curates exhibitions about the Holocaust. That's all I meant.'

'Where does he work?'

'He lectures at Columbia and curates at the Museum of Tolerance.'

'Goldenberg, you said? Thought I recognized it from when I used to work at Columbia.'

'Well, he knows you too, Dr Levene. Only by reputation.'

Denise began to search her memory for the name. 'What's his first name?'

'It's Aaron. Dr Aaron Goldenberg.'

Denise felt her heart pump. Any link just brought the tragedy closer. She paused and turned from the two cops, looking out of the window. 'I never knew him well. We probably met at an event. I don't think I ever met his daughter.'

'We know that.'

'So what are you doing here?'

'Truth is, this investigation is drying up fast. We've exhausted all avenues and Dr Goldenberg knows it. He's a very persuasive man, Dr Goldenberg. He wanted us to go one more round. He wrote a list. We always ask for a list. All the people who his daughter might have known, wanted to know or had been influenced by. If she's a runaway, she might go for someone she barely knows.'

'And?'

'You were on that list.'

'In which category?'

'She admired you, apparently.'

'Me? She didn't know me.'

'She wanted to major in Psychology. Her father took her to one of your lectures. When you left Columbia for the NYPD, she thought that was cool.'

'Cool?'

'Packing in academia for a real career.' Munroe tried a smile. Denise didn't respond. 'One in the eye for her old man, I expect.'

Detective Gauge stood. 'We've got her diaries. She mentioned you in there too. Not so much about the Psychology. She seemed to like your style, the way girls do. Thought you looked beautiful and confident. That's what she wrote.'

Munroe pulled out a copy of the diary entry and handed it to Denise. 'She was quite affected by your abduction too. She followed the case on the news. She wrote a few prayers for you.'

Denise felt her emotions stir and she tapped the wall hard.

'Dr Goldenberg has this theory that she might be disappearing to emulate you in some unconscious way. Maybe she sees it as a means of getting some attention. Her mother's a real live-wire. Doesn't have much to do with Abby.'

Denise shook her head. 'That's bullshit.'

'He's trying to imagine why she's not come home. He doesn't want to think she's just cut loose on him and run away with some guy.'

'And what do you think, Detective?'

'Looks like she planned to go away. She stowed her books and a set of clothes in a tree in the woods near her home. A dog-walker found them. She faked a phone call to a friend to get out of the house. We think she was going to meet someone. Maybe it was to run away, maybe she got into trouble.'

'If she was planning to run away, would she leave her diaries? This stuff is quite intimate. She'd know it's the first place you'd all look. She mention any boyfriend in the diaries?'

'No, she didn't.'

Denise turned. 'She's not a runaway. But you're not here for an opinion, are you?'

'Listen, we're ticking boxes here, Dr Levene. We've got a list, your name's on it. We got to ask. Have you seen her? Has she contacted you? Anything? This would've been a phone call if you ever picked up.'

'No. Nothing. As you know, I'm not easy to get hold of.'

Denise used the towel around her shoulder to rub her hair. She looked at Abby's picture again. She saw a bright, kind face, both cheeky and prepossessing. If she was to take a guess on the girl's attitude, she'd say that she was a fun-loving risk-taker who had her father wrapped round her little finger. The smile would get her a long way, not necessarily in the right direction.

'Is that all?' said Denise. 'I've got an appointment to keep.'

Chapter Seven

Apartment, East Harlem
March 7, 8.51 a.m.

The door to Harper's bedroom opened. The drapes were drawn back and Eddie Kasper stood over his partner, saying, 'What the hell happened?'

Harper's eyes remained shut. He lay flat out on his bed, his face all cuts and bruises, each one of which he felt reverberating through his head.

Eddie flicked the switch on the radio that lay askew on an old crate and turned the volume high. It blared out a news report complete with high-pitched crackles. The man on the bed failed to stir.

'The parents of the missing high-school girl, Abby Goldenberg, have made a fresh appeal for witnesses. Abby's mother and father have come together to make a video appeal to help find their daughter who went missing at 5.15 p.m. on February 26.'

'She's probably already lying dead someplace,' said Eddie and turned the radio off.

'Optimist.'

'So now you're awake.'

'What do you want, Eddie? I'm not on shift for two days.'

'Leave has just been cancelled.'

Harper turned and moaned. 'What's going on?'

'Just get up, Harper. I'll tell you all you need to know on the way. Come on, we got to go.' He threw a bag of grapes on to Harper's stomach. 'And there's some get-well-soon food for you from the girls at the precinct. They love a loser. Shirley was almost weeping when I told her about the fight, Harps. Weeping. You should think about it. She's not a bad-looking woman.'

Harper listened without response. He was finding it difficult enough to open his right eye. The left one was completely closed over. All he could see was a cloud of pinkish red. He was almost blind.

'I need ice,' he groaned. 'I can't fucking move.' He lifted his head and it shrieked like a train rushing towards a subway station. 'Get me something, Eddie. Codeine. Anything.'

'Hell, you're a sad mess of a man,' said Eddie. 'And it smells like a goddamn locker room in here. Harps, come on, what the hell are you doing to yourself?' Eddie threw open a window and headed into the tiny kitchen that was hidden behind a torn drape.

Harper moved his legs to the floor and lifted his torso off the bed. He sat for a moment, feeling the thumping of pain, then coughed violently and felt his ribs ache like they were broken in several places. He spat blood on to the floor, then looked out through a thin slit of light at the tall, slim figure of Eddie Kasper looming above holding a glass of water and a handful of pills.

'I'm guessing I didn't win,' said Harper.

'There we go. Make a joke of it. You could have got seriously hurt and I'm not going to be pushing you to no crime scene in a wheelchair.'

Harper grunted and tried to rouse himself from the bed but as he moved, his head thudded with bolts of pain. Every part of his face felt too large: his lips, gums, jawbone, and eyes. His chest, kidneys and stomach felt raw. Every muscle was yelling at him.

Eddie passed him the glass of water. 'Shit, I couldn't believe what I was seeing, Harps. I was not prepared. I am upset, man. I was feeling emotional for you last night. Nearly jumped in the ring myself.'

'Should've helped me out,' said Harper out of the corner of his mouth. His lips cracked and he tasted blood on his tongue.

Eddie walked close and pushed Harper's head back. Harper struggled with the pain. 'What the hell, Eddie?'

'I lost a hundred on you, Harps. I've got a very expensive date tonight and I've been promising her some fancy place. Now I got nothing. So much for a sure bet.'

'Then don't gamble.'

'What am I going to tell her?'

'I don't know, Eddie, just cut out the middle man and take her to bed.'

Eddie stood up straight for a moment. 'Not a bad idea, maestro. Looks like that little Italian didn't mess your head up too bad.'

Harper tried to stand and felt a fresh stab of pain across his chest and stomach. He sat down again and breathed deeply.

Eddie looked at his partner's face. 'You were never handsome, Harps, not like me, but you weren't no monster, either. But now, I gotta tell you, you look like someone took that ugly stick and beat you half to death with it.'

'You're way too sympathetic, Eddie, you know that?'

'What you want sympathy for? No one forced you to fight. We all told you to stay clear.'

'You're right, no one forced me.'

'A hundred bucks, Harps – where's the sympathy for my losses?'

'It's boxing, Eddie – remember not to bet on the white guy.'

'The other guy was a white guy, Harps.'

'Then I really was no good.'

Eddie took one of the coffees he'd brought with him from the deli in the street outside and handed it to Harper. He sat down and shook his head. 'Man, your face is like some close-up of a fungus. You should see a doctor.'

'I'll survive.' He threw four pills down his throat and gulped back water.

'And when the doctor's finished with you, you should go see the psychiatrist and get your head mended. And when the shrink's finished with you, you should take your gloves and throw them in the Hudson. You stank, man.'

'That bad?'

'It was like someone had switched you off. You didn't land a single punch, Harps. Not a single punch. You let him boss you round the ring. He was taking pot shots at you. Using that pretty face of yours for target practice. It was a massacre.'

Harper stared across, unable to smile. 'First time I slept that well in a long while, though.'

'Being unconscious doesn't count as sleep.'

'It gets you from night to day just the same. Look, these injuries may look bad, but he wasn't packing much in those punches. No lasting damage.'

'It upset me, man, and I don't like that. Come here, big guy.' Eddie pulled Harper to his feet, wrapped his arms around him and squeezed him tight.

'Go easy, Eddie,' said Harper, pulling away and reaching out for his phone. 'And where's that ice pack?' Harper looked down his messages. Lots of messages, probably heckling his performance, but nothing from Denise Levene.

He felt something like the beginning of grief again. Then it passed as the pain started up. He couldn't move his neck too well, so he presumed he'd been caught on the point of his jaw from a right hook, snapping his neck fast and twisting the spinal column. Rotational force. Sudden drop in blood pressure, brain slamming to the right as the skull went left – concussion maybe. He must've been out for the whole ten count.

Eddie returned and handed Harper an ice pack. He took it and held it to his worst eye.

'Seriously, Eddie, it's good of you to drop by. Appreciate it.' Harper walked to the bathroom.

'I care, Harps, you know that. But there was one other thing.'

Harper took a mouthful of water from the faucet and swilled it around his mouth, then spat it out. The white porcelain turned a translucent red.

'What's that, Eddie?'

'Captain's called Blue Team together again.'

Harper appeared at the bathroom door. 'What is it?'

'They found a body this morning in East Harlem.'

'They called the whole team?' asked Harper. 'Something I should know?'

Eddie nodded. Harper let the thought swirl around in his head and compete with the pain. Blue Team was the elite unit of homicide detectives from North Manhattan Homicide. The last time the whole of Blue Team was on a case, they were chasing a serial killer. Harper looked at Eddie Kasper, 'Well, you might as well tell me, I'm going to have to see it soon enough. What's the MO?'

'A body all wrapped up in barbed wire,' said Eddie. 'And Lafayette wants you to lead this one. It's nasty. Welcome back to our world.'

Chapter Eight

East 112th Street, Manhattan
March 7, 9.22 a.m.

East 112th Street ran all the way to Second Avenue and stopped adjacent to Jefferson Park. On Saturday morning, the pace was slow. The big blocks of public housing stood quietly in the morning sun. On one side of the street a gang of youths sat on a stoop; five big guys all stretching out, baseball caps backward, watching. The few stores were open, but there wasn't much going on. A couple of eateries, a grocery store with everything on sale, a mini-mart and a store selling nothing but wheel rims. But business was slow for the moment.

At the entrance to Jenson House XI across the street, a small dark alley ran behind the huge municipal trash loaders and led through to House VI. There was nothing remarkable about the alley, except for the single patrol car parked neatly in a 90-minute wait slot and a single uniformed NYPD officer standing beside a piece of yellow police tape.

Within seconds, the quiet street erupted with the sound of traffic. Left and right, trucks and cars started to stream towards the alley, except they weren't police vehicles. They were all marked with the bright logos of television networks.

About a half-mile away a red Pontiac belonging to Eddie Kasper swerved through the corners towards the crime scene. Harper kept his head low and his eyes covered with shades. His head hadn't let up the dance beat of pain. 'Promise me you won't ever drive an ambulance,' he said.

'I'd get to the hospital quick enough, wouldn't I?'

'Sure, but the question is – would you get there with anyone alive?'

Eddie turned to look at Harper and grinned. 'You made a joke, Harps! That's real progress. You keep up like this and you'll be human one day.'

He reached out and slapped Harper on the arm. Harper winced. The painkillers were only keeping out half of the pain coming from various parts of his body. Eddie swung into 112th Street. They came upon Jenson House XI almost immediately and Eddie slammed on his brakes.

Harper pushed up his shades and stared out. 'What the fuck is going on?' The street was log-jammed with cars and trucks. There were rows of TV trucks, seven or eight TV crews with reporters, cameramen, sound crews and even a few executives, all milling between the street and Jenson House. The presence of the networks had attracted a crowd of thirty to forty people standing round the fringes and trying to see what all the fuss was about. There were only a few patrol cars at the scene and the uniformed cops were having trouble keeping order.

Eddie pulled up to the curb and switched off the engine. The two Homicide cops glanced at each other.

Harper pushed his shades down again. 'What's going down, Eddie? I thought this was a fresh kill. Why are they all here?'

'I don't know, Harps. And how did they hear about it so quick?'

'Question is, why the hell are they so interested? There's been no ID, right?'

'Right.'

Harper pushed his body out of Eddie's old Pontiac and on to the sidewalk, a grimace crossing his face. A cold breeze ran across the street even though the sunlight was bright. The effect, through his bruised eyes, was surreal. It was like a circus had come to see a homicide in action.

Eddie moved around and said to Harper, 'Keep close, champ, or someone's going to mistake you for the victim.'

There was a battle going on up ahead, with the two police

41

officers trying to push back the TV cameras and reporters. Harper lowered his head, held up his shield and muscled his way through, ignoring the pain.

A smiling brunette from CNN spotted the shield and turned her TV crew through 180 degrees. 'We've got another detective coming through, let's try for a comment.' As she said it, a minor stampede headed Harper's way.

She moved across, ahead of the pack. 'Detective, can we get a statement? Can you confirm the identity of the body?'

Harper looked up. 'I just got here. I haven't even seen the body.'

The reporter saw Harper's beat-up face and shrank away. 'We all got an email, Detective, about a body found early this morning in a Housing Project in East Harlem. They are saying that it's Judge Capske's son, David. Email said it was a political statement for America. What have you got to say about that?'

Harper shook his head. 'I don't know nothing about this as yet. No comment.' He pushed forward, more confused, wondering why the networks had been sent this information. The press rounded on him, coming from all sides at once, throwing lights and microphones in his way. 'I'll give you a statement, ladies and gentlemen, if you let me take a goddamn look at my crime scene.'

Harper and Kasper made their way through to the rising volume of eager and excited questions.

Inside the makeshift compound, there were four police cruisers and a white truck belonging to the Crime Scene Unit. All the red and blue lights twirled without sound, hardly visible in the lights of the TV crews. Over to the right, a dark rectangle of shadow marked the entrance to the alleyway. Canary-yellow police tape crossed the crime scene and flapped in the breeze. They'd managed to get a rudimentary screen up, but Harper guessed that the cameras would've caught the image of the corpse already.

'Did the department get sent the same information about Judge Capske's son?' asked Harper. 'Is that why the whole of Blue Team got the call out?'

Eddie looked around, scanned the trucks and microphones. 'No, we didn't get shit. Must've gone straight to the TV stations.'

'Someone out there wants to cause maximum fucking chaos,' said Harper. 'Does anyone know what the hell's going on?' he shouted.

A tall cop standing in the shadow at the edge of the alleyway moved into the light, thumbs hitched in his belt. It didn't matter that there were several cameras pointed his way, world-weary nonchalance emanated from every pore.

Harper felt another sudden sharp pain cross his forehead, and he moved over the yellow crime-scene tape. 'You know what's going down here, Officer?'

'They just rolled in about fifteen minutes ago,' the officer replied. 'Said they got a warning. We were here quick, so I'd guess they were told before we were.'

Harper stared out at the circus and felt anger rising in his blood. 'I want this whole fucking street cleared, you hear? I need more patrol cars and uniforms right now.'

'The whole street?'

'The whole street. Every fucking TV truck. This is a crime scene, not a sideshow. Move them out now. Right out of my sight.'

Chapter Nine

East 112th Street
March 7, 9.28 a.m.

Harper spotted his team further up the alleyway, congregating as close to the corpse as possible, as if the lifeless body would somehow reveal the secrets of the crime as long as they got in tight enough. Harper knew that they weren't just clinging to the case, but that they were standing around the corpse clinging to the fragments of the victim's humanity.

Detectives Garcia, Greco, Ratten and Swanson, the other four members of Blue Team, were talking in brief sentences and looking around. No detailed forensics work going on – just experienced cops getting a feel for what had happened. Looking for the story, talking down options, trading insults and jokes. Each of them opening their account on the next dead body.

Harper moved towards his team. 'They're going crazy over there,' he said. 'The media said this is Judge Capske's son David. Has anyone ID'd our victim?'

'Can't do it. Take a look for yourself. Can't tell who it is.'

Garcia stopped as he saw Harper's face. 'Lafayette gave you the lead looking like that? You look like shit,' he said. 'And for the record, you fight like shit.'

'I'm leading this, that's right,' said Harper. It was going to be a day of soaking up the jibes and jokes.

Harper looked at the ground. There was a spread of white powder on the wet asphalt, with three or four small wraps, torn open. 'The email to the networks said this is a political statement.

That might or might not be true. Could be drug-related. A gang maybe? You know of any gangs with a barbed-wire calling card? Maybe it's some anti-drug thing. Vigilantes? Who the hell does this?'

'Never heard it used,' said Garcia, 'but, who knows, there's new gangs forming all the time.'

'Anyone going to ID this corpse?' said Harper. 'The reporters are going to break through sooner rather than later.'

'We can't get near the body. It's wound up tight. Crime Scene are just finished and the Deputy Coroner is on his way.'

Harper looked down the alleyway. 'I'm going to take a look.'

'Has anyone checked whether the body is infected?' Eddie joked. 'Our lead detective is carrying open wounds.'

Harper and Eddie walked towards the corpse, looking down at the body covered with a bloodstained sheet, the breeze lifting the edges and rippling the white cotton. A pair of bright white sneakers, spotted with black circles of dried blood, stuck out from under the sheet.

'Small feet,' said Eddie. He turned to Harper. 'How you feeling?'

'Don't ask. Let's take a close up.'

'Out of the way, people, we got the Cyclops coming through.'

'Concentrate, Eddie,' spat Harper.

'The humor is medicine, man.' Eddie patted Harper's back. 'Humor is the door out of the dungeon, that's all it is.'

Harper moved towards the body. 'Gerry,' he shouted. 'Get back to the precinct and find out everything you can about Judge Capske.'

Gerry Ratten nodded. 'Already done a quick search on my phone. He's the judge who shut down that New York local radio station after one of the shock jocks made death threats against the anti-gun lobby.'

Harper considered it. 'So this could be a political hit. We need to know more. Go and dig, Gerry. Find out what you can about David Capske too. Call me the second you got something. We're going to have to speak to the press within the hour.'

'I'm on it,' called Gerry, heading towards his car.

45

Harper glanced about. 'Garcia. Go and question the networks. I need to know what time the information came in. The exact message. Get me what you can.' Harper paused. 'Jesus.'

'What is it?' asked Garcia.

'Looks like some Colombian drug deal gone wrong. We're in fucking East Harlem.' He stared down at the wraps. 'Not enough to kill for, surely, but maybe they're just trying to smear Capske's family. Shit, if this is a political execution, then the organization responsible wants it known. Garcia, find out if any political organization has made any previous statement against Judge Capske.' Harper felt nauseous as he stared across the bloody asphalt. The whole alleyway was a big stage for someone's hatred. 'This set-up is too good for some gangbangers,' he said to Eddie Kasper.

'Premeditated,' said Eddie. 'Unless the gangs have started to carry barbed wire around with them.'

Harper stood for a moment in the dark of the alley trying to readjust his sight. He looked at the water that was still pooled in parts of the ground. 'Was it raining last night?'

'Yeah, some time early morning. Why do you ask?'

'Just find out for me. It's still wet in here, but the streets out there are pretty dry.'

'Not much of a breeze to dry it off down here.'

Harper stared at Eddie, then he noticed something. 'You were in those clothes at the fight. Same stupid T-shirt.'

'They make a good outfit,' said Eddie. 'Tried and tested.'

Harper nodded. Then he recalled the blanket on his armchair in the apartment. 'You didn't go home, did you? You were sitting in my apartment all night.'

'Hey, Harps, don't go fantasizing! I got a life to lead,' Eddie said and flapped a hand in the air.

Harper smiled briefly, then looked at the scene in front of him. Two different stories were forming in his head. The location, presence of drugs, reported gunshot and the victim's white sneakers all pointed to a gangland drug shooting. The barbed wire and the presence of the TV crews, the possible killing of a judge's son, all suggested someone with a bigger and possibly political agenda. But there was a third story forming in his head and it was an even worse one.

In the alley, the rain still sat in droplets all over the plastic trash sacks. Harper looked down at the body, at the shoulder of the victim peeping out from under the red and white sheet. The jacket hadn't dried off, either. Harper kicked a piece of trash away from the victim's legs and then reached out and pulled off the white sheet.

Harper stared down at the strange sight. The body had been tightly wound in barbed wire; it was so thick that most of the man within was hidden. There were so many cuts that the victim's clothes were all completely dark from the blood. The barbed wire continued over the victim's face and head. Harper moved in close with a flashlight. Many of the barbs were bent.

'That's some cruel work,' he said to Eddie. 'And the body's been rolled about, by the look of things.' He snapped the latex glove on his right hand and crouched by the corpse. He touched the barbed wire, its metallic surface hard against the softness of flesh. He spanned his hand between the barbs. 'Galvanized steel. The barbs are approximately seven and a half centimeters apart; each barb is two centimeters long. Nasty. He's got to be full of hundreds of holes.'

Through the gaps in the wire, Harper could see how the barbs had gone in deep and torn the flesh. The ground was covered in blood, seeping in every direction, smeared as the body was rolled or moved. The victim had clearly been alive for most of this ordeal, while his poor heart kept pumping fresh blood to the wounds. Someone was pushing this body around, possibly enjoying hearing the victim's cries of pain.

Harper tried to understand. He searched Eddie's face. 'This is some mean bastard. Are we sure that no one heard this? This victim must have been in excruciating pain. Eddie, I want a ground team talking to every person in these blocks. Someone heard this man dying. Probably lots of them heard it. Shake these people and shake them hard. I don't want any of the usual shit. Someone heard this man and I need to know about it.'

47

Eddie nodded and walked across to a heap of trash sacks. 'I'll set it up. Hey, Harper, have a look at these trash bags. Might just be some hobo, but it looks like someone's been sitting here.'

Harper looked around. 'Sitting and watching, maybe. Why? Torture? Punishment?' He let the thoughts move around his mind. Felt something come to the surface. 'It's like a body-cage, isn't it? Close containment, right?'

'What do you mean?'

'Once the vic is wrapped in wire, he's absolutely powerless. Our killer or killers might have enjoyed the complete control. Enjoyed watching the victim suffer. Sitting there, shining a light, maybe, waiting until he bled out.'

Harper found a patch of skin close to the temple that was not covered with blood. 'Whoever it is, they're Caucasian,' he said. 'I can't even tell if it's a man or a woman.'

Harper's sight wasn't great, with his bruised eye, but he slowly moved his good eye over the barbed wire, seeing if there was anything more he could detect. He was looking for the gunshot. At the forehead, he stopped.

'The wire's broken here. It's pretty blackened but I think I've found an entrance wound. Small caliber. Maybe nine millimeters.' Harper looked at the hole. Something wasn't quite right about it. 'Very clean wound,' he said. 'Lots of gas burn. The barrel was pretty tight to his head.'

Eddie came across and leaned over Harper's shoulder. 'What's your story so far?'

Harper thought for a moment. 'No question about whether the vic was killed here. The killer rolled the body, kicked it about, watched the vic die slowly, waited for the blood loss to take him to the very edge, then shot him to make sure. That's how it looks to me.'

Harper looked around. The ground was marked with the scrapings of metal on asphalt. 'We could probably get some sense of what happened if we tracked these scratches and blood smears. Looks like he rolled the body the whole way down the alley. He starts bleeding about a third of the way in and with each roll, more of the barbs dig in.'

As Harper knelt again and cast his eyes up the alleyway, Swanson walked across. 'Never seen nothing like this before, Harper.'

'Me neither. He might have taken the victim out of the trunk of a car, but he rolled him in the alley. You can see the marks left by the barbs. Some business, that.'

'Soles of his shoes will be cut up, right? He can't have been using his hands, can he?'

'Right. Eddie also thinks that he was sitting on the trash bags.'

'Cold bastards,' said Swanson. 'One guy couldn't do this. This is a two- or three-man job.'

Harper thought for a moment. 'Could be, but I got a single gunshot wound to the forehead. My take is that the killer sat waiting, watching his victim cry out in pain, then, at some point, executed him.'

'*Killers*, don't you mean?'

'I don't see any evidence of multiple killers but I'm not ruling anything out.'

'To roll a man in barbed wire would take a team of men.'

Harper scanned the scene. 'You could be right. Let's see what Crime Scene can tell us.'

'Shit,' said Eddie. 'I hate it when you get all mystical. Is Swanson right or not?'

'This is the thing,' said Harper. He took a moment, as if allowing his thoughts to settle into some kind of order. 'It could be a hit, it could be a drug shooting or it could be some political revenge. There's a lot of overkill. There's passion and hatred here.' He tried to imagine the killer, working at night, a roll of barbed wire at his side, a man screaming in pain, a maniac sitting on some wet sacks watching.

'Drug wars? Some kind of revenge gang kill? Trying to make out they're fearless?' asked Swanson. 'You know how it goes, building a reputation.'

'Maybe, but the body's white, there's drugs left all over the ground, and look at those hands, too. Not someone who's done much manual work.' Harper leaned further down and looked at the four fingers of the right hand. He lifted them and then looked up. 'Index finger shorter than the ring finger. Probably a male victim. Whoever did it is a sadist, for one thing. He's theatrical, for another. And this isn't his first kill.' Harper sniffed. 'I don't think he or they are finished, do you?'

He put his hand under the corpse. The ground was dry. Harper started to calculate. The dry ground and wet clothes gave them a timeframe. It depended on when the rain started. 'We need to officially ID this body,' he said. 'Check that Crime Scene have finished, Eddie, and get some wire cutters.' Eddie moved off down the alleyway, leaving Harper and Swanson.

Harper kept re-telling the story from different angles. But every time, there was something missing. It was Harper's way – you tell the best story you can, then you pull the story to pieces. Then you start again. Over and over until some threads remained.

Eddie reappeared with wire cutters, the Deputy Coroner with him. The latter shook his head. 'Some business.' He knelt down. 'CSU have cleared the scene. If you want to find out his ID, we need to cut this wire.'

'We'd appreciate it,' said Harper. 'Press have already been given a name.'

They watched as the DC snapped at the wire around the head of the corpse. With each cut, he carefully pulled back the wire. After a few minutes he'd exposed a blackened and bloody face. 'It's a guy,' he said.

The men stared in silence, an acknowledgment of the pain etched on the young man's face. The DC cut a line down to the chest. He pulled back the wires and reached into the jacket pocket. He fished out a wallet. 'We've got something here,' he said and passed it to Harper.

Harper opened up the wallet, which held one thousand dollars in fifties. He picked out a driver's license. The photograph showed a cheerful face surrounded by a mop of black curly hair. Then he saw the name.

'Okay,' said Harper. 'It's David Capske, which means that we have got to work fast. This has been labeled political so the Feds and Counter-Terrorism will already be applying pressure at Headquarters trying to pull this from us. Everyone's going to want to know what happened here and why.'

'What do you need from me?' asked the DC.

'Can you give this top priority for me? I want the autopsy within the next few hours. I need that bullet and anything else you can tell me.'

'I'll see what I can do,' said the DC. 'Dr Pense will handle it.'

Harper looked at the black curly hair sticking out between strands of barbed wire. 'Someone's tortured and executed the son of a judge and they're very proud of themselves. It's not going to end here.'

Chapter Ten

The drive took forty-five minutes in all. Denise sat in silence, ignoring the ramblings of the cab driver. She was unable to explain why she was still feeling so scared. Her therapy wasn't giving her what she wanted. Tom Harper had made the suggestion about Mac right after her ordeal. It had seemed stupid at the time. It had made her angry. Three months later, still terrified by people at her own apartment and unable to answer her own door, Denise needed to move on.

Tom had wanted to help, not with fancy theories but in a practical way. Denise stared ahead as the cab turned off the street. The out-of-town warehouse in the timber yard was at the end of a pitted road. The car rocked from side to side.

The cab pulled over. The whole place was deserted. There was no sign over the door and no indication of what this place was. 'This is the address you gave. You sure this is where you want to go?'

Denise pushed a twenty through the glass and nodded. She got out of the car and stood on the rough ground. As soon as she was out, the cab driver put his car into gear and drove away.

Denise watched the car's brake lights as it slowed at the junction and then headed into the distance. She breathed as she'd taught herself and looked around. It was an open space in the middle of unfamiliar and run-down buildings. She didn't feel good at all. And there was only one way out – through the unmarked black door. The cab had gone, there was nowhere else to go.

She knew Harper must have felt secure about this place and with that knowledge she started towards the door. The fear was growing inside her, a dark anxiety that had felt so close for months now. She tried to hold it back and looked up ahead.

There was no bell or buzzer, just a sheet of steel in peeling black paint. She pulled it open. It grated on an old metal runner. The sound shot right through her. Metal on metal. She knew that from the dungeon. She held the door and her breath.

There were no lights in the corridor, so she walked in and followed a narrow path around to the right. She stared ahead, where two dim yellow lamps lit the way. By the time she made it to the end of the corridor, Denise's heart was pounding. She came to another door and pulled it open.

A line of steel steps led down to a large warehouse space. In the strange space, there was a car parked next to a van, a small gym set up on one side, a few concrete stairs leading nowhere and a doorway just like in a house. All around were different scenes that looked like some fire sale from a film set. She looked at each in turn. The mood was strangely foreboding.

Denise descended the steps and called out, 'Hello?' Her voice echoed against the huge tin roof. From a door across the room, a man appeared. He looked up at Denise. He took her in slowly.

'I'm D—'

'Don't tell me a thing.'

'Tom Harper gave me your name.'

'I said not a thing. You don't owe me an explanation.'

Standing on the last step, Denise stared back at him. The man was rough-looking. About five feet eight in height, big and strong across the shoulders, hands like spades and a mean look in his eyes. She didn't like him. He was tattooed across his biceps and neck.

'Get in here.'

He walked back through the door. Denise stood for a minute. She climbed back up the stairs, took three or four paces and then stopped again. What was she going to do? Sit in the yard and cry? She knew that she couldn't be in danger. Tom would never send her into that kind of situation. She turned round and felt the steel under her feet as she made her way down.

Across the floor, the door was half open. She opened it and looked in. The short guy with the attitude was sitting on an old pommel horse in front of a group of seven women and one man. They were all hunkered down on the floor. The guy on the pommel horse pointed to the floor. Denise walked across and sat down.

'First things first. You never trust me, ever.' The guy jumped down off the horse and addressed his little group. 'Welcome, victims. I don't know why you're here or what happened to you, but I know by looking into your sorry faces that you have ignored your birthright.'

The guy stepped towards the group. They shied away in unison. 'You, lady,' he said, pointing at Denise. 'Stand up.'

Denise stood. This was clearly some kind of self-help group. Not the sort of thing she thought Harper would have been involved with.

'Where are your eyes, victim?'

'I don't understand the question.'

The guy moved two fingers up to her eyeballs. 'Where are my fingers coming from?'

'In front of me.'

'And what if I come from here?' He moved his hand round behind her ear.

'I can't see them.'

'Here?' he said again, moving his hand behind her head.

'I can't see them.'

'So tell me, victim, if you were meant to be scared of predators, where the hell would God put your eyes?'

'The side of my head so I could see them coming.'

'Fucking exactly. Go to the top of the class.'

'Can I sit down?'

'No, victim, you cannot.' He leaned in close. He smelled of two-day-old sweat and stale beer. Denise veered away.

'You don't like my smell?'

'No.'

'You think a rapist is going to smell sweet? Going to get all washed and put on his best cologne? You better get used to the thing you're going to learn to fight.'

Denise couldn't speak.

'I'm a pig, because that's what you've come to me for – to get rid of that stench he left on you. Am I right?'

Denise stared ahead.

'I said, AM I RIGHT?' He shouted hard, close up to Denise.

'Yes,' she said and looked down at her feet, her heart thumping.

'Sit back down, victim.'

He walked around the group, his eyes moving from person to person. 'We got work to do, victims. A lot of work. But you've all come here from something bad and you all don't like where it left you and I'll tell you why you don't like it. You're not prairie rabbits. You're not cattle or deer or ducks. You don't like being victims, people, because you are not *made* to be victims. You know what you are, people? No? I didn't think so. You're *predators*. Each and every one of you. Predators who have nothing to fear in the world but other predators. And you know what? Predators shouldn't ever be afraid. That's why your eyes sit right up there on the front of your skull. Front and center, to measure the distance between you and your prey accurately. You're made to hunt and kill and cause fear and maximum damage. You're not made to anticipate attacks and defend yourself. So I'm here to turn you back into predators. You understand? So sit down, listen and learn.'

Mac turned back towards the pommel horse, then stopped and faced the group. 'People who come here want to learn how to survive. Well, this is the right place. Welcome to Predator Class, victims.'

Chapter Eleven

Investigation Room, North Manhattan Homicide
March 7, 2.05 p.m.

'Wait up, Harper. I need to speak to you right now!' bellowed Captain Lafayette.

Harper was moving fast down the beige and brown corridor of the precinct house. 'I'll get back to you,' he shouted. 'I've got something that needs my full attention.'

Lafayette's face reddened and he marched up to Harper. 'Stop with the fucking games, Harper. I need to know, right now.'

Harper stopped and turned; he pointed his finger. 'You know and I know that someone is going to try to pull this out of our hands. The media are painting this as a political assassination so we're going to be dragged off-course unless we focus. We've got maybe twenty-four hours to make this our own.'

'Then help me to keep them off your back.'

'What do you need to know?'

Lafayette sighed. Harper looked bad and he felt wired. Everything was urgent, everything had to be done an hour ago. Evidence evaporated the moment it was born. Time was all they needed and time was the one thing that destroyed evidence. Harper had sent out his teams to interview witnesses, families, friends and anyone else who might have come into contact with Capske.

'It looks like a political attack, Harper. I got to explain to the Deputy Commissioner why we're closing the door to the Feds and Counter-Terrorism.'

'Don't close the door, just point them in another direction. Look, tell the Deputy Commissioner that, as it stands, there's not a scrap of evidence that this was political.'

'You really think that? The killer emailed the networks to tell them just that. Jesus, I thought this was an open and shut case.'

'You know Judge Capske and his wife had cut ties with David because he was marrying a non-Jew?'

'No, I didn't know that.'

'Did you know David Capske was big into cocaine a year back?'

'Come on. Harper, I know nothing till you tell me.'

'We can't presume it's political just because someone emailed. I've got the team bringing in evidence all the time. Just let me see this my way. What have the Feds got? Our victim's related to Judge Capske – that's it. You going to hand over every investigation on account of their parent's CV?'

Lafayette grabbed Harper's shoulder and turned him towards the window.

'Look out there, Harper. What do you see?'

Harper stared out of the sixth-floor window down to the street below. The crowd of news teams kept growing. The nearside sidewalk had already been filled, and new teams and the later arrivals from the print media had set up on the opposite side of the street. The whole mass of people seemed to be in constant circulation. 'I see about a hundred and fifty people down there telling some bullshit story before we've even got an autopsy report,' he said.

'What you see is pressure,' said Lafayette. 'By the fucking truckload. They've got Judge Capske's rulings and every third one is some battle with the gun lobby. He's been threatened a hundred times. They don't need an autopsy report to put two and two together. And someone called them, Harper. Someone wanted this to make the front page.'

'I get the connection, Captain. I get how we're supposed to read this, but we've got to work from evidence, not from what the media think.'

'That's how it used to be, Harper, but you know as well as I do that this is not how it is these days. The media is your biggest fucking threat. Worse than me, Harper. They apply the pressure, start questioning why a homicide team are leading on a political assassination, why we're ignoring the obvious, and we're history.'

'Looks to me that this is an East Harlem gang shooting. Cocaine found at the scene. All the hallmarks.'

'Don't bullshit me, Harper. Twenty-four hours, then I'm fighting our corner at a multi-jurisdictional meeting with the Feds and Counter-Terrorism, and you better give me something better than three wraps of cocaine and a smile.'

'If it's a political kill, then I'll back off, but until I get to look at the whole story, I can't lie down for the Feds or anyone else.'

The Captain stared down at the street. 'It's the way of things now. Trial by media. You don't want to get caught up in the middle of it.'

'We need time,' Harper repeated. He looked at the man who'd headed up North Manhattan Homicide for nine years and protected him for most of them. He knew Lafayette's intentions were good, but sometimes things got taken out of the Captain's hands. 'I'll get you something.'

Harper started down the corridor. Lafayette called after him, 'Why do you want to play it like this, Harper? A conviction on this isn't going to be easy. The media will want a fall guy. Who do you think that's going to be?'

'I am what I am,' said Harper. 'Let's just say I get excited by the complex cases.'

'This might be the shortest lead you've ever taken,' said Lafayette.

Harper turned. 'If I've got just twenty-four hours, I need help. I want Blue Team, plus four other detectives. No rookies – I want experienced guys. I want whoever it is leading the Federal investigation to come and tell me what he's got. I want a profiler from the FBI Field Office to start working on this. And I want someone to keep the press happy. I need a specialist team to respond to the calls. We're going to get a lot.'

'You finished?'

'For now,' said Harper.

He moved back into the investigation room. The overriding smell was of coffee and fresh paint; it wasn't a good mix, or a good time to start a major refurb. Three maintenance men in blue overalls were finishing up the latest addition to North Manhattan Homicide's investigation room – a new set of cubicles for each of the detective teams.

The rest of the room remained as it had for twelve years: a big open space with a dirty blue carpet and a long string of fluorescent lights that leaked out a dull yellow glow. Outside, the sun hit the building only to show up the haze of deep gray dirt on the windows. Beyond the grime, the heavy bass note of the city could still be heard.

Harper walked across to his old desk, his head swimming with details from the case that he needed to get down and think about. He didn't want a cubicle. Career advisers used cubicles. It wasn't right. Harper just wanted the old, worn, paper-stacked brown wooden desk that had been good enough for the last five years. Blue Team liked to spread and merge and, like all cops, they didn't like change.

Calls of, 'Hey, champ!' followed Harper through to where the rest of the team were setting up base camp. Cops didn't make a very sentimental bunch. It never took long to go from a hero to a zero in the eyes of your fans. Harper shrugged it off.

Eddie Kasper pulled out a chair and fixed his backside to it with a sigh. 'What did he say?'

'The press want it to be political. The Feds want to argue jurisdiction. I need something to give the Captain and the Chief of Detectives if we're going to keep this in house. And that means I need to know why Capske was killed.'

'What if it is some wacko from the gun lobby?'

'I got to tell you, Eddie, I'm not buying this Judge Capske thing. There are too many questions. Why the son not the father? Why has no political organization claimed the kill? They say it's a political statement but not what for or who made it.'

'You've got a point.'

'Then ask another question: why would they torture the guy? If it's a group, then they've got to be in and out fast. This feels different. This killer liked to spend time with his victim.'

Eddie narrowed his focus. 'You know something more than you're saying, Harper? You got that look about you.'

'Maybe this is about Judge Capske and some group who thinks he's a threat to American freedom, but if it is, they found someone who hated the victim. Hated him so bad they wanted to watch him bleed to death. Think about the mind that can do that, Eddie. If Denise Levene were here, she'd say the same thing. Overkill like this is pretty unusual – it's either a hell of a political statement or it's not political at all, it's something much more personal.'

Chapter Twelve

Denise spent three hours being spat at, hounded and abused – and what's more, she paid for the privilege. After the session, she didn't go home. She walked a while and thought about things. What Mac had done was not nice but it had left her feeling stronger than she had in months.

She grabbed a cab over to Missing Persons. All she was thinking about as Mac was screaming at her was Abby Goldenberg and what she might be going through. Abby Goldenberg who was just sixteen and had her whole life ahead of her.

Denise could help herself now, but if Abby was somewhere out there she wanted to try to help her too. The guy on the desk called upstairs and Detective Sarah Gauge came down, welcomed her and showed her into their offices.

At the squad room at Missing Persons, Abby Goldenberg's disappearance was cataloged in four large box-files and one chronologically ordered lever-arch file. The two detectives had gone through a lot of leads in the eight days since her disappearance.

Although they'd not voiced the level of their concerns to Dr Goldenberg, it appeared that they'd treated it as a potential abduction since day one. They'd even tried to get the detectives from the Major Case Squad to consider it a kidnapping. The latter had looked at the case-file and sent it back, saying there wasn't a single shred of evidence. Or, more importantly, the evidence they did have suggested she was a runaway.

Denise saw the problem. If the case stayed with Missing Persons, Abby Goldenberg would become another sad photograph on the NYPD Missing Persons website.

Denise flicked through the case-files. Munroe and Gauge had been working hard to find a break, often on their own time. Not many cops would've visited every last person on Dr Goldenberg's list, but they had done it. Was it something to do with the girl's beauty or her father's distress? It was difficult to say what moved cops to go the extra mile, but in the end it came down to a mixture of professionalism and personal integrity.

Denise pulled out the daily report summaries written by Munroe. The pair didn't seem to have taken a break in eight days. 'You've done well,' Denise said. 'You've kept the trail warm.' She flipped another page; pulled out an FBI profile. It was a one-page document, nothing more.

Denise turned to Gauge. 'You seem pretty convinced that Abby's not just a runaway.'

'I know runaways. What can I say? Some strike you that way, some don't. I can't see this Abby kid putting her father through this if she could help it. Not a chance.'

'So, if she didn't run, what happened?'

'Rape murder, most probably. The body buried in some shallow grave or cut up and stored in someone's ice compartment.' She saw Denise's face whiten. 'Sorry, Denise. But it's the truth. These things we know and it takes some doing to keep her old man from thinking them. I'm not cynical. I hope that she *is* a damn runaway. I hope she's on some romantic delusion with some idiot boyfriend – I hope she's screwing half of New Jersey to impress her mom. I hope she'll come back tomorrow, but they don't come back, not often, not after eight days. Not when they're sixteen and don't have a drug or home problem.'

'How much time you got left on the case?'

'None. We've been busting a gut to finish our other caseloads, working our own time, and generally lying and shit to give this case some light, but we're all done. The Squad Sergeant is going to move it to the back room.'

'And then what happens to Abby?'

'We keep in contact with her father every few months, we give the impression that we're still looking. Officially it's still an open case, but between you and me, it doesn't get a second of our time.'

'He's a smart man, he probably guesses. I was thinking that's why he mentioned me. I'm a link – Columbia and NYPD.'

'Yes, it could be. You want some time with this stuff?'

'Please.'

'Well, let us know if you think we've missed something.'

'What's the bottom line?'

'Unless you can find some physical evidence to prove to the Squad Sergeant that this is an abduction or murder, then it's over for Abby. She's a statistic.'

Denise nodded. She looked down at the FBI profile. 'They sent this through to you?'

'We made up some details about the case to get a second opinion.'

Denise read the profile.

'Any use?' said Gauge.

'Inductive profiling. It's pretty basic. They use the limited information they've got about known criminals and match them up with the crime under consideration. All this tells you is that in the last twenty years, the kind of person abducting teenage girls in this type of location tended to be men aged somewhere between thirty-two and forty-five years old who have previous convictions. It's not going to help you much.'

'It didn't.'

Denise took a pen and pulled a clean sheet of paper from the tray on the desk. 'Deductive profiling works quite differently. The Feds use statistical averages, but that's a blunt tool. Deductive reasoning is harder but it uses every piece of forensic evidence, every detail of the victim, the location and time of the attack to build an individualized picture of the perpetrator.'

'There's nothing for you to work on.'

'I can piece something together. At least, I can try.'

'Well, let us know if you need anything else,' said Sarah Gauge. 'Right now I've got a missing prostitute and an absconded husband to track down.'

Detective Gauge left the room and Denise was alone. A research psychologist by training, she had worked for years on the relationships between behavior and personality types, comparing these to criminal profiles and then analyzing where FBI and police profiles had gone wrong. It had drawn her into contact with killers across America, but always from a safe distance.

She took the job at the NYPD to get closer to the action and in a very short time, she was too close altogether.

Her research had shown her that inductive profiling worked in less than fifty per cent of cases. Human beings were not entirely predictable and Denise was interested in the fifty per cent who were more difficult to profile simply by using statistics. These were difficult because they were not normal. They were the criminals with psychologies so distorted and perverse that basic models and types didn't help. They needed individual attention.

On the piece of paper in front of her, she started to analyze the victim. It was often the biggest part of the profile, trying to understand why the killer was motivated to take this particular girl and for what particular reason. Denise wrote down everything she could about the kind of girl that Abby was.

The facts were simple. The last thing they knew about Abby was that she left home just before 5.15 p.m. and was last seen leaving the house by her father. A driver spotted her crossing Parkway, but didn't see anyone following her. There was a report that a truck nearly knocked her over. So presumably Abby was preoccupied. She was going somewhere secretive and she changed her clothes, so it would be something to do with a boy or a band. Denise couldn't really see another reason for her to deceive her father. And this was to protect him, not harm him.

Denise concluded that Abby was someone who was willing to listen to her own feelings and not be swayed by others. It seemed unlikely then, that she would have been seduced into a car, as some girls were by clever kidnappers who appeared injured, or seemed to need help or offer some inducement. She would also have had a high degree of self-confidence.

Abby was sixteen, pretty, adventurous and slim. A sexual motive was certainly possible, if not probable. She was also Jewish and Denise couldn't rule out that this might have been important to the killer in some way. There had been no contact with the family – no ransom request, and the family was not wealthy. Kidnapping for monetary gain seemed implausible. It was more probable, therefore, that it was someone she knew or who knew her family.

A personal motive seemed likely. It might well have been someone who had become obsessed with her. But the cops had exhausted that train of enquiry and found nothing. If it was a relative, a friend or a stalker, they'd kept their interests well hidden.

Abby had left the house in the dark just before it started to rain. It was not even a predictable event, as Abby rarely went out on a school night and this seemed to be a plan that she told no one about.

An opportunist would more likely be trawling in a car and would take someone waiting or in need of help, not someone rushing to meet up with the new man in her life.

No, Denise thought, Abby wasn't just unlucky – someone had targeted her specifically and either knew she was heading out that night or was following her. For that reason, Denise thought that the killer was likely to be known to the suspect and to live close. It might have even been a neighbor who saw her pass and decided to follow.

If someone had planned to kidnap the girl, it was likely that they would scope the victim's movements and choose a place and time that was part of the girl's normal routine. But this wasn't part of her normal routine and yet they somehow knew she was heading out and knew to be there. The perpetrator had to be very confident and very proficient to take someone and leave no evidence.

Denise pushed her short blond hair back and rubbed her forehead. She tried to clear her head. A moment later, Sarah Gauge ran back in the room. She walked past Denise and across to a couple of guys on the far-side desks. 'Guys, switch on the TV,' she said.

'What is it?'

'Captain says they've identified the body in Harlem.'

'What body?' called Denise.

'Unidentified bodies excite Missing Persons; they found one this morning in East Harlem.'

A couple of the guys from the squad started searching for the remote. Sarah walked across and reached up to the TV. 'It works with a switch, too, fellas.'

'Jesus, Johnny,' said one of them. 'Did you know they made them with switches? Is that like the latest thing, Gauge?'

'No,' said Gauge. 'The latest thing is a wise-ass cop with a face full of pizza.' The TV came on. It was an old model, pinned to the wall high on a metal arm. Sarah said to Denise, 'Lot of our cases turn up at the morgue as unidentified bodies.'

Denise rose and stood next to Sarah. 'It's a cruel job you've got.'

'It's nothing new. I've been checking every day for the bodies, hoping it's not Abby.'

The news channel was throwing out information about a crime scene up in Harlem. A dark-haired reporter with hair blowing about was live at the scene, speaking in an urgent voice with very little to say. The red tickertape across the top of the screen declared *Breaking News* and the voices of the two anchormen in the studio could be heard as they tried to piece together the story. Someone had died. It was someone connected to some case in the news, but they couldn't say any more. It was big news, but they were unable to report the facts until the family had been informed.

Denise leaned in and her hands started to shake. *A body found. As yet unidentified*, read the tape. Her mind immediately started to imagine how they might find Abby. But what was the likelihood? She stared at the screen.

'Over to Kirsty, down on 112th Street. Can you tell us what's happening?' There was a pause, a crackle, then a different tone as Kirsty's voice came on. Behind her, the chaotic noise of a hundred media teams clamoring for news.

'We've just seen another team of detectives head to the crime scene. As yet, the NYPD have not made a statement. We're just waiting to hear. That's all we can do. We'll let you know the moment things change.'

'But what do we know, Kirsty? Is anything confirmed?'

Kirsty pushed several strands of hair out of her face. 'All I can say is what we were told this morning. We received an early-morning email which told us that there was a body. It gave a name, but we can't confirm.'

Then out of the chaos, a familiar face appeared. Denise watched Tom Harper move towards the camera. He was surrounded at once by a group of baying reporters. He wasn't saying much, but was showing signs of irritation. The camera went in close. Denise saw his face – the bruised, swollen eye, the cut lip. She shivered. What had happened to him? She couldn't help feeling for him and it wasn't anger. That was strange. The anger wasn't there.

Denise remembered what her therapist had said. 'You've got to work out what's going on in yourself, in the past and in the present.' Tom Harper was in the present. It was the first time in three months that she'd seen his face, although not the first time she had thought about him.

Up to that point, she'd kept herself physically away from him, connecting him so strongly with her experience at the hands of a serial killer that she couldn't cope with the thought of seeing him. Somewhere in her mind, she blamed him for dragging her into the case and for what happened to her. But looking at the man on the television, she realized that he was just the fall guy. He was easy to hate, because Harper didn't want to be hated and Denise needed a reaction. Tears formed in her eyes.

On the screen, Harper was framed by the building and two other cops. He pulled out a piece of paper, stood still and stared into the camera. 'The NYPD were called to an incident early this morning. Two officers responded to the call and found a single victim. The body was tightly wound in barbed wire making identification difficult. We have now been able to confirm the identity of the victim and we have informed the family. I can now let you know that the victim's name is David Capske, aged twenty-seven. As soon as we have further information we will let you know. No questions, please.'

Denise felt a sudden strong sense of relief. It wasn't Abby's body in the alley. She turned to Sarah who seemed to feel the same.

She continued to watch as he came on screen again and appeared close to the camera. Tom Harper. He was her problem in the present, the problem she had to resolve. She had to let herself forgive him, but more than that, she had to let herself try to be part of something that mattered to her.

She stared at Harper – his hair ruffled, his damaged face, his coat torn at the shoulder. Tom Harper. Always at the scene, always in her thoughts, always at the center of everything, always where the trouble was. But if there was one man she'd like at her shoulder now, looking at the mass of information about Abby Goldenberg, it'd be Harper every time.

Chapter Thirteen

Harper returned from interviewing Lucy Steller and Capske's family. He called Blue Team together for a briefing and pulled up a chair.

'We've spoken to Lucy Steller. She's twenty-nine, works in a 7–Eleven store and writes novels. She's badly shaken up, but her story seems simple enough. She left the club with David, walked home but when they got to her building, David Capske received a phone call. He told Lucy that he had to go to help a friend. He wouldn't tell her why. He said he'd be an hour. The only other thing she said is that they saw a car outside the club. A red car. Someone inside was smoking. We're checking CCTV on that. Eddie's pieced together a tape of Capske's last walk.'

Eddie Kasper dimmed the lights and clicked on the laptop in front of him. 'We got every piece of CCTV tape between Lucy Steller's apartment and the crime scene. I've got Capske in seven different shots.' The team watched the grainy images of Capske walking up various streets.

'Here,' said Eddie, pointing. 'He took out a thousand dollars from this ATM. It was found in his wallet. Later, he received a second phone call. We've got to guess that the first phone call told him how much money was needed, the second was for directions. So this might suggest that he was lured up there due to drugs or some kind of deal or blackmail. We got nothing else, but we're going over this tape frame by frame.'

'We got a trace on these calls?' asked Garcia.

'Damn right,' said Harper. 'Greco, what did you find?'

'We've got one cell-phone number used in the two calls to Capske and the 911 call this morning. Untraceable account and the phone is not transmitting. The killer bought a cell, used it, dumped it.'

'So the person who called Capske also called the cops,' said Harper. 'Why did he do that? We need answers. What else? Ricky? We got any new witnesses with anything to say yet? I can't believe no one heard anything.'

'We've done four hours of door-to-door. We leafleted the whole area. We got a woman in Jensen House who heard a single gunshot at around 3.30 a.m. Two more witnesses give the same time.'

'That's good, we've got a TOD right there. Eddie, what's your best estimate on when he arrived at the alleyway?'

'Last frame is clocked at 1.38 a.m. It's five minutes from Jensen House. Let's say he arrived at 1.43 a.m.'

Harper stood up. 'We've got a guy leaves his fiancée after an unexpected phone call. It's something he doesn't want his fiancée to know about, so we presume it's trouble. He takes out a thousand dollars, walks to East 112th and arrives at 1.43 a.m. Between that time and 3.30 a.m. he is wrapped in barbed wire. That's an hour and forty-seven minutes the killer spent with his victim. Does that sound like a hit to anyone?' No one spoke up. 'Another detail we got is the weather report. Rain started at 2.41 a.m. The ground under the victim was dry. He was lying in barbed wire in that spot for fifty minutes before he was shot. Why?'

'Maybe the killer was talking to the vic,' said Mary Greco.

'Well, that's one possibility. One thing we can assume is that this killer is confident. More than that, he's fearless. Two hours with the vic in a public alley – that's no gangbanger or deranged killer. That's an organized and planned mind. Garcia, you getting anything on these right-wing groups who have been targeting the Judge?'

'Ratten found these right-wing assholes getting heated on the forums,' said Garcia. 'A lot of celebratory shit about the murder. They read it as a direct political attack.'

'Well, that's going to be front-page news by tomorrow.'

'Yeah, they're calling the killer a hero.'

'Fucking hard to believe these bastards,' said Ratten.

'Isn't freedom of speech just great?' mocked Harper. 'Can we trace them?'

'Maybe, maybe not,' said Ratten. 'It's a matter of priority. Could take two men four days to track this thread down and then you're going to find that most of them are just a bunch of inadequate losers, sitting in their bedrooms, kicking back Oreos, living with their parents and collecting welfare. Also,' Ratten continued, 'I did take a quick look and the key information is encrypted.'

Ratten moved across to a PC and tapped the keyboard. 'The forum is called the White Wall, but there's no overarching organization that claims to run it. Not that I can find yet. But a few of them claim to be part of something called the White Wolves.'

'Find out what it means,' said Harper. 'Give the lead to the Feds and get them to trace it. It might lead somewhere.'

'Sure,' said Ratten.

Harper pulled out a set of photographs from the alley. 'I got Forensics to give me something on the single or multiple killer angle. At the moment, they can only find traces of one set of boot prints in the wet. They aren't clean prints, but because kicking the wire has cut up the soles, they can ID each print and they're pretty sure that there was only one guy in that alley. Our killer's not just organized and fearless, he's strong and determined.'

Harper took a marker pen, wrote the name *David Capske* at the top of a clean white board and pinned up a big glossy photograph of the twenty-seven year old who seemed to have got caught up in a world where he didn't belong.

'Capske was also a user,' said Greco. 'Apparently, he gave it up after meeting Lucy Steller, but he might have been looking to score again. His friends still use the same dealer. We met him, but he tells us Capske's not using him.'

Harper turned to the team. 'Keep at it. Something will break. This whole picture doesn't add up. Someone lured him to that alleyway. Maybe the drugs were a lure, maybe it was blackmail.

He took out the thousand dollars for something. Keep looking.'
The team started to move. 'Oh, one more thing,' he added. 'Victim Support working with Lucy Steller told us that a reporter had already offered her money for the story.'

'A reporter? Seriously? You get a name?'

'No. But if it's not Erin Nash, I'd be surprised. Be aware, that's all.'

'She doesn't give up, does she?' said Eddie.

'No, she doesn't, so get moving. I need to know more about this killer. We've got the FBI profiler already working on a profile. All we know so far is that he's powerful, he's angry and he doesn't lose control for a moment. That's a pretty scary combination.'

Chapter Fourteen

The barking of the dogs announced his return. Abby's hands were handcuffed behind her back and her mouth was gagged with a leather restraint. The floor of the small room was covered in a thin mattress. The room, as far as she could tell, was no more than a closet. There was not enough space to lie flat. Abby could either lie on her side with her knees bent or sit up against the walls and stretch out her legs. She was wearing the same tartan skirt and T-shirt she'd put on eight days earlier. To one side of the mattress on the thin strip of bare concrete floor was a green plastic bedpan.

There was no direct light in the room, but the wall didn't quite reach the corrugated roof and light from outside filtered in. Not much, but it helped. Complete darkness would've been harder to cope with. Strange as it was, you were grateful for the smallest things. A thin mattress, a chink of light, a bedpan.

Sometimes Abby imagined the things that he might do to her. She let the horror snake around her and leave her cold with sweat. But he hadn't killed her or raped her. Yet. She attempted to convince herself that this was because he was trying to get money out of her folks. For days she tried to work out why the smell of his cologne was familiar. It was a strong musky scent, but she couldn't put a place or face on the smell. It was driving her crazy.

She tried to keep her mind from getting lost in the stupefying boredom by having imaginary conversations with friends, with her mom and dad, her grandparents. She visualized how they'd all react when she got out. How they'd be, what they'd say. She imagined the warm hugs, the wide eyes and big smiles, tainted with tears. She'd try to remember details from every part of her home, then she'd count the threads in the mattress and then recount them in different multiples. She had to keep her head straight. She was lucky she had her music, and in her head, she played note by note, practicing with imagined hands on an imagined saxophone.

Getting some kind of exercise was difficult, but there was enough space to stand and she spent some time each day standing and sitting, pressing her legs against the wall, turning, squatting, rising. It all helped to give some structure to the time.

On the wall she marked the days by dragging her cuffs in a single line across the brick. It was important to keep watch of time. The worst thing was the food. So little. Each day her abductor pushed a piece of bread, a piece of cheese and a cup of water through the flap. She would push out the bedpan. One little ritual.

She had tried to speak in the beginning, during the feeding times, when the restraint was removed. 'I'm missing my dad, you know. He'll be trying to solve this. Schoolwork will be piling up. My name is Abby Goldenberg.'

But he stopped it. Insisted on silence. The flap would shut and she would hear him move about, typing, changing clothes.

On the fourth day, she turned the mattress over and spent hours with her hands and teeth, pulling at a small tear. She had the idea that if she could get a rag of the mattress, by pressing her back to one wall and her feet to the other, she might be able to lift herself up to the roof and somehow push out a flag. It was not going to save her, but it might cause some attention and then she could hammer at the door with her feet. She'd tried that for hours already, but stopped out of frustration, and now tried it only every few hours. The thing was – her abductor was regular. He came at the same time each day. An hour or so before the sun went down. So she knew when it was safe to try to attract attention.

She was very cold. At night, all the time. Never anything but cold. She could hear cars and trucks and in the quiet hours, she

74

could hear birds. They sometimes landed on the top of the roof and she listened to their footsteps.

The dogs barked outside. She felt terrible panic and the instant retching of her guts. The outer door opened and he was inside. The dogs sniffed and ran about the room as they did every time. Their claws scratched on the hard floor, they wagged their tails and bumped into things. There were lots of them and they sniffed at her door. She tried to count them, but there were too many.

The dogs were shooed out. The flap opened.

'Hello,' she said. 'Can I come out . . . just for a second? Just for one second? Please let me. You've got to let me stretch my legs. You'll never guess, it's my sax exam tomorrow. If I don't practice, I'll fail. I want to talk to you. I understand why people do things. It might be good to talk about it.'

There was no reply. The bread and cheese were pushed through the flap. She used her feet to push the bedpan out. 'For God's sake, stop doing this,' she said in a whisper. The bedpan scraped across the ground.

Then his hand grabbed her foot. She froze. His skin was cold. His fingers closed around her ankle. She could hear him breathing. *Don't react*, she was telling herself. *Don't get angry*. 'I've been thinking about my mom,' she said. 'Missing her. She's not a great mom. She's a bit . . . selfish. You have to forgive people when they disappoint you, don't you? Everyone's got a reason to do what they do, it's just we don't always understand what those reasons are. Everyone's a mystery, right?'

The hand released her and she pulled her foot back through the flap. She was gulping for air.

'My name's Abby,' she said. 'I'm just sixteen. I'm scared. I miss my home. That's all, mister. I just miss my mom, my dad, my nana, my friends.'

There was no reply. The flap shot up and was locked.

Chapter Fifteen

Apartment, East Harlem
March 7, 5.55 p.m.

Harper crossed to the desk to sign out a department saloon. He needed to head up to the morgue and get the autopsy report. Dr Pense had said it'd be ready after 6 p.m. The guy on the desk raised his head and checked out Harper's face. 'Don't tell me, I should see the other guy!' he joked. Harper nodded, unsmiling, and took the keys without a word.

Harper walked down towards the car. He turned into the lot and stopped. Ahead of him, Erin Nash flashed a big cheap smile. The *Daily Echo*'s crime reporter looked lithe and purposeful, leaning on the hood of a parked SUV with one foot up on the chrome grille. Something about her had changed since he'd last seen her. He didn't know what it was at first. Maybe it was wealth. She had made a lot of money selling her stories.

'Erin, it's nice to see you. You spot an opportunity to fuck us over again?'

'Now, listen to you. I've come by to see how you are. Saw you at the crime scene. You look like shit. I was concerned.'

'Concerned enough to ride straight to the victim's grieving girlfriend and offer her money.'

'Harper, you know that's not ethical.'

'That's never stopped you before. I know it was you.'

'You're playing down the political angle on this murder, is that ethical?'

'I'm playing the percentages. If someone's targeting the govern-

76

ment, then it's the government's problem. I'm just trying to solve a homicide.'

'What about the coke? You seriously think he was shot while trying to score?'

'I think the drugs might be relevant.'

'I guessed you would.'

'What's that supposed to mean?'

'We've all got skeletons in the cupboard, right, including you, Tom Harper. A journalist's job is to sniff them out.'

'Yeah, well keep sniffing, I've got nothing to hide.' Harper stared at Erin Nash and felt the anger coming in spurts. 'What do you want?'

'I'm not into scandal-mongering, Detective, but an old friend of yours tells me that you were in rehab for something a few years back. Amphetamine addiction, maybe.'

'How much did you pay for that?'

'Listen, I don't want to make trouble and I wouldn't want to do harm to an investigation, but give me something. This Capske guy was dealing, am I right? Maybe he got in over his head.'

'I'm busy,' said Harper.

Erin Nash let out a little light laugh. 'Wouldn't it be nice if we could just walk away like that? You want me to run a drug story on you or on your victim? Nice simple choice.'

Harper stopped. He was running things over in his head. 'If you've got something to say about me and you've got the evidence, then print it. If not, go back to the sewer.'

'I wouldn't get so hung up, Tom.' Erin paused for a second. 'I wouldn't want to harm you just yet. You're a hero, Harper; people want to hear more about you. New case, first major one since your big moment.'

Harper looked to the ground. 'You want to know about David Capske, not me.'

'Come on, Harper. Just want to know what you're thinking? Trail a cop who's trailing a killer, that kind of thing.'

'Get this, Nash – it's a no. If you can't read it, put it in 72-point Helvetica like the rest of your headlines.'

'His father's a pretty important guy. A judge. This is going to run and run.'

'I got nothing for you, Nash.'

'Why were the media called this morning? What's the connection?'

'Not sure. Whoever killed Capske wanted a big audience and he knew how to get one.'

'Gun lobby would love the attention,' Erin said.

'You're a dog with a bone and you know I can't say anything, even if I knew something. Which I don't.'

'You know nothing, right?'

'And just for the record – you can't quote me on that.'

'I wouldn't dream of it, Detective.' Erin Nash took out a card and handed it to Harper. 'Just one more thing – here's my number. You scratch mine and I'll avoid pulling you off that great big pedestal.' She looked at him and locked eyes with his. 'So, soon as you get anything on this case, just holler.'

Erin Nash nodded and walked away. Harper watched her go. For a second, he wanted to reach out and shake her. Then his head started to pound again and he reached in his pocket for his painkillers, threw two pills down his throat and headed for his car.

Harper called Dr Pense from the car as the rain started to pound down again. 'Hey, it's Detective Harper. How's it going with my corpse?'

'Hell, Harper,' Dr Pense said. 'Well, it's not nice, but I'll be ready in thirty minutes.'

'Anything I should know?'

'I'll tell you in thirty minutes.'

Harper looked at his watch. He needed a shower, a change of clothes and some more painkillers, and since he had a few more minutes before heading to the morgue, he pulled out and headed for home.

Harper climbed up the stairs and entered his two-room apartment. He never used heating, and as a result the apartment was constantly damp. He took a quick shower, saw the extent of his bruises for the first time and was shocked at how he'd let himself get beaten up. He dressed and found more painkillers. Well past their sell-by date, but he figured they'd work as good as any. He went to the window, took a quick look across the street. The hookers were huddled out of the rain, trying to peer into cars from a distance. It wasn't working for them or the curb crawlers.

As quiet as Harper was, he found it hard to attain silence. His mind rarely stopped working. When he was on a case, that driven, tireless mind found a home and, for a time, his trait had a worthwhile outlet. As he was staring out into the rain, several thoughts passed through his mind. Each case was a puzzle that kept returning, and he knew that his mind was going back every few minutes to try to solve it afresh.

The shrill ring of the buzzer broke into his thoughts. He pushed open the window, took in the fumes of gasoline and rain and looked down to the ground floor – but whoever was there was taking cover from the cold sheets of rain. The ringing continued.

He walked to his buzzer. 'Hello.'

'Tom.'

Harper paused. 'Denise?' He felt his pulse rising with unexpected excitement.

'Yes, Tom, it's me.'

A line of heat ran along the underside of each of Harper's eyes. He pressed his head to the cold gloss of the door. 'Denise.'

'It's raining, Tom.' There was a silence. 'Tom, I'm getting soaked down here.'

'Denise,' he said again. He felt like a man encountering a ghost. It had been a long three months and she'd been in his thoughts every day. 'I just don't believe I'm hearing you. I called you – I left messages. You've never replied. I didn't expect to hear from you.'

'I got all your messages, Tom. Please believe it, and open the door. I'm freezing.'

Tom was on the stairs, heading down as fast as he could. He reached the front door and stared out. She was framed by the red wrought-iron bars that crossed the glass panel in the door. Her blond hair was shorter and plastered to her head, her face was charged with something he didn't yet understand, she had lost some weight, but it was Denise. He watched her a moment and opened the door.

'I can't believe I'm actually looking at you.'

'I'm sorry, Tom.'

'For what?'

'For being so . . . out of touch. I couldn't cope with you.' Denise's eyes fell to the ground. 'Sorry.'

'Forget it,' he said. He suddenly felt like the pieces of a puzzle he'd been struggling with for months had fallen into place. He was wide open. More open than he'd felt in months. Here she was. Denise Levene. He smiled.

'I've hated you, you know,' she said. 'I want you to know that's what's been going through my sick head.'

'You were always too honest. You could've kept that one to yourself for a while, at least.' Harper looked at her. 'Hell, maybe I've deserved it.'

'I don't think you have. I've been in a bad place. No idea how to get out.' The tone of her voice dropped a note and with it the volume. 'I went to see Mac.'

'I'm surprised, I thought that wasn't your thing.'

'Been to see every other specialist there is. Thought I'd give your recommendation a try.'

'What did you think?'

'Brutal, but it works.'

'That's good to hear. Come on, let's sort you out.'

Harper led her in silence up the stairs and walked into the apartment. She looked around in obvious dismay.

'Wow, you've decorated,' she said.

'It really makes a difference, doesn't it?' They looked at the one wall that had been half-coated in white paint. Harper went to a closet, pulled out a large clean towel and passed it to her. Denise ruffled her hair and pulled the towel around her. She sat down. She was shivering but still smiling. He went through to his bedroom and brought out a pair of sweatpants, a T-shirt and a hooded top.

'You should get into these, before you—' He stopped himself.

'Catch my death?' she offered.

He twisted his mouth. 'Okay, I'll cut out the fussing.'

Denise took the clothes and disappeared into the bathroom.

Harper stood at the door. 'So, what you working on?'

'What do you mean?' said Denise.

'I can read you, Denise. You didn't come here just because of my problems.'

Denise called through the door, 'You're still good on observations. What gave it away?'

'You've got a newspaper on you. You never liked newspapers. I figure you're looking for news, which means you're up to something. And, the big giveaway is you came here.'

Denise opened the bathroom door and stood there. 'I came to ask for help.'

'What is it?'

'An old colleague and a missing child. His daughter ran away or something worse. He doesn't understand. I went by to see him. He's a mess. He thinks something or someone happened.'

'And what do you think?'

'I agree with him.'

'What does he want you to do?'

'Prove that she didn't run away. Missing Persons are shelving the case. I'm all he's got.'

'You get anywhere?'

'I'm not a detective. But you are.'

Harper looked up. 'On a good day.' Then: 'Can I offer you something? A word of advice?'

'You can try.'

'Don't try to solve other people's problems because you can't solve your own.'

She looked up, hurt. 'That's unfair, Tom. I'm trying to get back to work.'

'You could have come to see me any time.'

'No, Tom, I had to know this was about me, about whether I could face this alone.'

'Come on, you're a helper, Denise – all your life, you've been saving someone, helping someone. That's who you are. You helped me. You brought yourself up. You saved your old man from losing hope when he was inside.'

'No, I didn't. I left him. I visited every week. That was all I could do.'

'Sure you did, Denise. He told you that you always had to have faith. The same faith you used to get you through. What did he call it? That thing in the dark that he said he always held every night and that kept him from being afraid.'

'His fantastic sparkler,' she said.

'That was you, Denise. That was you he was holding in the dark all those years in prison. His fantastic sparkler.'

Denise broke into silent sobs. Harper didn't comfort her. It wasn't pain that she was suffering. It was relief.

'What the hell do you want, you bastard? Making me cry and look weak and foolish. This is why I hate you!'

'I want to help you.'

'It's not that kind of help I want, Tom. I'm involved in this case because I think I can do some good. I went to see the case-files; I started a profile. Victimology.'

'What did you find?'

'A way in. I think there's something here.'

'Okay,' said Tom. 'I'm sorry. I'll help if I can, but I've got a big case just starting up.'

'I know. I saw you on TV,' she said. 'What's the deal?'

'Put simply, David Capske got wrapped in barbed wire and shot. Everyone has it down as a political killing.'

'But you don't see it like that?'

'No evidence. I know it's nice and neat, and someone wants us to see it like that, but I see something that I've only ever seen with sadistic serial killers.'

'What's that?'

'Someone who's got no real ulterior motive. The kill is the thing, the whole thing and nothing but the thing. Whoever killed Capske liked it. Liked it a lot and will do it again.'

'Gratification killer?'

82

Harper raised his eyebrows.

'You got a profiler working on this?' said Denise.

'Rookie that the Feds sent.'

'Any good?'

'Not good enough. We've only got twenty-four hours before Lafayette rolls over and the Feds come in and take over the investigation.'

'I could take a look,' she said. 'Offer a comment.'

'Tit for tat?'

'One good deed deserves another . . .'

'What do you want me to do on the missing girl?' asked Harper.

'I need some help getting access to the Hate Crime Unit.'

'What do you need them for?'

'A couple of months back, Abby was roughed up as she walked home. It's all I've got. A group of four young men. Hate Crime found them and took them in for questioning but couldn't make anything stick. A week later, there was a swastika painted on the Goldenbergs' front door.'

'You think it's related?'

'It's the only evidence of anyone targeting the family and my profile suggests that if Abby was attacked, then it was someone who knew where she lived, knew her name and wanted to hurt her and her family.'

'What are the guys called?'

'Raymond Hicks, Patrick Ellery, Leo Lukanov, Thomas Ocksborough.'

Harper wrote down the names. 'I know someone in Hate Crime. I can call him up, give you a good reference, get you some information.'

'Thanks, Tom. It might help.'

'And if you're going to help me, you need to take a look at this victim.'

'I suppose I'd have to.'

'It's not pretty. It's a hell of a way back in to your day job.'

'I'll cope,' said Denise. 'Or at least I'll give that impression.'

Chapter Sixteen

Office of the Chief Medical Examiner, Manhattan
March 7, 6.36 p.m.

Harper waited for Eddie Kasper to find his way to the department parking lot. Eddie got in the front passenger seat and turned round: Denise Levene sat in the back of the sedan. Eddie's eyes opened wide. 'Don't I know you from somewhere?'

'Yeah, maybe, but I'm not one of your conquests.'

'I wish,' said Eddie, 'but I don't go for smart women, they see right through me.'

'And see what? A good guy with a fine line in self-deprecation.'

'Hey, Tom, she's back, right? The mouth and everything.'

'Yeah,' said Tom, 'and everything.'

They drove by the city Medical Examiner's office and caught up with Dr Laura Pense, the Deputy Chief Medical Examiner. Denise stood at the back of the small group as they entered. She wanted to be closest to the door if the panic attack started.

Harper turned to Levene. 'This one is pretty bad, Denise. You sure you want to tag along?' She nodded.

The two detectives and Denise Levene walked inside and trailed down familiar corridors. Dr Laura Pense was sitting in a small windowless office, writing up paperwork. Harper knocked and stood at the door.

'Hey, Dr Pense, how are you?'

Laura Pense continued to hammer out something on her keyboard. 'All good, here, Detective, how about you?'

'He's a fucking mess,' said Eddie, 'but you already know that, right?'

Laura turned and saw Harper's face for the first time. 'Jesus,' she said. 'Were you assaulted or something?'

'Or something,' said Harper.

Laura Pense stood up, acknowledged Denise with a smile and then peered more closely at Harper's face. 'That's pretty bad. Abrasions to the nose, lips, jaw, eyes. Deep tissue bruising. Potential fracture on the left cheek. Is that sore, there?'

'I can't feel it any more.'

'He's popping four painkillers every hour.'

Laura Pense raised her eyebrows in disapproval. 'Don't tell me you've been boxing?'

'You're right, he wasn't boxing,' said Eddie. 'No, you couldn't call what he was doing anything more than giving someone target practice.'

'You been checked out?' said Laura.

'This guy?' said Eddie. 'This is a Neanderthal, Doctor, a throwback. You know, when men were men and pain was personal disgrace.'

'Macho men!' said Dr Pense. 'God, the amount of big guys I've seen who have been brought down by a spot of blood. Intracranial hemorrhages, Harper – perhaps you can fix that yourself, too.'

'Is that my report?' said Harper, pointing at the computer screen.

'Are you lead on the Capske case?' asked Laura.

'I've been given the honor. Blue Team are on the case.'

'Well, I'm just signing off.'

'Anything I should know?'

'Sure, come through. You got to see this.'

Harper felt reluctance stir inside him. He didn't feel too good already, but he followed Dr Pense through to the autopsy room. Eddie was even further behind with Denise.

Dr Pense put on a fresh pair of gloves and approached a gurney covered in a green sheet. She whipped it back like a magician.

The sight was not magical at all, but macabre and strange. The barbed-wire cage had been opened with wire cutters and each clawing strand of wire pulled back. It lay open like a metal ribcage or a huge barbed chrysalis. Beneath the barbed wire was a bloody carcass. The skin was punctured by hundreds of dark round holes and slits.

'Some of the puncture wounds are straight, but many have torn and ripped the skin where the victim has struggled. They're deep too, deep enough to get right through the skin. He lost a lot of blood. Practically bled to death.'

Harper and Kasper passed their eyes over the corpse.

'It's a vicious death,' said Dr Pense. 'I can't be exact but he's been left to bleed for an hour or more. Tortured, I should say. In incredible pain. He probably blacked out. Look at this.' She tilted his head so that one eye could be seen. The eyeball was punctured in two places. 'Every single inch is punctured. You can't imagine. You really can't imagine.'

'So, we got anything to nail his killer?'

'He was shot once in the forehead. Little black wound, right here. He must've been tight to the ground, the bullet went in through the skull, out, hit the ground, re-entered and mashed the brain like an electric whisk.'

They both looked at Laura. 'Nice image.'

'Sorry, I've been taking French cookery courses, you know, trying to keep alive.'

'That's nice. Did you find the bullet?'

'Yeah, sleeping like a baby in the left frontal lobe.' Laura picked up a little lump of metal with a pair of forceps and dropped it back into the tray with a jingle.

'It's not got much shape left,' said Harper. 'The wound is unusually small too. What's the exit wound look like?'

'Interesting that you should ask. Bullet left the skull here. Not a great piece of scalp knocked out. Looked like it zipped through.'

'It's unusual,' said Harper. He lifted the bullet with the forceps and turned it under his eye. 'There's something about this that isn't right. I want Ballistics to tell me what they can about this, Eddie. Can you get them to do it tonight?'

'Not much for Ballistics to go on,' said Eddie. 'But I'll give it a go.'

'Did you find a cartridge?' asked Dr Pense.

'No,' said Harper. 'You find anything more?'

Laura shrugged. 'We had samples taken; we did checks, but nothing to report, yet. I mean, we don't know what we're looking for, but his organs all look healthy. Apart from his septum.'

'The coke?'

'Yeah, signs of damage but it's healed. I'd say he used to be a user, but not in the last year or so. I won't know if there was any coke in his blood for another few hours. And another thing. We've got a lot of dirt under his nails.'

'What kind?'

'Petroleum-based with some black dye.'

'Meaning?'

'Boot polish.'

'So he cleaned his shoes before he went out dancing,' said Eddie.

'He was wearing white sneakers,' said Harper.

'You got any theories?' said Laura.

'Maybe he cleaned the killer's boots,' said Denise from the far side of the room. 'Punishment and containment. It wouldn't surprise me if he humiliated and demeaned the victim first.'

Harper and Dr Pense turned. 'Where did that come from, Denise?'

'Deduction. If it's not his boot polish, maybe this killer's got some big-time subservience thing going on – a malignant narcissist, something like that.'

Harper and Levene caught each other's eye. Harper sensed there was more that Denise could say, but he dropped it.

'Could be a small-time dealer. Selling to his friends. Got mixed up with some bad boys,' said Eddie.

'Not the usual MO for a gangbanger, is it? They shoot and scatter like rats,' said Harper.

'We've also got slight abrasions to his knees, just surface scratches.'

'Was he dragged across the floor?'

'No. Not dragged. This was like he was kneeling. Fits with Denise's idea that the killer made him polish his boots.'

'Kneeling?'

'At some point, before the torture and execution.'

The four of them stared down at the bloody carcass with the horrible possibilities reverberating in each of their thoughts. Harper gazed at Laura as the harshness of the word 'execution' hung in the air. 'Anything else?'

'Yes,' said Laura, 'but I don't know what it is.' She walked over to Capske's body and swabbed the corpse's chest until it was clear of blood. 'There,' she said.

'What are they?'

'Tiny needlemarks. Some have traces of ink, but the barbed wire has torn most of it to shreds.'

'They look like they form a series of lines,' said Harper.

'Yeah, there's a few more in the torn skin. Can't reconstruct anything. What do you think?'

'Tattoo,' said Harper. 'It looks like a home-made tattoo.'

'There was also a card stuck to his chest.'

'What?'

Laura Pense brought out a small rectangle of black card. 'It's got his name on it and the word *Loyalty*.'

'Where was it?'

'Inside his shirt.'

They looked at the card and then at Capske's chest where a series of small pinpricks stretched across the skin – but the tears and puncture marks obscured them. The marks ran across his chest and each line was in a different direction. Some were straight, others curved slightly, some were horizontal, others vertical.

Harper took out his sketchpad and drew the marks. 'It might be something important,' he said. 'Shame the barbed wire has ripped it all away.'

'The marks were made with a fine-point needle,' said Dr Pense. 'The killer took his time doing that.'

Harper looked down at his sketchbook. The marks led left to

right in a line and fell away to the right. All in all, there were about thirty-two tiny puncture marks. The others were lost in the torn skin. 'Denise, you got any idea?'

'Sociopathic not political. Maybe the killer thinks he's fulfilling some political purpose, but this kind of behavior is compulsive. The need to mark the corpse, to torture, to execute.'

'I agree,' said Harper. 'What about the word on the card?'

'*Loyalty*. It might give you a clue to the motive or it might be related to his conceptual framework, his ideology. He thinks this is purposeful, even necessary.'

'What do you mean?'

'A typed card in black. Like an execution card, right? Like his target has been pre-ordained.'

'Could it be from someone David betrayed?'

'He might feel that David has betrayed him. I wouldn't imagine that the betrayal is real. This is someone's psychosis working things through on real people. It's dangerous, Tom.'

'These other marks, what do they mean? Just dots . . .'

Harper looked down at the pattern on the page in front of him.

'What do you think it means?' he asked, looking at Eddie and Denise. They stared hard and shrugged.

'No idea,' said Eddie. 'If that helps.'

'Thanks, Laura,' said Harper. 'We'll be in touch.'

Dr Pense stood up and followed him out. 'Can I take a look at your face?'

Harper stopped. 'What for?'

'How's your sight?'

'Right eye good. Left eye not so good.'

Laura pushed Harper through the double doors into her office. 'Sit down. I want a closer look.'

'What for?'

'Because if I don't, no one will, right?'

Harper sat down at her desk and waited. Laura scrubbed her hands in a sink by the side wall, brought a pen light and pulled his head back. She shone the light into his eye and held it there for a minute.

'Feds are looking into it too,' said Harper. 'They want to know if it's to do with Judge Capske's ruling and the reaction from the Gun Lobby.'

'Is it?'

'I doubt it.' He looked up. 'What's the damage?'

Laura clicked the pen light off and put it in her pocket. 'I think you're okay. Your eye's responding well to the light. But you should get it looked at properly.'

'I just did,' said Harper, rising and offering his hand. She took it and they shook.

Chapter Seventeen

Hate Crime Task Force, Brooklyn
March 7, 7.03 p.m.

Denise stood outside the rundown precinct in Brooklyn that housed the Brooklyn Hate Crime Squad. Harper had squared things with the Lieutenant, a friendly cop called Phil Trigg. They'd talk to Dr Levene, give her some background and chase up the records of the four men accused of bias attack on the Goldenbergs. All she wanted was something to take back to Detectives Munroe and Gauge that indicated abduction or worse.

Harper went with Eddie to Ballistics. The mangled bullet was the only piece of physical evidence that came from the killer, so Harper wanted to know if there was anything in it. Time was ticking down fast.

Denise headed up to the fourth floor. She still had her Civilian NYPD ID card with her photograph against a blue background. She approached the tall gray-haired figure ahead of her. 'Dr Levene,' she said, and held out her hand.

Lieutenant Trigg shook it firmly. 'Harper explained,' he said. 'I've kept one of the team back for you. Detective Carney's the man you want to speak to. His knowledge of the area is second to none. He's got every hate group mapped and tagged. It's an impressive operation he runs.'

'I appreciate this,' said Denise.

'We all got daughters, Doctor, so if this might help some poor guy, then we're happy to assist.' The Lieutenant pointed. Denise found herself looking at the back of Jack Carney. He was tall, athletic with broad shoulders.

'Detective Carney,' said Denise.

Jack Carney turned. He stared across the precinct investigation room. His eyes were clear blue. He was handsome and confident. 'You must be Dr Levene. Good to meet you.'

'Thank you for agreeing to help.'

'Not a problem. Harper gave me four names: Raymond Hicks, Patrick Ellery, Leonard Lukanov and Thomas Ocksborough.'

'You know them?'

'I know them as Ray Hicks, Paddy Ellery, Leo Lukanov, Tommy Ocks. I've done a quick check. I know a couple of them pretty well. That's not usually a good sign.' He smiled. Denise smiled back.

'You married?' he asked.

'No,' she said. 'Is that relevant?'

'I don't know yet,' said Carney. Denise stared. 'Come on, I'm kidding you. You got to loosen up, Doctor. This is no comedy show down here, so we've got to cheer ourselves up.'

'Can we concentrate on these four guys, rather than my marital status?'

'Sure,' said Carney. 'Let's go find a seat somewhere.' He led Denise into one of the interview rooms, asking, 'You got any indications of hate crime on this missing girl?'

'Such as?'

'Words, symbols . . . any indication that it was because of her religion?'

'No. There's nothing except this attack which happened much earlier.'

'But you think these guys might have held a grudge?'

'That's what I'd like to take a look at. Where do they hang out?'

'Brooklyn.'

'Any chance you can take me on a tour? Maybe speak to them?'

'These aren't nice characters, Dr Levene – you sure you want to?'

'I'm sure as long as you can spare the time.'

'You're not going to like what you see. They're sick little thugs and they believe what they spout. It's pretty hard not to react and I know you're the kind to react.'

'Don't worry about me,' said Denise.

The third name on the list was Leo Lukanov. Carney and his partner muscled up close to the door. They were an intimidating pair. They knocked hard and loud and shouted out 'NYPD – open up!' They kept it going until the person inside felt that this was drawing too much attention to him.

The door opened. Leo Lukanov stood there. Close-cropped blond hair, pale blue eyes, full red lips. He was wearing a tank top, the number eighty-eight tattooed on one shoulder above an iron cross, some SS symbols on the right. Denise shied away immediately. She hadn't expected the Nazi symbols.

Carney stared at Lukanov. He was strong and wiry. He didn't smile or speak.

'This is Dr Levene, Leo. Now you be nice and answer the lady's questions or I'll serve this warrant here and tear your digs to pieces.' Carney waved a warrant. Denise had been told that it wasn't real, but it didn't need to be. Leo Lukanov's eyes settled on her. 'She's working on the disappearance of Abby Goldenberg,' added Carney.

Denise looked at the big tattooed figure ahead of her. He was cold, difficult – not bright, she guessed.

'Mr Lukanov, you were questioned in relation to an alleged bias-attack on Abby Goldenberg,' said Denise. 'Do you remember the allegation?'

Lukanov smiled and leaned against the door. 'The girl who thought someone grabbed her ass and shouted "Let's fuck a Jew"? It was just wishful thinking. She couldn't even say who grabbed her ass and who shouted something.'

'Is that right?' said Denise.

Leo leered forward. 'Some girls just want to improve their bloodline,' he said. 'Maybe you like the look of what you see, too?'

The back of Carney's hand hit Lukanov's shoulder. 'Be polite, retard.'

Denise flicked open her notes. 'This your line, Leo, sexually motivated hate crime? You into that – hate and lust? That make you tick?'

'We didn't do nothing. She imagined it. We were shouting all kinds of things. Just walking and shoving. Nothing about or against anyone. She must've got confused.'

'You're wearing some Nazi symbols,' said Denise. 'Do you hate Jews?'

'I don't take political stances, lady.'

'She also heard someone say, "Die you kike bitch".'

'She misheard.'

'She heard it twice.'

'She misheard it twice. Some kids, some Jews, they've got a persecution complex. One of us says something innocent and because we're wearing Nazi symbols, they get confused and bitter. We're the victims, here.'

'I think we all know you're lying, Mr Lukanov. Those symbols are offensive.'

'HCU will tell you that it ain't a crime. Pro-Nazi symbols aren't anti-Semitic in their own right, did you know that?'

'Is that right?' asked Denise.

Jack Carney nodded and twisted his mouth.

'You heard or seen or know anything about Abby's disappearance?'

'Uh-huh.'

'You know anything?'

'No,' said Lukanov. He took a rolled cigarette from behind his ear and lit it.

'You ever think about going round to her house after she reported the four of you to the police?'

'No, we never thought that.'

'Don't get smart, Leo, or I'll put it about that you're an informer.'

'Sorry, Detective.'

'You be very sorry, Leo, now answer the questions.'

'Look, lady, we might do some shit, but we don't do no serious shit.'

94

Denise looked at him. She sensed that he was capable of cruelty. 'I'm just saying, Mr Lukanov, that one story going around my head is about the four of you, becoming angry that some little high-school girl gets you all a night in the cells. Must've been embarrassing. Two of you lost your jobs on account of it. What do you say about that?'

'I'd say you should stop telling stories,' said Lukanov.

'You have a few drinks, decide to go see her. Maybe you follow her into the woods. Maybe things got out of hand and maybe you hurt her, maybe worse.'

'Fuck you. Is she allowed to make these fucking allegations, Detective? Fuck you, bitch.'

Jack Carney moved in close and pushed Leo's head against the door. He held it there tight. 'Don't you ever speak like that to anyone in my company, Leo, or you'll be in serious trouble.'

'You got a car,' said Denise, 'between you?'

'Answer the question, deadbeat,' said Carney.

'Yeah, Paddy rolls.'

'What is it?'

'Red Ford.'

'We're going to check this car, we're going to check your story, Leo. I want to know where you were at five-fifteen on Thursday, February 26.'

'Don't remember,' said Lukanov.

'Try,' said Carney.

'Do whatever, some kid runs away, that's all and I get the fucking shakedown.'

'What were you doing?'

Leo thought for a moment. 'Nothing. Finished work, probably having a drink with Paddy.'

'Where?'

'We go to the pool hall.'

Denise nodded. 'Thank you for your time, Mr Lukanov.'

They left him at the door, returned to the car and drove off.

'What did you think?' said Carney.

'Nice boys,' said Denise. 'Leo's the one hiding something, though.'

'You think?'

'Yeah. The other two we found didn't seem as cagey or as aggressive.'

'He's bad news all right. A little sadist. You should try to get a warrant to turn him over.'

'I've got nothing at all to put him at the scene.'

'Well, I hope it helped,' said Carney. 'You want to try Tommy Ocks? He's not blessed with looks or brains. And his politics stink too.'

'Let's make it a full house,' said Denise.

Chapter Eighteen

Crown Heights, Brooklyn
March 7, 9.03 p.m.

Brooklyn wasn't Brooklyn any more. That's what Martin Heming was fond of saying. He walked with his head high, an odd little twitch in his neck making its presence known every few paces. Heming was born and bred in Brooklyn, schooled and beaten and mugged in Brooklyn. His first kiss was a Brooklyn kiss, his first love was a Brooklyn high-school beauty queen whom he had won, married, beaten and lost. And now, the whole world was caving in, even in Brooklyn.

He paced up the sidewalk with Leo Lukanov at his side. 'What did the bitch have on you?'

'Nothing. Not a thing. Just went on about the time we put the frighteners on the girl.'

'Her name?'

'Denise Levene.'

'Another Jew,' said Heming. 'Look at these people, Leo.' They stared across the street. The black and whites were out and about in numbers. Alien faces, alien customs, alien dress. Heming felt the anger well up. It was happening all over and now they were hanging around in his street. In his own fucking street.

'We should teach this Jew cop a lesson.'

'I'd like that,' said Leo. 'She needs a slap.'

'She needs to know she doesn't fuck with us,' said Heming.

Leo nodded and bristled, his shoulders moving back and forth, a kind of semi-conscious limbering up. 'What are you looking at?'

he shouted across the street. He licked his upper lip that carried a line of hair, masquerading as a mustache.

Heming and Lukanov each had a fist of leaflets. They'd produced them themselves. It was important, as a cell, to become active and to keep active. Heming said it every damn day – they spent too long waiting around doing too little as these immigrant communities grew stronger. Action made sense. It was an imperative. Every moment of inaction tipped the balance against the future for real Americans.

As they walked, they dropped a leaflet every few yards, scattered them outside the Jewish schools, up the pathways to synagogues, in parks and along busy walkways. The type was in a gothic script, chosen on Lukanov's computer in his dirty little room in a poor part of Brooklyn. A neat little Swastika had been cut and pasted in each corner and in the middle they'd typed three bold words:

KILL ALL JEWS

The message had the desired impact on the local Jewish population. It created outrage and outrage was good. It made Section 88 feel strong and powerful.

Heming was twenty-eight. Lukanov was two years younger. They'd met at a neo-Nazi rally, when Heming and his Section 88 gang started to turn up the heat in Brooklyn with placards and signs declaring *God Hates Jews* and more. Heming had been involved in the neo-Nazi movement for over eight years before he set up his own group two years earlier.

Heming knew that attacking illegal immigrants would find sympathy in the jobless communities in Brooklyn; graffiti on synagogues seemed to capture people's hidden internal hatreds.

Heming sent orders down the line, where he wanted more or less action. He followed political elections, trying to ramp up pressure on the liberal Left and secure greater popular appeal for his movement from the far Right. His gang organized small riots, attacks on immigrant communities, right-wing graffiti, harassment and – the pinnacle for any Section 88 member – violence against persons of Jewish or non-white origin. The 88s even had a tattoo, worn like a badge of honor, that members were entitled to if they spilled the blood of the undesirables. It was a blue eagle.

Heming and Lukanov threw the last few leaflets down on the sidewalk and continued to walk. Heming had been working closely with Lukanov for a few months, trying to get him more involved. Lukanov was strong, stupid and impressionable. He'd kill if you told him to, and that made Heming excited.

Across the street, a group of Hasidic Jews stared at them. One of them was showing a leaflet to the other men. Their mutterings in Hebrew started low and secretive, but they soon became louder. Their long curled strands of hair started to shake and they pointed across the street at the pair.

'Get the fuck out of here!' shouted Heming.

There was a switch in Heming's head and he didn't know much about how it got there, but once it was turned on, he felt anger welling up like water in a blocked drain. Over time, the little things had become the big things: a feeling of being an outsider turned into anger against the invader, a feeling of being judged became harsh judgment, a feeling of being spat on and disenfranchised by the American government became a need to express hatred. Now he hated the Jews, the Federal government and non-whites in that order.

'I just want to hurt them,' said Heming, staring hard at the group of angry men. His tattooed knuckles twisted into fists. His gun was tight in his waistband. He touched it with the heel of his hand for reassurance.

'They're so fucking in your face,' said Leo. 'What do you want me to do, Martin? Talking that shit. This is America! You want me to hurt them?'

The group of men continued to stare. It felt like a challenge to Lukanov and Heming.

'Fuck them up,' said Martin.

'I'll do it, Martin, I'll do all of them.' Lukanov felt a jerk of excitement. He pulled a switchblade out of the back pocket of his jeans.

'Turn away! Turn your fucking eyes away!' shouted Heming, but none of the seven pairs of eyes moved or seemed to understand. They looked like a group of deer staring up at a distant noise. Heming stepped out into the street. 'Stop fucking looking at me, you fucking Yids.'

Lukanov moved past Heming and started to march across the street. The rising tide of anger was impossible to contain.

Heming strode with confidence towards the group, a step behind Lukanov. One or two started to say something. But they didn't scatter and that annoyed Heming even more. 'Cut them, Leo,' he shouted.

Lukanov flicked open his blade and held it at arm's reach, pointing towards the seven men. He felt good now, he felt like a hero, ready to clean up his city. He just wanted to cut, wanted to kill. 'Now, Martin?'

'Make them run, Leo.'

Leo ran at the sidewalk. The group didn't wait any longer to find out if this thug was willing to kill. They scattered both ways.

'Do not stare at me, not in my fucking street. You hear? Not in my fucking street!' shouted Heming.

He stepped up to the sidewalk. The men were running away in both directions. Leo was breathing heavily. 'That fucking showed them,' he panted. 'They fucking scattered like rabbits. You see them dance?'

'You did good, Leo. You're a real rising star.' Heming was still. His eyes stared with something close to longing. 'You want to go after that cop, Leo? Call some boys together. You feel ready to lead your own team?'

'Sure,' said Lukanov. 'I'm ready. I'm more than ready.'

Chapter Nineteen

Salsa Club, Upper East Side
March 8, 1.30 a.m.

Harper arrived alone at the Dancer Downstairs. The club was closed and shuttered. A sign on the small door at the bottom of a flight of steps expressed sympathy for the family of David Capske and said they were closing for two days. He knocked for several minutes, but no one was there. From the street the club was hardly visible. He took out his watch and started to walk the route that the murder victim, David Capske, and his fiancée, the writer, Lucy Steller, had walked the previous evening.

It took Harper twenty-five minutes to reach Lucy Steller's apartment building. He headed off again, following the route David Capske had walked to the alleyway before he was killed. It took him just under an hour. It was quite a walk for someone rich and white, traveling into the heart of Harlem at night. Harper knew that Capske had reached the alleyway at 1.43 a.m. The caller in the apartment building said that a shot was heard at 3.30 a.m. If the rain started at 2.41 a.m., then the victim was lying on the ground in that spot for a long time, all wrapped up before he was shot. So between 1.43 a.m. and 2.41 a.m. what happened to Capske was still uncertain. However, after the visit to the morgue, it was clear that the killer had spent some time tattooing something on to David Capske's chest.

Harper looked around him. Two uniformed patrol cops stood at the alleyway and nodded. He pulled out his shield and waved it towards them. Alleyways in East Harlem were dangerous places.

There were limited exit routes for one thing, and victims didn't stroll into alleyways too easily for another. Would Capske have gone into a darkened alleyway with unknown dealers? How did the killer lure him?

Harper tried to imagine how a man would have been able to wrap another man in barbed wire, unaccompanied. It wouldn't be easy.

Surely the victim would have to be unconscious in order to allow the killer to start to wrap him. Harper made a mental note to ask the Medical Examiner about head wounds. If a man did this alone, his best bet would have been to knock the subject out, bind him, roll him, then wait until he came round. Harper thought about the timescales. It was possible, wasn't it?

Perhaps Capske was just unlucky. Perhaps he was on his way to meet a dealer when someone in the alleyway hit him, dragged him unconscious into the dark and wrapped him as he lay flat out. That would explain the marks across the ground. If the body was flat out, the only way to bind him would have been to push the body across the wire. Harper pulled out his sketchbook. There were two places where the body had lain still. The first was halfway up the alley, but the majority of the blood was to the right side of the alley and it was less than the size of an entire body. The second spot was where they found the victim and there was blood the whole length of the body. How did that happen?

But a random attack? It seemed highly unlikely. Capske had been targeted specifically and he had been punished. And furthermore, someone had informed the police and the media.

Harper's flashlight criss-crossed the alleyway. He'd found something that fitted, something that explained the situation, the strange time-lag and the marks across the ground. Harper let a smile cross his lips.

He thought about Denise Levene. She was back and had already spent the evening tracking racist thugs in Brooklyn. Whatever Mac had put her through, it had given her the confidence to start again.

Some of the guys in Blue Team, earlier in the day, had gone back to a multiple attacker theory. The Captain had lapped it up. Harper was now sure that what they were looking at was something darker. A solitary killer, a night stalker, waiting in an alleyway, ready with his cosh and barbed wire.

What kind of animal hunted like that? A political killer? No, not to his knowledge. Political killers tended to be martyrs who sacrificed themselves. This was someone who liked to kill for the sake of killing. If there was a political issue caught up in this kill, it was not the prime motivation.

He needed to know if the victim had been unconscious. He took out his phone to call the Medical Examiner's office. He direct-dialed Laura Pense. It was a long shot, but a moment later she answered the phone.

'You work nights too,' said Harper.

'Everyone else decided it's vacation time. What do you want?'

'I'm at the Capske crime scene and I've got a theory. What I need is a blunt-force trauma to the head and I've got a full house. I think he must've been knocked unconscious. Do you have that card?'

'No. There's no blunt-force trauma to the head. But there *was* intracranial hemorrhaging, so he got hit somehow. He was probably hit on his jaw. There's a fracture running across his left side. X-rays just came back. Couldn't see the bruising because of the tears in his cheek.'

'That's useful, thank you,' said Harper. He suggested she go home to get some sleep and hung up. So that's what had happened: the killer caught the victim on his jaw hard enough to give him brain damage. While he was knocked out, he taped his hands and ankles, wrapped him in barbed wire up to his chest, then he tattooed him. That was the first resting-point, with blood from the abdomen and legs. Then he waited, rolled his upper torso and head and shot him.

Harper imagined Capske waking up in his steel cage. He could feel the horror, the constriction. He could see the face of the attacker above him. Smiling, laughing? A terrifying end. But why would a killer wait to shoot him? Denise was right. It wasn't just political. He wanted to hurt and punish Capske. Or maybe there was something else. Harper took out his sketchpad and opened it. He stared at the sketches of the crime scene, the placing of the body.

In his mind, he saw the corpse. There was something there, but he couldn't bring it to mind. Harper nodded to the patrol still guarding the entrance of the alleyway as he headed out of the darkness.

Now he had the MO, the how and the what, the next thing Harper needed to work out was the why – the motive was everything. And this murder had many potential motives – drugs, politics, anti-Semitism. But none quite accounted for the ritualized kill scene, the sudden, brutal ambush, the waiting game and the execution, except for Denise's description of some form of deranged narcissism.

Harper walked across the street. They'd not found a single piece of the kill kit. They'd been chasing down CCTV from every municipal and private source for five blocks. They had plenty of people on tape, but it was impossible to judge if any of them were involved. No one on the tape was seen carrying anything. So either the killer was in a car or, if he was on foot, he dumped his kill kit as soon as he used it.

Harper looked up and down East 112th Street. There were CCTV cameras at either end of the street. Rows of garbage from the cafés and eateries lined the sidewalks. Harper looked across again. Even if the killer cut through the housing project up to East 113th Street, the CCTV tapes would have caught him coming out further up. No, thought Harper. We would've found the kill kit. Somehow he got the stuff taken away.

He watched as the garbage truck turned up, and the men threw the bags lining the streets into the back of the truck. Harper looked at his watch and cursed. It was only 1.45 a.m. He had imagined that the killer might have waited until 3.30 a.m. in order to catch the garbage truck, so that he could dispose of his kill kit as he left the scene. But it was too early.

Harper crossed the street. A surly garbage man was tossing bags into the back of the loader. 'Detective Harper, NYPD, can I ask you a question?' said Harper.

The guy looked up. 'Go ahead.'

'We had a murder at this site last night. We reckon the victim got here at around this time – one forty-three a.m. He was hurt real bad. So bad, he must've been screaming at some point. Were you working this route last night?'

'Sure was, and every other night.'

'Did you see or hear anything?'

'What time you say?'

'The victim arrived around this time.'

'Well then, I heard nothing and saw nothing.'

'Why's that?' asked Harper.

'We're a couple of hours ahead of schedule tonight.'

'So what time did you get here last night?'

'Last night? About three-thirty a.m., give or take a few minutes.'

'Last night, you were here at that time? You see anything?'

'Not a thing worth noting.'

'Where do you go from here?' said Harper.

'We got this street, then we complete the round.'

'Then where do you go?'

'Queens.'

'What for?'

'To unload. You're very interested in garbage for a cop.'

'Can I ride with you?'

'Ask the driver. I don't see why not.'

Harper jumped up to the cab and introduced himself. 'Can I ride with you, ask some questions?'

The driver shrugged. 'Whatever turns you on.'

'Where do you unload?'

'Queens.'

'I know. Where in Queens?'

'North Shore Marine Transfer Facility.'

'And what happens to the trash at the North Shore?'

'It gets loaded into a container. When it's full, it gets put on a barge and it sails away, to where I do not know or care.'

'What about last night's garbage? Will it have gone already?'

'Hey, what do you think I do, keep tags on my garbage? I've no fucking idea, Detective.'

'That's okay. I can find that out.' Harper took out his cell and called Eddie. He answered on the first ring. 'You at the Station House, Eddie?'

'Still chasing down these leads, but getting nowhere fast.'

'I think I might know where the killer dumped his kill kit.'

'What are you thinking?'

'This killer is smart,' said Harper. 'And if he's smart, he's going to dump it somewhere we won't find it.'

'They checked the storm drains, the sewage, the trash, the streets, the houses, the roofs, the alleys; they've been everywhere, Harper,' said Eddie.

'I've been wondering why he waited until three-thirty a.m. to shoot this guy. It's risky, right?'

'It's damn risky.'

'Maybe he was waiting for Department of Sanitation.'

'How so?'

'Garbage trucks, Eddie. On Saturday, they collect around three-thirty a.m., and all our killer has to do is take his bloody clothes, the barbed-wire spool, the gloves and maybe even the murder weapon, put it out on the sidewalk and watch the city pick it up and take it away for him. Then he walks.'

'That's brilliant. Where are you now?'

'In a garbage truck on the way to the North Shore Marine Transfer Facility in Queens. Meet me there in one hour with Blue Team and Crime Scene Unit. See if you can get the Logistics and Operational Manager for the Facility. We need to trace last night's garbage.'

'I'm on it, Harps. They work the same routes each night, right? We just need the truck number and the dumpsite. It's going to be a dirty night's work for someone in the Crime Scene Unit.'

Chapter Twenty

North Shore Marine Transfer Facility, Queens
March 8, 2.23 a.m.

Harper arrived at the huge blue warehouse at the North Shore Transfer Facility. Eddie Kasper, the team and two CSU trucks were sitting there waiting. Harper thanked the driver and jumped off. The air was cold next to the river, and in the distance he could hear the industrial hum of hundreds of loaders, dump trucks and garbage trucks transporting New York's waste to someplace else.

'Quick work, Eddie, what have you got?'

'Dogs are on their way. We've got David Capske's jacket coming across from the OCME to give them something to work on, but the handlers aren't sure how they'll cope. Depends on how rancid the trash is.'

'That's great, Eddie. What about the location of our load?'

'We've dragged the Logistics Supervisor out of bed, the Operations Manager and the roll-on team. We've got tonight's team on hold. Nothing leaves until we find our trash.'

Harper looked at the tired faces of the people in front of him. Two men who looked like they just got out of bed stood shivering in the wind. Behind them, three more of the team from the Transfer Facility. Their faces were cynical and bored.

Harper walked across. 'This is a homicide investigation, gentlemen. I apologize for the disturbance, but we need your help. You'll go back to bed when this is over, but our victim never will. So no wise-ass bullshit. We're serious about finding that kill kit and we'll keep the whole plant closed down until we do. Understand?'

The men nodded one by one. 'That's good. Now let's locate the dock and the barge.'

He turned as the CSU trucks started to unload. Several men and women all wearing white suits tramped across the concrete.

'First up, what happens when the trash gets here?'

The Operations Manager took Harper through the routine. Eddie Kasper took the Logistics Supervisor back inside with the truck number.

Within fifteen minutes, they came back together. Harper gathered the team.

'We're in luck,' he said. 'Our garbage is sitting on a barge in Dock Four. It's due to leave later tonight, so we just made it. The garbage truck unloads in one of bays sixteen to twenty-two, which means the trash will be on the right section of the barge. We've been through the options. There's no way we can jump on board and start sifting. We're going to crane the rubbish back on shore, and sift it load by load. Any questions?' There was silence. 'Well, let's get going.'

Harper searched with the team throughout the night, staring out over the vast mountains of trash as far as the eye could see. It seemed like an impossible task. At six, he lay down on a bench in the warehouse and closed his eyes. An hour later, he felt someone pushing his shoulder. He looked up.

'Eddie, what've you got?'

'We got something,' said Eddie. Just then, Rick Swanson burst in. His blue suit was stained at the knees with dark wet patches, his hands were black with dirt, his jacket was covered in unpleasant-looking detritus. Behind him, Mary Greco was a five-foot-two picture of perfect cleanliness in a plain white tank top and jeans. She was wearing gloves and holding a plastic bag high in the air.

'Five fucking hours in Harlem's shit for forty-two-thousand dollars a year, Harper! No sleep, no nothing. It smells worse than a body in that dump,' said Swanson.

Harper clapped. 'But you found it! You're a hero.'

'Six fucking hours.'

'You said five,' said Eddie. 'Either I'm not hearing things right or that's one quick hour.'

'Fuck you,' said Swanson. 'Six or seven hours, what's the difference?'

'How comes he's all dirty and you're clean, Greco?'

'They offered us white suits, but Mr Macho found the onesies a little effeminate.'

'I'm not wearing a fucking Babygro.'

'No, you're wearing cabbage and diapers by the smell of you.'

'You got it, though, am I right?' said Harper.

'Yeah, we got it, all right,' said Swanson.

'What's in there?'

Swanson took off his jacket and threw it straight into the bin. 'I can't wear this no more. It's going to remind me of stamping through a container of putrid Harlem crap.'

'What's in the bags, Swanson? Focus.'

'He's not as smart as he thinks,' said Swanson. 'He's bagged the lot together. We weren't getting anywhere until the canine unit brought in the sniffer dogs.'

'We would've been another twelve hours,' said Mary. 'And this macho pig moans like a girl with a broken nail. Every five seconds. I couldn't stand it any more.'

'We got a rag of Capske's blood from Forensics and they found it. You know what? I hate being second to a dog.'

'In every way, Swanson,' said Mary Greco. 'In every way.'

Rick Swanson muttered something. He pulled off his shoes and put them in the trash too. 'The fucking canine unit . . . if they'd come first, I wouldn't have ruined my suit and shoes.'

'The department will clean your suit,' said Harper. 'For the last time, what's in the bag?'

'The whole shebang. Gloves, remnants of wire on a wooden spool, knife and overalls.'

'Weapon?'

'No gun.'

'Let's get it straight to the lab.' Harper looked at his team. 'That's good work, guys. Real good work. Let's hope they find something for us to go on.'

Chapter Twenty-One

North Manhattan Homicide
March 8, 11.30 a.m.

Denise Levene was wearing a smart black suit, a white blouse and glasses. She breathed slowly, trying to control the nerves that were making her hands tremble. It was impossible to know if what she was doing was right for her, but it no longer mattered. She needed progress.

She walked right back into the North Manhattan Homicide investigation room and stood there. She felt her world begin to click back into place. No one looked up. No one noticed her. She looked down at the old blue carpet, at the tar spots, at the discarded gum that had turned gray.

She held back tears, but they were not tears of fear, they were tears of pride. She had made it through the door. She had thought about it a hundred times, and every time she'd backed out, unable to even make it to the door. Now she was there.

Mark Garcia turned. He was wearing a pink shirt and even from a distance, Denise could smell his cologne. It took a moment for him to identify the woman in front of him, to place the pale face that he hadn't seen for three months. Then recognition dawned on him. 'Hey, fellas, look who's come back home!'

The other detectives turned. Apart from Gerry Ratten, they'd all worked the American Devil case. Harper felt the hairs on his neck stiffen as he turned and saw Denise standing there in the doorway, in the same black suit that she'd worn the day he met her, when she was safely ensconced in One Police Plaza as a psychotherapist who looked at the aftermath of trauma and kept her distance from the streets.

Rick Swanson had pulled on his gym kit, a Yankees sweat top and a pair of black sweatpants. He was a mean and cynical son of a bitch, but even he felt the atmosphere and smiled.

Garcia took a glance around the room. The detectives of Blue Team were a tight group and Denise had worked with them and suffered for it. A team didn't forget that. Garcia started to clap. The others joined in. And Denise Levene stood, her cheeks flushed red, not knowing where to look. Harper stared at her, brimming with pride and a strange fear. Whatever she'd been through, they had to make sure it wasn't repeated.

The clapping died down. 'How the hell are you?' said Swanson. 'Took your time. I thought as a psychologist you could've healed yourself.'

'I'm wondering how you've all got time for applauding some amateur profiler when you've got a case to work. I hear it's a bad one.'

She walked directly to the coffee pot and poured herself a cup. Harper sidled up. 'Denise,' he said. 'I—'

'Don't say a goddamn thing or I'm going to break here.'

Harper closed his mouth, took a step back, let her regain composure. 'Welcome home, Denise,' he said.

Denise leaned her back against the wall and took a look around the room. 'Feels odd to be back in here. Nice cubicles. You've been busy building.'

'You haven't seen the Captain since he spent some time in the Bronx.'

'Always captures the big ideas, doesn't he?'

Harper nodded. 'You get anywhere with Abby?'

'Yes, thanks to you. I met some real morons. The worst was Leo Lukanov. Leo gave a false alibi for the evening when Abby disappeared, and it transpires that Dr Goldenberg saw him the day before in a car outside the house. So we've got extra time on the case.'

'That's good. You were brave to go over there.'

'Well, I'm feeling better. I'm here to return the favor.'

'Profile?'

'I can try.' Denise spotted a wiry fair-haired man in one of the new cubicles, who had eyed her a few times. She nodded towards him. 'Is he the competition?'

'The kid in the corner with the snarl? He's the FBI's boy. New profiler from the New York Field Office. He's squaring up for a battle. He's heard about you. You're all we talk about.'

'Only to piss him off, I hope.'

'Yeah, only to piss him off. Second-rate, unfortunately, even though he's trying.'

'Well, let's hope that's good enough.'

Harper laughed. 'You're going to kill him. It's not a fair fight. Not fair at all.'

'Where are you on the case?' asked Denise.

'We're waiting for something to break,' Harper told her. 'We found the killer's kill kit last night. We're just checking out leads.'

'Good, that's progress.'

'Well, I've got the case-files set up for you. Take your time, just as long as you've got something by this afternoon.'

Denise looked up. 'No honeymoon period? This really is like old times. Where are you headed?'

Harper picked up his coat. 'I'm going to check out some barbed-wire manufacturers.'

'Lucky you,' said Denise.

Chapter Twenty-Two

North Manhattan Homicide
March 8, 12.30 p.m.

Harper arrived back at the precinct. He had news about the barbed wire to give Lafayette. What he had was good but he needed something more. He approached Eddie. 'I got your message. Where are they?'

'In the interview room.'

'How sure are you?'

'It's good, Harps.'

They headed straight for a small interview room that had been set up with three phones. Three Chinese cops were on the phones, speaking in Mandarin.

'They traced the number, like I asked?' said Harper.

'Just like you asked.'

'And they got something?'

'They did. Harps, you were right.'

'I don't care about right, I care about catching this guy. Let's see what they got.'

'The purple serial number you found on the spool was our only lead,' said Eddie. 'We've been chasing that number all morning. We reckon the barbed wire is a Chinese import, and the serial number had an import number next to it. We traced the import number through shipping number via customs. We're tracking down manufacturers.'

Harper looked around him. 'In China?'

'There aren't too many barbed-wire manufacturers importing to the US, so we're down to the last one. But I don't know that the number will give us anything. Even if we find where it came from, we might not see where it went to.'

Harper put his hand on the shoulder of one of the guys. 'Anything?'

Detective William Hong nodded. 'We think we've got the manufacturer. They're tracing that batch number, might be able to tell us where it was sent.'

'Call me the second you know,' said Harper.

He walked back into the investigation room and sat down by Denise, on an old plastic chair. 'How's it been?' he asked.

'Okay.'

'No progress?'

'Not yet. I'm just absorbing all the details. It's not nice.'

'No,' said Harper.

'There's nothing on the bullet. You anywhere with that?'

'They can't ID the bullet. It's so mangled. It's just a lump of metal. I'm going to get it looked at. There's something more to it. Why, what are you thinking?'

'I need to know what kind of gun he used. It might tell us something.'

'Like what?'

'Confidence with a gun, military background, who knows.'

'They say it was a 9mm bullet.'

Denise nodded. 'I went through the sequence of events, the witness statements, the confession letters, the forensic details, the autopsy protocol. Then I went through it all again.'

'And?'

'He's not a political animal. He's a sociopath. I agree with you – I think there's something else, too. Something . . .'

William Hong emerged from the interview room and called across. 'Harper, we've got it. This consignment was headed for Washington. Then headed for a commercial supplier.'

Harper turned. 'And where did they send it?'

'It's been a ride. The commercial supplier sent it to a local state

115

wholesaler. They found the order. We know the shop this spool was bought from.'

Eddie Kasper took the faxed copy of the import order. Chinese letters across the top of the paper. 'If he's a right-wing pro-America freak, Harper, do you think he knew he was buying Chinese barbed wire?'

Harper felt the release in the tension with the breakthrough. 'We got to get up there, have a look at the layout. See if they have CCTV. But first, I've got to tell Lafayette that we have a lead. It'll buy us a few more hours.'

In the background, Denise looked through Harper's murder book. A sketch of a wind-ruffled falcon graced one page. She turned over and saw the strange sketch of dots and scratches that they'd seen at the morgue.

'Sorry, Denise, you were about to say something?'

'No, nothing really. Hey, you thought any more about this?' she asked.

'No, why?'

'Another strange sense I get. I think I half recognize these marks, but I don't know why or how.'

'Well, give it time – it'll come.'

Levene drifted into thought. An image from her childhood emerged deep from within her memory, but it was so vague she couldn't capture it. Perhaps it was some picturebook her father had showed her. If so, it was before he went to prison, when she was nine years old. She didn't remember the book. She remembered black and white photographs, her father not speaking, just turning the pages in silence, then when she turned, seeing her father's tears. His large leathery hand stroked her hair. She could taste his pipe smoke in her throat and hear the accent that never left him.

Her hand reached out and moved across the scratches. Something appeared, a pattern of some sort, but she couldn't read it. Not yet.

Chapter Twenty-Three

Lock-Up, Bedford-Stuyvesant
March 8, 1.05 p.m.

He parked his old sedan three streets away, put on an overcoat and baseball cap, then walked the rest of the way, past derelict housing blocks and shuttered shops scrawled with graffiti.

He reached the razor-wire fence and pushed through a small gap at the side into a grassy alley between two buildings. He walked through to a wide patch of scrubland that was once the backyard of a clothing business that had long ago closed down.

Several stray dogs appeared from each corner of the square, eager-eyed and barking. The man took out his bag of meat, which consisted of cheap scraps that he collected from the meat market. The dogs ran towards him, yapping and jumping, saliva dripping and swinging from their jowls. There were about sixteen strays of all types. He took out handfuls of fatty meat and tossed them around the yard.

The dogs were his homemade security force. He'd started to feed them a few months back, after he'd found the abandoned garage on one of his tours of duty. He knew that a lock-up without additional security would not last in that part of Brooklyn, so he'd spent the time trying to get the dogs to see the garage as their place and defend it. No one would try to get past a pack of wild dogs. Not even gangbangers.

He got to the door of the garage and unlocked each of the three padlocks. The dogs surrounded him, yelping and circling tight around his legs.

He pushed open the door and flicked on the light. The dogs ran in all around him and their barking filled the room and echoed against the tin roof. He threw more meat down and filled three bowls with water.

He sat in a battered armchair and started feeding some of them by hand. They fed furiously, angrily, gulping down the lumps of fat and gristle with excited glee. They were a pack, a team, but underneath that organization, they were out for themselves. If one of them got injured, they'd tear the animal to shreds.

The man stood up and went back to the door. He threw the remaining lumps of meat into the yard and watched them tear out of the room. He slammed the door shut and breathed excitedly. Around the room, there were several scaffolding poles that leaned against the walls, and bags of sand and cement piled in corners. Outside the garage door stood a large pallet of bricks. He'd brought about four dozen bricks into the room and had started to mark out two internal walls along the floor, coming out from the back wall. He'd been planning on a building project for a while now, but was waiting for the right kind of girl. It was going to be a room within a room, a very special room. One he'd dreamed of his whole life.

The large brick garage had been empty for years. A piece of derelict real estate in a part of town no one wanted to live in. He had a new door fixed, new bolts and padlocks. He'd bricked up the one small window. Across the garage was a second door which once upon a time housed a bathroom. The cistern and sink had been smashed. He'd cleared the room out and sealed it up as best he could.

He took a metal plate from a shelf next to the door. Removed a piece of dry bread and a small piece of cheese from a tin, and put them on the plate. He then poured some water from a bottle into a metal cup. He placed both at the bottom of the door where there was a hinged flap.

He stood at the door, knocked twice and pulled back a small slot that he'd cut in the wood. He stooped and stared into the room at the bundle lying on the floor.

'Stand,' he ordered. The prisoner did as he requested. He did

118

not listen to her when she spoke or cried. He had taught himself to believe it was another language. The language of lies. She stood and turned her back to the door. He moved his hands through the slot and unbuckled her wrists and then her mouth restraint. Then he shut the slot and pushed the metal plate through the hinged flap with his foot.

A few seconds later, a bedpan was pushed out. He picked it up, took it outside the door and threw the contents on the ground. The dogs ran at the sewage as if it were more food.

As she was eating, he started to undress and place his clothes in a wooden trunk. From the trunk he took out another set of clothes. He was going hunting again. He dressed in his hunting uniform, slowly adding each item of clothing that he'd carefully sourced over the years. He pressed his hair flat to his head and looked at himself in a jarred fragment of mirror. His eyes flinched at the sight of his own dark hair and olive skin. He moved his gaze quickly to the uniform to stem the self-loathing that flooded within him at the sight of his own features. He shifted nervously from foot to foot, letting the whole effect grow in his mind and now feeling excited by the transformation.

He walked to the cell and knocked. He kicked the clean bedpan through the hinged flap. A moment later, the empty plate and cup appeared at the bottom of the door. He knocked again, opened the slot and the prisoner stood again and turned. He stared into the tiny cell, and opened the door.

Every day, it was the only interaction he allowed himself with the prisoner. Distance was important.

He walked the girl out into the room, where she picked up the tin of boot polish from the table and a rag and knelt at his feet. She started to polish his boots as he stared down at her.

'That is good, Abigail. You are behaving well today.'

'I hope you're pleased with me,' she said. 'I try to please you.'

He pulled back and looked down at his boots. 'Good,' he said. 'Now stand. I need to inspect your cell.'

Abby moved away as he leaned into her cell and checked the door hinges and the mattress.

'I recognized your cologne. I've smelled it before. I just can't think where.'

'I've been close to you a number of times, Abigail. I came close to taking you but each time something got in the way.'

The memories suddenly clicked.

'The man in the dark. You pushed into me.' She felt a shiver of fear, then anger, a fury that she couldn't control. She picked up a brick started towards him.

He heard the movement behind him and turned. The girl was running towards him. He was shocked for a moment. A brick hit him hard on the side of the head. He stumbled backwards into the cell, his hand grabbing on to the door frame. She smashed the brick down on his hand and he let go, tumbling backwards. She pushed the door shut on him, but he wasn't unconscious. His boots, bright black and shining, kicked the door open. The girl was hit but did not give up; she approached again with the brick.

He stood up, a trickle of blood over one eye, cradling his left hand. She stared, panting, the brick raised.

'It's wrong, what you're doing. It's sick and it's wrong and I want to go home,' she shouted. 'I won't stay here. I won't!'

He moved towards her. 'You betrayed the trust I put in you, Abigail.'

'Don't come any closer or I'll smash your filthy head in.'

'Will you?' he said, and closed in on her. The girl raised the brick, but he was expecting that. His arm came across to bat it away, but the brick didn't move; her body shifted and her left leg rose high in a karate kick and the side of her foot hit his chin. He reeled backwards.

'Don't come near me,' she shouted. Then she stepped towards the door. 'Help!' she screamed. 'Help!'

'You will be punished for this, you realize. And I will make your father aware of every moment of your suffering.' He stepped towards her, his face angry now.

'Get away from me. You find suffering a turn-on, do you, you sick bastard?'

He moved quickly. She threw the brick at his head; it glanced off his shoulder. She twisted, punched and kicked. But he came too fast and his bulk pushed her back and pressed her against the wall. He held her there, his mouth close to hers.

'They will find you dead, Abigail. A naked corpse on your father's doorstep – half-eaten by dogs. But I want to find out how close to death you can go. How slowly I can kill you.'

She was shivering. His hand tightened around her neck. He leaned back and smashed his forehead against her nose. 'You will not be beautiful any more.'

He gritted his teeth. He shoved her hard into the chair, took out a knife and started to chop away at her hair as she wept and screamed. She stared into the shard of a mirror leaning against the wall. The girl she knew, the girl everyone knew, was disappearing. All around her, her long brown hair lay discarded on the floor.

'We will not call you Abby any more.'

'What?'

'You are an experiment now, not a person. We will call you 144002.'

'Fuck you,' she spat.

He breathed, his hand so tight around her arm that he could feel the bone.

'We will call you 144002.'

'No.'

He pushed her head back violently and she stopped speaking for a moment, but she needed to know. To know why.

'What are you doing this for?'

'144002 must be quiet. 144002 speaks again and I will cut out 144002's tongue.'

The girl stared across. Her eyes fixed on the red and black insignia on his arm. He smiled. 'You can't believe it, can you? But it is real. It is very real. This is not a dream. You will not wake up. You will never wake up from this.'

Chapter Twenty-Four

Eastern Hardware Store, Maywood
March 8, 1.50 p.m.

Harper and Kasper headed out of town. They pulled up at a hardware store off the Interstate. It was a vast warehouse structure, a rectangle of steel and plastic thrown up in what looked like a matter of days. The whole complex was a sprawling mass of similar buildings, all with their own large, bright signs.

Kasper parked close to the entrance. Harper was speaking on the phone to base, but no one had anything. Harper looked around. 'Big.'

'Sure is,' said Eddie. 'This isn't going to be easy.'

They met the manager of the store, and followed him up a long, wide aisle of fencing, rails, pipes and tubes until they got to the barbed wire. It was sitting on huge wooden pallets, three different grades, and three different types: razor wire, barbed wire and galvanized barbed wire.

'This the only place someone can get barbed wire in the store?'

'Sure is.'

Harper looked up and down the aisle. 'Okay. I want this aisle taped off and dusted for prints.'

'I'm not closing an aisle. It's a big sales day for us.'

'I'm trying to stop a killer, Sunday or not. I could close the whole store if you'd prefer.'

The manager shook his head.

'Eddie,' said Harper, 'I want this whole area dusted, then the cash register area. We know he's been here.'

'So have thousands of people,' said Eddie.

'We might get lucky.'

Eddie's eyebrows rose slow and high. He took out his phone. 'I'll get Crime Scene across here.'

They spent an hour with the manager going through the sales data and receipts, picking out every sale of barbed wire. 'We've got hundreds,' said the manager. 'No telling which one bought your roll.'

'We'll take all the names, and follow them all up.'

The manager handed a printout to Harper. 'Impossible to tell which one. The digital readings are our own – they only have the product, price and date. No import number, no license. But the batch you're after – it only came out of the back store nine days ago.'

'Let's try CCTV,' said Harper. 'You keep it?'

He nodded his head. 'We keep one week of tape. If it was within the week, we might see someone.'

'Eddie, try to find him.'

'Will do.'

Within the hour, eight CSU detectives arrived. Their supervisor, Detective Ingleman, moved straight across to Harper. 'What are we looking for?' he asked.

'Someone was in here in the last nine days buying a roll of barbed wire,' said Harper. 'I've got a guy here from the cleaning company, and he's going to tell you where they wipe down. We know whoever bought it was over in the barbed-wire area, by the cash register, and at the door. We think the door and checkout counter get wiped. I just wonder if you guys can find a needle in a haystack.'

'You're kidding? You want us to dust a whole store?'

'Not the whole store. The barbed-wire aisle to start with.'

Ingleman followed Harper to the aisle. He walked up to the pallet. 'What's he going to touch, apart from the roll he's buying?'

Harper shrugged. 'It's a long shot. He may have touched other rolls, the price tags, I don't know, but this killer is going to kill again. We've got to do something.'

The supervisor walked off, shaking his head. He had a team of top detectives and he was going to ask them to dust a store. He went outside to the vans and organized his teams, shaking his head so much that his jowls wobbled.

Harper sat down at the computer in the store's back office. He called Denise. 'You been getting on with our young profiler?'

'He thinks this was a group attack. That's going to go to the Captain and he'll lap it up and pass it to the Chief of Detectives. I need to stop him.'

'So what do you think?'

'Single male, early- to mid-thirties, delusional fantasies, but nothing that would prevent him from operating successfully. You want your type, think controlled, obsessive, and this guy's got hooked on a clean-up.'

'Like a prostitute killer – a moral cleaner?'

'There's something in that, something of the cleaner, but it's strange. Like a military operation, taking out numbered targets.'

'Ex-military?'

'Not possible to say right now. But could be. How's it going up there?'

'Time is short, the work is slow.'

'Well, let's hope for something.'

Harper hung up and wandered out of the small office and into the aisle. He walked up to the team, slowly taking prints off every surface. 'How's it looking?'

'We're getting so many prints, Harper, we'll be here all day and then it'll take all night to get them uploaded and checked.'

'We haven't got all night.'

'There ain't no short cut.'

Harper walked away. He sat down. Another hour slipped by, his mind going over the case, detail by detail.

Eddie came through at 6 p.m. He was nodding.

'You got something?' Harper asked.

'Come see.'

Harper and Eddie sat together in the security room. Eddie pulled the tape back and then played it.

'We've got a guy here coming out with a cart three days ago.' He froze the tape. 'Can you see it?'

The grainy still was difficult to read. Harper moved closer. At the edge of the man's arm was a cross of wood. 'That's the barbed wire spool?'

'Looks like it.'

They watched the man push the cart across the parking lot, until he was nearly out of sight behind two other cars.

'Problem is,' says Eddie, 'we don't see his face or his car.'

'You looked back and forth?'

'Sure have and it's empty. Sorry.'

'You must have quite a few guys buying barbed wire – why'd you focus on this guy?'

Eddie smiled and then pushed in another tape. 'This is from the camera on the checkout.'

Harper watched. 'He keeps his back to the camera, the whole time. Like he wanted to keep his identity hidden.'

'And he pays cash,' said Eddie, as the man leaned across the counter to hand cash to the guy on the register.

'That's it?'

'He's pretty suspicious for a man in a hardware store, but no, that's not it. Look at this.' Eddie moved the tape back and zoomed. There was a close-up of the man's forearm.

'What is it?'

'The words.'

Harper looked down. '*Loyalty, Valiance, Obedience*. The word *Loyalty*, you mean?'

'That's what it said on the Capske black card, right?'

'That's right.'

Harper watched the tape again. He stopped it. 'It's got a time and date here. Does that cross reference with the man at the car?'

'Yeah, two minutes later.'

'Go speak to the manager and find out who was serving on the cash registers at that time and then get him here and get a description from him.'

Eddie stood up. 'I'm on it.'

Harper took the sequence back to the beginning and watched it. He repeated it three more times. There was nothing to go on. Then he took out the disk and put in the film from the parking lot. Again, there was nothing to tell him who this guy was. A blue hooded top, white sneakers, blue jeans. The man could have been anyone. He went through it again, right to the point when the man was only distantly visible by his car.

Then Harper stopped the tape. He zoomed in and peered into the grainy image.

'Eddie!' he shouted. There was no response. Harper moved across to the door. 'Eddie, get back here.'

Eddie ran back in. 'What is it?'

'Come here.' Harper's finger touched the screen. 'You see?'

'No. What is it?'

Harper pulled back the tape. 'Just describe what he does.'

Eddie watched. 'He wheels his cart between two cars, and then stops. He leans forward. He's unlocking the car, maybe. He picks up something from the cart. Can't see what, puts it in the trunk. He stops, leans up against the street lamp, does something with his foot.' Eddie stopped. 'Aha!'

'You see it?' said Harper.

'I see it. Hell, man, that's good. That's very good.'

Harper ran across the store and shouted up the aisle, 'Ingleman, I've got something for you!'

Ingleman moved away slowly from his team. 'I hope you don't want the whole store dusted, Harper.'

'No, but I think I've got you a print.'

'Where?'

Harper led Ingleman into the security room and ran the tape. 'See there?' said Harper. 'He puts his arm up and leans on that street lamp. High up. You think he might have left a print?'

'I like that,' said Ingleman, nodding. 'That's good thinking. How do you know this is our man?'

'We don't. It's not a hundred per cent but it's all we've got.'

'Okay,' said Ingleman, 'let's see if we can get a clean print.'

Within the hour, the print had been lifted from the street light in the center of the parking lot. The team traveled back to Manhattan and went directly to the Latent Prints labs. In the meantime, the print had traveled electronically to the crime lab and was being enhanced and analyzed.

The prints team worked fast and the print was soon scanned into the national print database. Within a few minutes, a match had come up on screen.

By the time Harper and the team arrived, it was all completed. The team saw two prints sitting side-by-side, green on a black background. The red hieroglyphics of the points of comparison showed an identical print.

'That's what I call a breakthrough,' said Harper.

'We're lucky he's in the database.'

'So who is he?'

The technician clicked on to the personal file. 'His name's Leo Lukanov.' A photograph of a muscular white man in his early twenties came up on the screen. He was covered in tattoos.

'That's our guy?' said Eddie. 'Like Frankenstein in jeans.'

'Shit,' said Harper.

'What?'

'Where's Denise?'

'She's gone home.'

'Try her for me, Eddie.'

'What is it?'

'Leo Lukanov was involved in an attack on Abby Goldenberg. Denise went to question him yesterday with Hate Crime Unit. If he's involved, then Denise is in danger.'

'I'll call,' said Eddie. He left the room.

'What's his record?' asked Harper.

'Assault, robbery . . . small-time stuff.'

'He got an address?'

'Yeah, here it is.'

Harper took the address and rose from his chair. 'Get moving on a warrant, but we haven't got time to wait for it. Let's go.'

Chapter Twenty-Five

East 1st Street, Manhattan
March 8, 7.05 p.m.

The man in the long gray coat walked down First Avenue, close to the gutter. He kept his head low and peered out from under a heavy brow. Fourteen minutes into his tour, no sight of his target.

On the corner of East 1st Street, he saw the preacher emerge from a doorway. The old man was draped in a torn coat that was stained brown from sleeping on wet ground. His nose was broken. One of his nostrils was missing. The wounds were fresh.

The preacher pushed a sign high above his head. It read *Jesus Loves You*. He started to speak. 'I am the voice of one crying in the wilderness.'

The man stopped. His fingers flexed in his leather gloves. He hated weakness. He wanted to puncture the preacher's lung with a sudden blow. He wanted to watch him cough out his last sermon. Weakness, filth and arrogance. He hated it all.

'It has happened before,' the preacher shouted. 'And it will happen again. The beast will appear. A righteous beast. He will destroy the unrighteous. And he will take down the innocents with him.'

The man was the only person listening in the heat of the night. He stood at the edge of the sidewalk nodding. The preacher was right about the beast, he thought.

He leaned into the wind and moved back towards his car. His tour of duty was not yet complete.

'It has happened before,' he repeated as he drove away.

The streets were busy with traffic making its way down East Houston Street and Baruch Drive. He drove slowly, keeping a close eye on the streets and cursing the careless drivers cutting in as they passed. He traveled under the Williamsburg Bridge and parked again. He crossed the footpath over FDR Drive on foot.

He walked at a pace, a sweat beginning to form under his heavy coat. He was thinking. There was no difference in his mind between then and now – the line was crossed a long time ago, not by him, but by another man in the shadows. Perhaps the circumstances were easier then. Or perhaps it always felt like you were going upstream.

The dark skies above Manhattan were closing in with cloud. He watched the stream of white and red lights rushing by, then looked at his watch. Time to go again.

His next tour was half a mile from the river. Half a mile meant a good time outside the safety of the shadows. He walked away from the wailing of cars as they hit the shell of the Williamsburg Bridge and slipped out beyond it.

He walked up Delancy and glanced into Downing Park. The trees ahead were covered in pale flowers. They looked ethereal and beautiful. He walked down Abraham Place, stopped and stared across Grand Street. The large apartment block was a grey mass in the darkness, scattered yellow lights like golden bricks trailing up the side of the building. He took out a Black Card. The name was typed. He mouthed the syllables slowly, his spit sticky in his mouth.

The sky reflected in the puddles on the ground. He decided to take another turn around the block. He didn't want to be seen waiting for too long. He turned left and walked down to Abraham Kazan Street, circled and returned. Up ahead a figure came into view, walking towards him. He slowed his steps. If it was her, she must've been at her mother's apartment later than usual.

The figure – a woman in her twenties with brown hair – walked along the side of the road opposite, her heels clipping the asphalt and echoing. Then she slowed. No doubt she had spotted him. He didn't mind that. People were very predictable. They rarely ran unless directly threatened. He could get very close before she tried to defend herself, and by then it would be much too late.

He watched the hesitation in her step. He was enjoying it. Fear was growing inside her. It was what his hate fed upon. People's fear: their open-mouthed horror and pain.

He had plans for Marisa. He wanted to see how long she would survive in the river. He wanted to watch the cold snake up and grab her, the horrible pain of the cold. She would be subservient then. She would not complain and throw her human rights in his face. She would plead like a dog for her life, for an end of the pain.

And then he would give her what she wanted. Salvation. A bullet through her head.

He could tell she was looking at him. She had seen him silhouetted against the dim light and was calculating as women had to do. *What are the risks?* If only she knew how big the risks were, but the future is blind except to those who are going to hack out a pathway. Only they know the future – the leaders, the visionaries. The victims are always blind.

He turned and walked away, playing with her state of mind, knowing that she would feel sudden relief. But at the top of the road, as he felt her eyes on him, he turned. How easy to double fear in an instant. Offer a way out, then bar the door. Each glimpse of an escape only increased the fear.

He stood still and stared directly at her. He saw her take out her cell phone.

She crossed the street, her phone to her ear as if that would save her. His eyes peered at her as she continued to walk quickly through the trees. She didn't call out. He imagined she was telling herself that he was just some jerk.

He let her walk on for fifty yards. He imagined her heart racing as the light hit her eyes, now slowly returning to normal, her mind beginning to tell her she was safe. The road ahead was brighter and she was nearly there.

A cool wind ran down the avenue and shook the trees along the park. They rattled up above like a child's toy. The woman shot a look over her shoulder. He wasn't there.

He had moved closer and darted into a doorway. He hid for a moment, until he heard her footsteps. Now she was ripe. Now she was confused. He moved out of the doorway and started to run. He wanted to get her as she passed the entrance to the park. It was darkest there, and the park gave him cover. He looked up and down the street and there was no one around.

He pushed hard against the ground, the wind at his back. The thrill rose up through his body and left him light-headed. When she heard the sound of his boots on the ground, she turned. But he was ten yards away by then and traveling at speed. She didn't stand a chance. He was a hunter and she was his.

A whoosh of air from her left side and suddenly she was reeling. Her phone fell from her hand and smashed on the sidewalk. She stumbled and fell. He stood above her, opened his coat and took it off. The uniform was very striking. It was the part he liked to play most of all. It gave him such a sense of power. He towered above her, resplendent.

'Your name.'

'What do you want?' she said.

'Your name,' he shouted.

She was shaking and breathing hard. She didn't understand. Above her, his wide eyes stared out. He pulled her into the park, into the undergrowth, his hand over her mouth.

'I will shoot you like a dog if you disobey me,' he whispered in her ear.

Marisa shook visibly. He let his hand drop from her mouth. 'Please don't hurt me.'

'No talking.'

'My mother is dying. Please. Please don't hurt me.'

She felt the barrel hard against her skull. She was crying in fear.

'You will be punished for talking. Kneel.'

'I don't want to die. What do you want?'

'Kneel,' he spat.

The woman fell to her knees and looked up. He pressed the barrel of his gun to her forehead. The thin skin creased against her skull.

'Clean my boots,' he said.

She stared at him imploringly. He liked that look, the look of the dying animal. It pleased him.

'I am Officer Sturbe of the SS. Now, clean my fucking boots.'

Chapter Twenty-Six

Brownsville, Brooklyn
March 8, 7.49 p.m.

Denise ran down Manhattan and across the Brooklyn Bridge. She ran up street after street. Pounding for mile after mile. The high-rise blocks gleaming in Manhattan started to disappear behind her. In their wake, as she passed through each Brooklyn neighborhood, things got meaner and sharper. It had felt good to get back into work, good to help the Missing Persons investigation, good to start profiling. It had been good to be working closely with Tom Harper.

The streets were full of people like her and not like her. They belonged to some different world, but she was born in Brooklyn and she enjoyed going back. Harper had triggered some deep memories.

Denise pounded up Brownsville, past stooping old black women carrying plastic bags of overpriced food from the only convenience stores that would locate outside the wealthy areas.

She turned off Riverdale and noticed a black sedan crawl past. It didn't stop but carried on right up to the lights. Denise looked over her shoulder. She felt her heart rate rise and she noted the license plate. The car took a right at the lights. Denise looked ahead. A long empty road lay in front of her.

Denise tried to ignore it. She was running. It was what she needed. The cool air and the ache of muscles. Sweat poured from her. She needed to see the abused face of the city. She ran up through deserted lots, abandoned buildings, through housing project after housing project. The spent lives stared back at her, hard and pitiless. No one cared about no one and that meant they certainly didn't care about you.

Faces, cold and stern, stared out at her. Old men sitting in beach chairs on the sidewalk, lazy hoods on the stoops, crackheads and hobos. Everyone just looking for the next drama.

The sedan rolled past again. It turned and then followed her up the street. The windows were blacked out, but she knew the kind of people who were inside. It was the second time the same sedan had rolled by and in Brownsville, that wasn't good news. In the projects it wasn't going to be a welcome party.

Chapter Twenty-Seven

Crown Heights, Brooklyn
March 8, 7.56 p.m.

Three cars drove at speed through the streets towards an address in Brooklyn, a four-story public housing block on the edge of an Orthodox Jewish area. They had traced Leo Lukanov quickly. He wasn't good at hiding his tracks, especially when he'd been claiming welfare.

Harper was feeling afraid, the adrenalin pumping through his blood, since they hadn't been able to contact Denise Levene. He'd sent a squad car over to her building, but they'd come back with nothing. She wasn't at home or at work, and Harper didn't know enough about her to guess at where she would be.

In the car, the team were staring out, steely eyed and focused. Harper knew what was going on inside. Eddie kept making light, but he felt it too. Levene had been targeted before. It couldn't happen again, could it?

They parked side-by-side in a deserted lot and all six detectives got out and walked towards Leo Lukanov's apartment. Harper directed Swanson and Greco round the back of the building. The rest headed up the stairs.

Leo Lukanov lived along a dark brown corridor with a single window at the far end. His apartment was a small one-bedroom, three quarters of the way along the corridor. As Harper and the team walked towards the door, they could smell marijuana and hear distant voices – an argument, followed by a baby crying. Harper took out his Glock and knocked on the shabby door. Kasper and Garcia had their guns out too. Gerry Ratten leaned against the wall. Harper glanced at him.

'I don't always carry my gun,' he said.

Harper raised an eyebrow.

'He makes a good shield, though,' said Garcia.

'Then keep a watch,' said Harper.

Harper listened. There was no reply. He knocked again. Shouted through the door: 'NYPD, open up!'

Nothing.

They looked at each other for a moment. Harper tried the door, but it was locked. They hadn't had time to get a warrant through.

'He might have left already,' said Eddie.

'We need to find him, quick,' said Harper as he put his shoulder to the door and leaned his weight on it.

'You do that and anything we find is inadmissible,' said Garcia. 'We need a conviction on this, Harper.'

Harper held his shoulder a second. He let the thought go twice round his mind, then he barged his weight against the door and it flipped open. 'It's about saving lives. Now let's see if we can do something.'

The apartment was a hell of a mess. The smell was bad but the pictures and symbols were worse. Every wall was covered in neo-Nazi slogans and images. There was a large red and black Nazi flag, several large black crosses and slogans: *The triumph of the will. The final solution.*

'He's not sane,' said Harper.

'He's sane enough to have kept out of prison,' said Garcia.

Harper started at the desk drawers, Garcia went for the small wardrobe and Eddie started pulling out boxes from under the bed.

A moment later, Ratten walked in, licked the sweat off his mustache and twiddled his stubby fingers. He watched the frenetic search, then calmly walked up to the desktop and switched it on.

He laughed to himself. Loud enough for Harper to hear. 'What is it, Gerry?'

'You lot, searching like some cops out of the Dark Ages. People don't keep their secrets under the bed any more. They keep them online.'

Mary Greco looked around the room, flicked through his bookshelves.

'What are you thinking, Mary?' asked Harper.

'History books,' she said. 'He's interested in fascism and there's a few seminal texts here in the demented white supremacist line.'

'He's one of them, for sure,' said Harper.

Gerry connected to the Internet and opened Leo Lukanov's browser history. 'Little bastard wipes his history.' A couple more clicks and he was looking at the systems files, the temporary Internet files and Internet cache. '*Voilà*!' he said. 'Look at that – Leo likes to paint on the White Wall. This is his last post. He even calls himself Goering. Nice to model yourself on a mass murderer, I always think.'

'No delusions of grandeur, then,' said Eddie from the bed.

Gerry brought up the White Wall and started to look for posts by Goering. He found the latest thread. 'Look at this shit. Pretty vicious.' He read down the threads. 'Now look at this. As soon as they get interesting, it goes into runic fucking symbols. I've been working on this site for a day and a half and I can't understand it all. They use code.'

Harper stood up. 'It's going to take too long. If he's out there, he might not be coming back.' He pulled a bank statement from a drawer and looked down the list of items. 'Gerry, keep at it and I'll stick to paper. There are basically four locations on this list. There's a bar he hangs out in, a pool room, a shop he goes to. There's an ATM he frequents. I'm going to take a look with Eddie.'

Harper stopped and looked down at the bin under the desk. He lifted it up on to the desk. 'Wait up,' he said.

Harper pulled out eight small pieces of black card and placed them on the desk. Eddie and the rest of the crew came in close. Harper moved the small squares of torn black card around, matching up the rips. In the top corner, the word *Valiance* formed. Harper moved the three pieces that crossed the middle line. Two words appeared in front of them. Harper and the team stared in silence. They weren't just words. It was a name. A name they knew well. *Denise Levene*.

Chapter Twenty-Eight

Brownsville, Brooklyn
March 8, 8.19 p.m.

In Brownsville, the car slowed to a crawl as it passed her, then went straight up the street. She watched it, then she turned left into a smaller street, hoping to avoid a third sweep.

She continued running through the vacant lots and low-rise housing projects surrounded by wire fences. She glanced to her side. The sedan was right there, out of nowhere. Four guys in the car. Two guys hanging out of the window, tracking her. Not gangbangers. White guys. Two she recognized as Tommy Ocks and Leo Lukanov. She looked ahead. There were no other cars on the street. No people. This was a ghost town.

'Hey, Jew, you want to make a complaint about us?' shouted one of them, his hands drumming on the side of the car.

'We found ourselves a stray kike bitch,' called the other.

'Come on, lady, you want to stop and talk about missing Jews?' All four men in the car laughed.

Denise stared straight ahead, her pace increasing, her heart rate speeding up. Adrenalin starting to make her muscles feel weak. Condition red just around the corner.

A baseball bat appeared through the blacked-out window in the back seat. 'You want me to take her Jew legs out? That'll slow her.'

'Not yet, fool, back off,' said Lukanov.

'Let me take her out, man. Let's take the bitch home and keep her for a while.' The drumming on the side of the car intensified.

Denise kept her eyes on the road ahead. She was so scared, her legs felt like Jello – so weak and tired that she couldn't even coordinate her strides.

'You talk about us again, Jew, and we'll cut you to pieces.'

The sedan drove on ahead of Denise and then stopped. Denise slowed her pace. Two guys got out of the car. They were both over six two. Tommy Ocks was dark and mean. Leo Lukanov was pale and intense. They sneered, hitched their low-slung pants, jiggled their shoulders. Behind them, the background vocals from the sedan was a low persistent abuse.

Denise was fifty yards away. Life was a fifty-yard play.

'Hey, Jew, we're gonna show you how to behave right.'

Denise stepped off the curb and ran across the street. The two guys jeered.

'You want us to hunt you down? We can do that too.'

Chapter Twenty-Nine

Apartment, Lower Manhattan
March 8, 8.39 p.m.

Harper sat in his car outside Denise's apartment and continued trying to call anyone who might know anything about her. He called the building manager at her apartment, her neighbors, her colleagues and her therapists, but no one knew where she might be. Denise had kept herself to herself over the last few months.

Eddie appeared at the window and handed Harper a piece of paper. 'That's his cell.'

Harper nodded and called Daniel, Denise's ex-boyfriend. He introduced himself.

'Not you again – what the hell do you want?' said Daniel.

'Denise might be in danger, Daniel. So let's forget our hang-ups. Try to help us here.'

'What kind of danger?'

'Just answer my questions.'

'I'll try. What do you need to know?'

'Denise started running after the abduction.'

'Yeah. Obsessively.'

'We've been in her apartment. Her running shoes are missing, but her cell phone was still there. We guess she's out there running somewhere. We've got an APB on her. You any idea where she might be?'

'Brooklyn, I guess,' said Daniel.

'Brooklyn's a big place,' said Harper.

'Listen, she has a GPS wristwatch. She downloads her routes

and times on to her PC. If you can get on to her computer, it'll have all her routes mapped.'

'That's great, Daniel. Thank you.'

'Let me know when you find her.'

'Will do,' said Harper. He called across to Gerry Ratten and sent him up to Denise's apartment. Harper and Eddie followed closely behind. 'Call Dispatch, get some squad cars ready in Brooklyn.'

Gerry stopped and turned. 'Harper, you drive across to Brooklyn – I can talk you through the routes by phone. No point in us all sitting in her apartment.'

Harper stopped. 'Yeah, let's do that. It might save us a few minutes.' He watched Gerry lumber into the building. 'Let's hope he finds something.'

'If it's on her PC, Gerry will find it,' said Eddie.

Chapter Thirty

Brownsville, Brooklyn
March 8, 8.52 p.m.

Denise felt her heart pounding even faster now. It was hitting dangerous levels. She saw them head out towards her. She turned, started to run back towards Manhattan. A long way away now. Her head was hazy and confused, her vision began to tunnel.

'Fuck you, bitch.'

The two neo-Nazis went back to the car, slipped in quickly and the driver pressed the gas hard. The car lurched off the curb, screeched as it reversed and turned.

Denise was sprinting. How long could she keep it up? After an hour's run, not long. With her heart racing in fear, even less so. She felt her legs pounding. She could only hear the sound of her feet; all her senses had hollowed out a focus about a foot in front of her face. The sedan raced by, a hand slapped her ass, then laughter pealed ahead. The car ripped across her path, the suspension hitting the curb with a heavy clunk. Metal on concrete. Two guys jumped out. The slam of the car door. Quicker now. Closer. The last ten yards. Endgame.

Tommy Ocks smiled. His thick biceps were covered in tattoos. The sickening feeling of fear was drowning her. The debilitating fear.

'She's all hot and sweaty,' called out the guy.

'Just shoot her on the street, man. Don't want my car messed up.'

Denise shouted but she had no voice.

'You gonna repent, Jew? You gonna accept that you're the inferior race?'

Denise looked to left and right. She was paralyzed and confused. There was a wire fence to her left. A small opening at the bottom where local kids slipped under to play in the abandoned lot.

'Or I can make you repent,' said the second guy, taking a step towards her. Denise took her chance and darted towards the fence. The two big guys lurched after her. She made it through the hole in the fence, but it was much too small for the broad-shouldered neo-Nazis chasing her. She stood. Across the vacant lot, she could see Riverdale. There were cars and people on Riverdale. She started to run.

Chapter Thirty-One

Crown Heights, Brooklyn
March 8, 8.56 p.m.

Harper and Eddie were driving fast through Brownsville.

'Where are you?' asked Gerry.

'We're coming back the same way,' said Harper. 'Is there no other route?'

'This is pretty obsessive stuff, Harper. She runs the exact same route, has done for three months. She times it and tries to beat it. She's brought her time down by twenty minutes. She's got some strength.'

'But she's not here,' said Harper.

'Keep circling,' Gerry told him. 'I'll keep looking.'

Harper turned to Eddie. 'She's gone off the path.'

'Or someone made her.'

Harper felt the flurry of anxiety again. 'I called Hate Crime. They can't find these guys anywhere.'

Eddie turned the car and they started back up through the streets of Brownsville.

Harper's cell went again. He picked up. It was Gerry Ratten. 'What is it?'

'I had a thought. If her GPS watch is sending out signals and getting pinpoint location . . .'

'Can you trace it?'

'I'm waiting. I called the company. They want a warrant. They can't release location information.'

'They're sticking to that?'

'Seems so.'

Harper hit the window. 'Come on.'

'So,' said Gerry, 'I tried a little trick or two I know.'

'And?'

'The watch sends signals back to base. You can get your runs logged in real-time to share with others and race with others. I've signed her up for this service. It's just loading up.'

Harper held his breath. Gerry kept them waiting. 'It's worked,' said Gerry. 'I got it live. Not quite live. But three minutes ago she was two blocks west from where you are. Then left.'

'Let's go, Eddie. Two blocks.'

Chapter Thirty-Two

Behind her, she heard them curse and start climbing the fence, but Denise was fast. She was halfway across the lot by the time they jumped down. Her eyes were scanning the fence ahead. She spotted another gap, a vertical cut, and headed off to her right. She was going full speed but they were gaining on her quickly.

Five yards to the fence she felt a hand slap her back. She hurtled forward and rolled, with laughter following her. Footsteps skidding on the gravel. The gap was close enough now and she scrambled through. A hand caught her ankle. She turned over and stared at his face. His name was Paddy Ellery. He was sweating, his eyes were brimming with excitement.

'I'm just going to hold the Jew bitch here. You jump over and help her back through.'

Denise watched Tommy Ocks move down to a post and start to climb. Paddy held her ankle hard and watched, his chest pounding. 'God, you're pretty for a Jew,' he said.

Denise felt the fear subside for a moment, to be replaced by a sudden clarity. She had to do something. 'I'm not a victim,' she said. 'I'm a predator.' Her eyes peeled around. As Tommy Ocks reached the top of the fence, Denise saw a beer bottle lying on the ground. She pulled and leaned towards it, twisting her upper body, and grabbed it. She sat up and smashed the bottle on the ground. Then she jerked towards Paddy Ellery and drove the jagged edge of the smashed bottle into his arm. Ellery looked up;

146

he didn't seem to feel much, then he saw the deep cut and the bottle gleaming with his blood.

Ellery screamed as he let go, his arm oozing blood. It gave Denise the time she needed. She pushed herself up as Tommy Ocks jumped down from the fence and looked for instructions. He took too long and Denise edged back, her hand holding up the bloody broken bottle.

She turned and ran straight into the street, but the sedan had circled and cut off her path. It drove right at her. Denise jumped to one side. Ocks and Ellery started to move in from the right. The car was advancing from the left. Denise saw no escape. Only an alleyway.

She backed into the alleyway, turned and ran, only to come up against a locked garage door and a brick wall. She looked round: the car had turned and the light cut into the darkness. Ocks and Ellery appeared either side of the car.

'Now, let's do this,' said one of them. 'Let's finish it.'

Chapter Thirty-Three

Brownsville, Brooklyn
March 8, 9.08 p.m.

The car screeched around the corner. Harper spotted the black sedan at the head of an alleyway. They pulled to a halt, rushed out and ran across the ground, guns out.

The sedan was blocking the entrance. Harper jumped on to the trunk and leaped on to the roof and across the hood. Eddie followed. There, in the headlights of the car, four men were standing around Denise Levene.

She was in the center, a jagged broken bottle in her fist.

Harper jumped off the hood and into the alleyway.

'Police,' he shouted, raising his gun. 'Move away!'

Tommy Ocks grabbed Denise and pushed her out in front of him. 'You going to shoot? Then shoot.'

'That's dumb, that's so fucking dumb,' said Harper. He took his gun and handed it to Eddie. 'No chance for a shot. This has to be done by hand.' He moved fast down the alley, took the first thug by the collar and pushed him to one side. There was no reaction. He shoved past Leo Lukanov and Paddy Ellery, then stood in front of Tommy Ocks. He took Denise by the hand. 'You're coming with me,' he said. 'You okay?'

'I'm okay,' said Denise. She stared with anger at her four attackers and Tommy released his grip.

'Let's not make this worse than it is,' said Harper. He patted Tommy Ocks on the shoulder. 'Because I would just relish the opportunity too much.'

Denise walked back up the alleyway to Eddie. Harper held them in his gaze for a few seconds. 'Uniform are on their way. Empty your pockets.' He spat on the floor.

Tommy Ocks was first. He landed a heavy blow on the back of Harper's neck. Harper fell to his knees. Eddie darted forward and raised his gun. Harper looked up to Eddie. 'Take her to the car, Eddie. Call back-up.'

'I can't leave you,' said Eddie.

Harper pushed himself to his feet. 'Take her to the car, Eddie, and call back-up.'

He watched Eddie leave and then turned and looked at the four guys. 'Your third dumb move.' Harper considered. Four to one. The odds weren't good, but he was feeling something he'd not felt for three long months and it was running through every vein and artery, pulsing in every muscle.

Running away was not an option. He'd needed this feeling in the ring, but it'd deserted him – yet it was there now, like a fire. His fists clenched, his body felt strong and agile, his eyes narrowed. Tommy Ocks positioned himself on his front foot. His aim was to hit Harper hard on the side of the head. The other three thugs had already closed in.

Harper moved so quickly and decisively that they had no time to react. He threw his foot out wide in a great sweeping movement, hooking the feet of Tommy Ocks and jerking his ankles back with sudden force. Ocks lost his footing and fell flat on his back, his arms in the air.

'Fucking help me,' shouted Tommy.

Paddy Ellery and Ray Hicks moved in. Harper caught Leo Lukanov circling round behind him. He turned, but Lukanov wasn't coming round for an attack, he was heading up the alleyway.

Harper pushed a boot into Tommy Ocks's neck and held him on the ground. He eyed Ellery and Hicks. 'You've got to make a calculation here. You must be half-smart. So far, you've got harassment. That's not good, but your chance of getting away is quite high. You want to add assault on a cop?'

He watched the two guys move nervously on their feet.

Lukanov was getting away. It was Lukanov he wanted. He had to act.

Harper felt Tommy Ocks try to rise. He pressed hard on his neck. Ocks screamed. Paddy Ellery pulled a knife out of his jacket. He smiled like some moron who felt he'd suddenly got the upper hand.

Harper's right hook was so fast, that they only saw the recoil. By which time, Paddy Ellery was lying on the ground with his nose mashed up. Ray Hicks ran in and kicked.

Harper reached out, grabbed his leg, locked it, jerked it up violently and threw Hicks on the ground. He looked down on all three. 'Now, I can hand you over to my partner.'

Harper raced up the alleyway. Lukanov was in the sedan, staring out from the driver's seat. The car's engine growled. 'Eddie,' shouted Harper, pointing at the car. 'Help me out here. Block this bastard in.'

Eddie's Pontiac roared across the back of the sedan and screeched to a halt.

Harper raced to the door. Lukanov pressed on the gas and swerved the wheel towards Harper. The car lurched forward, scraped the wall and jammed Harper against the car. Lukanov shoved the door open and clambered out. His big fist hit Harper hard on the side of the head. Once, then twice. Harper felt the power of the blows and struggled to get his arms free as Lukanov came in again. Harper swerved his head and the third shot missed his face and landed hard on the wall. Lukanov cried out and Harper saw his chance. Leaning back, he threw the whole weight of his head forward. His forehead connected hard with Lukanov's face and the big man dropped against the car. Harper squeezed out from behind it and grabbed Lukanov's collar.

'Leo Lukanov,' said Harper, breathing heavily, 'I'm arresting you for the murder of David Capske.'

PART TWO

Chapter Thirty-Four

Forest Park, Brooklyn
March 9, 9.55 a.m.

Denise Levene stayed in the taxi for a few minutes, staring across the road at the unremarkable suburban house in a row of other unremarkable suburban houses. She had coped better than she'd expected with the ordeal in Brownsville. Maybe Mac was helping, but she wasn't feeling sorry for herself; she was feeling angry. She wanted to do something. She needed to.

The driver didn't speak English too well, but he was happy to keep the meter running. She looked down at the note in her hand. Detective Gauge had provided her with the home details, but had warned her that it wouldn't be easy. No one coped well, and Dr Goldenberg was worse than most.

She noticed that the drapes were shut in every room. Maybe he was sleeping. Sometimes it was the only way if the worry and the strain kept your mind whirring all night long.

She'd called a colleague at Columbia and heard that Dr Goldenberg hadn't gone back to work. He was on compassionate leave. Since Lukanov's arrest, she had tried not to imagine what might have happened to Abby. But she felt the sadness deeply. There was nothing here to hate: a small suburban lot and a divorced man bringing up his daughter. Now it was shot to pieces. He was in hell because of racists like Leo Lukanov.

Denise had spent the morning reviewing the case with Harper, gleaning what she could from the new information. Abby was the golden girl by all accounts – a grade-A student with charisma, musical ability and an independent mind. It was terrible to imagine that people like Lukanov could take it all away for nothing, for some messed-up sense of history.

Denise handed a twenty through the Plexiglass and got out. She steeled herself, walked to the door and rang the bell.

Dr Goldenberg answered quickly, almost as if he was expecting Abby or news about Abby at every moment. Behind him, the house was in darkness. His eyes took a moment to adjust to the light.

He was dressed in a plain blue two-piece suit. His hair was almost completely gray and he wore dark-framed glasses. Denise recognized him as the colleague from Columbia University, but a changed man.

He was shrunken by a few inches; his shoulders dipped forward and his clothes looked baggy. His skin was gray. His eyes were creased so badly that he looked like a victim waking up from major surgery. They were rimmed with red and there was a strange depthless quality to his stare, as if his body was going through the motions, but his soul or heart, or whatever it was, had flown.

'Hello, Dr Goldenberg.'

His hand reached out and grasped hers. It was soft but it gripped her hand tightly and didn't let go. His eyes rose, almost as if he'd seen a glint of hope.

'Dr Levene,' he said. 'Thank you so much for coming by. On the phone, you said you had news?'

Denise stood with her hand gripped by his, looking into his eager eyes. 'I'm so very sorry,' she said. 'I've got some news, but it's not necessarily positive.'

'What is it?'

'Please, could we go inside?'

'I understand, of course,' said Dr Goldenberg. His eyes were now trying to read hers. 'Tell me, please.'

Denise pulled her hand from his. 'I wanted to say how sorry I am. I just want to say it.'

'I appreciate it,' he said. 'We can talk all about it later, but just tell me, what have you got?'

'Of course.'

154

Dr Goldenberg's mouth creased with some memory of his daughter. 'Abby is . . .' He stopped mid-sentence and Denise watched as his whole face contorted in silent pain.

He brought himself under control.

'Please – come in, Dr Levene.'

They walked through the house. It was quiet and felt unlived in. Goldenberg switched the light on in the living room and motioned impatiently towards a seat.

'What have you found?'

Denise pulled out a folder. 'Nothing conclusive. Last night, the NYPD arrested four men. Leo Lukanov, Patrick Ellery, Thomas Ocksborough and Raymond Hicks.' She showed him the photographs.

'The four men who attacked Abby?'

'Yes. I went to speak to them.'

'You?'

'I thought they might know something. They came after me.'

'Oh, I'm sorry. Were you hurt?'

'No. I was frightened,' said Denise, 'but I wasn't hurt. The cops got there real quick.'

'Have they told you where Abby is?'

'No. We can't even be sure they're involved, but something spooked them. Why come after me, try to frighten me, if they didn't have some connection to Abby?'

'Could you try to tell me what happened?'

'I went to see these four men with officers from the Hate Crime Unit. Next day, they came after me.'

'There's more,' he said. 'I heard the news.'

'There may be a link.'

'With the murderer of David Capske? Please don't tell me that.'

'Lukanov bought the barbed wire that was used in the murder of David Capske.'

'You think my Abby could have been a victim?'

'There's going to be an investigation. Homicide will look into it. It means that she's going to get more time.'

'That is something.'

'Not much, I know.'

'I appreciate it, Dr Levene. I know this is not easy. Do they know why these men might have been targeting people?'

'It could be something to do with anti-Semitism,' said Denise. 'But we can't be sure, yet. I'll keep you informed.'

'Thank you.'

'Could I see Abby's room?'

'Yes,' he said. 'Anything specific?'

'No, I just want a sense of her.'

Inside Abby's room, Denise felt the horror of her disappearance again. Life was made up of the tiniest fragments. Memories, loves, events. Denise saw the pop posters, the half-naked men, her wide-ranging intellectual interests, her passion for music, her adoration of her father, her love of her mother, her independence, her eccentricity, her karate skills, riding skills, ballet.

Denise sat down in Abby's room, the drapes drawn, and opened her diary from a year earlier. She had no idea what she was doing or why, but she felt unable to leave without engaging as much as she could, for an ex-colleague she barely knew and a girl called Abby, whom she knew even less, but for whom, for some reason, she felt responsible.

Chapter Thirty-Five

Harper left the interrogation room and slumped down in the darkened observation room. Denise watched him closely. 'We need more time,' she said. 'That's all. He's tough. You should've seen Abby's room. She's just a kid, Tom. If Leo killed her, we've got to find out where she is. The question is, *if*.'

'You don't seem convinced?' said Harper.

Denise moved across to the window. She prodded it with her forefinger. 'I hate him, Tom, I hate everything about him. He's a vicious little racist, a bully, a coward. He's everything I hate about people wrapped up in one ugly package, but he's not bright, is he? He's not got an organized mind.'

'I've been thinking the same thing.'

'We've got to find another way to get him to talk.'

Harper nodded. They both stared into the small interview room as two more detectives entered and started going through the routine. One prowling, one sitting. One getting close, the other keeping in the background with threats chipping away at the nerves.

Harper leaned on to his elbows and stared into the room. Eddie entered the observation room, carrying three coffees. 'He's a hard nut, this one,' Eddie said. 'A real thick skin. Or maybe just real thick.'

Harper took his coffee. 'Thanks, Eddie. Anything more from his apartment?'

157

'Shitloads of racist crap. Shitloads of it. But nothing to tie him to Capske. Not yet anyway. Forensics will be days going through all his stuff.'

'He's part of some organization, though. You find anything?'

'He's definitely part of something, but it seems he's a pretty small cog within it. We've got the other three guys locked up in the cells. They're all scared of something, so no one's saying anything. I don't know who's leading this operation, but they are real spooked.'

'Lukanov hasn't given you a single name,' said Denise.

'Why do you think it is, Denise? Maybe he's just as scared as the rest.'

'Could be. We've all seen it before. Gangs don't dare rat people out. I think he knows he's got to stay quiet.'

'There's plenty of vicious hate gangs in prison. He talks, gives people up, they're going to hurt him bad.'

'Yeah, maybe, but I think it's something else,' said Denise.

'What?' said Harper.

'There's someone pulling the strings. Someone he's really terrified of.'

'That's my thought too,' said Harper. 'Which leads me to something I've been thinking since the arrest.'

'What's that?' asked Eddie.

'Read Lukanov's record. Every time he's been arrested, it's for some group attack. He's one of those men who get brave when it's five to one. I just don't see him as a lone wolf, which means that it's unlikely he killed Capske. Denise, what do you think?'

'It's difficult to call, Tom. He could be capable of operating alone, but I'd agree with you. Most likely scenario, Lukanov is only violent within the group.'

'Another thing. He didn't want to get involved in the alley. He kept back.' Harper stood up. He drank down his coffee and took another look at Leo Lukanov through the glass. Lukanov was unshaven and tired. He'd taken off his denim shirt and was wearing a white tank top.

Harper pointed at Lukanov. 'Look at his arms and hands. There isn't a single scratch mark on his skin. You ever tried to work with barbed wire? The killer was working with barbed wire in the dark with a victim. It's not evidence, but if it's not Lukanov, then whoever it is, he's still out there.'

Harper took Eddie to the side of the investigation room. 'I want you to look into something for me.'

Eddie forced a smile. 'What?'

'There's no match on any of our databases or ViCAP for this kind of MO. The barbed wire, the torture, the point blank gun-shot. We came up with nothing. Denise, how long before a serial killer gets so deluded, they think they can do anything?'

'Can happen after one kill in some cases,' said Denise. 'There's a moment when every repeat killer is sitting in their apartment thinking about what they've done, when they suddenly realize that no one's come calling for them. They've done the worst thing they can and they've gotten away with it. They get to think they're immune or invincible. Or, they get angry, because they wanted to be noticed and they wanted to be understood.'

'Eddie, our killer could've killed before, got no reaction, so upped his game with Capske.'

'And this time, he made sure he had an audience. He called them,' said Eddie. 'So we've got to find that kill. If it's Lukanov, then it'll only help to link him.'

'Leo Lukanov's linked with two attacks, both of Jewish victims. If we count Denise as well, that's three attacks. Eddie, I want you to search out every crime against anyone even remotely Jewish. See what you get.'

'I'll do it,' said Eddie. 'I'll find something.'

'Denise, I suggest we take a walk in Forest Park.'

'You serious?'

'It's a material link to this case. You were looking into something and Lukanov or someone connected to Lukanov wanted to hide that so much, they were willing to attack you.'

'God, I'd hate to think what guys like that would want to hold someone like Abby for,' said Denise.

'Try not to think about things like that.'

'I'll stay here and search ViCAP,' said Eddie. The Violent Criminal Apprehension Program was a database of all recorded crimes across the States.

'If we get something from ViCAP or Forest Park, it's going to be easier to give Leo Lukanov a hard time,' said Harper.

Chapter Thirty-Six

Forest Park, Brooklyn
March 9, 10.10 p.m.

They stood at the end of Park Lane South and looked across the street to Forest Park.

'Do you have any idea what the connection might be?' said Harper.

'At the moment, the only connection with Abby is circumstantial,' Denise told him. 'These Nazis seem to have chanced across Abby and hassled her. She complained and then the graffiti appeared and they showed up near her home. I don't know how it links with Capske or even if it does.'

'No, the only connection is that Leo Lukanov was involved in both, and both victims were Jewish. The MO is very different,' said Harper.

'We don't know that. Abby might have been murdered in the same way.'

'True, but there's no evidence that either the disappearance of Abby or the murder of Capske was because they were Jewish.'

'No, there's no evidence yet, but that's what we're here for.'

'So talk me through it,' said Harper.

'Abby crosses the road here. She was nearly knocked down by a delivery truck. The drivers came forward. They say she gave them the finger.'

'Spirited girl.'

'Yeah, she actually is pretty tough. A Black Belt in karate too.'

'What happened next?'

Denise led them across the street. 'She was heading this way and then she disappeared. A dog walker found her clothes and books carefully stowed in a tree in the woods.'

'You said it was raining that night?'

'Yeah, but not when she left.'

'So let's imagine she's off to meet some secret boyfriend. She fakes a study session with a friend, hides a short skirt under her top. She takes off, changes in the woods and heads up to Myrtle Avenue. From Myrtle she takes the bus to wherever she's going. So far, it's pretty normal for a sixteen year old, right?'

'Yeah, except she doesn't get to the bus stop. None of the drivers remember her and she's a pretty striking girl.'

'So she didn't make it to the bus,' said Harper. He pointed. 'Whatever happened to Abby probably started in those woods. Have they been searched?'

'There was a community search. Mainly friends, family and volunteers.'

'They would've been looking for a body, not evidence of what happened. Let's take a look.'

'Any evidence would've been washed away by now, wouldn't it?'

'Not necessarily. We don't know what we're looking for yet.'

Harper and Levene clambered up the small bank into the woods and started to walk.

They walked up the whole path and back, then through four other routes. The site of the hollow tree where Abby had left her books and clothes indicated the main path she'd taken between Park Avenue South and Myrtle. It would've been very dark under the canopy that night.

'Let's suppose she ran off the path. Where would she go?' said Harper.

They tried several different routes off the path but didn't find anything. Then they traveled back up to Myrtle. Harper started walking in and out of the trees, trying to imagine where he would hide if he was an attacker. He stopped at one tree that gave him cover from both the road and the path. It also gave a perfect sightline. He smoothed his hand over the bark.

'What's this?' Harper said, staring at the tree trunk. Denise moved over and looked at the carving. '88,' said Harper. 'What does that mean?'

'I don't know,' said Denise.

'I'm going to get Crime Scene to look at this. Someone needs to check the Capske crime scene again. Maybe this killer likes to leave a signature.'

'If it's his.'

'So, look, if it is his, then he's waiting here, right by Myrtle Avenue. You know why?'

'No.'

'Come on, Denise. Why doesn't he go deeper into the woods?'

'He needs to be near his vehicle.'

'That's right. There was no body found in the woods, so dead or alive, he took the body someplace else. But there's no sign of a struggle. Let's imagine he meets her right here. Let's imagine she manages to escape. Where does she go? Let's play it out.'

'Just like old times,' said Denise.

'Go and get ready. You play Abby.'

Denise walked down the path and turned. She walked back towards the tree. As she approached, Harper jumped out. 'Now, let's imagine I'm right-handed, so this arm comes out here and grabs you. What do you do?'

'I pull away.'

She pulled away and broke his grip. Her body flew off to the left.

'Okay, where now?'

Denise looked. She only had two options. 'I wouldn't take the path. He'd catch me. If I'm familiar with these woods, I'd chance this overgrown path.'

They both looked into the path. Harper walked slowly along it. 'It gets thick here. Look, broken thorns and twigs. Not too fresh.'

Denise peered around. 'She could've come this way.'

They followed the half-track. It opened out at one point. Harper

163

pointed to the ground. 'Look at that root. In the dark, would you see it?'

'I doubt it,' said Denise.

Harper knelt. 'She may have stumbled. Then what?' He looked around, spotted something about three meters away. There was a tiny glint of some unnatural color. He got up, walked towards it and knelt again, taking out a pocket-knife. The object was bright pink. He scraped away enough of the mud with the knife and read the label.

'Denise, come over. There's something here.' Harper pointed at the small pink cylinder. 'The brand name is Hot and Pink.'

'What is it?'

'It's a girl-friendly brand of pepper spray – eighteen grams. The safety lid is open. It's been used.'

'You think it might be hers?'

Harper stood up. 'I don't know if your guy, Dr Goldenberg, knew whether she carried pepper spray?'

'She did. Pepper spray and a rape alarm. He made her.'

'I'll call CSU – this might be a crime scene. You call Dr Goldenberg, see if Abby used Hot and Pink.'

'How long before you can get a print?' asked Denise.

'If there's one on there, we could have this case opened in under an hour.' Harper walked Denise away from the scene. 'Keep off the evidence. How long has she been missing?'

'Nine or ten days.'

'For nine days whoever took her has been getting his kicks, thinking that this girl is never going to be looked for. He's probably feeling good about himself. This is going to change things for him. Suddenly, the game shifts. We're hunting a potential killer here. If he hasn't contacted the family, this doesn't look good for Abby.'

'What odds do you give her?'

'Someone took her with minimum hassle. He either killed her after he raped her and put her body somewhere safe, or he's got her somewhere.'

'Why would he do that?'

'I don't know.'

'What do we do now?'

'Shake the tree, Denise. Shake the tree. Make him do something. If he's listening and if she's out there, let's tell the media that it's a murder enquiry and see if he wants to change our minds about that.'

Chapter Thirty-Seven

Forest Park, Brooklyn
March 9, 3.06 p.m.

Aaron Goldenberg opened the door. His eyes were already red. He saw Tom Harper behind Denise Levene. He was just the kind of big, brutal cop that he'd expected. Since Abby had disappeared, Aaron Goldenberg had imagined the moment he was told about her death.

In fact, he rehearsed it every day. He imagined that it was about to happen every time the mailman called, every time the paperboy came by, every time visitors rang the bell; and every time the phone went, he waited for the news that would tear him to pieces. He knew that he would never get up again after he heard; that his body would sink and die. As it should. He'd make it his duty never to allow himself to get up again.

He heard Denise Levene say something. He tried to listen. She repeated it.

'Sit down, please, Aaron,' she said.

'Please tell me. If you have bad news, please be quick.' Aaron stared up at Denise, imploring her, desperate with fear.

'I need you to keep calm, Aaron.' She leaned in and took his arm, sitting with him on the couch. He glanced across to Harper.

'Is he the one? You're only a psychologist. It has to be a cop to give the bad news, right?'

'This is Tom Harper. I told you about him. He's a very good cop. The best. He said he'd help.'

'Thank you, Detective Harper. Thank you for helping.'

Harper nodded and stayed quiet.

'Aaron. You told me when we first met that you made Abby carry pepper spray and a rape alarm,' Denise said.

'Yes, for her protection. What else can a father do?'

'Do you remember the brand of pepper spray?'

'Brand? No. It was pink. I bought her pink. I thought she would be more likely to carry it.'

'Detective Harper here thought Abby might have cut through the woods to get to the bus stop.'

'Why would she try to get to the bus stop?'

'I'm not saying she was trying to run away, sir, only that she was going somewhere she didn't want you to know about.'

'I see.' Aaron lowered his head.

Denise took his hand. 'We searched the path. We found a discarded canister of pepper spray. Pink.'

Aaron's eyes glanced rapidly between the two cops, trying desperately to make sense. He couldn't. 'What does it mean? She is dead?'

Harper stepped forward. 'Sir, we got a clean thumbprint off the lid of the spray. It matches Abby's.'

The man's eyes seemed wild with pain and anguish. 'Is she dead?'

Denise shook her head. 'We don't know. But it means that it's unlikely that she ran away. It looks like she was heading through the woods and somebody came across her.'

'Was the spray used?'

'Yes. The whole canister.'

'She's a fighter, Abby. She wouldn't just let someone take her. She would fight.'

Denise and Tom Harper stared on, unable to speak or help the man.

'We've got the woods closed off now. We're doing a full search,' said Harper.

Aaron's lips stared to tremble as dark thoughts clawed through his mind.

'It doesn't mean she's dead, sir.'

'No? What does it mean?'

'Keep hoping, Aaron. There's no saying what will happen,' said Denise.

Harper pulled out his sketchbook. 'We found these symbols on a tree near to the entrance to the park. They mean anything to you?'

Aaron took the sketchbook. 'It's used by neo-Nazis,' he said.

'How do you know that?'

'I'm Jewish, I was brought up in Brooklyn. I'm a Holocaust specialist. Nazi graffiti is a perennial flower.'

'So what does it mean?'

'Eighth letter of the alphabet.'

'H?'

'That's right.'

'So what does H mean?'

'It's double H, as in HH. Which stands for Heil Hitler.'

Harper drew breath. 'It's unbelievable. Do they not know what the Nazis did? What they stood for?'

'I doubt it. Or they find it powerful because they feel weak. Evil has that capacity to captivate those who feel hard done by in life.'

'Could this symbol be traced to anyone?'

'No,' said Aaron. 'It is too common.' He watched Harper closely. He felt there was something more. He stood up.

'What is it, Detective? You want to say something.'

'I want to go public with your daughter's disappearance. I want to call it a homicide.'

'But you don't know that she's dead!'

'You have to trust me, Dr Goldenberg. My feeling is that it plays into his or their hands to have Abby labeled a runaway. That way, the cops don't make these links. If we call it a homicide, he just might have to prove she's alive.'

'If she is alive,' said Aaron.

Chapter Thirty-Eight

North Manhattan Homicide
March 9, 4.49 p.m.

Lafayette sat on the desk. 'Where you been, Harper?'

'Collecting symbols.' He threw down two photographs. 'We found these 88 symbols at the woods where Abby Goldenberg was taken. So I went back to the Capske crime scene – and guess what? He left an 88 on the corner of the alleyway.'

'Might not be him.'

'No, but it's another link, Captain, between Capske and Abby. We could have a Nazi killer on our hands. An 88 Killer.'

'Let's not jump to conclusions.'

'I won't. How did things go at your meeting with the Feds?'

'They want us to keep them informed.'

'So they backed off?'

'They backed off. Your print and link to Lukanov was enough.'

Harper hit the desk. 'That's good. Now I need another favor.'

'What?'

'Abby Goldenberg. Can you swing it under our jurisdiction on the evidence of these 88 symbols and the Lukanov link?'

'I think I can pull it off Missing Persons. They don't want it, but she's not necessarily dead, is she?'

'We're hunting a killer and she's linked, let it be enough for now.'

'Okay, Harper, but keep me right up to speed on this.'

Harper agreed and headed down to the investigation room. He met up with Eddie. 'What you got, Eddie?'

'We've got nothing,' said Eddie. 'We cross-referenced homicides with reported hate crime and Jewish identity and we got nothing. Sorry.'

Harper sighed. 'You go take a break. I'll give it a go.'

Eddie pushed back from the desk and swung his legs out. 'Thanks, I need to eat. You want something?'

'Yeah, anything you can get.'

Eddie left and Harper sat in his seat and looked at Eddie's searches. He'd tried everything. There were four murders highlighted. Two more drug shootings involving Caucasian victims, one Brooklyn murder and one Brooklyn mugging-homicide. Harper read the details. The two drug shootings belonged to the Bronx. The two white kids had been dealing under the noses of the suppliers. They were punished.

Harper stood up and walked around the precinct investigation room. The killer had killed before, so what were they missing? Maybe he had killed and taken the bodies like he might have done with Abby.

Harper logged in again. He tried to cross-reference missing Jewish girls with the MO. Harper looked down list after list. He felt the thud each time the unimaginable crimes flickered to life on his screen. Faces of the dead, bodies photographed in harsh light from every angle. No crime scene on TV could ever convey the banality, the lack of humanity. But there was no link.

Harper trawled through, going through month after month, not knowing what he was looking for, feeling like he was struggling through the darkest jungle, with predators all around. People shot, stabbed, battered, crushed, raped, torn, slashed. Words mingled in Harper's mind with the images and he had to bat them all aside to keep the emotion away.

A thought hit him as he went through each murder. What if it wasn't an unsolved murder? What if someone had been put away for the murder? Miscarriages of justice weren't all that rare.

Harper realized that they hadn't searched solved homicides, only cold cases and open cases. He put in his search parameters.

Single gunshot wound, Jewish victim, writing on the body. He was seven victims down the search results, when he stopped.

Her name was Esther Haeber. She'd been killed in Brooklyn two months earlier. Esther Haeber, possibly the first victim of the 88 Killer, now resting in the Records Office with someone else paying for the crime. He noted the Investigating Officer and signed off.

Chapter Thirty-Nine

East New York
March 9, 5.06 p.m.

She'd hidden it well from Harper and the team, but the attack in Brownsville had gotten to Denise, no question about it. Her pulse had hit dangerous levels, she had felt the panic drain her legs, but she hadn't looked away. She had run through Brooklyn on her own towards her own crime scene. She had been terrified as they blocked her in that alley. She hadn't panicked, though. She'd fought back and held it together. The session with Mac had helped.

She'd been tough on Tom, but she didn't want to be a victim, not in her personal or professional life. She wanted to say what she thought and avoid getting herself caught out. Hard as it was to say it, part of the reason Abby was attacked was that she made herself an easy target by straying away from other people. Just as she herself had done.

Now she was back, sitting at the front of Mac's class, listening intently. Mac stood front and center, his fingers jabbing the air.

'Okay, people, this is for real. You've got to know some techniques so that you can go back to living your lives. These techniques are not here to frighten you or make you into some terminator. But they will save your life and they will prevent you from becoming a victim ever again.

'In every event, the key is to avoid ever getting into a situation when you are in close contact with another predator, but sometimes it happens and someone has got close to you. Now there are two main problems with your behavior – passivity and non-aggression.

'These are social aspects of your character. They are appropriate when ordering a pizza or waiting in line at the bank. But when someone grabs hold of you, all bets are immediately off. No more social behavior. You got to dig down under that superego and find the id. Inside you is an animal, so find it. Inside you is the will to live at all costs, find it. And I'm going to teach you how.'

Mac stood and stared at the crowd of women. 'Levene, stand up.'

Denise stood. She walked towards him.

'You know I'm stronger than you, right? I look stronger, I can probably hurt you in a few seconds so you also believe I'm stronger – but am I?'

'Yes.'

'Wrong. It's not a question of strength but of what you're willing to lose. If you're willing to fight to the death, you will fight very differently and you will be stronger. Your attacker will not be willing to fight to the death. Your attacker wants to rob, rape or hurt. He does not want to injure himself. He's probably got a wife and a mother he has to go home to. You must fight as if every fight is your last. So, you need to be a predator, and the moment your attacker realizes that, you'll have bought yourself enough time to get away. If we've both only got our lives to lose we're equals. Okay?'

Denise looked around. Seven other women sitting in fear.

'So let's try,' said Mac.

Mac lunged at Denise and held her. They struggled. She tried to nip at him with her teeth, scratch at him, kick him and elbow him. Mac stopped and stood back.

'If I'm stronger, taking that number of different approaches only strengthens me. Each time your change your strategy, I feel stronger. And none of them actually hurt me.'

'So what can I do, if you're stronger?'

'Intention is what's terrifying. Find one thing, choose it and go for it. Whatever that is, it doesn't matter, but if you want to unhinge your opponent or make him think twice, it is the fear of the intention. I want you to choose something. One thing, then to try to get me. Think – he can do what he wants, but I will gouge his eyeball. Or I will bite off a piece of his cheek. And then go for only that one thing. Make it your entire goal.'

'Okay,' said Denise.

Mac waited for a second and then lunged. Denise had one thing in mind and that was to bite him. They wrestled hard, but every time Denise had a half-inch of space, she lunged her teeth towards him. The fight went on longer and longer.

Mac finally pushed her away. 'How did that feel?'

'Better,' she said, breathing hard.

'You have a target, you think less about your pain, your passivity, his strength, or how tired you get. The predator always has a single target. It is what makes him a predator. Even under attack, never play the victim, always play the predator. When you have confused him or frightened him or made him question himself, you'll have the opportunity to get away. The predator needs to remain intact. Intend specific hurt. He has that in mind, which makes him dangerous. Have that in mind too.'

Denise walked back to her seat and sat down. Her body was still thrilling from the fight, tingling with adrenalin that felt more positive than usual. She suddenly realized why: she was not using it to defend but to attack. She was becoming a predator.

Denise felt the power of the session. Somewhere inside each of their minds, they were beginning to remember those events, those terrible events, but now, they were facing them not with the terror of being unable to defend themselves, but with the questions: *What could I have done? How and when?*

Chapter Forty

The walk up Essex was unremarkable. It was an ugly stretch of road with a huge municipal parking lot opposite the retail market. The sidewalks were busy with young Asian students and the odd guy with seemingly nothing better to do. Harper crossed Rivington and Stanton and found Detective Jack Carney's building opposite a bright public-school playground. The kids were all at home and the playground stood empty.

Jack Carney worked Brooklyn Hate Crime and had lived on the Lower East Side for most of his life. The city had changed a great deal since he grew up on the streets of Lower Manhattan, but Jack insisted that there was nowhere else that felt like home.

Harper took out the address, which was scribbled on a small scrap of brown envelope. He looked up at a dirty black building. Under all the grime it was quite an ornate piece of architecture. But the carbon emissions had brought it down to earth.

Tom Harper pressed the buzzer. He had called Jack in advance, to let him know he was coming by. Jack was off shift for two days, but didn't mind helping out an old colleague. He waited and pressed again. Then he checked the address. After a couple of minutes, a voice came through the speaker.

'That you, Harper?'

'This is me, Jack.'

Jack Carney laughed. His voice was deep and filled the tinny speaker until it crackled. They'd never been close, just went through training together, remaining aware of each other, the way two lions are.

'You know it all comes flooding back. Come on up.'

Harper pushed the door and found his way to a small elevator. He reached the fifth floor and walked down the dark corridor to Jack's apartment. The door was open.

'Come right in, buddy.'

Jack Carney and Tom Harper were of similar height, but apart from that they were about as different to look at as you could get. Harper was big, strong in the shoulder and with strong features. Carney was like a dark wiry animal you'd find surviving some terrible arid landscape on scraps. He was hardened Brooklyn stock.

'Jack.'

'Tom.'

'I could've met you somewhere.'

'No need, I don't want to put you to any trouble. How's Dr Levene?'

'She got pretty shaken up by those four thugs.'

'They don't play by normal rules,' said Carney. 'Been dealing with them for years and they continue to surprise. We've got all our ears to the ground down at Hate Crime. Is that where your investigation is heading?'

'Lukanov is involved. We also got an 88 moniker at the crime scenes of David Capske and Abby Goldenberg. You ever seen that?'

'Sure, neo-Nazis use it. Means Heil Hitler.'

'Yeah, that's what I understand. We're going to need your help, Jack.'

'Any way we can.'

Harper looked directly at Jack. He looked good. Still sharp. 'Shit, you look ten years younger than me.'

Jack's blue eyes searched Harper's face. 'You think? Maybe it's just because you look like shit.'

'I got my ass kicked in the ring.'

'You could handle yourself better than that – what happened?'

'Shit happened.'

'I guess. Was he that good?'

Harper smiled. 'No, he wasn't. I was that bad.'

'Now that's what I've been telling people all over. There's something up with the world. The strong are being ousted by the weak, you know. Who was it, Tom?'

'What do you mean?'

'Someone took the focus and fight out of you – who was she?'

'There wasn't anyone, just had a bad night.'

Carney smiled. 'Sure. I've had bad nights like that plenty of times. You want a drink?'

'No, thanks. I want to find out about these fucked-up groups. These neo-Nazis.'

'They come out of the woodwork. America has lost its confidence, right? An economic ecosystem, just like the dust bowl – you take too much and the whole thing turns to desert. People are losing their livelihoods out there. So they find someone to blame.'

'You notice it in Hate Crime?'

'Sure do. The economy goes down, hate crime goes up. Being rich is the only way to fight against racism.'

'Horrible thought.'

'The worse things get, the more scary the politics get, the worse it is on the streets. Low-level frustrations tipping over into full-scale turf wars. Poverty and desperation are only half of it.'

'And the other half?'

'Politics. The rhetoric from the government, the ruddy-eyed American dream. People on the streets hear it and it creeps into their blood, but it's nowhere to be found where they live, so they get to think that someone stole it from them.'

'Understandable.'

'Leo Lukanov. People like that. They're told that the Mexicans or the Koreans or the Jews have taken their dream. You need to look carefully at dreams, Tom. Yours too. The dream is always a fake, and the man who sold it to you is long gone, so you need someone to blame.'

'Yeah, I guess.'

'Someone once told you that you'd be happy, didn't they? But it went belly up, right? The girl left, the world became gritty and real. It's called waking up. Hardest thing in the world is waking up.'

'Waking up isn't hard, it's keeping clean once you see how things are.'

'Damn right,' said Carney.

Harper looked around the apartment. 'You push two ends of a piece of metal and at some point, it buckles. That's all it is. We're the buckle.'

'Hey, I like that, Tom. Look at us. Old buddies.' Jack laughed. 'Where the hell did it all go wrong? You married, Tom?' And when Harper shrugged: 'That's what I'm talking about. The dream didn't turn up, did it? I'm living in this tiny room and working my ass off for less than 40K. Happy? When did the pursuit of happiness get so fucking hard, Tom?'

Harper shook his head. He felt it too. It was hard. Life had fragmented – communities blistered and split apart in the heat of poverty and need. Everyone was on their own. There was no community.

'If I could afford it, you know what I'd do?' Jack went on.

'No.'

'Buy a plot of land and farm the soil.'

Tom laughed. 'I just can't see you as a farmer, Jack.'

Jack smiled. 'Maybe you're right. All dreams are bullshit.'

There was a silence. 'Enough of that,' Jack said finally. 'Let's talk about your case.'

'We're not sure about Lukanov.'

'You're not sure it's him or you think there are others involved?'

'He attacked Abby and Denise, there's no question about that, but we've got nothing on the Capske shooting. And it seems a different crime altogether. Much more brutal.'

'Except the barbed wire? That's a physical link between Lukanov and the crime scene, right?'

'Not quite. The print was on the post, not the barbed wire. It wouldn't hold up in court. We're trying to match up some fibers.'

'What kind of fibers?'

'Looks like wool. Left on the barbed wire. Probably from the killer's coat.'

'You ransacked Lukanov's place?'

'Yeah. He's a member of this neo-Nazi group. We haven't got the name.'

'They're called Section 88,' said Carney. 'They're new or it's a new set-up. We've not got much on them.'

'But there's something more. Lukanov's scared.'

'What of?' asked Carney.

'Something, someone – not sure. Maybe the organization itself. Any evidence they hurt their own?'

'It happens, yeah. Usually in prison, if word gets around that someone's talked.'

'No big player out there frightening these lowlifes?' asked Harper.

'Unless it's the leader. But we've not been able to infiltrate the hierarchy. They've kept themselves hidden and they never talk even if they get caught.'

Harper stood up and walked about the small apartment.

'There's something else,' said Jack. 'Let's have it.'

'I want to talk about Esther Haeber.'

'Who?'

'Esther Haeber. Two months ago, you were involved in the investigation. I spoke to the Investigating Officer, Hilary McCain from Brooklyn Homicide. She's a tough investigator, but she's not stupid. Far from it. She got a prosecution out of it, but she wasn't a hundred per cent on it. She said you knew the case. The perp was one of your regulars.'

'That's right. So what's the problem?'

'I don't think your man did it. I think it's one of our guys. You know what else? I went to see the crime scene and guess what I found?'

'I don't know, Tom.'

'An 88 scratched into the concrete, about twenty yards from the body. This killer can't help himself.'

'Come on, Tom. An 88 that could have been scratched there by any lowlife. The perp was good for this.'

'I don't buy it. Esther Haeber goes walking late at night wearing gold jewelry in a part of Brooklyn that she should've avoided. Just like Capske. She's carrying five hundred dollars that's not taken from her purse. And yet, the story is, this killer follows her, then tries to rob her. She struggles. Maybe she screams. He gets scared and pulls out a gun.'

'He panicked.'

'Panicked? He left five hundred dollars on the body and before he shot her, he cut off each of her fingers, one by one. That's not panic, Jack, that's fucking pathological.'

'I remember. He cut off her rings. They were worth something.'

'Then he shoots her. The bullet goes right through her carotid artery, shatters her seventh cervical vertebra and lands in a beautiful brand new Porsche Carrera on the side of the street.'

'Yeah, that's right. The owner was sick – that's an eighty-thousand-dollar car,' Jack Carney said.

'Detective McCain didn't find any leads to anyone else, but this guy fell into her lap.'

'It was a homicide. Wasn't my case.'

'Why did they bring you in?'

'Homicide wanted to see if there was evidence of hate crime. Someone heard some racial slurs about a half-hour before the murder. We looked into it. Impossible to get anywhere, and by the time we'd done the rounds, they had their man.'

'Was there any racial motive?'

'The killer was a racist, but he seemed to want money more than anything.'

'How confident were you that the suspect was the killer?'

'He had a history. They found her jewelry in his apartment. Still blood-smeared.'

'Yeah, I've been through the case. Careless to keep that kind of thing.'

'Damn right.'

'But the crime scene left nothing. No prints, fibers, nothing.

The bullet was in no shape to be analyzed. Seems incongruous.'

'Mind that can cut someone like that isn't thinking straight,' said Carney.

'Anything odd about the crime scene?'

'I wasn't at the crime scene, Tom, I was just advising. I was looking for evidence of hate crime.'

'The killer who worked on David Capske wasn't new to the game. He's killed and hurt people before. I think Esther Haeber was one of his kills.'

'Shit, you really think they jailed the wrong guy?'

'I can't be sure. But if you can remember any more detail, Jack . . .'

'I'd need to revisit the case-files, try to jog my memory, see what I can come up with,' said Carney.

'I'd appreciate it.'

Jack nodded. 'You're either inspired or you got too many bumps to the head, Tom. Not sure which it is.'

'Me neither. But Esther Haeber is supposed to have been mugged – yet the killer cuts off her fingers for some cheap jewelry and takes a fur coat, but he leaves her purse. I read the report, it doesn't add up.'

'He got spooked maybe. It happens.'

'I'll tell you what's bugging me about this case. Simple as this – staging.'

'What?'

'This woman is staged to look like she's been mugged but she hasn't. But the cops look around, there's no other motive so they've got nothing else to say. So they guess she struggled or he got scared and didn't get to finish the job.'

'She fought him, he reacted.'

'I looked at the report. No scuff marks, nails unbroken, hair wasn't even messed up. No sign of a struggle or fight. She must've been unconscious when he cut off her fingers. Else, there'd be more to see.'

Carney shrugged.

'He had Capske out cold while he rolled him in wire. One more question. Did she have anything tattooed or written on her chest?'

'Not that I know of.'

'I just want the truth, Jack. The truth.'

'You look long enough into the abyss, it starts to look back at you.'

'And what's that supposed to mean?'

'You seem wired. Keep things in perspective, Harper. You're under a lot of pressure here and nothing's breaking. Lukanov's been found. Don't go looking for the extravagant theory, when you've got your man in the can.'

'I know, I know, I've had all those doubts myself, but I can't stop thinking that there's more to it.' Harper pressed his hand on Carney's shoulder, then headed out the door.

Chapter Forty-One

Midtown, Manhattan
March 9, 6.43 p.m.

They had not found her yet. The thought pleased him. She was still there, tied to the post and dragged by the currents. He had submerged Marisa in the East River in the dark night, sat by her side as the cold water stripped away her body heat. He had read much about these experiments, he had absorbed every detail, every statistic, but nothing compared to the cold reality. He had kept his stopwatch close to his eyes as her lips turned blue and her head shook above the water. She wanted to submerge herself, to drown, but he wouldn't allow it. Death belonged to him, not her. How long would she last? Would she die first or ask for salvation?

Under forty-five minutes. It had surprised him. She hadn't lasted as long as he had anticipated. Hypothermia was a curious death. Dying while fully clothed as the traffic roared by on FDR Drive. He could still remember the distinctive sound of her teeth chattering above the water.

It was his need, to take these people apart, to absorb their life as they died, to feel them slip away as he grew stronger. She managed only minutes before she was blue with cold. Then he fished her out, revived her on the wooden platform until she showed signs of life. Then he put her back in.

It took three submersions until Marisa was nearly unconscious with the cold. He smiled as he shot her through the top of her head. Orders were orders.

The smoke twirled in his car; he stared out, excited by the experiments, the slow precision of his deaths, the fear that grew as the knowledge that there was no escape ripened in their minds. These inferiors wanted you to want something – sex, revenge, money, something tangible. They couldn't conceive or cope with the glaring eye of impartial observation, or the brutal logic of the fanatic. They were not human to him, they needed to suffer as a means to his own survival and to the growth of knowledge.

He watched the people pass him on the street. Small-minded people living limited lives. They had no purpose. The next victim hadn't arrived yet. She had been harassed by the bottom-feeders of Section 88. A series of minor attacks. She had informed the police. It was her only mistake to try to use the police. He was the force in power, not the NYPD. He didn't like to be undermined. It was ironic that her attempt to find help was the reason she would die slowly and without pity.

What was startling to him was his own capacity for death. His appetite was growing and his hunger came back every day. He knew the police were closing in, too. He felt their proximity; he felt harried. Perhaps that's what it was, an awareness that time for the project was short. He needed more to die.

She had children, two of them. They would be orphans soon. He would take her and continue his experiments. How much pain can someone stand? He himself had borne much. Much more than they had and he was still alive. But they were weak.

He could see Rebecca Glass laughing and joking as she walked along the street, swinging arms, singing a song with her two children. Recently divorced, after her husband's affair was discovered. She seemed to be coping, but he suspected she cried at night and wondered if she would always be alone.

Crimes were crimes, though, thought the killer, and no amount of forced happiness would protect her from the necessary – the arrest, interrogation, torture and execution. It was what was required and he would not fail in his duty.

He had to wait until she was alone, that was all. He had read about a new experiment for this victim. Then, when she had suffered all she could suffer, when he had wrung her out like a wet cloth and all that was left was a soulless carcass, then and only then would he allow her to die.

Chapter Forty-Two

Lower Manhattan
March 9, 6.58 p.m.

Harper stopped on his way to Ballistics. He parked his car and got out to look over the river. He put his binoculars up to his eyes and started to scan the bridge and the nearby rooftops. It was nesting time for the winged predators of the city. He looked out across the sky for peregrine falcons. The city was now home to over a dozen pairs. It'd taken years to reintroduce these raptors but they'd taken to the city well. Strange as it seemed, it was a home away from home for the birds – except these cliffs and mountaintops were made not of rock but of concrete, iron and steel.

As he watched, he could hear the chorus of dawn song against the sound of traffic already making its way into the city from Brooklyn and beyond. Harper moved slowly across the ramp and down towards the water.

After a couple of hours, he spotted a peregrine swoop across from a building on Dover Street to the vantage point on one of the Gothic pylons of the bridge. It might even have been nesting there on the makeshift cliff face.

Harper focused on the bird, its head making rapid movements left to right, its dark glossy eye alert, its body holding an imperious pose. The peregrine – known as The Wanderer.

There were no other birds in flight – the presence of the falcon had scared them all away. The falcon was the supreme predator. It could dive at speeds no other animal could reach – up to 240 m.p.h. had been clocked by a diving falcon. The impact of those claws at

186

that speed, taking out a pigeon mid-flight, was something to behold.

Harper's cell phone vibrated. He pulled it out quickly, thinking it might be Denise Levene. It wasn't. He put the cell to his ear. 'What is it?'

'Man,' said Eddie Kasper, 'you really got to work on that phone etiquette.'

'I've got a Ballistics report to pick up.'

'I got something.'

'What is it?' Harper repeated.

'You ask nicely and I might tell you.'

'Sorry, I'm outta polite.'

'You're your own special category of impolite, Harps.'

Harper put his binoculars to his eyes as the falcon rustled its feathers, flexed its wing muscles and pushed off from the pylon. It was a magical sight, watching it climb higher and higher above the river.

'You found us a new body?'

'I didn't say it's a homicide,' said Eddie.

'I don't get any other kind of calls, Eddie.'

The falcon rose higher with an effortless beat of its wings, its head scanning the air below, looking for prey.

'I got wind of a homicide down in South Manhattan with some similarities to our case. I thought you might want to hustle your way in.'

'What are the connections?'

'Female. Single gunshot wound. Name's Marisa Cohen.'

'She's Jewish?'

'She's called Cohen.'

'It's not Lukanov.'

'Or it's not only Lukanov,' said Eddie.

Harper picked up the falcon riding a thermal, silent, with wings outstretched. He felt the hairs on the back of his neck rise and his fingertips tingle. His case had jumped back to life.

'This is escalating way too quickly. I'm at the Brooklyn Bridge,' he said. 'Get right over here, Eddie.'

Harper put his phone back in his jacket and looked up at the sky. The falcon was focused. It had seen its prey.

In Lower Manhattan, Eddie and Harper drove up to Downing Park where the body had been found. South Manhattan Homicide was already on the scene in numbers. Harper got out of the car and looked at Eddie.

It was getting gloomy. The two detectives squinted into the bright lights of the crime scene. Another body meant that Lukanov wasn't the killer or that there was more than one.

Harper walked across. The crime scene was next to the park, in the courtyard of a haulage company working right on the river. Up above, they could see traffic all the way along FDR to the Brooklyn Bridge and beyond.

'This road never gets quiet, not even at four a.m.,' said Harper.

'What's your point?'

'The point is, if this is the killer, it's something I didn't consider from the first kill. He might get excited by the idea of getting caught, so he commits crimes close to where people can see. Esther and David were both murdered in public places. He might like the risk. I think he might get off on it.'

'I don't know what you got in that head; all I see is the world's dullest haulage lot.'

Harper walked over to the entrance to the haulage park. He signed them both in on the crime-scene log and wandered to the edge of the platform. There weren't any boats tied to it. Maybe they didn't use this place any more. The water was sparkling in the dark. Ink black and flecked with gold.

Harper found Detective Johnny Selinas walking the perimeter, kicking up dust as he shuffled his feet across the ground. Harper shook his hand. Selinas was a veteran. Twenty years in Manhattan South, in which time he'd expanded from 150 lbs to 300 lbs.

'What you doing here, Harper? Don't you get a nosebleed if you come this far south?'

'I try to avoid it, but I think we've got something for you.'

'What's that?'

'We're investigating the David Capske murder uptown.

188

Gunshot to the head, Jewish victim. Thought I'd check out any similarities. Let you know what we have.'

Selinas led Harper over to the body. 'I don't know what this is, Harper. Her name is Marisa Cohen, if her purse is hers. She's been in the river a day maybe. Can't tell much about the COD. Maybe she drowned, maybe she was strangled and thrown in. Who knows, but she's also got a gunshot wound right on the crown of the head.'

Harper looked down over the edge of the wooden platform into the water. Her body was hanging about a meter and a half below the platform. Both hands were tethered to the upright wooden stanchion. The wrists were bruised and the flesh torn, the wounds black against her white skin.

'What else have you got?' he asked.

'Nothing yet. It's early days.'

'She married?'

'Yeah. But separated. He's with someone new, they were together.'

'You have suspicions?'

'Wife found bound and drowned, and the husband off with his new mistress? Who knows?'

Harper got down flat and peered at her head wound. It was difficult to tell through the matted hair, but it was a neat little hole. Close range.

'When do they think they can get her out?'

'Two boats are on their way. Coroner's also coming. Couple of hours.'

'The Capske killer liked to look down on his victim,' said Harper. 'Shot him through the forehead from above.'

'What else you got for me?' Selinas said.

'Look for dirt under her fingernails. If it's boot polish then we might have a match.'

'What's your theory?' Selinas wanted to know.

Harper looked at her hands. It looked like she had the same black dirt under her nails. 'Someone likes to torture his victims. He likes to draw it out. He goes through some ritual with boot polish. We guess he makes them kneel and clean his boots. There's writing too. Our guy had the word *Loyalty* written on a card that was left on his chest, and some unreadable scratches that looked like a homemade tattoo. Put it all together and you've got some sociopath with a lot of hatred in his blood. It might be linked to a series of neo-Nazi assaults. Check if she reported any hate crimes.'

'Marisa Cohen fits most of your killer's MO,' said Selinas.

'Look at her hands,' said Harper. 'She's been tethered. I don't think it's to prevent the body floating away. I don't think he cares about the body once it's dead. As if it's meaningless then, like a piece of garbage.'

'Then why tie her there?'

'She's hanging there, isn't she, with her head just out of the water. He didn't want her to drown. In fact, he's tried to prevent it. She's tried to struggle. Why?'

'To get away?'

'Look at the rope marks. She's tried to pull downwards. That would take her closer to the water.'

'What for? To escape?'

'No, I think it was because she wanted to die. She wanted to drown. Because he was keeping her alive for as long as he could.'

'Sick bastard. Why?' said Selinas.

'Because that's his thing. That's what excites this maniac.'

The two men let the thought dwell in their minds for a moment.

'When did you get to the body?' asked Eddie.

'We had a team here yesterday afternoon in the area but we didn't find her until this afternoon.'

'Why were you searching? Someone call it in?'

'She called a friend just before she disappeared. The friend missed the call, but she listened to the voicemail and then called the cops. We got another call from some building by the park. They heard screaming.'

'So what, patrol searched the area?'

'Exactly.'

'Then he wanted us to find her. He's getting even more fearless,' said Harper. 'He's taking risks. He might have taken her out by the park and transported her here. Pretty risky.'

Harper let the thought take him. Marisa was different. She hadn't been staged to look like something else. Not this time. Maybe the killer was feeling the urge and losing his control. Maybe he was feeling the pressure mounting.

'I hope you find a slug in her body somewhere.'

'No doubt,' said Selinas.

'Listen, get it to Ballistics, tell them to give me a call.'

'Will do.'

Harper looked down at the brown-haired woman at their feet. 'If the bullet and the boot polish match up, then I'm going to ask to take this over. Sorry to butt in like this.'

'Reckon you might need to,' said Selinas.

'I'll get Lafayette to square it with your squad.'

Harper moved in and sat on the platform by the body. His mood changed. He wanted to reach out, put his hand on her, pull her out of that horrible painful position. Even though she was dead, you still empathized with the body. It still hurt to see it cold and in a position of pain.

Why had the killer gone for Capske and now Marisa Cohen? Were they randomly chosen? What if Abby Goldenberg was linked somehow?

Harper wasn't sure. Even if Marisa Cohen was also the victim of some hate crime, David Capske hadn't been. Or, Harper suddenly thought, he hadn't reported it. The link was Leo Lukanov or someone connected to Lukanov. He called Eddie across.

'Eddie, see if you can talk to Lucy Steller and any friends of David Capske. Ask about hate crime. Did he ever get targeted?'

'I'll get on to it,' said Eddie.

Harper looked at the hands again. The marks of someone thrashing about for freedom. The water must've been so damn cold. How long would a body last? An hour at most.

Harper stood up. He turned to Eddie. 'He was here for an hour, sitting by the water's edge as she froze to death. Tell Crime Scene. He might have left something.'

Harper looked down and shone a flashlight into the dark water. 'Eddie, I don't think she's got a blouse on. Tell Selinas to keep a look out.' Harper leaned out further and tried to peer through the water. The woman's bra was dark against her white skin. He felt intrusive, like a voyeur, but he leaned in closely. 'Come on, you bastard, what were you doing? Did you tattoo her too?'

Harper walked along the sea front, trying to locate the position the killer would have watched from. He knew that the killer liked the excitement of getting seen, so he presumed he'd sit somewhere he could see the floating body and the road. Harper moved right to the edge of the platform, out to the last raised post. He knelt and looked. It didn't take long. This killer wasn't hiding his mark. There it was, a small, neatly carved 88 on top of the post.

Chapter Forty-Three

Harper sat with Blue Team watching Garcia interrogate Lukanov. 'It's not him,' said Harper. 'He might be a little cog in this wheel, but he was in here when Marisa Cohen was killed.'

'How tight is the link?'

'I followed the body to the morgue. Dr Pense looked it over. Three similarities. The boot polish, the same caliber bullet with a close head-shot, and she had something tattooed on her chest.'

'What was it?'

'88.'

'Shit.'

'And then something indecipherable.'

'No idea what it says?'

'We don't know yet, but it's our guy.'

'So Lukanov is out of the picture.'

'For now,' said Harper. 'Denise is working on this new information. She says that the writing on the corpse is important to him. He does it before they're dead. It might dehumanize them.'

'What about Esther? Did she have a number on her?'

'No, there's no record of it. I've got the autopsy photographs coming across, so we'll have a look ourselves. Seems that they ignored the overkill once they had evidence linking this mugger to the crime.'

They looked through the two-way. Garcia slapped the table and stood up. A moment later, he appeared in the observation room.

'He's trained,' said Garcia. 'No other explanation. They've trained him. I've seen it before. No answer is the only answer. Or else you just tie yourself in knots. Martin Heming is their lead, right? He might have a military background. We should check it out, find out what we're up against.'

Harper looked across. 'You've got no subtlety, that's the problem.'

'Fuck you,' said Garcia. 'You going to do better?'

Harper went to the wall and picked up a big file of information. 'The game has changed. If Lukanov didn't do it, then we need information from him, not a confession. Information needs a different approach. I got a lot of background on this Leo Lukanov from Eddie and you guys. We got plenty of stuff on him. Let's draw him out.'

Harper stood at the door of the interrogation room and stared at the sad figure before him. He sat opposite the big man as Eddie slipped in behind and leaned against the wall. 'You remember me?' said Harper.

There was no response. Harper nodded. 'You fought well in the alley. Hit me hard. You got the build. Could be a fighter if you put your mind to it.'

Leo Lukanov continued to stare at the table. Harper pushed a packet of cigarettes across to him. 'Take one. You've had a tough night.' Harper paused. 'They set us up when we're useful, then abandon us, don't they? This is what they do.'

Lukanov looked up. Harper caught his eye. 'I'm talking about bosses. People in charge. People who think they know better. You know the kind of people I'm talking about, Leo. People with all the orders – but you know what? Where are they when the shit hits the fan? Where are they, Leo?'

Lukanov reached out and took a cigarette. Harper waited. He needed the man to engage. Harper withheld the matches and stared up at the wall. Finally, Leo looked up. 'You got a light?'

'Sure,' said Harper. He leaned forward and struck a match. Lukanov dragged hard on the cigarette.

'People like you are in the front line. You're taking all the risks,

194

while someone sitting back there is drinking a cold one. I tell you something, Leo, if I could have my way, I'd get rid of bosses and orders. The reason they give orders is because they're too scared to do the job themselves. Look at this. Will you take a fucking look at it.'

Leo looked up, as Harper flicked through a sheaf of paper. 'You know what this is? This is paperwork. They want us to go out and risk our necks and they want fucking paperwork.'

'It's bullshit,' said Leo.

'It is bullshit. But if I don't do it, I get canned. You don't follow orders, what do they do? Smash your car? Beatings?'

Leo turned his head away.

'I know about the beatings, Leo, and the threats – they told me.' Harper watched. It was a bluff, but not a big one. 'Think about this, Leo. When you joined up, did they ever tell you that they wanted a fall guy, someone to go down, while they escape? I bet they didn't sell it like that, did they?'

'No.'

'Let's just complete this paperwork and get you out of here. Far as I can see, you didn't lay a finger on anyone until things got intense. You hit me, but you could argue you didn't know who the fuck I was. I didn't show any ID, right?'

'That's right.'

'Any lawyer with half a brain could get you off. So let's just get this done right now.'

'How so?'

'Ticking boxes, Leo, that's all I'm doing. I'm a trained fucking box ticker. You think cops are thick? Now you know why.'

Leo laughed.

'That's right, Leo. We're a bunch of sheep. No one's independent. No one's operating from personal integrity. I bet it feels like that with you, doesn't it? You don't call the shots any more.'

'I just get told.'

'That's right, you get told, like you're some fucking ninth-grader. Tell them to go fuck themselves, Leo.'

'Yeah.'

'You're taking this shit because some asshole told you to do something you didn't choose yourself. I tell you, I bet if you'd done it yourself you wouldn't have got caught, either.'

'No damn way.'

'Let's get ticking,' said Harper. 'Then you can go focus all that energy on something worthwhile. Make something of yourself while you can. You're still young.'

Leo Lukanov's head nodded a little. Harper looked at him. Lukanov was listening. Harper was trying to feed him a story, a way to understand his behavior, then he wanted to give him a door. The door would come later; first, you had to prime people. He continued, 'We all get angry, Leo, but you don't want to spend your life in jail. It's a shit place to be. You don't want that. So here we go.'

Harper spent ten minutes going through all the information he already knew. Age, date of birth, conviction records, alias, known associates. Leo just agreed as things progressed.

'Okay, next question. What's the name of the other guys you were with?'

'I'm not giving no names.'

'Shit, Leo, I'm trying to get you off here. I've got the fucking names written right here. Look!' Harper showed Leo the three names. 'I got all this information. We're just signing it off to please the Captain.'

'Okay.'

'So again, who were the three guys you were with in the alleyway?'

'Ray Hicks, Tommy Ocks, Paddy Ellery.'

'Right, we've finished another page. Well done. We're nearly there. Okay, now this bit is tough. We need to know how to explain the barbed wire, or else you're going to go down for the murder of David Capske.'

'I didn't kill David Capske.'

'I know that – you know that – but my guys upstairs want to pin it on you. Your guys out there are pinning it on you. They're all just looking out for themselves.'

'No, they're not,' he said. 'Not my guys.'

Harper opened the file. 'Oh no, big man? Well, in that case, they didn't tell us that it was you who received the black card for the Denise Levene attack. Yeah, Leo, that's what they said. That's how the operation works. Your so-called buddies told us. The lead guy gives out a black card with a name on and you do the person on the card. Is that right?'

'Yeah,' said Leo.

'So, as far as this goes, I got to say here who was the lead. At the moment it was you. As far as your guys are concerned, it was you. If you're the lead, Leo, then this looks ten times worse. If you're the lead on this operation and it's premeditated, that's a very serious fucking crime. The lead is responsible. So, Leo, let's check this box. You weren't the lead, were you?'

He shook his head. 'No, I wasn't the lead.'

'That's right, Leo, you weren't the lead. Smart boy.'

Lukanov swiveled in his seat and dragged on the cigarette.

'Next up, who's the lead?'

'Fuck you.'

'If it's not you, it's got to be someone. Just give a name, Leo. The name of the guy.'

'There is no guy. I got the card. The card just comes.'

'Fuck that. No one goes and fucks people over for a card through the mail.'

Lukanov breathed deeply. Harper shifted in his chair. 'I just need to get this signed off. The thing is, Lukanov, I'm in a hurry.'

'I got all the time in the world.'

'You do?'

'I got nothing on.'

'Eddie, give me an update.'

'She's already been found. The media are all over her.'

'You need to go home, son,' said Harper.

'What do you mean?' said Leo. 'Who's been found?'

'Media got your name, Leo. We tried to keep it quiet, but the Capske thing is fucking major. I mean, everyone wants to know. So now your name's out there. They've got your home address, Leo. And now they've found your mom's address.'

'What the hell does this have to do with her?'

'The press don't give a flying fuck for you or your mom.'

'What the fuck are you talking about?'

'They'll be hounding her, raking through her trash, searching records, speaking to neighbors, work colleagues, phoning, knocking, hour after hour. She'll be a prisoner too, Leo. All on her own, I understand.'

Leo rose; the handcuffs clinked taut. 'Let me go.'

'Give me the name, Leo.'

'No.'

'Be a fucking man, you coward. Be a fucking man, for once. Look after your family, right? Your mom. Look after her, not some lowlife who set you up.'

'What do you mean, set me up?'

Harper tried his trump card. 'I think this scumbag set you up. How the hell do you think we got to that alleyway? He set you off, then called us. He probably wants you to go down for the Capske murder.'

'He fucking called you?'

'He killed David Capske but he wants you to burn for it. He chose the barbed wire because you bought it.'

Leo bent over and hit his head on the table. 'I need to go see my mom.'

'Leo, be smart. You let this asshole put this Capske killing on you and you're the number one hate figure. Even if the evidence doesn't stack up, by then, your mom's life will be fucked to pieces. Her life is hell. They're going to hunt her in packs until she tells them something. Then they're going to hunt down your ex-girlfriends, friends, brothers, sisters, until they're painting ugly pictures of you all over. Fair trial? Not a chance. Unless you act smart and speak, you're going down for stuff you didn't even do, Leo. And in prison, they're going to smash up a poor white racist like you.'

Leo stared at Harper. He was breathing heavily. 'You'll let me go?'

'I'll do my absolute best. We'll try to spring you and you can walk free, go see your mom. You've got to trust me, Leo. I don't want you locked up in here, but you bought that barbed wire and that barbed wire killed David Capske.'

'I give you a name, I walk?'

'You give us what we need to nail Capske's killer, and we make sure you've got a way out.'

Leo paused. 'I didn't kill no one. We were building fences. That's what the barbed wire was for.'

'What fences?'

'Upstate. At the compound.'

'What compound?'

'He bought five acres.'

'Who bought it, Leo? They're going to come in here in ten minutes, bag you up, shove you in a truck and send you off to the state penitentiary. They want someone for this, Leo. They don't care who it is, they just want someone.'

'We were fencing off our land.'

'What land?'

'We just want a place we can call our own. A white homeland.'

'I want that name.'

Leo Lukanov looked up. His eyes wide and open. 'I get off? That's for real?'

'You get off the Capske murder. You walk.'

Leo Lukanov stared at Harper. 'What about protection?'

'From whom?'

'I just need to know. If he finds out, I need to know.'

'Who, Leo? Give me his name and we'll look after you.'

Leo Lukanov twisted his hands into a hard knot. The fear was visible in his eyes. 'Heming,' said Leo. 'Martin Heming.'

Chapter Forty-Four

Harper sent out word to the team. They were hunting a man who went by the name of Martin Heming. He called Jack Carney with the same information. An hour later, Jack Carney turned up at North Manhattan Homicide carrying a box.

'Jack,' said Harper. 'I didn't expect a personal call.'

'I needed to come, there's so much shit on Heming.'

'What have we got? Is he someone?'

'We've got a pretty substantial file on him,' said Carney. He dumped the box on Harper's desk. 'He's a long-time agitator. A neo-Nazi. He's got his own set-up – website, blog, pamphlets and publications. He even self-published a book called *The Desire of the Will*.'

'What's it about?'

'Evolution, social science, politics, history. But in a nutshell, it's about how bad the Jews are and why it's true that they really are trying to destroy America.'

'I get so angry at this stuff, Jack. This is hateful shit. How do you stand it?'

'Same as you. We hate it, so we try to clean it up.'

Harper nodded. 'Associates?'

'He's clever, Heming. He seems to be in charge of operations but there's no direct link. He's been arrested a couple of times, but for low-level offenses.'

'Addresses and haunts?'

'Yeah, a couple of places he goes to, and the apartment in Crown Heights.'

'Thanks for this, Jack, I appreciate it.'

'Listen, Harper, it's not all altruistic. I want to jump into bed with you on this one.'

'Your knowledge is going to be useful. What are you after?'

'You're going to be getting to the heart of some of these neo-Nazi groups. This could crack open a lot of our cases. And we might be useful to you. I can put the Hate Crime team at your disposal.'

Harper shook Carney's hand. 'Let's find this sick bastard,' he said.

The teams went out searching for the leader of Section 88, Martin Heming. They tried all the known haunts and addresses. Everyone came up blanks. There was no question about it, Heming knew and had gone into hiding.

Harper returned to his desk and received a report from Forest Park. They'd found blood on the bushes. Abby's blood. Harper put the report down.

His plan was simple, but dangerous. He walked to Lafayette's office, thinking it through. The Captain beckoned him in.

'Any news?' said Lafayette.

'Denise has gone across to see Dr Goldenberg. We found Abby's blood on the bushes.'

'What about this Heming guy?'

'The thing is,' said Harper, 'we've got this guy on the run. He knows we're chasing him. We've got his place under surveillance and all known haunts, but he's gone. He's going to be difficult to find.'

'You think he might have gone out of state?'

'Denise and I think that he's still here, and that Abby is somewhere close. I think he needs this. He killed Marisa after we arrested four of Section 88.'

'What are you suggesting, Harper?'

'We don't sit and wait. We set a trap.'

'What kind of trap?'

'We release Lukanov and follow him. Either the killer will come to him or he'll go to the killer.'

'You think?'

'Heming will know that Lukanov has said something. The killer's got to be worried about these guys being inside, talking to us.'

'You got a point. You think it'll flush him out?'

'They'll make contact. Even if by phone or email, but that might be enough.'

Lafayette stared at Harper for a moment, then nodded. 'Okay, get it done.'

Chapter Forty-Five

Forest Park, Brooklyn
March 9, 9.17 p.m.

Denise Levene sat next to Aaron Goldenberg. 'You wanted to speak to me,' she said.

Aaron tried to appear calm, but his eyes were anxious. 'Have they found anything in the woods?'

'They found a small amount of blood on one of the thorn bushes. It's Abby's. Looks like she crawled into a bush, scratched herself.'

'Who would do this? Who'd want to hurt her?'

'I don't know,' said Denise. 'There's nothing on the attacker. The rain hasn't helped and the time.'

'But at least you're investigating. You said you wanted to shake him out of the tree.'

'Yes, we released a story that this was being looked into as a homicide investigation.'

'I think you shook the tree well.'

'What do you mean?'

Aaron stood up and walked to an antique bureau in the window. He took out an envelope. He returned to Denise.

'What is it?'

'The kidnapper wrote to me. I received it this morning.'

'The kidnapper?'

'She may be alive,' said Aaron.

Denise put her arm around him. 'Yes, she may be, that's good.'

He placed the envelope on the table. Denise looked at it. 'Aaron, you know sometimes sick people get involved in crimes they had nothing to do with.'

'What do you mean?'

'I mean this could be a hoax. Until we get it analyzed, we can't be sure.'

'Oh, I am sure,' said Aaron. 'I am very sure.'

'Have you called the cops?'

'No, I called you.'

'Munroe or Gauge?'

'They've moved on, passed their information to Homicide.'

'Let's take a look,' said Denise.

Aaron nodded. He went to take the letter, but she held up a hand.

'Don't touch it any more. It may contain evidence. They can find a lot from a letter.'

'And what about you? What does this tell you as a psychologist?'

Denise took out a set of latex gloves and put them on. 'It tells me that he needs to be caught.'

'But what else?'

'I think he's escalating. I think he's changing. He started this as a secret and private thing. He went to some lengths to hide what he'd done with Esther and Abby, even changing the MO. Then things exploded with Capske. He went public and he started to show how dark he was. The barbed wire was a particularly evocative touch.'

'It fits.'

'What do you mean?'

'He hates Jews. He imagines himself part of some powerful Nazi project. They work in groups. They need each other to keep the delusion going. That's why they come together. It is difficult to be a lone Nazi, because there is nothing but madness in it. But they need more than a group. They need the ideology, the symbols, and the dress. With all this paraphernalia, they can believe that their hatred is real. Then they need to focus all that hate and all that delusion on an object. On a Jew or a homosexual or a gypsy or an immigrant. They get reactions, they get to feel the excitement of hurting others. It begins to feel like their project is more real than anything else, so real that the rest of the actual world disappears. But even this is not enough. They need to kill and hurt as Nazis. They need to scrawl Nazi images on sacred buildings. They need, in this case, to use barbed wire, the image of the Holocaust, to hurt someone Jewish. A double attack.'

Denise picked up the letter. 'You see this in Esther, too?'

'Yes,' said Aaron. 'Cutting fingers off to get gold rings. This is how they treated people in the death camps.'

Denise stopped. 'Marisa Cohen was found half-drowned.'

Aaron stood up. 'I have thought about that too,' he said.

'And?'

'Whoever this is,' said Aaron, 'he may be copying Nazi experiments.'

'Go on.'

'They used Jewish prisoners to test how long soldiers could last with hypothermia. They put these poor people in iced baths and timed them until they died. They wrote the results down in charts, as if what they were doing was simply scientific.'

Denise held his hand. 'Your knowledge will help solve this, Aaron. We need to tell Harper. But, first, this letter. When did it arrive?'

'This afternoon.'

Denise picked up the letter and opened it. She read it once through. It was short and to the point. Her nerves crackled as she read.

Report 1:	March 8
Subject:	Abigail Goldenberg
Number:	144002
Initial weight:	120 lbs
Initial blood pressure:	114/64
Week 1 weight	108 lbs
Week 1 blood pressure	109/60

Denise re-read the letter. 'She's losing weight.'

'Maybe she's refusing to eat. Maybe something else. I don't know.'

Denise suddenly understood. 'You know what he's doing, don't you, Aaron?'

'Yes, I think so,' he said.

'How do you know this is from the kidnapper?'

He looked Denise straight in the eye. 'It has a lock of her hair in the envelope.'

'Is it hers? Can you be sure?'

'It smells like her.'

'We'll get it tested.' Denise stood up. 'I've got to take this back, right away. Keep thinking, Aaron. I'll be in touch.'

Once outside the house, she called Harper.

'Go ahead,' said Harper.

'Dr Goldenberg thinks the killer is copying Nazi atrocities and experiments. I'll explain when I get back. There was something else.'

'Go on,' said Harper.

'Tom, the killer wrote to Dr Goldenberg. I'm bringing the letter over.'

'And?'

'If we can believe it, then there's some good news. It indicates that Abby's alive.'

'And the bad news.'

'It also seems to indicate that he's starving her to death.'

Chapter Forty-Six

Harper stood up in front of Blue Team. 'Let Lukanov go. Sign him out, tell him we've got nothing.'

The rest of the team looked up. 'What's the story?' said Garcia.

'He's giving us nothing.'

'He's our prime,' said Swanson. 'Let's get the judge to give us some extra time. We can break him.'

'He's a foot soldier,' said Harper. 'Maybe he bought the barbed wire, maybe he took it to the compound, but he isn't our guy. He gave us Heming. We need to concentrate on finding Heming.'

'What about the compound?' said Garcia.

'We checked it out. It's been torched. Presumably because of the heat on Section 88.'

'What makes you so sure Lukanov wasn't part of it?'

Harper looked across at Denise Levene. She nodded. 'He's part of the organization, all right, but he's not the killer. Marisa Cohen was killed after he was arrested.'

'He attacked Denise and you. We don't let some sick racist scum out for nothing. He's still the only suspect we got.'

'He's our only link to Heming. We got to take a chance.'

'There might've been a few guys. This guy might've been there, watching.'

'Eddie, give them the low-down.'

'His girlfriend puts him at home all night.'

'His fucking girlfriend. The bleach blonde in the hot pants with the Nazi tattoos? Like she's a good fucking alibi.'

Harper nodded and looked across. 'There's enough to discount him. But listen up. He's involved somehow, he's just not the main man. And I want the main man. He's our lure. Leo Lukanov will lead us to the killer.'

Harper set the surveillance operation going. The team set up the rota for a tail on Lukanov. They would let him go before midnight.

At 11.57 p.m., Leo Lukanov was released and left standing on the steps of the precinct in a state of confusion. He looked like he wasn't sure whether it was a sick joke by the cops or just luck. He went straight home to his apartment. Behind him, just out of sight, Swanson and Greco kept up the tail.

Twenty minutes later, Lukanov took off. He got the bus to his mother's place. Ratten and Garcia were already sitting outside in a car. No doubt he was surprised to find that the media hadn't been anywhere near his mother.

Ten minutes after arriving he left and visited his girlfriend's place. Harper and Kasper were sitting right outside.

Lukanov made several phone calls from his girlfriend's house. The cops couldn't trace them, but they could be used in evidence later.

After four hours, in the dead of night, Lukanov left his girlfriend's building and walked home. It took him an hour to walk the streets. Harper and Kasper had to get out and follow on foot.

He entered his own apartment building for the second time at 5.08 a.m. Harper returned with Kasper to their car and headed back to the bunkhouse. Likewise, Garcia and Ratten. Swanson and Greco were the unlucky ones. They sat outside his apartment, with an unmarked police car at the service entrance at the back. At 5.42 a.m., the lights in Lukanov's apartment finally went out.

Chapter Forty-Seven

Apartment, Crown Heights
March 10, 5.10 a.m.

Lukanov wasn't stupid. He knew he had a tail. Anyhow, even if he had missed it, Heming had told him he was being tailed. They had a routine. He called a cell number three times, waited forty minutes then called a public booth from his girlfriend's place. By that time, Heming was there to answer the call. Heming had told him to keep his mouth shut, go home and stay put.

Lukanov intended to follow the instructions. He opened the door to his apartment. The lock had been busted, so he only had to push it. He pulled off the remnants of the police security stickers pasted across the frame. The cops must've kicked the door down, fucking assholes.

He entered the room for the second time that morning. Most of the room was wrecked. Everything was tipped out, the floorboards ripped up, wallpaper torn down. A note from the police department had been left, with details of how to get compensation. Assholes. This was what Heming had told them all about. The cops were part of the problem.

Lukanov stared at the mess and then heard a noise in his kitchen. He turned. He suspected cops. Maybe they were going to get in a reprisal for attacking Denise Levene or for punching Detective Harper.

He called out, 'Who's there?' No one replied. Was it just rats? The cops had left food and shit all over the floor with the door open. Could even be cats. He hated cats.

Lukanov heard a low cough from the kitchen. Not cats, then. An open apartment in this kind of building with the door kicked in would be quite a temptation. It might be kids or some hobo.

Lukanov picked up his baseball bat from the floor and headed towards the kitchen.

He pushed open the kitchen door and peered in. Someone was there, staring out of the window. A figure.

'Who the fuck are you?' shouted Leo, and he raised his bat.

The man spoke. 'How long does it take you to find someone in your own apartment?' He turned. 'Hello, Leo.'

Leo let the bat fall. 'Is that you, Martin? You scared the shit out of me.'

Martin Heming stood tall and powerful in front of him in a suit. He was clean-cut and had shaved. 'I look a little different. I had to be careful. Police are tailing you and they've been hunting me. They're searching for some tank-top-wearing, unshaven thug, so I just put on a suit, carry a briefcase and wander around Manhattan.'

'That's a great idea, Martin, but why are they tailing me?' said Leo. 'They let me out.'

'They let you out to lure someone else out. I can't think of one other fucking reason, Leo, why they'd let kike-hating scum like you out of the slammer. Why would they? You raced down a cop. You hit a cop. You got caught. Ellery pulled a knife.'

'I didn't hurt anyone.'

'It doesn't seem right to me, Leo.'

'What do you mean?'

'I just got a nose for it. What did you tell them?'

'Nothing. But they told *me* something, Martin. Told me you set us up.'

'You think I'd do that? Why?'

'To pin Capske on us.'

'Like they're going to believe you lot could kill Capske. You can't even rough-up a woman.'

'They found us, somehow.'

'They probably tailed you.'

'I promise, Martin, I said nothing to them.'

'You lying piece of shit.'

'No, Martin. Not a thing.'

'You fucked up. You had the operation. Your first independent and you fucking embarrassed us.'

'The cops knew.'

'So that's what they told you?'

'How else did they get there so quick?'

'They got there so quick, Leo, for two fucking reasons. The first is that you didn't wear gloves transporting the barbed wire. The second is that you fucking emailed your squad and left the black card in your apartment.'

'I needed the team quick. I couldn't get hold of them on the forum.'

'What's the problem with email?'

'It's traceable.'

'Right, the forum is anonymous.'

'Sorry, man, sorry.'

'You going to be sorry to me or you going to tell me?'

'What?'

'You tell them about Sturbe?'

'No. You think I'm stupid?'

'He's in the fucking bedroom, waiting. He thinks you told them. He's going to be coming in here and pulling your teeth out one by fucking one.'

Lukanov went pale. 'Fuck you.'

'You want me to call him out?'

'No.'

'Sturbe's angry.'

'I took a hit for you.'

'You're out, no one else is. Not Paddy, Ray or Ocks. Just you. You know what that tells me?'

'I didn't get caught hitting someone.'

'You hit Harper. No, Leo, it means that you gave them some information.'

'No, sir, not me.'

211

'You know what that's called, Leo?'

'No.'

'High fucking treason.'

'I did nothing. No treason, nothing.'

'You're not safe, Leo. You're like a weak point in a wall and the thing is, the weak point is the point where the wall breaks.'

'I'm not a weak point, I swear.'

'I'm going to go in the bedroom, talk to Sturbe; we're going to decide what to do with you.'

Leo watched. 'Fuck you, Martin. There *is* no Sturbe. You fuck. You're just trying to spook me. We all know that Sturbe's just a fucking game you play. You can fuck off and die, Martin.'

'Really? You think that, do you? You think that this has no one behind it? Really? You think this is just me?'

'Fuck you, Martin. We've all been up to the compound this Sturbe wants us to build and none of us have seen him.'

'You've got to watch yourself, Leo.'

'Do I?'

'Sure you do, kiddo.'

'Why's that?'

'You know what happens when you stop believing in the bogeyman.'

'What?' said Lukanov, his head twisting to look over his shoulder.

'The bogeyman comes to pay you a visit.'

Chapter Forty-Eight

Apartment, Yorkville
March 10, 6.45 a.m.

The autopsy on Marisa Cohen found a third bullet. Harper had it in his hand. He needed an answer soon. Even if they caught Martin Heming, they'd need some evidence to link him to the murders.

Each bullet was too mangled and, without a cartridge, there was no way of matching it to a gun. But Harper wanted to know more.

Eddie was working with Hate Crime, conducting interviews with friends and relations of Marisa Cohen. So Harper brought Denise with him.

Denise sat in the car. 'Where are we going?'

'I need someone to look over the three bullets. Ballistics have nothing much, but I gave them to someone who used to work with us. He's retired, works the odd case with the FBI. He's one of the best. Hans Formet.'

'What are you looking for?'

'These bullets look different to me – so do the entrance wounds they leave. They're tight, no expansion. Look, Hans is a genius. If anyone can find something, he will.'

'Anything on the tail?'

'No, he's still in his apartment. Sleeping. He didn't get back until after five a.m. What about Abby?'

'We're working on the note. Nothing yet. What am I here for, Tom?'

'You're here to certify I'm of sound mind and let me know if I'm not.'

'But if you're not, you wouldn't believe me.'

'Then get me to a psychiatrist as soon as you can.'

They both smiled.

'I want to hear more about what Aaron said. You can talk on the drive over.'

Harper pulled out. Denise filled him in on the Nazi symbols used in the three murders and Harper listened intently. 'It makes sense,' he said. 'You're beginning to understand him.'

'With Aaron's help, I am.'

Harper and Levene arrived at the home of ballistics expert Hans Formet and walked up the steps.

'What did the CSU find on the Capske bullet?' asked Denise.

'The initial ballistics report was inconclusive. They carried out some ballistic imaging on the bullet, but nothing came up on the National Network. There was too much damage.'

'No way to tell if it was the same gun that fired both bullets?'

'If the gun that shot this bullet had been used before, we wouldn't be able to tell from the mangled slug we've got. We didn't find the cartridges. They'd tell us more.'

'So what the hell can Hans Formet tell us?'

'I don't know, but we're going to find out soon.'

Harper rang the bell and waited. After a long while, Hans Formet appeared.

Hans was of Austrian origin. A short, balding man with small intense eyes, he was in a white coat, the picture of the anti-social scientist. Harper said hello. Hans smiled and stared at Denise.

'How you getting on?' said Harper.

'Who's this? Some inspector?'

'Dr Levene. Psychologist. Working on the case.'

'Don't try to read me, Dr Levene, okay?'

'We're interested in bullets, not therapy,' said Denise.

Hans eyed her for another second, then seemed to let it go. He turned to Harper. 'I found something interesting,' he said. 'Something very interesting. You should come in.'

'Thanks,' said Harper, and the door opened.

Hans stared at Harper for a moment longer than was comfortable. 'If you want something done properly, you come to me. Those new recruits at CSU are full of techniques, but they have no depth of knowledge. Everything is from a computer. No real-world experience.'

Hans smiled thinly and led Harper and Levene down to his lab. He waited for Harper to say something. Clearly Harper was supposed to acknowledge his old-school brilliance. Harper didn't. He looked around at the images on the walls – all of them bullets and cartridges. 'You like bullets, Hans?'

'Yes, I like bullets. That's called dry humor, isn't it?'

'If you ever got caught up in a murder investigation, you'd be a prime suspect,' said Denise, staring at the obsessively neat close-ups of bullets.

Hans led them past the workbenches to a desk with three computer screens side-by-side.

'So this is where you get to play now?' said Harper.

'Since I retired, yes. Anyway, I like to do my own work out here away from those new guys with their smart shirts. I don't like bright colors, you see. What did they find in these bullets?'

'Nothing,' said Harper. Denise watched from a distance.

'Nothing is correct, Detective. But what did I get?'

'I don't know,' said Harper. 'What have you got for me?'

'What have I got for you? Here,' said Hans. A picture came up on the screen.

Harper looked at two close-up photographs of the twisted gray bullets. 'What am I looking at?'

'It didn't take long – not long at all, considering that no one else spotted it. There is something unusual in your bullets. Your instincts were right, Detective.'

'What did you spot?' said Harper. 'Come on, he could've murdered again in the time you've taken building up to the show.'

Denise Levene felt her interest growing as she stared at a magnified picture of a used bullet. A bullet that had passed through Esther Haeber's body.

'Look, here's the Capske bullet. And here's your bullet from

Esther Haeber. They are both badly damaged. Much more deformed than you would expect. You can see that right away. I presume that is why the young technical specialists at the CSU labs could not identify them. They only know modern bullets. But even for me, this is not something I've seen outside of museums and I've seen everything post 1961. So that led me to believe that this was older.'

'Seriously?'

'Yes. This, Detective Harper, is, as you know, a 9mm Parabellum. But it is an unusual 9mm. Firstly, the metal is different from usual and so is the color.'

'Looks like it got burned.'

'It's a different metal. Not a metal anyone uses to make bullets.'

'What is it?'

Hans Formet put his hand on top of Harper's. He whispered, 'This, Detective, is an iron bullet.'

'An iron bullet – what does that mean?'

'Very rare in this size of ballistics. Very rare. So rare, in fact, that you have a connection between your apparently unconnected murders.'

Harper put the third bullet down on the desk. 'This came from our next victim, Marisa Cohen.'

Hans pulled it out of the bag with forceps and turned it under his eye. 'It appears the same,' he said. He dropped it into a small dish and squeezed some droplets on it. They changed color. 'Iron,' nodded Hans.

'But an iron bullet isn't conclusive, is it?'

'Iron is made strong by the addition of various impurities. Pure iron is very soft, whereas iron with the right mix of impurities becomes steel. So I had the iron content analyzed. The proportion of iron, carbon and other impurities.'

'Okay, I get iron, Hans, but what does it tell us?'

'Well, guess what I found? An exact chemical match. Not only are these bullets of a similar type, they are from the same batch.'

'Is that admissible?'

'Who knows what the DA would accept, but for a detective,

knowing there is a real link is worth something in its own right. Correct?'

Harper's skin was tingling. Hans was a showman all right. This was the first piece of real physical evidence, providing a link between the three murders.

'The bullets might not be from the same gun, but they were manufactured in the same factory, at the same time, is that right?' said Denise.

'Yes.'

Harper caught Denise's thinking. 'A munitions factory must make a million bullets of the same type at the same time. How does this give us a link?'

'It's not absolutely conclusive. I never said it was. But who makes iron bullets, these days? And iron is different from lead. This match is not close, it's identical. Same batch. How many killers are there in New York using old iron bullets?'

'You'd say not many,' said Harper.

'One. No more,' said Hans.

'Can you tell me anything more about these bullets?' said Harper.

'I have to continue my work. At the moment, I don't know what they are or where they were made. I will try for you, Detective.'

Harper stood up and let the idea swim in his mind. It was a material link between the cases. And that meant that he now had evidence linking three Jewish murders. It was potentially explosive.

Chapter Forty-Nine

Harper's head was full of iron bullets as he ran up to the investigation room with Denise. She put her arm out, touched his. 'What do you think it means?' she asked.

'Our killer is not new to this game. He's tried before.'

'What else?'

'He's not politically motivated. He's killing people because they're Jewish.'

'Can we be sure? There's just three murders.'

'Each killed in similar ways with iron bullets. He doesn't want to get caught, does he?' Tom said. 'If we're right, then the man in prison for killing Esther Haeber is the wrong man.'

'And that adds something vital to our profile. He's stalking these people, killing them, then setting up other people and staging it to avoid us joining the dots.'

'Intelligent, strategic, psychotic,' said Tom.

'Add brutal and determined. He wants to carry on. He really enjoys this. Like some . . . necessity, you know.'

'A religious killer?' asked Harper.

'Yeah, that's what I was thinking. It has that visionary zeal about it.'

'God help us, then.'

'Or just avoid helping him, if at all possible.'

Harper left Denise and marched into Captain Lafayette's office. 'I got a link for you.'

Lafayette stood up. 'Really? Evidence?'

'Yes, real evidence.'

'Go on, tell me.' Lafayette moved round the desk. 'We're getting busted on this by the hour. They want to know why Lukanov walked. I need some good news.'

Harper produced a printout of Hans Formet's photographs. 'We've discovered a link between the bullets found at the Capske scene and the Esther Haeber and Marisa Cohen scenes. It links each murder.'

'What's the link?'

'The bullets are all made of iron,' said Harper.

Lafayette looked at the pictures. 'What's the significance of that?'

'Iron was used to manufacture bullets at some times in the past, but it's rare. These bullets are very rare, therefore linked, Captain.'

'Coincidence?'

'No.'

'Come on, what you got? Three bullets made of iron, separated by four months, one on a case with a conviction? You know, Harper, even your fans wouldn't buy this.'

'It's a link.'

'Could it be contamination?'

'Please, Captain. This is a breakthrough. I nearly choked. There's some animal on the loose, taking these people out because they're Jewish. I think we've got a serial killer at work.'

'It's not a complete picture, Harper.'

'Complete enough. I need to take these homicides together. We need a task force. I'll want a liaison with Brooklyn Homicide. We have to reopen the Esther Haeber case.'

Captain Lafayette sat back down and directed one of the fans on his desk towards his face. 'Are you sure it's enough? I know you want this, but we've got to be sure, Harper.'

'Captain, I need some authority here. I need to take this forward. You've got to trust me on this one.'

'The iron's not enough. I need more. Go and check out this guy who got jailed for the Haeber murder.'

'I'm on my way soon as we're through here. But you've got to understand that the iron matches. There's an exact chemical fingerprint to iron. These three bullets were from the same batch.'

'You got anything that matches that bullet to a particular gun?'

'No, it's mangled all out of shape. But the chemical properties are identical.'

'Bullets are made in big batches, Harper. Big, big batches.'

'But this is not what bullets are made of now. No one uses iron today. These are incredibly old bullets. Possibly antiques.'

Lafayette pushed his chair back and stared up. 'Okay, Harper. I'll take your word. We'll get some help. Run with it. But we got to talk to people about how to handle this. You know what this is.'

'Of course I do. Some psychopath is killing Jews.'

Chapter Fifty

Eddie and Denise nodded silently as Harper talked through his visit to see Bruce Lyle, the man imprisoned for the murder of Esther Haeber.

'So you've got nothing to show for your efforts?'

Harper shrugged. 'He's not the guy, in my opinion, but we need evidence to get the case re-opened and that means catching the real killer. He says he was framed – that someone planted the rings. I think our killer chose an easy target. They found illegal firearms and cocaine in his place, so he's got three violations to serve.'

'But he's no killer?'

'No.'

'What else you got?' said Eddie.

'We've got something on the note from the kidnapper. It's got mildew on it, so it was written somewhere damp. But the main thing is the typeface and ink. It's strange.'

'How?'

'They've got a pretty full database of typewriters and fonts down there. They tell me this is something unusual.'

'Just like the bullets.'

'Right,' said Harper. 'They say this is from an antique typewriter. German make, around 1934. They are pretty sure it's a Torpedo Portable Typewriter. It was designed for military use and only wrote in black. Not red ink.'

'What the hell does that mean?' said Eddie.

Denise nodded to herself. 'This guy is delusional. Aaron noticed the Nazi symbols in the way he kills. Now an antique German typewriter. He's not a neo-Nazi, Harper. He thinks he *is* a Nazi, one of the originals.'

'It's a very rare model,' said Harper. 'Not many people deal in these. We might be able to track something.'

'Give me the printout,' said Eddie. 'I'll see what I can do.' He got up and walked towards Gerry Ratten.

Harper's cell phone rang and broke the somber mood. It was Hans Formet.

'You need to come round,' said Hans. 'You need to come round now.'

'What for?'

'I know what your bullets are. I know where they come from. And this is strange.'

'That's great, Hans, we'll be there as soon as we can.'

Within the hour, Harper and Denise were back in Hans Formet's homemade lab, with a cup of coffee each, listening to the long rambling story of the man's genius.

Hans clearly had not moved much since they'd last been there. He was bleary-eyed, with his hair sticking out in every direction. He sat on a stool with his computer screen to his side.

'An iron bullet is rare – a 9mm Parabellum made of sintered iron is extremely rare. Take a look at this.' Hans brought up a photograph of a bullet with a cartridge. The cartridge was black.

'Looks like there's a tux on a bullet,' said Harper. 'Like a bullet going to the Oscars.'

Hans laughed. 'That's a very good joke, Detective. A good ballistics joke.'

'Come on, Hans, spill.'

'So I sent the information across to some people I know, then I put it up on the web and got a hit. They said it might be an antique bullet. Something from the Second World War.'

Harper and Denise felt the thoughts rushing through their heads. 'Tell us more,' said Harper.

'The Parabellum itself was introduced for the German Service

222

revolver, the Luger Pistole. It's one of the most popular cartridges in the world now. But back then, it was new.'

'So this is a German bullet?'

'Oh, yes. Manufactured in Poland, probably.'

'Go on.'

'Okay, well, sorry for the history lesson, but the Parabellum originally had a lead core. A better bullet, of course. An iron bullet is too hard. The purpose of a bullet is to cause damage in the flesh. An iron bullet can zip right through the body with no expansion. It is the expansion that brings someone down. However, in about 1942, war-time lead supplies were running low so they started making the Parabellum with an iron core. *Miteisenkern*. They had stocks of these bullets left over after the war. Quite often, if you try to buy a bullet from that time, it will be an iron-cored bullet.'

'Always the pragmatists, the Germans.'

'Yes, indeed. Now, the bullet with the iron core was given a black jacket to differentiate it.'

'So what more do we know? Why is someone using antique bullets?'

'Come on, Harper,' said Denise. 'They're not just antique bullets, they're army supplies. These are Nazi bullets, Harper – original Nazi bullets. He's playing the whole part, he *is* the whole part.'

Harper felt the hair on his neck rise.

Chapter Fifty-One

Apartment, Crown Heights
March 10, 2.10 p.m.

Denise Levene headed off to see Aaron Goldenberg. He was a curator at the Museum of Tolerance. If anyone was going to know how to source Second World War artefacts, it would be him. He had also been working on a couple of other pieces of information. The number on the kidnapper's note and the words *Loyalty* and *Valiance* on the black cards.

Harper found Eddie and headed out to Lukanov's apartment. He called Swanson and Greco.

'I'm on my way. Any movement?'

'No one in or out. He's probably still sleeping.'

Harper and Eddie drove over. Eddie explained what he'd done so far. He had passed the information about the typewriter to Ratten, who had gone out over eBay and two or three Internet groups asking for a 1934 Torpedo Portable Typewriter. He'd already had two hits. Someone who had one and someone who might have one soon.

'He'll have a list of dealers by the time we get back.'

'Good. But I doubt we'll be able to trace it. If this guy's really delusional, he could've bought it years ago.'

They turned into the street and saw Swanson and Greco's car. They pulled up and got out. Greco and Swanson drove up to them.

'Good luck,' said Swanson.

'Which is his room?' said Harper.

Greco pointed. 'Third-floor corner.'

Harper stared up. 'Windows open all night?'

'Yep. Lights went off at 5.27 a.m.'

'Strange,' said Harper.

'Why?'

'People close their drapes to sleep.'

'His bedroom is at the side,' said Greco.

'I know,' said Harper, 'and the drapes aren't drawn.'

'Maybe he sleeps heavy,' said Swanson.

'You see anyone come and go?'

'Not a thing. Just other residents.'

'How many?'

'Several. We got pictures, if you want.'

'You kept an eye on the back entrance?' Harper asked.

'Sure. There's two cops there.'

'They say they saw anyone come in or out?'

'Nothing.'

'Girlfriend?'

'No.'

'Anyone else?' said Harper.

'A cop.'

'What cop?'

'The guys at the back saw him. They didn't see him go in, but a cop came out with a perp in cuffs this morning.'

'One cop?' said Harper.

'Yeah, one cop. Suppose the second cop was in the car.'

'You said he was leading a perp?'

'Yeah.'

'They get a good look at that perp?'

'No. He had a hoodie on.'

'Fuck,' said Harper.

'What? It was a cop.'

'Maybe it was a cop, maybe it was Leo and one of his crew.'

'No, they were sure it was a cop.'

'You don't know that. Let me ask you.'

'What?'

'How many cops do you see making arrests from the projects

225

on their own?' The two detectives shook their heads. 'Is that never? Or do you want more time?'

'Hardly ever,' said Greco.

Harper sighed. 'Come on, he's gone. Somehow, he's fucking gone.'

Harper and Eddie ran up to the house, Swanson and Greco behind them. They entered the building, raced up the stairs to the third floor.

Harper stared at the door. 'Who's done this? Who kicked this in?'

'You did,' said Swanson.

'I barged the door. The Crime Scene team bolted the door. It's been kicked open. Careful, there might be prints.'

Harper pushed open the door. He called out, 'Police.'

Not a sound came back. They stopped still. Were hit by the smell of urine.

They opened the door fully. 'Looks like he's gone,' said Eddie.

'How fucked up do we want to be? We lost our one lead,' shouted Harper. He moved through to the bedroom, pushed open this door in turn. 'Shit,' said Harper. 'I don't think he's gone.'

'What? He's sleeping?'

Eddie joined Harper. There was Lukanov, lying naked on the bed. Gunshot wound to the head. Feathers everywhere, a pillow marked black with residue. His torso was ripped across with the number 88 in large bloody tracks. A small black and white cat was licking at the wounds. It paused and stared at them.

Harper turned and pushed past the two detectives. 'They killed him,' he said. 'He didn't come or go, you fucking imbeciles, but someone fucking did.'

'Who? We were supposed to tail the guy, not fucking nurse him. We weren't looking for someone going in, were we?'

'I guess not. Another fucking dead end.'

The body was pale, the blood dried black. Covered with Nazi tattoos from neck to ankle. The red calling card ripped across it.

'A foot soldier,' said Harper. 'Dispensable. Someone they knew had betrayed them.' He turned to Eddie. 'We're getting close.'

'How do you figure?'

'Serial killers who attack random victims according to type are difficult to trace because there's no connection between the motive and the victim. There's only the unlucky fact that the victim was the type.'

'I know that.'

'But this is no random victim – this man was killed because he knew, because he was a threat.'

'So what?'

'We're in his lair, Eddie, we're right in the heart, in the control center, with links and evidence.'

'That's good, right?'

'Sure, that's good.'

'You don't have the face of a man who thinks it's good.'

'No. He's playing a different game now. Either he's going to pack up, go quiet, move town and hope we never catch up with him, or . . .'

'Or?'

'Or he's going to feel our breath on his neck and start enjoying it, like it's some game, and then things are going to escalate fast. So fast, I'm scared.'

'Why?'

'Because, Eddie, these people think they're right, and if he feels he's pushed into a corner, if he feels that there's no way out, he's going to start thinking about doing some permanent damage, maybe on a different scale.'

'A kill spree.'

'Yeah. That's what I'm worried about. Three kills in three days. He's not just a pattern killer, he's a deluded soldier who thinks the war's fucking started. And he's in New York.'

Chapter Fifty-Two

The door was yanked open and he stood in a rectangle of moonlight. The darkness of the garage made him pause for a moment. The smell of mold on clay bricks, the human smell somewhere in the background. His hand moved out and flicked an old plastic switch. Lights flickered dimly in the gloom below.

The killer stepped into the garage. He moved sideways past piles of bricks and scaffolding poles. At the side of the room stood an old desk facing a mirror. An old-fashioned reel-to-reel tape recorder sat on the desk with a small square-headed microphone attached.

The killer put his notebook beside the tape recorder and stared into the mirror. His hair was slicked flat to his skull, and he was wearing a uniform, a full uniform, with the blue eagle on the arm. The uniform made him feel stronger.

He stood in front of the mirror and tried not to look at his face. His uniform couldn't disguise his features. He was no Aryan, but in the low light he could believe it more than usual. There had never been, to his knowledge, a connection between the expression on his face and the feelings and thoughts beneath.

His whole life he had played a calm game, smiling and getting by, but everything was conditional, nothing was absolute. Perhaps it was just like that with some people. Even as a child he experimented with faces, hiding the feelings below with a mask. With the uniform and the formality of the army, it was different. You were what you appeared to be.

He appeared to be an SS officer because he *was* an SS officer. He could kill when he liked. When Jews were in the ghetto, when they were out of the ghetto, during the day, during the night. If they broke the rules by being out after curfew or by wearing fur coats or gold rings. All of this was illegal. He could dismiss a Jew with a ragged bullet-hole in an instant. Feeling was action. The manifold between the two worlds had never been complete until now.

He loved this new life he had created. His reanimated life. The life of the past, of past certainties, of past glories, of power, hunger and the Third Reich.

He sat, awake and alive from watching himself in the mirror. He had a small and simple Anglepoise lamp on his desk. This too was an authentic 1940s build. He opened his notebook and looked ahead.

One night, many, many nights ago, he had run away from a persecution of sorts. A beating by some other boys who were supposed to be his friends, who thought beating a Jew was all the more fun for its sudden and unexpected nature. But he wasn't a Jew, they were mistaken. He had taken on the suffering of a race of which he was no part. He had felt the blows, he had heard the insults. 'I am not a Jew!' he shouted.

He ran from them that night. By the time he turned for home, he found he was lost. What happened that night in the dark, alone and terrified? Did the anger and frustration pass into his blood-stream then, at the height of fear? Did the man who now made him feel warm and safe find him in the dark wood? A boy, alone at night, shivering and terrified by every insect and breath of wind. The Jew who shouted out aloud that he was not a Jew.

Out of his pocket he took a scrunched-up piece of white cotton and placed it on the oak table-top. Then he produced a small square of paper. There was a paragraph of writing on it. He pressed the cotton to his nose as he read it. There were 88 words on the piece of paper. He read them as if he needed their power.

He reached down to the right-hand drawer; it pulled easily on its old worn runners. The desk was made in 1933, the year Hitler became Chancellor. He fumbled around inside for a bottle. He lifted it out and looked at it under the light. He peered through the bottle, three quarters empty. He put it on his desk and stared ahead. His fingers were grubby and oily. He continued to stare as he unscrewed the top of the bottle. He removed the cotton from his nose, swigged and then stroked the cotton. He then pushed it from his desk on to the bare ground.

Somewhere behind him, there was a moaning sound. He listened, then walked across the ground and switched on another light. A brick cupboard with a wooden door was suddenly illuminated from the inside. The light shone out through gaps around the door. Inside was a girl. He leaned against the wall and felt the stirring of desire. She was the most beautiful of all. He had to destroy her, day by day, to watch her body turn to gray sacking, to watch her teeth fall out. He wanted only to find her disgusting.

His hand pressed flat on the wooden door. He picked up a chart from the wall. Looked at it. '144002. No food at all. You are still alive. You are strong.'

He opened the door and looked down. The body was lying on its side, barely moving.

'You will not last more than another week or so. You are the lucky one.'

She groaned. Over the past few days, he had conducted several experiments on her. He had noted down all the results.

He knelt down and put his hand on her skin. He still felt the desire. 'I shouldn't feel like this, you know?' he said. 'It burns inside me. I must fight it.' He stroked her arm and then pulled back. He felt the disgust at himself rise and merge with a strong sense of guilt and failure. 'The flesh of a Jewess. It is base. It is vile to want you but, Jewess, my whole body yearns for it.' He grabbed her head and pressed his lips hard against her mouth. Then he pulled back and spat at her. 'Your sickening seduction must end.'

He moved back across to his desk, took out a cigarette and lit it. 'You're a filthy whore, Abby, you understand? A filthy whore!'

Desire was hard to control. Desire needed to be destroyed. He sat down in his seat and looked over his shoulder towards the dark corner of the room where he could hear the faintest shuffle. Then he turned back, opened another drawer and took out an apple. He peeled it and ate it slowly. He clicked the tape recorder, moved the old tape round and clicked it again.

The spool ran, caught up with itself and slowed. He rewound, then pressed another lever and spooled by hand to a small chalk mark. He stopped. He breathed, and then clicked the recorder. He watched the whole mechanism move and the tape start to run on the rollers through the pick-up.

He raised his head again and cleared his throat.

'Josef Sturbe reporting for duty. I have conducted the third day of the survey. I have much to report. Marisa Cohen is dead. She was found out after curfew. I conducted a rudimentary experiment on her, which is all in my written report. The woman Rebecca Glass is next on my list.'

He turned the page of his notebook; continued with his list of details from the tours. He coughed then turned another page. He leaned to one side and picked up the cotton underwear from the floor. He flattened it on his desk, smoothing it back into shape. It was stained all over with the dirt from his boots. They all cleaned his boots with their own underwear. Destroy desire. Belittle it. But it excited him. He shot them because he must not desire the thing he hated. He knew that things must happen more quickly now. The desire was destroying him, but he had to win and he could only win by destroying desire once and for all. He turned back to his report.

'New York City, I saw four complaining Jews this week. One target is still outstanding. She will be punished, but today the opportunity did not arise.' He paused. 'The powers are rising in opposition. They are all here. It is as I have read and all on our streets. The filthy disease-carrying parasites, the greedy, lazy perverts worshipping their God and money with trickery and deceit. Deviants, rats – spreading their Jewish secrets. The Jew is the parasite of humanity. A demon in flesh. We must start to consider a more devastating solution. A bigger solution.' His face strained. The light clicked off. He felt her underwear again. He was embarrassed. He desired her and despised himself for it. He turned to the door in the corner. He knew the pamphlet word for word. He pressed his face to the wooden door and whispered through the cracks: ' "Jewry undermines every people and every state that it infiltrates. It feeds as a parasite and a culture-killing worm in those lost people. It grows and grows like weeds in the state, the community and the family, and infects the blood of humanity everywhere.

' "It is the pestilential nature of Jewry against which every people, every state, every nation must and should want to defend itself if it does not want to be a victim of their bloody plague." Do you hear me, Abby?'

PART THREE

Chapter Fifty-Three

Auto-parts Yard, Brooklyn
March 10, 6.05 p.m.

Karl Leer's autoyard was used by Section 88 as a safe house. Karl wasn't an activist himself; it wasn't in his nature to do that. He liked his workshop and didn't want to risk his livelihood. Karl was more of an observer. He kept himself to himself and, more importantly, he provided Section 88 with old vehicles when they needed them – vans so old they couldn't be traced.

Heming looked around the yard. The dogs behind in the scrublands barked incessantly. If he was being watched, they were keeping themselves well hidden. Karl had given him the all clear. He was sure there was no one around. Heming had got sick of being cooped up and, anyway, he needed to be out. He had a lot to do. He had a lot on his mind.

He looked towards the veranda where the office door stood wide open and then at the small table set up by a heap of old engine blocks. Karl Leer appeared from the office. His eyes opened in surprise.

'Thought you was hiding?'

'I need a beer,' said Heming.

A train passed by not far from the workshop. The tools rattled. 'Could've been worse,' Karl shouted over the roar.

'Just how so?' said Martin Heming.

'You could've gone out with them, been arrested yourself. The way it is, they'll be back on the street soon enough.'

'I can't work with them any more,' said Heming. 'They make

mistakes. Everyone's a fucking incompetent. Lukanov was a fool – no good. I thought he was better. I was wrong.'

'He wanted to do good for you.'

'Yeah, well, he failed. He was a liability.'

'Was?'

'Sturbe killed him.'

'How do you know?'

Heming looked up. 'How do I know? I was right there. I saw him do it. He enjoyed it.'

The passenger train rumbled into the distance. Heming's voice lowered. 'Detective Tom Harper took out my whole team.'

'He must be something to do that.'

'He must be a sonofabitch.'

'You should go sort this cop out,' said Karl.

'I should, you're right.'

'Everyone else turned up at the meeting house, you know.'

'Last night?'

'Yeah.'

'I told people the meeting was off,' said Heming.

'Six or seven turned up. Didn't get your message. Cops were waiting right there. They took their names and addresses.'

'Anyone mention me?'

'Don't think so. But you're not exactly low key. Got your own website. They only need to look you up.'

'They're probably at my apartment. I can't go back.'

'You should do something about it,' said Karl.

'That's right,' said Heming. 'I ought to.'

A silence fell between them. They reflected on what they had left unsaid for a moment. Heming looked into the office. 'Karl,' he said. 'Get me a beer, would you?'

Karl shuffled across to the fridge and took out a key which hung on a chain around his neck. He knelt down and unlocked the padlock. He pulled a cold beer from the icebox.

'I should just lay low, keep out of trouble,' Heming said. 'It's too difficult to keep going while all this Capske shit is brewing.'

Karl nodded and placed the beer on the table.

Heming shook his head to some internal argument. He drank from the bottle, before wiping his forehead. 'We can't sit on our own and grumble. It ain't us who are cranking this up. It's them that are infiltrating every fucking place. Judges, lawyers, bankers, politicians, businessmen. They own the system now, Karl, that's what we're up against. These people are everywhere. Immigrants and Jews fucking running the place.' He rose up. 'I hate them, man, you know? I just hate them so fucking much I can't focus on anything else.' Heming's cheeks were bright red and his forehead was glistening. He looked into the middle distance as if possessed by a terrible vision.

'Why so much, Heming?' said Karl Leer.

'Why so much? Are you kidding? I'll tell you straight up: I love my country and they are destroying it. It's an act of self-defense. Would you protect your own children? Don't answer me, that's all I'm doing. Protecting my children. My children's children.'

'You don't have children,' said Karl.

'Fuck you,' said Heming.

Martin Heming stood still for a moment as though something had just been clarified in his mind. He drank until his beer was gone, then went and opened the door of the icebox. Let the cool air drift across his face a second.

'Some guy has done some research and you know what he found? He found that the Jews and the Arabs and the Blacks are all part-Neanderthal. They did some genetic experiment and found this out. They carry the genes of the Neanderthal. Doesn't that blow your mind? They're infected with the genes of a dumb animal. Neanderthals. You can see it in their faces.'

Karl let out a laugh. 'Sure they are, Heming.'

'What are you saying? You saying that I'm lying?'

'You're not lying; you're just being selective. We're all of us part-descended from Neanderthals. All of us have that gene. I read about it too.'

'Not all of us, Karl. You, maybe, but not me.'

'It's not something you choose.'

'It *is* something you choose,' said Heming. 'I choose not to be a dumb fucking animal, I choose to rise above. I choose to further our race and not let it be diluted by theirs. You go eat with the animals, Karl, but not me. I'm no fucking violent Neanderthal ape.'

Karl stifled his rising laughter. If Heming was trying to be comic, he wasn't showing it.

'You take a look around you,' continued Heming. 'See who's doing what and who's suffering. This is everyone's problem. You think you're immune to it? You can just walk about, go about your business? Look at your fucking shop! Do you get everyone coming here? No. Where do they go? They got a monopoly, go to their own shops. It's one rule for us and another for them. They're squeezing guys like you out. Good guys like you. They're the Neanderthals, they're trying to destroy America from within, trying to fuck up our gene pool. Infected, they are, infected with this ape-gene. I love this country, man. I love it. But it's got a disease right here under the skin and it's carried by all those fucking types.'

Heming took another beer and pressed the cool bottle to his cheek. His pale blue shirt was stained with sweat under both arms. He carried three days of stubble and his eyes glowed red from staring into the dark, night after night, alone with his mind-rotting theories.

Karl reached out towards a chipped wooden bench and felt for a wrench. He found it and moved across to the open hood of an old car. He leaned into the engine. Heming watched for a moment. 'These people have tentacles. They control Wall Street – and if they control finance, they control government – right? They've got us wrapped around their fingers. And what else? Out there, in the world, we were once a proud nation. Now we're drowning in shit with our reputation dying because they got us into a war with the whole rest of the fucking world. Playing second fiddle, maybe even third fiddle.'

Martin remained by the open fridge letting the cool air dance around his heated face. He drank in quick gulps. Then he turned to the car that was absorbing Karl Leer more than he was managing to do.

'You see, Karl, you got to go to the top of the mountain to see the lay of the land. The spread, the forces at work. You've got your head stuck down in the valley. Heh, listen to me, don't be getting distracted by the fucking car.'

'I'm working, Heming, I got rent to pay. You don't work, you've got it easy, you got time to get all worked up. You should do something positive.'

'Don't tell me what I've got. They've taken the lot. My wife, my money, my freedom. Don't tell me what to think, Karl, they took it all and they'll take it from you too, if you sit back and let them. This government is destroying us. Our own government is infected with their thinking. We need to do something.'

Martin wandered back to his seat with another cool one. He twisted open the bottle and put it to his lips. The cold beer passed across his tongue and down his throat. He wiped his mouth. 'I should do something positive, you're right. You're right, Karl, I got to do something real positive. Not wait around for the fucking world to change. Do something. You hear that? We got to do something. You got that fucking right.'

Chapter Fifty-Four

North Manhattan Homicide
March 10, 6.23 p.m.

Harper walked out of the investigation room, leaving Denise to work on the profile. He took two more codeine pills, knowing that in fifteen minutes he'd feel the subtle change of mood, a feeling of peace – happiness even. It was low enough, background enough to carry on working.

He felt in his pocket for the small piece of card. What did he do now? He pulled out the card. Erin Nash's name in red lettering. She knew something and was interested in what was happening out there. She would sense what was going on. Erin Nash would maybe write an article that could help them to steer things.

There was plenty to write about, Carney had been clear about it. There was hate crime all over. Maybe Erin could upset the ship a little, warn the public about this freak. Maybe get Heming's picture out there.

He dialed her number. Erin answered immediately. 'Who's calling?'

'Detective Harper, NYPD.'

'So formal. Tom, good to hear from you. I'll book us a nice cosy table in Greenwich Village.'

'What?'

'You want to talk to me about this serial killer, I'm guessing, so why not talk somewhere comfortable?'

'How did you know what I want?'

'I've got many friends. They all like to talk to me. Some like more than that.'

'What are they telling you?'

'That Harper thinks there's a hate killer out there. A pattern killer. Maybe a killer with a racial motivation.'

'You work this out?'

'I heard about the new body on Lower East Side. I also heard you were looking into the Esther Haeber murder. That's three dead Jews, Harper. I can count, you know. That makes a series.'

'How do you get all this information?'

'I don't know – I think it's something to do with my nature. People just like to open up to me.'

'I know your nature and you'll do whatever you have to in order to get information, including debasing yourself.'

'Nothing debased in sleeping with a cop, Detective. You should have more self-esteem.'

'Well, I don't.'

'Come on, Harper, lighten up. I like you, let's get together. See what happens.'

'To talk about the case.'

'And that too,' said Erin.

'Two Jewish women and one Jewish man got shot. But there's no real connection. I might be way off-track.'

'That's not your style, you're usually spot on. Of course, you might not have been calling about the case at all. Let's consider that for a moment. I look forward to seeing you, Tom. Be nice working together – unless, of course, it's something else you're after.'

'What's the restaurant?'

'Little deli. Nice place. Mosha's.' She gave him the address. 'See you in one hour.'

Harper ended the call. Erin Nash was used to using people, but in this case, Harper had an idea, a way of getting a great big spotlight turned on these murders. He needed Nash, because he needed the public to start giving him information.

Chapter Fifty-Five

Mosha's was a simple table-screwed-to-the-floor Jewish deli that had once had a reputation for the best something or other, but had long since stopped giving a damn for quality just so long as things were served quickly and people were happy.

Jake Mosh, the owner, still worked the front desk. Harper arrived before Erin Nash and waved towards a seat. 'I'm waiting for someone,' he called across to Jake.

'No way you wait for someone. You order something. This is not a bus stop.'

'Get me a coffee.'

'Coffee is not good for you, a man needs to eat. I get you a waiting plate.'

'Okay.'

'One waiting plate for the cop.'

Harper looked around.

'What? You think you look like you write novels in Greenwich Village? You got that cop look, always checking out all the things. Cops have the wandering eye.'

'You always like this?'

'Like what? Like noticing things?'

Harper sidled into a tight space in a corner. A cop seat. No one behind him, a good view of the whole deli. He was only just in his seat when a teenager with dark hair put a coffee cup in front of him.

242

'Taste it. Best coffee in the world.'

Harper nodded. She was obviously trained by Mosha himself. He took out his cell and checked the bird news. There were reports of Snow Geese upstate, flying high and honking through the night. It was enough to take him away for a moment.

The door opened and in walked a small woman dressed up with several bangles on each arm. She jangled to the counter.

'Erin, my beautiful bride. We get married soon – you promise?' said Jake.

'Oh, yeah, Mosh, very soon. Just after I've tried every other man in New York.'

'I will wait. My wife understands. She was only ever a stand-in.'

Erin was wearing a party dress. Black and silver. Hair done up high on her head. Not the weasel in jeans that Harper had got to know standing outside the precinct. She was looking pretty and elegant.

Erin turned and looked. 'See my friend took the seat.'

'I knew he would.'

'The test always works.'

'I didn't know he was yours.'

'He's not mine yet. He's a cop.'

'I know he's a cop. Who else wears cologne like that these days?'

Erin Nash walked across and sat opposite Harper. 'Mosh tells me you're wearing cologne.'

'I shaved.'

'For me?'

'To avoid being picked up for vagrancy.'

'Nice and smooth.'

'This guy, Mosh, he's a talker.'

'Yeah, he talks. He'll shoot you too if you don't buy something.'

'I got a waiting plate.'

'Then you're in trouble.'

'You eating?'

'Mosh will bring me something I like.'

Harper looked at her arms. Thin. Four small tattoos on the under-side of each arm. Possibly Celtic, possibly Chinese. He couldn't quite see, but that was the gist – origins. Usually someone else's.

'You look different.'

'Are you flattered that I put on a dress?'

'It doesn't take much.'

'Don't be, I've got a launch party. Friend wrote a terrible book and we've all got to turn up and smile about it.'

'What's it about?'

'I don't know. I didn't ask. You know why? He's a liberal with too much free time.'

'A friend.'

'Yeah.'

'Let's cut to the chase, Erin. I don't want to ruin your evening.'

'You won't. I might take you with me. You don't look so bad.'

A moment later, two waitresses appeared from the side. One carried a small bowl of soup and placed it before Erin. The next moved beside Harper and placed an enormous platter in front of him. It contained everything. Herring, chopped liver, gherkins, a salt-beef sandwich.

'Jesus.'

'Not in here, Tom. It's David and Abraham all the way.'

Harper smiled. He needed someone to bounce ideas off. Someone outside of the NYPD. Erin was not Denise Levene, but she was smart and cynical and she could get his story the angle he needed.

'Tell me about your family,' said Erin. 'I guess you came from a stable little well-meaning unit out in Brooklyn.'

'You been reading up on me?'

'Couldn't get much.'

'Not much to get. Parents separated. Mother's English, she took off back to the UK some years back. Father's a drunk, he took off to Chicago. My sister still lives in the city. She's a lawyer. Two kids. Great kids. Me and my sister have never been close, though. Hardly speak now. I've lost touch.'

'She's older, right?'

'Right.'

'Always bossing you around?'

'Yeah, she's the one in command.'

'Smart too?'

'She was always smarter than me. Went to college. Got a degree. Law firm. Worked hard. She's bringing up the two kids well. I wish I could get to see them more.'

'Such a tender story. Why you both in law?'

'Do I need to tell you?'

'Why? You think I should be able to work it out?'

'No. I know you will have already found out. Erin Nash wouldn't come unprepared now, would she?'

'Okay, I did a little research. I was interested.'

'I'm flattered. What about you, Erin, what's your background?'

'God, we're like some soap opera. My story is simple. I was born like this. I was spoiled by my old man and hated by Mom. I learned to enjoy annoying her. It became an art. I now use the same tactics to get under other people's skin.'

'What tactics are those?'

'All people like flattery, right? You work your way in, be real nice, make them feel that you're in need of them until they let down their guard. Then when they've revealed an itsy-bitsy bit of weakness, you snap their hand off.'

'I guess, in telling me this, you're not trying to impress me.'

'I like you. I'm not playing games with you. You know the score. You do the same with interrogations, I bet. Soft soap followed by sudden attack. So, I'm just being honest.'

'For a change.'

Tom pushed a gherkin around his plate. He thought of Denise, then looked up at Erin. He didn't know what he was feeling at the moment. Hurt, mainly. The boxing match plus a couple of hits from Lukanov had left him with a few wounds. But beneath that, he was pleased to be working again, working with Denise.

'Okay,' said Nash. 'Now let's get down to business. Tell me about the case.'

'Look, Erin, this isn't official, but we've got unconnected Jewish deaths. Capske, you know about. I've got Esther Haeber from a few months back – and she's Jewish. And South Manhattan found the body of a Jewish woman yesterday, apparently killed for no reason. Her name is Marisa Cohen. What's more, about ten days ago, a Jewish high-school student was abducted.'

'You've got links, haven't you?'

'I think so.'

'What have you got?'

'These three Jewish murders are all linked by an "88" written at the scene and by the use of iron bullets.'

'What's the significance?'

'Being blunt, he's using Nazi symbols and Nazi bullets and he's attacking the Jewish community.'

'You've just written tomorrow's headline story. What do you want from me?'

'We need help. We're searching for a man called Martin Heming. If we could get some public help on this, we might be able to stop him.'

'You need pressure put on him.'

'I need information. He's speeding up. The time between kills is falling rapidly.'

Erin Nash listened for another twenty minutes as Tom spoke and worked his way through his waiting plate. She nodded appropriately.

At the end she said, 'Hell of a story, that, Harper. I can write this, you know.'

'I know, but you can't say anything definite yet.'

'I wouldn't need to, Harper, that's the beauty of journalism. You have to *prove* your case while I just have to *throw* my case to the public. We're talking about the police linking the murders of Jewish people across the city.'

'Don't name me as the source.'

Nash looked into Harper's eyes. 'Don't worry, Tom. I understand. And thanks, this is another big break for me. Means I won't have to do the story on Detective Harper's addiction problems.' She drank up and smiled.

'You leaving?' said Harper.

'Yeah. I've got a party to go to.'

'On your own?'

'Wouldn't be the first time,' she said. 'I like to travel light. Company gets in the way of a good story.'

Chapter Fifty-Six

Denise met Harper outside her building. 'I need sleep,' she said, and looked at Harper. 'You more than me, maybe.'

'We can sleep when this is over. What did you get?'

'I've been working all evening. First thing is that Aaron called. He found a link between the words. You know, the words *Loyalty* and *Valiance* that were printed on the card.'

'Yeah, so what do they mean?'

'The motto of the SS. Loyalty, Valiance, Obedience.'

'The SS, as in the Nazi Party SS?'

'Yeah. We think he's playing a part. Trying to make it as authentic as possible.'

'Anything to help find him or nail him?'

'Not yet, but I spent some time thinking and then it came to me – where I'd seen those marks on David's chest. My father used to show me images from the Holocaust. I think I might have another link between David and Abby.'

'What?'

'The tattoo on David Capske's chest. I think it was a number.'

'Marisa Cohen had something written on her chest too, but the water washed it away. They found some residual signs of ink. And he'd removed her blouse.'

'He writes numbers on their bodies,' said Denise.

Harper noticed the heavy tone in her voice. He pulled out his notebook and flicked through. Stared down at the marks. 'Could

248

be,' he said. 'You got a theory for me? The guys at Forensics were trying to match letters.'

'They look like prisoner numbers, Tom. After Aaron found the SS link, I just went with the idea. The SS ran the concentration camps. They numbered prisoners' chests. They're not letters,' she said, her fingers running across the scratches in ink. 'They're prisoner numbers. He thinks he's running some prison camp.'

Harper felt his breath catch. It was so obvious, but they'd missed it. *He'd* missed it. She leaned over his shoulder. He felt her closeness.

'What's the number?' he said.

Denise stared hard at the scratches, trying to discern a pattern.

Then she smiled. 'Well, although numbers are infinite, in fact, in our limited numerical system, there are only nine numbers and one zero.'

She took a pen and scratched a number four through the second set of dots. 'Looks like a four.'

'Could be a one or seven to start with,' said Harper. He watched the numbers emerge on the paper below. 'There's a cross on the third. Got to be another four,' he said quickly. They continued to stare at the marks on the page.

'744 . . .' said Harper. He turned and looked at Denise.

'Or 144,' she said. '144003.'

'That was quick. You know that number?' Harper asked.

'Abby Goldenberg's kidnapper sent a letter to her father. It gave her weight and blood pressure. And it gave her a number. It was 144002.'

'David's the next in the sequence,' said Harper.

'So Esther was presumably the first kill,' said Denise. '144001.'

Harper wrote down the four consecutive numbers: 144001, 144002, 144003, 144004. Would the sequence continue? Who would be number 144005?

'What do the numbers mean?' he asked.

'I'll see what I can find.'

'Find it quick,' said Harper. 'We're getting somewhere.'

Chapter Fifty-Seven

Museum of Tolerance, Brooklyn
March 10, 11.51 p.m.

'Thanks for meeting me here,' said Denise. 'I can't imagine how hard it is to come back here.'

Aaron Goldenberg stared out glassy-eyed. 'What can I do? My only daughter is out there – I must do everything I can.'

Denise felt the rise of tears but pushed them away. It wouldn't help to be emotional. 'The police won't give you the whole story,' she said, 'because everyone's afraid to speak.'

'What about?'

'A serial killer attacking Jewish victims.'

She saw something move behind Aaron Goldenberg's eyes. 'Killer? But my daughter was kidnapped.'

'I can't tell you a lie,' said Denise. 'We now think your daughter's kidnapping is linked to three other murders. David Capske, Esther Haeber and Marisa Cohen.'

Aaron Goldenberg shook his head as if it was the only thing keeping him from being swallowed alive by the yawning abyss. 'My only daughter.'

Denise watched him fall forward on to the glass case. Beneath his outstretched arms and tearful eyes, were photographs from Auschwitz and Belsen. Naked Jewish men, women and children, lining up for execution, modestly covering themselves although they were moments from death. The look of agony and uncertainty in their faces.

'What do you know?' he said.

'Not enough. Your daughter and David Capske had consecutive numbers used to label them. Abby had the number 144002 on her report, David had 144003 scratched on his chest. Do you have any idea what the number 144004 means?'

'No. I can look for you.'

'Please,' said Denise.

Aaron Goldenberg thought for a moment then let out a sigh. 'The number of Jews who will be saved.'

'What is?'

'Maybe the 144 refers to 144,000. It is in Revelation. It is a contested number. It may refer to many things or nothing at all, but it is said that it related to 144,000 Jews converted to Christianity.' Goldenberg walked to the side of the room and entered his office. He came out with a copy of the New Testament. He spent a minute flicking through it, then showed it to Denise:

Then I looked, and behold, on Mount Zion stood the Lamb, and with Him 144,000 who had His name and His Father's name written on their foreheads.

Denise read the passage. She looked up. 'The 88 Killer is trying to save Jews?'

'There are some who see the number like that, to mean that 144,000 Jews will be redeemed.'

'Our killer's a delusional fanatic. The bullets they found in three of the bodies were original Nazi bullets.' Denise lowered her head. In the museum, they were surrounded by examples of the horrors of the Holocaust, the mindless and ruthlessly inhuman destruction of millions of people. It was hard to imagine that the lessons of history had been lost so quickly.

'What do you want from me?' said Goldenberg.

Denise put out a hand. It rested on his shoulder. 'You need to help me profile this killer. If he's delusional, then I need to profile the projection as well as the man. I need to know what he's doing.'

'Committing crimes against Jews!' said Goldenberg. 'Playing God. Perhaps he thinks he is working in a concentration camp or a ghetto.'

'The ghettos were just holding compounds for the camps,' said Denise.

'That's right, Dr Levene. And it was happening all across Eastern Europe. When the Nazis invaded and took over areas, they created walled cities within cities. Policed by vicious soldiers, sometimes Jewish police. People were crammed into these ghettos, disease spread – but you knew this. The Nazis liked to associate the Jews with disease. Infected bodies were kept behind barbed wire. There were outbreaks of typhoid and cholera. They starved the populations, feeding them so little that they had to burrow out through the walls to find some food. You once said that one of the victims was found without a coat.'

'Esther Haeber.'

'In the bitter winter, they outlawed winter coats and fur coats.' Dr Goldenberg sighed heavily. 'In the Warsaw Ghetto, the Nazis outlawed the owning and wearing of winter coats upon pain of death.'

Denise listened. The full horror of what she was hearing opening inside her mind.

'He's doing the same.'

'So it would seem,' said Goldenberg. 'It doesn't end.'

An hour later, Denise dropped Aaron Goldenberg back at his house and called Harper.

When Harper answered, his voice was strained and tired. 'How did you get on?'

'Good,' said Denise. 'He's not just a Nazi.'

'So what is he?' said Harper.

'He's living like a Nazi. I think he's a copycat.'

'Of what?'

'Of Nazi crimes, Nazi murders.'

'A copycat. These are real historical crimes?'

'I think so. They echo what happened in the ghettos. I think he's delusional. I think he even thinks he's policing the ghettos and punishing crimes. The number 144 might be a Biblical reference to 144,000 Jews who would be saved.'

'He thinks he's saving them? What about Abby?'

'Starvation. It's how they killed great numbers in the ghetto. But there's something else.'

'What?'

'Aaron Goldenberg told me something he feared. They sometimes used Jewish women for prostitutes. They kept these women in brothels.'

'You think that's why he took Abby?'

Denise paused and then whispered her answer.

Chapter Fifty-Eight

Crown Heights, Brooklyn
March 11, 7.55 a.m.

Harper and Eddie spent the night in the car, searching around the various locations that Jack Carney had given them for Heming's whereabouts. Conducting surveillance was never easy and the night had been cold and long. There wasn't much hope of finding anything, either, but they needed to keep busy and keep the team active. The interviews had revealed nothing. The killer seemed to come and go without ever being seen.

Harper pulled over at a news-stand. 'We're going to see some reaction now,' he said. He handed across a dollar bill and took a copy of the *Daily Echo*.

Eddie looked and sighed. 'There'll be protests and marches. This is going to cause real outrage.'

Erin Nash was focusing on the murders of David, Marisa and Esther. Two big pictures of confident women stared out, smiling, with David in the middle. Denise read Erin Nash's report.

NAZI HATE CRIME IN MANHATTAN

On a quiet Monday afternoon earlier this week, in downtown Manhattan, a 32-year-old Jewish woman was found tethered to a piling in the East River. She had been submerged and then shot through the head. A small symbolic number was carved into a nearby post. It was the number 88.

She was the third Jewish New Yorker murdered in the past two months, the second in the last three days. The question needs to be asked: is this a series of hate crimes against the Jewish community?

Marisa Cohen, a PR consultant recently separated from city lawyer Daniel Cohen, had been missing since Sunday evening. A police source said that she was half-drowned before she was shot. A death that is so horribly violent and cruel that it takes your breath away.

This attack comes only a few days after another Jewish citizen, David Capske, was found dead in East Harlem, his body wrapped in barbed wire.

And now a police source is saying that two months ago, in a similarly random and brutal attack, 29-year-old Esther Haeber was shot in a vicious robbery. The thief cut off her fingers in order to escape with her gold rings. Although officially a closed case, police are investigating the possibility that this was a hate crime.

All three victims may be among a growing number of victims of a new and vicious breed of American hate crime. Brooklyn's higher rate of anti-Semitic hate crime seems to be heading across the river to Manhattan.

Right-wing organizations like the American Brethren, the White Wolves, the Neo-Aryan Alliance and Legend 88, have been growing in recent years as unemployment and international and national crises deepen the sense of disorder and chaos.

In communities across America, youths are seeing right-wing rhetoric as an attractive way to cope with social and national insecurity. In places like Brooklyn, Jewish communities are concerned by the rise in verbal and physical intimidation.

Even with their own security force, the community could not prevent several attacks in recent months. A schoolgirl on her way home; a mother pushing a stroller with twins; a shopkeeper closing for the day; a businessman getting into his car. All of these people were assaulted and beaten to the accompaniment of racial taunts.

Lieutenant Tierney of the Hate Crime Task Force said yesterday, 'There is nothing more despicable than crimes of bias and we will seek out and prosecute every one of them. But there is little actual increase in crime figures. We are reporting more because we are *better at identifying them. In the past, many hate crimes would not have been reported at all. We're now hearing about them, and can act.'*

But is it true to say that communities feel less safe than a decade ago? Hate has come back and, as David Capske, Marisa Cohen and Esther Haeber lie dead, we must all ask ourselves: do we have a Nazi serial killer or, as the police have named him, the 88 Killer, stalking New York?

Harper waited as Eddie read and reread the article.

'What do you think?'

'It's what you wanted her to say. I'd even go so far as to say she's been a little reserved.' Eddie passed the paper back to Harper.

Harper said, 'Let's see what kind of a reaction we get.'

'The Captain will know it was you.'

'I know, but he won't be able to prove it.'

Chapter Fifty-Nine

Midtown, Manhattan
March 11, 8.42 a.m.

Becky Glass had been unsure about the job from the start. She'd never done anything like it. Never even anticipated that she'd end up in this position, but money was money and she needed a new place to live, her kids needed new shoes and everyone had to eat. Since the divorce, her husband's checks were not reliable and she had to work for herself.

Becky continued to stride up the avenue, a child attached to each hand. Her pace was quick. She was already fifteen minutes late.

Out in Brooklyn, she had a part-time day job, but it paid very little. Prior to the arrival of the children she had been a bank clerk and now she needed a full-time job again. She had to focus on moving forward as an independent single mother.

She had to shut the door on her emotions. She'd deal with them later, when the children were older. It was a fact of life, no one else was going to jump in and save you, at least not if you were thirty-six with two kids in tow.

The job had been advertised. She'd called them up. She had the right experience and they told her to come by. She'd let her old boss know she needed full-time work and he was kind enough to put in a good word with the company. The location on Manhattan would present problems, but the pay was good.

That morning, things hadn't gone to plan, though. It was a teacher day at school, her babysitter had called in sick and her friends couldn't be rounded up at short notice. She had a brief meltdown, shouted at both kids and then pulled herself together. She got herself dressed, decided she wasn't going to let this small obstacle get in the way of a new life, and brought the kids with her to the interview.

'I can't walk any more,' said small, round-faced Ruth.

'Well, it's just round the next corner,' Becky replied with a jerk of her right arm. Her daughter skipped forward. 'Come on! I can't be late for this. Mommy needs a job. Ruthie needs to eat.'

Ruth and Jerry were both seven years old. They weren't twins, there were ten months between them, but for two months each year they shared the same age and the younger Jerry teased his older sister about it until she lost her temper.

Out on a Manhattan day trip from Brooklyn, or that's how they saw it, they didn't quite understand their mother's impatience. Mom had always been there just for them.

Becky was excited about getting back into the routine of a job. She knew it was the right thing to do. She was a little scared, of course, not sure if she had the skills or attitude they were looking for, but she came with a very good résumé and she was determined.

Now, standing in front of the huge office block, dwarfed by the gargantuan glass building zigzagged with windows as far as the eye could see, she could feel her fears rising.

She looked at her kids. 'Mommy is now officially terrified. Say a little prayer, won't you?' Neither child responded. 'It's just an interview. I shouldn't be more than fifteen minutes. Wish me luck.'

They both turned their heads up towards her bright blue eyes and stared.

'Good luck,' came a staccato reply.

'Come on, you can't wait for me out here. You can wait at reception. I'll ask the receptionists to keep an eye on you, but no moving and no talking to anyone. I called and told them my problem. They said they'd be pleased to have you. Anyone apart from them talks to you and you go straight to reception, they know where I am.'

Becky pulled both children up to the top of the steps. Jerry was preoccupied. He was pointing down at the street. 'Mommy, that car's on fire.'

'Shhh, no more talking,' said Becky. She looked across the street at a red car. 'Someone's smoking in the front seat, that's all.'

Becky walked across the marble floor to the glossy receptionist, half dragging both kids.

'Becky Glass. For an interview.'

'Fourteenth floor, Ms Glass. Take the first elevator and report to reception.'

'Thank you. I realize that it's a bit of an imposition, but would you be able to keep an eye on my children? I called – you might remember. I had a problem with my babysitter and had to bring them with me. They have promised to behave.'

'Of course, I'd be happy to. Good luck and have a nice day.'

'Thank you, that's very kind of you.' Becky looked around one last time. It was a very nice-looking building, safe and open, with security on the door and three receptionists.

She turned to her kids. 'Now, look, it's safe here, the receptionist is there if you need anything. You've both got reading books in your backpacks, now go and sit on that bench and be good. I won't be long. If you move from here, I will not be happy.'

The two kids muttered under their breath and hauled themselves on to the bench.

'Can't I come in with you?' said Jerry.

'No, Jerry, you sit and read.'

'I don't want to be left alone with her.'

'She's your sister.'

'I know and she stinks.'

'She's just the same as you. If she smells, so do you.'

Jerry said something under his breath. Ruth glared at him and pushed him with her leg. He pushed back. Becky scolded firmly, then moved towards the elevator, walking backwards and wagging a finger.

She gave them one last look as she stepped into the elevator and shouted out, 'Now, don't move from here. I love you. I'll see you in a little bit.' The elevator door shut. Becky felt the cabin shake as it rose. She took out her résumé, panic swelling in her throat. What was she getting herself into? Could she even hold down a job with her two children?

As soon as their mother was out of sight, the children glared at each other.

'What are you staring at?' said Ruth.

'The ugliest thing I ever saw.'

'That's because you've never seen yourself.'

'I'm not staying around here with you, stinker,' said Jerry.

'You heard what Mama said. You're not allowed to go anywhere.'

'I can go wherever I want as long as that lady on the desk doesn't see me.'

Jerry jumped off the bench and started to walk towards the big glass door while keeping a close eye on the receptionist. He pulled the door open and felt the cold air again. The sound of the traffic excited him as he moved outside and let the door swing shut behind him. He'd prove who was the bravest.

Ruth looked around her. She wasn't going to be left alone, that was for sure. She quickly followed Jerry out of the door. She caught a glimpse of her brother as he disappeared around the corner of the building, his two hands formed as if carrying a handgun, the imagination already in overdrive.

Ruth hung on the rail and then sighed. She'd have to follow. Otherwise Jerry would get himself into trouble and she'd get the blame.

Chapter Sixty

Harper arrived back at the precinct as Eddie was heading out. He stood across the road and stared at the media. He decided to go no further but hung back and waited for Eddie.

The article had provoked an enormous response. There were Jewish groups protesting at Police Headquarters and the Mayor's Office, and the press were still sniffing around Blue Team.

Eddie came out and joined him. 'Thanks for getting back. You heard?'

'No, what is it?'

'Another body, Harper.'

'Is it Jewish?'

'We don't know yet.' Eddie moved towards his car.

Harper took a look up to the sixth floor. 'I ought to check in with Lafayette.'

'No time,' said Eddie. 'Press will be at the crime scene before we know it.'

Harper followed Eddie to the car. They got in and Harper asked, 'How did things go with the Nazi bullets and the typewriter?'

'Very difficult to trace the Internet sales,' said Eddie. 'They're often not identifiable, but we might get them through credit-card or PayPal details. There are relatively few agents dealing with this kind of memorabilia and we're checking them all out. We're starting by asking them about Martin Heming, seeing if he ever bought anything, but then we're asking for their full records.'

'What are the numbers like?'

'In terms of clients, there are thousands,' said Eddie. 'The main problem is that the agents don't want to get involved.'

'Why not?'

'It's a closed world, isn't it? They don't want to be seen as Nazis or to be seen as outing their customer base.'

'How did you get them to talk to you?'

'I took your lead. I said I'd simply pass their names on to Erin Nash of the *Daily Echo*, explaining that they didn't want to assist with the investigation into these Nazi killings.'

'Did it work?'

'You bet. New York is a dangerous place to be if you're seen to be against this investigation. This is a liberal city, Harper. They'd be hounded out.'

Harper stared out of the window. 'Where are we heading?'

'Midtown. Woman killed, found in an alleyway.'

Eddie threw the car into gear and pulled off at speed. They drove up to the crime scene and found the squad cars sitting outside an alleyway.

'Anyone tell you anything about this one?' Harper asked.

'Not a thing,' said Eddie.

'Another alleyway – maybe there is a connection.' said Harper.

'Seems likely, doesn't it?'

They pulled themselves out of the car and moved towards the scene.

'What you got?' asked Harper at the tape.

'Two months and I move to Suffolk County,' said the First Officer.

'Yeah, well I hope the pay makes up for the company. Tell me about the body.'

'It's a woman halfway up.'

Harper walked under the tape and down the long black tunnel of the alleyway. 'Let's get thinking, Eddie.'

The alleyway was wide, with two dumpsters at the far end. They arrived at the corpse. Two other detectives were already there, sketching and taking notes.

'How you doing?' asked Garcia.

'Not great,' said Harper. 'You found anything?'

'We just got here.'

Harper turned to the body. The victim was propped up against the wall of the building. There was a cloth over her face. Harper moved in close. He lifted the cloth and saw the star-shaped wound on her forehead. 'Why did no one tell me? It's a gunshot wound to the forehead. Did Lafayette know this?'

'Dispatch didn't know what it was. First Officer said it was a rape murder.'

Harper shook his head. 'Rape murder, my ass – this is the 88 Killer. Look around for his symbol.' He lifted the cloth again. 'It's another small entrance wound, very similar to the others.'

'Yeah, we saw the hole in her head, Harper,' said Garcia with a laugh.

'It's shaped like a little six-pointed star,' said Harper. 'This is the fourth homicide with a point-blank gunshot wound to the head or neck. The killer's made an error. Or he's done this purposely.'

'Why would he do that?'

'They get decadent, they want more attention, they want people to know how they operate. He tried to hide at first; now he figures that we know it's him, he wants to entertain us.' Harper turned to Eddie. 'He shot her point blank, Eddie. Point blank. With the muzzle tight against bone.'

'Okay, man.'

'You know what happens?'

'Not sure, I've never been shot through the head – but please, Harper, enlighten me.'

'The gases can't escape so they get out through the skin. It's pretty unmistakable. The gun was closer than it was on Capske and Esther Haeber, though.'

Harper knelt by her side and tried to get a closer look at her face. He moved her hair back. 'She's in her late thirties. Looks . . . worn out.'

'She a whore?' said someone from behind.

Harper ignored the comment and looked at the body. 'Both shoes are missing.'

'We got them, Harper. One over by the restaurant trash and one just to her side.'

'No pantyhose. You find that?'

'Yeah. We think. Tan pantyhose over here.'

Harper looked again at the body. The upper body was clothed but the victim was naked from the waist down. The pants were thrown to one side.

'You find any underwear? You find that?'

'No. Nothing else.'

Harper was letting the scene piece together. Was it a rape and execution this time? A change in MO? Or just something staged to look like that?

He stood up and looked round. 'I need light.'

Three sets of flashlights flicked to his feet.

'We're looking for one bullet, one cartridge.'

The team of four detectives started scouring the scene. 'Crime Scene will get this, Harper, why we doing their job for them?'

'Because, Garcia, it might link this case with the Capske case.'

'As much as it pains me, I think you might have something,' said Garcia.

Harper moved back to the corpse. He took out his gun and held it in front of him. He looked again at the head wound. 'The angle's all wrong. She wasn't here when he shot her.'

'Where?'

'Maybe further up the alleyway.'

The other cops spread out. No cartridge. He looked across at the wall, tried to work out the angles. He started to move along the wall, taking in a three-foot-high band and looking closely. He saw a tiny glint of metal; moved up close. The bullet-hole was there, but the bullet had been taken already. 'I got the slug-hole, gentlemen. Anyone got the slug?'

'No one's touched a thing,' said Garcia.

'Then the killer did it. He's reading our reports and taking the piece of evidence that links these things. Still, there are fragments in here. We'll know if it's iron.' Harper watched the CSU detective remove the tiny fragments in the bullet-hole and bag them.

Harper was closely examining the walls but there was no 88 to be found. He went back to the body. 'Our killer's changing. This is designed to shock. Naked from the waist down and up against the wall.' He moved in close, peered beneath her smart black jacket: her white blouse was bloodstained, the buttons were undone. 'I've found the 88,' he said. 'He's cut her.'

'So what's the scenario?' said Eddie.

'Not sure this makes sense to me.'

Kasper pulled up close to Harper. 'What is it?'

'Motive?' asked Harper.

'Staged to look like a rape, maybe. So the motive is different. He kills because he's a fucking psycho, but he puts her like that to confuse us.'

'Yes, but she's got bruising all up her arm and her pantyhose are ripped.'

'What are you thinking?'

'Why bother to stage it? Why write 88 on her chest like some big signature? I don't think this was staged. I think he wanted to rape her. I don't think he necessarily did, but he sure wanted to. Seems like he's punished her for his desiring her.'

Harper crouched again. 'She's got dirty fingernails. Dirt across both knees too. She's been kneeling in this alley. Just like Capske and Haeber.' He stood and looked around the alleyway. 'What do you suppose she was doing here? How did she get into this alley? She looks dressed for work.'

'He's brought her here or he's forced her here.'

Harper suddenly stopped and listened.

'What is it?'

He walked towards a dumpster and pulled his gun out. 'There's something in that dumpster.'

'It'll just be rats,' said Eddie. But he drew his gun too and headed towards the sound.

Harper shouted, 'Get out of there, right now!'

Nothing moved.

Harper moved in close. He moved behind the dumpster and yanked aside a large piece of cardboard. Two sets of eyes stared out at him.

'Jesus Christ,' Harper exclaimed. 'We got two kids back here.'

Chapter Sixty-One

Denise Levene and Tom Harper sat across from Captain Lafayette, who was scowling. 'I'm going to have to bawl you out about that Erin Nash article, but this takes precedence,' he said. 'What you got on the victim?'

'Nothing. Not even a name. We've tried dental records, prints . . . She wasn't carrying a phone or a purse. Maybe they were taken. No ID.'

'What about the kids?'

'They won't talk. They're not talking to anyone. Not a single soul. Shut up tight. The psychiatrist says it's trauma, so I'm guessing that they saw the whole thing. Makes you want to hurt someone, doesn't it?' said Harper.

'They won't say a thing?'

'Not a word. Doctor says it's not voluntary,' said Denise. 'I spoke to him in person. He says they've frozen. I'm going to see them, see if I can get through, but I'm not promising anything.'

Captain Lafayette walked across to the large blue board that Harper had started to use to pin up images of the unidentified Jane Doe. Either side were the four other boards in chronological order. Haeber, Goldenberg, Capske, Cohen and Jane Doe.

Photographs of the crime scene and body were all they had and they made for a grim spectacle. 'What do you make of it, Harper? This is his work, right?'

'Yes. It's his. Iron was found in the bullet. He wrote 88 on her chest.'

'But she's half-naked.'

'Yeah, but we just got back from speaking to the Medical Examiner. We wanted to see right away if there's any DNA or semen. There's nothing. No evidence of actual rape.'

'He's losing control,' said Denise.

'How so?'

'I think all his kills have been sexual, but he's been repressing it, made it about hate. I think he's finding that hard. He *wanted* to rape her. He staged it so it looked like he did, but he couldn't do it, or hates himself for it, if that makes any sense.'

'No, it doesn't.'

Denise stood and pointed at the photograph. 'He's left her in an explicit pose to humiliate her, but he's covered her face. He's never done that before.'

'Why?'

'He's ashamed. Not of killing her, not of raping her. He's ashamed of letting his desire control him. He didn't plan to rape her, that would be my guess, which would mean that he might have left semen or pubic hair on the scene.'

'Before you ask, we're checking it, Captain,' said Harper.

'Do you have a story? Why the kids?'

'We're walking the streets, talking. She looks like she was at work or going to an interview.'

'Anything else?'

'Crime Scene found spit on the ground. Her spit. Quite a lot of it.'

'Strange.'

'She appears to be on her knees, leaning on one hand and she's either dribbling or spitting. They reckon it's spit.'

'How?'

'There's a spray pattern.'

'This some fetish we ain't heard about?'

'We've got to re-enact it, get some people to look at the possibilities.'

'If only the children could talk.'

'It'd save a lot of time, I know that, but for their sake, I hope they didn't see anything.'

'Unfortunately, the psychs think they saw the shooting,' said Denise.

'How did they get to be separated, unless they heard something and went to hide behind the dumpster?'

'He couldn't have known that they saw him, is my guess, or else he might have killed them too. At the moment we don't even know if they are connected to her. We've got to keep their existence tight.'

'No way we can do that, Harper, not long-term.'

'Then our only alternative is to catch this guy soon.'

Lafayette remained silent. 'Tell me what you've been itching to tell me,' said Harper.

'I had a call about the kids. I didn't want to say. It might not mean anything.'

'Is it bad?'

'Both the kids are wearing Magen Davids around their necks.'

'Wearing what?'

'Jewish Stars of David,' said Denise.

Harper stared back. 'So this is definitely our fifth Jewish victim?'

'And they gave the kids paper and pens. All the boy has been doing is writing 88 all over the paper. It's compelling, as you say. See if you can find anything more. As soon as you get an ID on this body, I want to know. The press is going to make some connections of its own, you know? If I could prove that you spoke to the press as I imagine you did, I'd discipline you so fast you wouldn't know what hit you, Harper. It's caused me all kinds of shit upstairs.'

'It's good to know you're helping, Captain.'

'With the Capske and Cohen murders going national on every channel, another murder of a Jewish woman is going to give the media plenty to report. So we need some results now. People are getting spooked out there and we need an answer for them.'

Chapter Sixty-Two

Denise appeared outside her apartment block and Harper felt a surge of admiration. She was dressed for work, wearing a black suit with a white shirt, and looked every bit the young, ambitious, go-getting star she had been a few months earlier.

She got in the car beside Harper.

'You ready for this? We need something from the children.'

'Sure, I'm ready. At least we managed to get an interview with the psych team. I had my doubts.'

'Lafayette got the Chief of Detectives behind us.'

'The brass are beginning to believe us then?' said Denise.

Harper nodded. 'Reluctantly. The boy scrawled 88 all over his coloring book. He saw something. They can't ignore that.'

'Or heard something,' said Denise.

'Right. We only have one shot, though.'

'I understand.'

'You think you can argue your way in?'

'What do you think, Tom?'

Harper smiled and started the drive across town to the children's hospital. The kids were in a secure ward with police protection.

Despite several attempts to get to talk to the children, the psych team had refused on the grounds that the welfare of the children was paramount. The police needed someone who could convince the psych team to give them access to the children. Levene was a specialist, not a cop, but even so, it had taken some persuasion to set up the initial meeting, and there was no guarantee that the psychologist would allow them to actually meet the children.

As they went up to the seventh floor Denise straightened her jacket.

'You look good,' said Harper. 'Don't worry.'

'You notice how I look?' said Denise.

'I notice. You've chosen pink nail varnish,' he said. 'I guess you've chosen a gentle color for the children. You usually wear a stronger color – crimson. The pink's a little soft for you.'

Denise looked across at a now smirking Harper. They waited for half an hour before they were summoned into the room to see the children's social workers. Denise pushed Harper out of the way. 'Okay, now it's my world, Tom. Let me do this alone.'

He took a seat, as directed by Denise, outside the room.

The psychologists sat in front of a big empty polished table, all with notebooks and case-files open and ready. Denise introduced herself, shook each hand and opened her own notebook.

'This case is our number one priority at the moment,' said the consultant child psychologist. 'There are indications of extreme psychological trauma, which has unfortunately increased over time. Your friends at the NYPD don't do subtle. Our staff have been given a hard time.'

'No, they don't do subtle,' said Denise. 'That's why I'm here.'

'Listen, I'll cut to the chase,' said the consultant. 'Our recommendation is that we do not allow any questioning until we can see how these children are coping. They have suffered and will suffer even more trauma if we allow further access to them. They need time to recover.'

'I agree with you,' said Denise. 'I understand what you are saying – and I don't mean to be rude, but there's an important principle here that I would like you to acknowledge.'

The consultant looked up, his expression indicating surprise but a grudging respect for Denise.

'Your concern is for the welfare of these two children,' said Denise. 'And you're right: an experienced detective will naturally exert psychological pressure during an interview. Two big guys in suits are scary. Guilt is scary. These children are suffering fear and guilt – that's not the way to ease their pain. I entirely understand that you would not want them interviewed. In fact, normally I would support it, Doctor. There is nothing more important than the welfare of these two children.'

'Thank you, Dr Levene.'

'But here's my point,' Denise continued. 'These two children, we believe, have lost their mother. What I want to offer, Doctor, is a chance for them to close this primary trauma, not shy away from it. I want them to understand who killed their mother and why, then you can work on the secondary trauma, their fears. They have seen irrational violence. We need to show them that a man, who was very sick, and very wrong, did this thing and is now locked up. Until we can tell them this story, they will not heal.'

Denise stopped and held the psychologist's gaze. When she saw the movement in his throat, the tiny muscle twitch in his eye, she knew she had him.

'So, Doctor, for the welfare of the children, I am suggesting that we need to know how their mother died and who killed her. If we find these two simple facts, we can begin to piece their world back together.'

She saw the consultant swallow.

'First, though, you will need to know what I am asking for. I need three sessions, each lasting thirty minutes. I will ask them a single question about the event. I won't repeat it. I've written the question here for you.' Denise handed the piece of paper to the consultant. He read it, nodded, then passed it around the table. He waited, looked at each set of eyes.

'Okay, Dr Levene. I'll give you the three sessions, but no one else speaks to the children.'

'No one but me.' She reached out her hand and the consultant shook it. He held it a moment too long, just as she'd expected.

Chapter Sixty-Three

Children's Psychiatric Unit, Harlem
March 12, 9.00 a.m.

The room was a small ugly square. It had the lack of generosity and aesthetics of every municipal building. Denise had asked for the three sessions to be held in a single morning. It wasn't ideal. It would have been better to hold them on consecutive days, but time was too important.

The first two sessions had gone reasonably well. The kids didn't utter a word, but the odd nod and their facial expressions showed Denise that they were paying attention.

The third session was the important one. Harper sat at the back, watching, with his sketchpad open. Denise talked about her own mother. The kids didn't seem to care.

Denise knew she didn't have long to get a connection with them. She took her question out and smiled at the two kids. 'We've got to go now, unless there's something more you want to tell us?' She searched their faces. They had no idea what to say or why.

She toyed with the question in front of her. She turned it in her hand, let the time slip by. Finally, she looked up.

'Is there anything you can tell us about what happened in the alley that might help us catch the man who hurt your mother?'

She waited. The boy's face seemed to show thought. His eyes moved around. The girl didn't even look up. She hadn't once held Denise's gaze.

Nothing. Two minutes passed. They had all said that the boy knew something. He gave out more clues with his non-verbal communication, as if he needed to get this horror out of his system.

In the corner, Harper sketched a falcon from memory, the pylon below. Denise watched the children closely, then spotted something. A small, perhaps insignificant thing. She honed in on the girl and flicked a quick look over her shoulder. The girl was watching Harper.

What was interesting her? Denise waited another two minutes. Again, the girl's eyes rested beyond Denise's left shoulder.

Denise leaned back in her chair and reached her arm out. 'Can I have your sketch?'

Harper let her take his notebook. Denise started to look through the pictures, concealing them from the girl. She needed to know what was interesting her. Another two minutes passed. The second hand on the white clock-face was slipping by. She didn't have much time left. Then it happened again. The girl looked up through her bangs. She looked first at Tom but then quickly searched the room and rested her eyes on the book in Denise's hand.

It was not Tom she was interested in, it was the book. Denise placed it in front of her. She slowly lifted her eyes again and stared at the picture of a falcon. There was a moment of apprehension, then she reached out and touched the picture of the bird.

'Do you have the crime-scene sketches in here?' said Denise.

'Few pages back.'

Denise took up the book and flicked back to the scene of the alleyway. It was drawn several times, from different angles. She chose the one from the perspective of the far end where the dumpster was. She placed it in front of the children.

They both stared at the alleyway. The little girl reached out her hand and touched it.

'Tom, draw a figure in the alleyway.'

Harper moved across and sketched a person standing in the alleyway. The two children watched intently.

'Okay, draw another figure.'

Tom drew another figure. The mother this time, wearing a black suit. The little girl's hand reached out and touched the figure.

'Good. Now draw a third figure.'

Harper moved in again and drew a third figure next to the first. The girl's hand darted out and she started to shake her head vigorously. Harper took his pen and scribbled over it. The girl calmed.

'Okay, this is good. It's one guy.' She looked at Tom. 'Draw me the dumpster.'

He did. The children looked at it. Presumably, they had heard people coming up the alleyway and had scurried behind it.

'Draw them. Draw the boy watching but the girl hiding her eyes.'

Harper drew, but the girl's head started shaking again. Tom sketched the boy hiding his eyes. He then showed the girl watching. There was no interference. 'It was the girl who saw what happened,' said Denise. 'No one's ever asked her. We've all just presumed the boy saw it while the girl hid.'

Harper drew a gun in the man's hands. The girl pointed to the page. Harper seemed to understand and changed the man's arm to point to the ground. Then the little girl pointed to the sketch of her mother and then at the man's feet. It had been Harper's instinct that she'd been kneeling and polishing his boots. He drew. The girl rested her finger on the man.

'What?'

She took the notebook and turned a few pages back. She found the bird and pointed at it.

Harper and Denise stared for a moment. They didn't understand. The girl then turned back to the alleyway and she pointed to the man.

'A tattoo?' said Denise.

Harper drew a small bird on his arm. The girl nodded. Harper then drew three quick sketches of birds. She chose the picture of the American Eagle, its head to the side, its wings arched.

'Unbelievable,' said Denise. 'She was ten yards away.'

Harper looked at the girl. Her features were like her mother's. Blue eyes, freckled cheeks. He drew her mother from memory and put it in front of her. The girl stared down. It had been only a day since the children had seen her face. Her brother looked away, biting his thumb, curling all his limbs inwardly.

The girl's hand reached out and touched the face on the page. Harper handed her the pencil. She took Harper's pencil and wrote two numbers beside her mother's face. Two number 8s, side by side. Then she looked up at Denise and Harper. 'Did he say anything?' said Denise.

The girl looked up. It was the first time she had spoken and her voice was clear and unemotional. 'He said his name.'

Harper and Levene held their breath. 'What was it?' asked Denise.

'Something I don't remember,' said the girl.

'Josef Sturbe,' said the boy. 'I heard it.'

'What did he say?'

'He said, "I am Officer Josef Sturbe. Clean my boots".'

The girl and the boy stared at them, clear-eyed.

'It's going to be okay,' said Denise. 'It's going to be okay. Do you think you could tell us your names?'

'Ruth Glass,' said the girl. 'This is Jerry. We're both seven but I was born first.'

'Thank you, Ruth. We're going to go now, but we'll find the person who did this to your mother. I am so sorry she's been taken away.'

Denise stood up as the social workers walked in. Denise thanked them again as she walked out. Harper waved at the little girl and drew a quick smile on a face on his sketchpad. As he showed it to her, the little girl forgot herself for a single moment and smiled back.

Chapter Sixty-Four

Myrtle Avenue, Brooklyn
March 12, 4.06 p.m.

He sat outside the garage, drinking coffee from a Styrofoam cup.
His eyes were fixed on the small TV screen. He'd bought every one
of the papers but none of them mentioned a blue eagle from the
murder. He liked reading about his dead. He liked to see how
dumb they all were, how little they understood. He liked to keep
the clippings about them. But he didn't understand how someone
had seen the eagle.

They'd found the body of Becky Glass a day earlier but the TV
reports were now talking about the latest NYPD discovery. They
were looking for a man with a blue eagle tattoo. The image they
had was of a small blue eagle with its wings outstretched. It was
more of an American eagle than the one on his arm, but it was still
shocking to see the image in connection with the 88 Killer. It
shouldn't have happened. How did the cops have a picture of the
eagle on his arm? He considered it closely.

He hadn't removed his coat until he was alone with Becky
Glass. He had waited outside the alleyway until she walked by.
She looked distressed. She was searching for her children. He was
an opportunist. He'd told her they were in the alleyway.

She ran in, all on her own. Stood there and looked around her.
Then he put the gun against her head and told her to take off her
pants.

He only wanted her to do that in order to remove her underwear.
It was important that she was degraded and humiliated. He had

not intended to rape her. She had fought and cried and disobeyed him. He had to hit her face. He had to rip off her clothes. The attack excited him. He was ashamed. He made her kneel at his feet and wash his boots clean with her spit.

No one but the victim should have been able to see the blue eagle.

He let his mind return to his victim kneeling in front of him, thinking about angles. Perhaps someone had seen him from the street. He had pushed a large metal bin in the entrance to the alley, but someone might have looked round it.

He didn't usually kill in the daylight, but he couldn't help himself. It had been a mistake. He had lost control. He had only meant to trail her. He had been trailing Becky Glass for a while. He knew she had two children. They were even there with her at the interview, but they'd run off before she made it back down to the reception area. She was searching for the children. That's why she went into the alleyway, to look for them, and that's why he had acted. He hadn't planned to kill her so soon, but it just overcame him and he couldn't resist. He didn't even bother to check to see if the children were in the alley. He had been foolish. The urge was too strong; the pressure of the press and the cops was getting to him.

He knew that Becky was a single mother. She had told him as much as he placed the gun at her head. He had listened to her pleading on behalf of her children as he dragged the clothes from her body. He hadn't imagined for a moment that her children were watching, but, thinking logically, where would they go?

He recalled the scene. She had polished his boots. It had made him feel better. He had said he was pleased. He remembered her anxious gaze around the alley.

It was obvious and he wanted to kick himself for being so stupid. He had presumed that she was looking for help. But she had been terrified about her children witnessing the scene rather than what was happening to her. Witnesses. The children had seen him kill her. He leaned back against the garage. The children would be able to identify him. That couldn't be allowed. That would put an end to his plans.

Chapter Sixty-Five

Museum of Tolerance, Brooklyn
March 12, 4.42 p.m.

Denise sat in the large glass atrium of the museum waiting for Aaron Goldenberg to appear. She had already scented the 88 Killer and thought she understood the way his mind worked – from the clinical bullet-hole to the forehead to the brutally angry use of barbed wire. One mind, twisted beyond normal limits, a man with a need for control – surgical control – and a deep, deep pain that needed to be screamed from the housetops. But he was losing that control. Which would make him even more dangerous.

She looked down at her notebook and took up her pen. She kept seeing the number that Ruth Glass had written on the page. She wrote the words across the top. *Profile of the 88 Killer*.

Denise was in the process of unpicking the killer's mind. Like an expert unpicking a lock, she would press each lever in turn, teasing and testing until it fell in line and suddenly the whole row would be along the shear line and the lock would open. That was all she was after – the killer's shear line.

So far, she had written: *He's male, early- to mid-thirties, gifted, but a failure in something, single, unable to form strong relationships, with a background in security or military-type work. A man without siblings, a lone child, probably with a normal-looking family, a family he felt never knew what he was, never accepted him. Possibly adopted.*

She looked at the words and felt the give of the first lever of the lock. She continued to write. *He's used to being alone, it's not a problem for him to be alone. He's been alone his whole life, he can take it. But he needs to be understood and that's confusing him. He feels a dual push to keep hidden but to be understood. His latest kills show an increased stress level. He is getting more extreme, his attacks becoming regular, necessary. He is not a neo-Nazi with Nazi sympathies, it is stronger, the identification almost exact. He is a Nazi.*

Just then, Aaron Goldenberg appeared, holding a sheaf of papers and folders. He looked at Denise's notebook.

'It should say *Profile of Josef Sturbe*,' he said.

Denise turned. 'Aaron. How are you?'

'Better now. It has been so many days with nothing to do. Now I can work.'

'So what did you find? Is Josef Sturbe a real identity or an assumed one?'

'I will let you know what I found out,' said Aaron. 'But how did Harper get on?'

'Detective Harper has tried every database that he can find and there's nobody coming up with that name. The Feds have nothing on him either. They think it's a name Martin Heming uses. A pseudonym.'

'Then they'd be wrong,' said Dr Goldenberg. 'Very wrong.'

Denise raised both eyebrows. 'He's real?'

'Yes, Josef Sturbe is real, all right.'

'How the hell did you find a man when the combined forces of the NYPD and FBI couldn't?'

'They weren't looking in the right places.'

'Then what are the right places? Where can we find him?'

'We can't find him, but we know who he is. Josef Bernard Sturbe was born in Bavaria in 1923. We don't have any records of him until 1943 when he turns up in the Warsaw Ghetto.'

'He was an actual Nazi?'

'Yes. A member of the SS. Of the feared *Totenkopf* – Death's Head Division. According to reports, he believed he was fighting only for the Führer. He was fascinated by Hitler's *Mein Kampf* – obsessed by eighty-eight words from its text. "88" is not just a code for *Heil Hitler*,' said Aaron. 'It also refers to the following passage. Let me read it to you: *What we must fight for is to safeguard the existence and reproduction of our race and our people, the sustenance of our children and the purity of our blood, the freedom and independence of the Fatherland, so that our people may mature for the fulfillment of the mission allotted it by the Creator of the Universe. Every thought and every idea, every doctrine and all knowledge, must serve this purpose. And everything must be examined from this point of view and used or rejected according to its utility.'*

'He was into eugenics? What was he?'

'A curious case. After the war, they could not find Josef Sturbe. The Nazi Hunters had him on their wanted list but he didn't turn up. Many Nazis, members of the SS, went to South America after the war. There was a Network, ODESSA. It helped members of the SS to escape. They think Sturbe went to Argentina and ended up in America.'

'Was he ever found?'

'No. Never.'

'What was he famed for?'

'He was a murderer. Very vicious. A serial killer in the ghetto. A man who was so desperate to prove his loyalty to the Führer that he hunted in the ghetto after dark. He kept a record of how many he had killed. He conducted experiments, trying to emulate men like Dr Joseph Mengele. But he was an amateur. In SS circles, he was mocked. Sturbe had a secret, though.' Aaron paused. 'He was a Jew.'

'What!'

'The son of a young Jewish girl who had got herself into trouble, he was adopted by a German family. The Sturbes pretended the baby was theirs. His papers proved he was a German, but he looked Jewish. All through the 1930s he was bullied and mocked. He joined the Hitler Youth, but they could see he was no Aryan. He tried to change his appearance. He bleached his hair, but it made them ridicule him more. He joined the SS when they only allowed pure Aryans. He was obviously not, but they accepted him based on the ancestry of the Sturbes. It was on the eve of his acceptance into the SS that his father told him the truth.'

'What did he do?'

'He never spoke to his father again. But this knowledge was like a canker inside him. It was as if he could never outstrip his own identity. He hated the Jews even more than the other officers did. He started to murder in the Warsaw Ghetto. He was insatiable, proving his hatred every day.'

'And no one knows what happened to him?'

'No. The SS all had their blood group tattooed on the inside of their upper arm. After the war, the Nazi Hunters found a man in Boston who they claimed was Josef Sturbe. He was recognized by someone who lived in the ghetto. But he had no mark under his arm, so they let him go. Fifteen years ago, the Sturbe myth surfaced. Someone found Sturbe's notes and in it, he stated that he never allowed them to tattoo him, because he feared that they would be able to detect his Jewish ancestry in his blood.'

'He was insane?'

'Yes. He was insane. I doubt he was the man in Boston, but we shall never know.'

'So what do you think this has to do with our 88 Killer?' Denise asked. 'Josef Sturbe would be about eighty-seven if he was alive.'

'I expect our killer has taken him as a model.'

'Our killer feels the same? A fraud? A fake?'

'I think it might be something like that,' said Dr Goldenberg, 'but we must continue to search.'

'I think our killer is afraid of Jews. I think he's deeply afraid of them. It's why he caged Capske, it's why he's starving Abby. The Jew has a hold over him, a power. In his imagination, it is a terrible power. He's trying to reduce it, to lessen the power, the anxiety.'

'Maybe not a terrible power,' said Dr Goldenberg, 'but a terrible secret.'

Chapter Sixty-Six

North Manhattan Homicide
March 12, 7.14 p.m.

Harper walked into the investigation room with Denise Levene. They had to share what they had. They'd both worked through the night, hadn't slept at all and looked ragged and exhausted. Harper had received a call from Jack Carney. The Hate Crime Unit had picked up some information. The remaining members of Section 88 and a couple of sympathetic organizations were planning a night of attacks to show solidarity with Leo Lukanov. His death was being treated as a martyr's sacrifice. They also heard that Martin Heming might try to turn up to soak up some of Lukanov's martyrdom.

Carney and Harper had set a night of joint surveillance between Homicide and Hate Crime. Harper wanted the whole of the task force to get out on the street, trail the Hate Crime Unit and their usual targets and see what these neo-Nazis were capable of. He wanted to help Hate Crime to cut out this terrible cancerous growth of anti-Semitism.

Harper looked across the room at the blank faces of the team who had been working flat out for days. Garcia wasn't around. He pulled up a chair and sat down in the center of the room. 'Guys, close in a minute. We've got in touch with Becky Glass's husband. He's been out of town speaking at a conference with a thousand delegates. He can't tell us anything.'

Denise sat near the front. There was a freshly printed profile on her knee that she needed to share with Blue Team.

The team turned to face Harper. Harper spoke slowly, conspiratorially. 'Listen, this is going to take a while to settle. We've found some new information about the killer. Denise has been working with Dr Goldenberg. It's quite unusual stuff, but stick with it.'

Denise filled the team in on the background of Josef Sturbe. She gave his life story and then walked up and down the room. 'In summary, gentlemen, our killer has assumed an identity. His identity is strange. It is of a man who is so ashamed of his origins and his race, that he becomes an extreme version of those he wants to impress.'

'What can we use?' said Swanson. 'You think our killer is an eighty-seven-year-old man?'

'No, I don't,' said Denise. 'I think he is a deluded narcissist. He wants power, he wants accolades but he's got a big secret. Perhaps he's like Sturbe, someone who feels his identity is fake. I'd say we ought to work from two assumptions. The first is that the killer is adopted. The second is that he was adopted from a Jewish to a non-Jewish family.'

'He's a modern-day Sturbe?'

'It's just a theory. I don't know what he is. I've got a couple of other Nazi elements,' said Denise. 'The 88 moniker is code for *Heil Hitler*, but it's also a reference to a passage from *Mein Kampf*, Hitler's ruminations on power and eugenics. It's not his name, it's a salute after his kills, and it's his mission statement. We're looking at a man driven to kill by hatred, because somehow he's got the idea that Jews are the cause of his problems, that they are less than human. But I think it's himself he feels is inhuman. That's why he identifies with the Nazis – because he thinks he's subhuman himself. I think that he's killing his own identity.'

'He's a Jew?'

'Most serial killers attack their own kind. I'd say, yes, he's Jewish.'

The room was silent. It was a complex idea to take in. They didn't know how to respond.

'We can't go around saying that the Nazi Jew Killer is a Jew, Denise. We'll be pulled apart as racists.'

'You know the Atlanta Child Killer case?'

'Remind me.'

'A number of black children were killed over a period of time. Same kind of outrage, and everyone thought it was a racial crime, except that there was no political statement or claim by any group. In the end, they found him. He was a black man. He was attacking his own. That's what a serial killer is, someone attacking their own identity; that's why they repeat – it's a process. It's themselves they're killing.'

'That's good,' said Harper. 'It gives you all some background. Anything else?'

'How close is that profile to our prime suspect, Martin Heming?' said Mary Greco.

'There's very little match,' said Denise. She opened her palms. 'I wish I had something more concrete. I'll keep trying.'

Harper stood up. 'You all understand?' He looked around. 'No word of this to anyone. We need to be further along before this comes out.' There were nods throughout the room.

'Now, why you're all here. You want to hear about the operation – Operation Sturbe. There's to be no more waiting around. We need to be out there watching them. We've got to find him, people. We're going out to Brooklyn to work some overtime. We've set up a surveillance operation with Hate Crime. We're going to track them, as many as we can, all across Brooklyn and see what we can find.'

Chapter Sixty-Seven

Brownsville, Brooklyn
March 12, 8.01 p.m.

Harper crossed town with Blue Team. There was a sudden sense of potential, and the whole team felt it. A feeling that they just might have something that cast a net around this killer.

They headed towards their meet with Hate Crime.

Harper, Levene and Kasper stopped outside a worn-out shop on the edge of Brownsville in Brooklyn. Behind them, the cars of Blue Team pulled up and a series of doors opened and shut.

The team leader, Jack Carney, was organizing the op on the ground for Hate Crime. He walked across. 'Hey, Harper. Let me walk you through it.'

Harper introduced his team. They all shook hands. The night was damp and the temperature was dropping. It felt chill and gloomy.

Jack Carney walked by Harper's side. 'We've got surveillance going on most of the remaining members of Section 88 and seven other groups which are marked as code A through to G. We think they're going to try something. They're hurting after you took Lukanov and the gang. The word out here is that he didn't kill himself, that police killed him.'

'If only,' shouted a voice from the back.

'They're after a conspiracy and that's what they want to believe.'

'It all fits with their view of authority,' said Harper.

'The key point is that they are angry and want to do something. We've been seeing a lot more activity. They usually use a public place to talk. We think that they're going to use a big restaurant off the main road. It's called McRory's. There's a big parking lot, a large drifting clientele. A busy place they can get lost in. They tend to get take-out and sit in the cars out back.'

'Any sign of Heming?' asked Harper.

'Nothing,' said Carney. 'He's either flipped out or hunkered down somewhere.'

'Do we know their targets?'

'We don't. We're still not sure how it happens, but we think they are told by someone, maybe by text even. When they've been told their hit, they travel out. We've got evidence of Section 88 using black cards as a way of putting hits out on their victims.'

'I'm interested in our 88 Killer. Josef Sturbe.'

'We got to follow the groups and see what we can. If he's connected to Section 88, like you think, then this is the best way forward. You want Heming? We think he'll turn up if he's around. You take Unit C. These guys are on the edge, Harper, so steer clear unless you've got support.'

Harper looked down at the map on the hood of Carney's car. 'We just follow them?'

'That's it. Follow, get them caught in the act, then rumble. Backup will be with you on each unit. Now, come and meet the guys.'

They walked over to the Hate Crime team. Carney waved his arm. 'You take them through your operation and why you are looking at Section 88,' he said. 'Then let me take over.'

'This is the deal,' Harper called out. 'We know that Section 88 are involved in organized hate crimes. We also think that the organization is responsible either directly or indirectly for the murders of three women and one man. All the victims were Jewish. We're looking for a lone wolf who may be feeding off this group, or he may be heading this group. His name is Martin Heming but he may be using the pseudonym Josef Sturbe. Most hits involve low-level intimidation, but that's not what we are here for. We're after our lone wolf, and his style is to pick off victims of hate crime and execute them.'

The men and women in front of him nodded. 'This is a joint op, people. What we're looking for is the main man, so try to hold off so that we can track these guys. See what they do, where they go, who joins them.'

Carney then took over. 'Just a word or two. These guys get pumped up when they're out on a mission, so roll with them, keep your distance and keep in contact. As soon as you see Heming, just shout. As soon as you see anything even close to looking like trouble, call in the support team. Okay, let's move out.'

The team rolled out in a variety of vehicles and drove to McRory's. They pulled into the parking lot and spread out. Each unit had a different target. The radio link between the vehicles was open. Harper was in the car with Denise Levene. They sat and stared out.

'It's a good spot,' said Harper. 'Maximum crowds, large numbers of people, so they wouldn't be spotted. But we've got to get out and get closer. We'll see nothing in here.'

The three of them got out and started to walk towards the center of the parking lot where the first of the suspects were congregated.

Chapter Sixty-Eight

Brownsville, Brooklyn
March 12, 10.05 p.m.

Blue Team and Hate Crime spent almost two hours watching, but nothing seemed to go down until one set of guys started to shake hands. It wasn't a normal goodbye shake. They went down a line, high-fiving people in a pumped-up manner. This was celebratory.

'We've got that truck covered,' said Carney. 'The rest just keep watching.'

The truck rolled out with four men in it. A few seconds later, a battered Hate Crime Unit panel van pulled out into traffic and started the tail.

Then the call came through. 'Harper, you wanted to see how these guys operate, roll in and take the lead. This is a strong unit here. If Heming is around, he might want to make contact.'

Harper gunned the engine and pulled his car around. He overtook the HCU truck and followed behind the white van and hung back. There was silence in the car. The hunt was on.

The night air was chill and damp. The gang in the truck were traveling north from McRory's and still drinking. They were easily visible from Harper's car and the jokes seemed to be flying.

Right behind Harper, Jack Carney followed in his car and behind him was the HCU truck with the support team.

McRory's disappeared behind them. The pink neon lights and big crowds were silenced by distance. The team had no idea what was ahead. The groups didn't seem to speak on their cell phones and there was nothing they could find on the forums. All Hate

Crime Unit had managed to find out from informants was that tonight was a joint operation – a protest at the treatment of Leo Lukanov. Carney had heard that the leader of Section 88, Martin Heming, could be joining the post-attack celebrations.

Tom Harper turned to Denise. 'Why do they do it? What's in it for them – attacking defenseless people?'

'They believe they're right,' said Denise. 'That there is someone on their patch who is causing them harm, and they don't see the government doing anything about it. Or the NYPD.'

Section 88's van turned. Carney and the support truck fell in behind. The truck turned off the major road and with the lack of traffic, the train of following vehicles was too conspicuous. Harper called Carney. 'You and the van take the next left and carry on. You can re-join further up the street. I think they've clocked us.'

Harper watched the white van and Carney's car veer into a side road and disappear. He continued to follow the truck.

They seemed to be heading towards Borough Park, one of the largest Jewish communities in the States. Harper followed until the group's truck pulled off the road and into a side street, where it stopped. A sedan pulled up beside it. Harper stopped and they watched. Someone from the sedan jumped into the truck and then someone from the truck passed a duffel bag to the driver of the sedan.

Harper called Carney. 'Jack, you need to pick up a dark blue sedan – it's coming your way. You'll be face to face in a moment. Looked like some drop. Maybe drugs.'

'That's how they fund their operations,' said Carney.

Harper thought back to the three wraps in the alleyway beside David Capske. It seemed more likely than ever that this was a Section 88-sanctioned attack.

He called the driver of the white van on his radio. 'This is Detective Harper, we're following south of Lewton. Where are you?'

'We've come up to a block. A truck ahead of us has got a flat and can't move out. Carney got past but we're stuck. We're going to try to back up.'

'You want me to drop off the tail?'

'No, keep contact and keep in touch.'

Harper waited for a few minutes before turning into the side road. Up ahead there was nothing to be seen. It was a long narrow street surrounded by high buildings. Harper drove slowly, his eyes searching.

Five hundred yards down the street, Harper stopped at a junction. He pulled out and looked both ways. The Section 88 truck was parked to the right. He could just see its tail lights shining in the darkness. Harper turned and drove close enough to be able to see and the three of them sat and watched. Up ahead, the guys in the truck didn't even look around; four of them were already on foot, heading down an alleyway towards the back entrance of what looked like a kosher bakery. Three were carrying sledgehammers and one had an ax. The lead guy, a huge muscular skin-headed man, called for the rest to follow. A fifth man got out of the truck carrying a can of gasoline.

'What now?' said Harper over the radio. 'They are out of their vehicle and are heading to the street.'

'Call for more backup. Do not try to stop them yourselves. We can't be there soon enough. We've got reports of other groups heading to that area.'

Harper looked across to Denise and then to Eddie behind him. 'What do you think?'

They could just see the group formed at the alleyway. It was 10.29 p.m. They seemed to be waiting. All five men pulled masks over their faces as the time clicked over to 10.30 p.m.

'What the fuck are we going to do?' said Eddie. 'We can't let this happen.'

'Wait,' said Harper. 'Just wait for a moment.'

Then they heard a shout and further away, another shout and another. It wasn't a secret assault, it was a war cry. 'Let's get out there,' said Harper. A moment later, they heard a huge smash of glass, followed by another, and suddenly the whole street was ringing with car alarms, shop alarms and broken glass.

'*Kristallnacht*,' said Denise. 'They're smashing Jewish shops and buildings.'

Harper got on the radio. 'This is Detective Harper. We've got major rioting starting up down here in Borough Park. We need SWAT, we need support. It's big.'

Harper, Kasper and Levene ran down into the street. Then they stopped and drew back. Thirty or more hooded Nazis were running along the street with hammers, axes and baseball bats. They'd coordinated the seven teams. It wasn't seven separate hits, it was one major assault. The shop fronts were exploding with fragments of glass, the doors smashed open. There didn't appear to be any looting. The rioters would simply rush in and destroy what they could.

Across the street, people started to pour out of the Jewish restaurants screaming in terror. Gasoline was being splashed through the broken shop fronts and the sudden whoosh of fire exploded on to the street.

'We can't just watch, Harps. We got to do something.'

'I'm thinking about how to get out of this without getting anyone killed,' said Harper. 'If all these rioters were being tailed by our operation, then we've got support.' He got back on the radio, listened and turned. 'They're here.'

The joint operation involved over eighty police officers, who streamed into the street. Harper, Eddie and Denise were joined by ten or twelve other officers and they began to sweep towards the rioters. The other officers came from the west. The rioters gradually became aware that they weren't going to smash and run like they had planned.

'Do not draw your weapons,' ordered Harper over the radio. The streets were full of people running, some starting to fight the Nazi rioters. 'We can't ensure the safety of the public. Tackle them safely, but take them down. Now.'

The police ran forward. Two to one, grabbing the rioters, chasing them through broken and flaming streets. The rioters were flung to the ground, and cuffed, then left to struggle. Members of the public began to attack the rioters: there were groups kicking cuffed men on the ground. Harper moved forward. 'Get the public off the streets.'

He ran up to one group. Two men and a woman were screaming at one of the cuffed rioters, dragging his balaclava off. 'Get out of here before I arrest you,' said Harper. 'Don't become one of them.' He moved them off and up the street, saying, 'Denise, can you direct these people out of here before they land themselves in prison.'

Harper and Eddie then raced across to a jewelry store, where two big guys with hammers were smashing the cabinets. A lifetime of work broken in a moment. Harper flew in and grabbed the first. He pulled the hammer from his hand, smashed his jaw with his forearm and threw him out to Eddie. The second guy watched, then dropped his hammer and let himself be cuffed.

Outside, there were seven or eight rioters still evading the police, but the majority had been downed. Harper looked at the damage. Twenty or thirty shops smashed to pieces, several burning, billowing black smoke. If they hadn't been trailing these guys, it would've been a hundred times worse; the gangs would've attacked people. There was no question, a much worse situation had been avoided.

Harper called through on the radio: 'We're nearly there, people. Get the rest of them cuffed and move them out of here. We need to get this whole place cleared.'

Harper saw the big guy from the truck disappear down an alley with two other rioters. Not wanting any of these cowards to escape, he darted after them, back up the alleyway. As they headed back to their truck, Harper pulled out his badge and called: 'NYPD. Stop! Drop your weapons – now.'

The lead guy stopped and turned. He saw that Harper was alone. Harper saw them come at him. Three of them and he was the only thing stopping their escape. A hammer flew at him, hard and low. If it hit, it would break his leg. Harper jumped out of the way and the hammer smashed into the brick wall.

'I didn't appreciate that,' said Harper. 'Not one bit.' The second hammer rose high and flew across him. It was easy to avoid. Hammers were slow and heavy. Harper pulled the rioter towards him. He landed a boot in his groin and butted him to the ground.

The other two came in fast. One jabbed at Harper with the ax, while the second guy threatened a big blow to his head.

Harper backed to the wall. An ax, a hammer and two frightened and desperate rioters. There was no fear, just the thumping of his pulse and the softening of the boundaries between his mind and his body. He could hear the screeching of alarms in the background. He could smell the smoke. He could even see the fear in the two sets of eyes staring out through their masks. He felt the wall at his back, the ax-head thump in his stomach again, the hammer press against his shoulder, being driven backwards like some beast.

Harper calculated they were just out of reach of his fists. He needed to get closer, inside the range of their weapons. He ducked, pushed the hammer away with his right shoulder, and moved inside the ax-head using his left arm. It gave him what he needed: something within his reach. He came up from below, delivering a thunderous uppercut to the hammer guy and an elbow to the lead. The hammer guy dropped his weapon and crumpled, dazed. The lead guy was shaken but not out. Harper moved in. This was no boxing match, this was a street fight. His right boot scraped hard down the man's shin and dug into his foot, while his arms reached up, grabbed the masked head and tugged it forward at speed. His knee then came up hard to meet the head. There was a loud crack and then a thud as the guy hit the ground.

Harper knelt down and pulled off his mask. 'You want more?' The man's nose was split wide open, and his eyes had that lost look that Harper had seen so many times in the ring. 'I said, *do you want more?*'

The man shook his head. Harper grabbed him. 'Where's Martin Heming?'

'Fuck you,' he gasped. 'Heming isn't here. Heming is cleaning up.'

'What do you mean?'

'Yeah, like I'd tell you.'

Harper raised his fist, then stopped himself and stood. He had to use his head now. What would Heming be cleaning up?

Chapter Sixty-Nine

Harper was sitting on the hood of his car looking out over the destruction with Denise. Eddie Kasper was in the back of an ambulance talking to a young female paramedic with cute dark brown eyes. *Any opportunity*, Harper thought.

'What now?'

Harper looked at Denise. 'We've got twenty-four more individuals to talk to, so we can hope that they've heard of Sturbe or that they know where Heming is hiding. But how helpful are they going to be?'

'No sign of Heming, then?' she asked.

'He wasn't here. The guy I took out said he was "cleaning up".'

'What does that mean?'

'I've been trying to work it out.' Harper took a call on his cell phone. It was Mark Garcia. 'Where are you?' said Harper.

'Just taken our arrests to the cells. I'm back at McRory's. Where are you?'

'I'm still at the scene. You found something?'

'Yeah, we found the black cards. They all just have the address in Borough Park. They were ditched in the toilets, torn-up and flushed. They weren't careful. Quite a few pieces were on the floor.'

'So what's the news?'

'One of the cards didn't have the address on it.'

'What did it have on it?'

'We only got two pieces of it. On the right hand side it just says

295

SS and 88. The word *Obedience* is in the top right corner.'

Harper said, 'Thanks. Not sure what it means. The SS, the 88 and the motto . . . Hold on, Garcia.'

'What?'

'The other cards. Did they have the 88 on them?'

'Not that we found.'

'Neither did the card we found in Lukanov's place with Denise's name on it. Keep that card, Garcia, I want to see it. It might be the killer's card, which means he might be out tonight, with a new target. Oh, and one more thing . . .'

'What's that?'

'We need the name on that card. They could be in danger. Get the sewers checked out. The card might be somewhere.'

'You're kidding? You want me to search the sewage?'

'It's someone's life, Garcia, and I never kid.'

Harper called the investigation center and got through to Swanson, who had returned earlier.

'What you got, boss?'

'We've got the potential of a hit tonight,' Harper said.

'What's the lead?'

'Black card with the moniker 88 and the letters SS.'

'No name, I guess.'

'No name. We just got the half with the SS and 88.'

'What do you want me to do?' Swanson asked.

'I want to see if we can get as many patrol cars on the streets of Manhattan as possible.'

'Yeah, right – double overtime. I'll ask, Harper.'

'Put me through to Lafayette, can you?'

'Sure, but he's gonna say the same thing.'

Harper waited. The SS. The Nazis' elite force. The previous card didn't have the SS written on it. Perhaps there were different cards for different things. Some with names, others not.

Lafayette picked up. 'Yes, Harper.'

There was silence on the line. Harper was thinking again. *SS* . . . Then he made a connection. What was Heming going to clean up? He was going to clean up any shit that could incriminate him.

'Jesus!' shouted Harper. 'We got to go!'

'Harper, what is it?' demanded Lafayette.

'I got to go,' Harper repeated. He disconnected and slid across the hood of the car. 'Get in,' he ordered Denise.

The car was moving in an instant, eating up gravel and screeching out of the gates.

'What is it?'

'They found a black card with the letters SS.'

'So what? We know Sturbe was a member of the SS. Our killer likes to use these monikers and symbols.'

'Yeah, that's what I thought too. If I'd seen it, I'd have known immediately, but I didn't. I just heard over the radio.'

'What would you have known?'

'The SS doesn't stand for the *Shutzstaffel* or whatever it was. It's the last two letters of a name. All the cards have names on, right?'

'Becky Glass,' said Denise. 'Was that Becky's card?'

'Not Becky Glass,' said Harper. 'Becky Glass is dead.'

'Then what?'

'There's only one possibility. Her kids – Jerry and Ruth Glass.'

Chapter Seventy

The Safe House, Manhattan
March 12, 11.47 p.m.

Jerry and Ruth Glass were being held in a well-used temporary safe house in the city on 14th Street. It was a two-story building with an anonymous-looking façade, a used Chevy out front and a yard scattered with kids' toys like any normal family home.

Inside, a female cop was sitting reading, as the social worker assigned to the children sat beside her watching television. Upstairs, the two kids lay fast asleep in the same room, where they felt safest.

There were usually two cops on duty, but at the moment there was only one. The rota only changed one cop at a time to ensure continuity, but that meant that often, the cop at the end of his or her shift would leave dead on time, while the relief cop often turned up late – so at shift changeover, the house was at its most vulnerable.

Unknown to anyone in the safe house, a car was heading towards them, the driver looking down at his watch. His slot was narrowing. A few minutes had gone already. He had to be quick.

On the other side of town, speeding towards the house, were Denise and Tom. Harper reached his hand out of the open window and put a siren on his car. He drove like a bullet through the greasy streets. It was coming together in his head.

'How do you read it?' she asked.

'Someone made the connection. We put out the information about what the child said. We didn't mention the children, but the killer must've worked it out. The papers were full of it. And they reported the fact that Becky had two children. He spotted the link.'

'Who called it?'

'They're protecting the organization, I guess. Heming might be on it himself, or even Sturbe.'

'You think they're different people?'

'I don't have time to think. I know we've got two names, that's all.'

They shot through dark streets, their fear palpable. Harper called through to the house, but the line was dead. They called the police radio. It was switched off. A major violation. Harper hit the steering wheel.

He then called the precinct. 'Swanson, I've got someone after the kids in the safe house. I need a number. Find out the name of the officer on duty or the social worker, and get me a cell-phone number.'

'I'm on it,' said Swanson.

The killer turned into the street. He felt his neck tensing and twisted his head around. He was gripping the wheel too damn tight as well. He parked on the opposite side of the street and got out of his car. He breathed deeply. He was a little late. The world seemed silent for a second. He moved around to the trunk and opened it. He took out two body bags, a thick rope and a climbing grapple. Then he walked across the street, checked his gun and looked up. He saw the lights go out in a downstairs bathroom. They were not expecting any trouble.

He walked around the back of the house. He needed to silence the children. It was as simple as that, but it didn't feel good. It wasn't part of what he wanted to do. He felt angry about it, angry and disappointed that he'd left a clue. He looked up at a large oak. It wasn't close enough to the window, but that didn't matter. He climbed up the tree, eased himself out on a branch, and then tied the grappling hook to the rope and swung it in a large circle. He released it. It skittered on the tiles and slid down, missing the chimney stack. He tried again, leaning out more. The throw went further. The hook slapped on to the higher tiles and went over the peak. He tugged slowly until the hook bit, and then dropped the rope. It hung down the guttering and right in front of the bedroom window.

He climbed down the tree, sweating from the exertion. When he reached up and tested the rope, it was fixed nice and firm.

He put one hand as far up as he could and jumped, reaching up higher with his second hand. His upper body was strong and he slowly pulled himself up the rope. One hand over the other, slowly advancing towards the window where the kids were sound asleep.

Harper's cell phone finally rang. He switched off the sound of the siren and answered.

'Garcia here. I've got the cell phone of the officer.'

'Go ahead.'

Harper took the number and immediately cut Garcia off and dialed the officer. He waited as the ringer started up. The cop finally answered. 'Hi there, it's Candy.'

'Candy, nice to know your first name. My name is Detective Tom Harper of North Manhattan Homicide. Are you with anyone?'

'Just me and the social worker.'

'Where's the second officer?'

'They haven't turned up yet, but they should have been here by now.'

'Okay, Officer Candy, listen up. We've got reason to believe that someone has the location and identity of the kids. Have you seen or heard anything at the house?'

'Nothing, Detective, it's all quiet here.'

'That's good. But this killer is smart. Listen to me. Don't get alarmed, but I want you to stay on the phone and go upstairs.'

'Have you called patrol?'

'Yeah, everyone's on their way. We're on our way. Just keep calm.'

'Okay, I'll go check.' The officer stood up and walked to the stairs. She pulled out her gun and switched on the light. The cell phone returned to her ear.

'Anything?' said Harper.

'Nothing,' she said.

'Check the kids.'

'I'm going up,' she said and walked slowly up the stairs. She felt a cool breeze down the corridor and edged into the children's room.

'What do you see?' asked Harper.

'They're both sleeping,' she said, feeling relief rise in her stomach.

Harper thought for a moment. 'How about the window?'

'It's wide open. I'll shut it.'

'Was it open when you left them?' said Harper.

'I don't think so,' said Candy.

'Then it might be too late,' said Harper. 'Pull your gun. He's there already.'

'Oh, Jesus Christ, oh no,' she said.

'What?' Harper said urgently. 'Come on, Candy, keep it together.'

'Shit, shit, shit.' Her voice was high and trembling.

'Help me here, Candy.'

'I'm looking outside. There's a rope hanging down from the roof.' She leaned out of the window and saw the rope swinging right down to the ground. Across the street, she noticed a red car that hadn't been there before.

'There's a car parked across the street. It wasn't there earlier. It's red. License-plate is not visible.'

'Shit,' said Harper. 'Check the beds *now*.'

The police officer raced over to the beds. Neither child was visible. For a moment, she dared not look, the only sound Harper's breathing in her ear.

'Are the kids there?' said Harper. The officer placed the phone on a bedside cabinet, took a deep breath and pulled back both covers. She picked up the phone.

'Harper,' she whispered. 'They're safe. Still sleeping.'

'Thank God. We're on our way – we'll be there soon as we can.'

The police officer put down the phone and checked the children's breathing, the fear subsiding slowly. She turned to the door and the fear returned immediately.

He was standing in the dark, behind the door, no face, a gun out in front of him. He motioned her towards the window, his finger on his lips to indicate that she should remain quiet. Her heart felt as if it had stopped.

He pulled the gun from her hand and threw it on the bed. He then took her handcuffs and cuffed both hands behind her back.

The officer couldn't help herself. 'Please stop. You can walk away from this. This house is surrounded by cops. You'll never get away. Just leave the kids and walk. You've still got time.'

He pulled the rope through the window, wrapped it three times around her shoulders and arms and tied it.

'Please don't hurt the children,' she said.

He forced her to the window and pushed her out. She dropped a few feet then jerked to a halt. Her body strained as the rope pulled around her shoulders. She dangled there beside the tree.

The man turned to the now waking children. He opened his backpack and took out the body bags. He looked at the phone on the side. All he could hear was a voice calling for the officer. He picked up the cell and put it to his ear, then he killed the call.

On the other end of the line, Harper hit the wheel. 'We've been cut off.' He screeched around a corner.

'What?' said Denise.

'It means he's in the house.'

Chapter Seventy-One

The Safe House, Manhattan
March 12, 11.59 p.m.

As they arrived at the safe house, Harper looked for the car parked across the street. It was gone. Harper got out of the car, Denise following quickly behind. He told her to wait at the entrance and walked around the house. At the back of the house, he saw a strange shadow. There was something large hanging from a rope.

He felt his pulse quicken and for a moment he thought the figure was dead. Moving closer, he saw a female officer with the rope pulled tight around her shoulders.

She saw Harper in the dark and called out, 'He's gone. He's taken the kids.'

'We'll get you down,' shouted Harper.

'No,' she said. 'You've got to get him. I think they're alive. I caught his license-plate as he drove off.'

Harper was astonished. 'Well done, that's got to help.'

'I feel so guilty,' she said. 'I was looking after them.'

'You shouldn't have been alone,' said Harper. She told him the license-plate and Harper called it in immediately to Dispatch.

With a racing pulse, he moved quickly into the house. The social worker was sitting in an armchair facing the TV, motionless. Denise flinched. 'Are you all right?' Harper asked.

'He said he'd kill them if I moved,' she explained, a look of terror across her face.

'Did you see what he looked like?'

'No,' she said. 'He was wearing a balaclava.'

'Stay here,' said Harper. Denise sat beside the woman and comforted her while Harper ran upstairs. A moment later he reappeared in the living room. 'There's nothing there. He was hiding in the closet. I need to haul the officer in the window. Denise, I need your help.'

He turned to the social worker. 'What happened? Just tell me.'

'He took them, in two bags. Black bags.'

Harper called base and gave them the lowdown. They'd send an ambulance, and backup was already on its way. He then took Denise upstairs and together, they pulled Officer Candy Simons back through the window. They untied her and she flung her arms at them. 'Leave me, for God's sake. Go after him.'

Harper and Denise headed for the car. They had no idea which way to turn.

'What about the car, Tom? Where do we go?'

'I'm thinking,' said Harper.

'So am I. And I think the reason the kids aren't dead is because he's not tortured them yet. That's what he needs to do before he kills. Mark them and torture them. We've got time, but it's not much.'

Harper looked at her for a second. 'Let's go.'

As they sped back to Brooklyn, Harper reckoned that the kids would soon be in a lock-up or worse. He knew the driver of the red car wouldn't risk speeding, but would keep to the legal limit. That was their advantage. They had the license-plate out there. Someone had to spot it.

He called up Eddie Kasper who was back at the scene in Borough Park, helping the clean-up. 'I need to know the places these guys go when they've got something to hide. You've got twenty or more prisoners – find out which ones are most afraid and cut them a deal. I need a lock-up, a location, anything.'

'I'll see if anyone knows anything,' said Eddie.

Harper hung up.

'How did he know where they were?' asked Denise when they arrived at McRory's.

'I don't know,' said Harper. 'But I will find out.'

It took ten minutes for the red car to turn up on the police radio.

'What have you got?' asked Harper.

'There's a red car parked in Bedford-Stuyvesant. Plates match. It's just been taken inside a lock-up of some sort.'

'Don't spook him,' said Harper. 'He's got the two children. Just give us the location and tell them to set up roadblocks. If he drives off again, I don't want him getting far.'

They traveled for about ten minutes. There was silence in the car. Harper turned into the street that Dispatch had given him and killed the lights. He then called the patrol car.

'I'm going in direct. Got to see if the kids are still there. Most likely, he's switched cars, come from the side street.'

Harper and Levene got out of their car. Ahead of them was a row of lock-up garages in a courtyard. Tall buildings flanked the lock-ups and two alleyways led between these buildings on either side.

'You hold back,' said Harper. Denise stood at the car as ordered. She watched as Harper walked towards the row of garages. He looked inside the one that was open, but it was pitch black. There wasn't much light in the courtyard. The greasy asphalt shone in the moonlight, but the whole area was full of shadows and alleys. Whoever had taken them could be anywhere.

Harper held his Glock firmly in his right hand. He crept to the left of the lock-up, down a side street then came back. Hearing something, he turned quickly. It was a low thump. He listened intently. Someone was inside the garage, kicking at something. That meant that the driver had probably left the kids.

His pulse raced. The two children were still in the car then, still alive. Harper started to run back towards the lock-up. He only half-caught sight of something over to his right – a red cigarette end or a glint of light. The sound of a gunshot woke the night. A bullet hit the ground by Harper's feet and ricocheted into a large metal door. Harper heard the patrol cops in the distance; they had started to run towards the sound. He pointed his gun into the alley and fired six shots into the darkness.

Nothing. Whoever had been there, had gone. Harper stared at the scene, trying to work out what had happened.

Denise was standing by the car, hidden in darkness. Harper decided he couldn't wait another minute for patrol. He had to chase the killer down. He got up and started towards the alley, trying to get cover before heading into the darkness.

Harper hit the wall and leaned into the alleyway, gun first. It was too dark to see a goddamn thing. He stepped into the shadows. It was a risk, but he figured the sound of the uniformed officers running and shouting could have spooked the killer.

As Harper disappeared into the alleyway, a figure appeared from the next alleyway up and moved to follow him.

From the far side of the alleyway, Denise stared out, her hands shaking. Alone and exposed, she could hear the running footsteps of the two patrolmen coming up behind her and suddenly felt afraid. Her heart beat fast, and her legs felt weak.

'It's all going to be okay,' she told herself and moved a couple of steps towards the alleyway. She stopped by the side of the car. At that moment, a shadow emerged about fifteen yards in front of her – a figure holding a gun. Denise stared across at the killer. The shaking moved throughout her body. She steadied herself and tried to breathe.

From where she was, she could see the garage and the alleyway where Harper had followed the killer, but the killer had doubled back and was now behind him. What could she do? Her throat was dry.

Denise tried to remember what Mac had told her, but she couldn't. The whole psychological change that Mac talked about was already happening to her. 'You've got to be a predator to stop your body preparing yourself to die.' She knew she couldn't shout to Harper. She was unarmed. The killer would turn, take her out and then wait for Harper.

She reached into the car and pulled out the keys. Slowly, she moved around to the back of the car and lifted the trunk, her eyes on him as he walked down towards the first alleyway.

She reached in and felt around until she gripped the handle of the lug wrench. She pulled it out and felt the weight in her hand. 'Become the predator,' she whispered.

Denise needed to get across to the killer just as he turned into the alleyway. She would have to move silently, so she removed her shoes. Watching and waiting, she was the predator now, both eyes forward, body still, ready to pounce. He was moving to the corner of the alley: if she left it any longer, he would be able to catch up with Harper. She had to act now.

Denise sprinted across the open ground, her feet making a low slapping sound, nothing more. She hit the wall within a few seconds and moved quickly to the corner. She leaned in, held the wrench hard, raised it to her shoulder and then turned the corner. *Think Predator. Act Predator. It's life or death.* She needed all her power, but it was working. She wasn't scared. Not at all. She was angry. This killer had Abby, had the two kids. Denise moved lightning fast, reaching him in two large strides. He heard her and turned, but that didn't help him. As he turned, Denise smashed the lug wrench across his temple. The killer's head twisted. She saw the whites of his eyes, white teeth and that was all. He was falling in front of her.

His head twisted into the ground, he lost control of himself and his gun hit the ground and skidded into the dark.

'Harper!' shouted Denise. 'I got him!'

The killer rose slowly. 'What the fuck . . .' he said, but the lug wrench came down again, hard on the head. No mercy. One specific target. She hit him again on the same spot. 'On the floor!' she screamed. 'On the fucking floor.' He didn't obey. She hit him twice, as hard as she could. Blood splattered her hand, but she kept him there and screamed, 'On the floor, flat on the floor!'

She could hear Harper running up the alleyway. The man stirred and tried to speak. She hit him again. 'Do not move,' she shouted.

The body at her feet lay still on its front, a large wound on his head, blood creeping across his skull and on to the ground.

Harper appeared, his gun trained on the body on the ground. 'What the hell?' he cried. 'Who is it?'

'It's him, Tom. He doubled back on you. I saw him coming after you. I had to take him out.'

Harper just stared. Denise stood, her heart pounding, her body feeling strong and powerful, the lug wrench poised for another blow.

The killer lay prostrate, groaning in pain, his right hand clutching the wound. Harper flashed the light over him then pulled out his cuffs and jumped on the body, cuffing him.

'Well done, Denise,' said Harper. He rolled the body over. 'Let's see what we got.' Harper's flashlight illuminated the face staring up at them and he felt the shock jolt him.

'It's Jack Carney,' said Harper. 'You've attacked a cop.'

Carney groaned. 'I tried to fucking tell her. She's brutal. Just kept hitting me. Jesus Christ, my head.'

'Save your strength, Jack,' Harper said. 'Where did you come from?'

'Hate Crime Unit got the call from Dispatch. We got here a few minutes before you.'

'I'm so sorry,' said Denise. The lug wrench clattered to the ground. 'I didn't realize.'

'You didn't fucking check,' said Carney. 'Just lucky you didn't have a gun.'

Harper knelt and uncuffed Carney. 'Where are they, Jack? Did you see?'

Carney motioned to the building opposite. 'There's a garage. Second along. He parked in there, then I heard him lock the front, so I went around the back. He's gone already. Are the children okay? I didn't check if they were in the car.'

'We don't know. We hope so. Can you walk? We need to stick together.'

Jack was helped to his feet. Denise decided to say nothing and just looked at the ground. She picked up Jack's gun and handed it back to him. 'I'm sorry.'

'Listen, lady, this goes nowhere, right? Nowhere. No one finds out I got pummeled to the ground by one of our own, by a civilian. By a woman.'

'All right, Jack, this stays here, but let's get back to the garage,' said Harper.

'I got the whole thing on the radio, got here fast as I could. I should've identified myself. I didn't fucking see her. She must've been hiding.' Carney grimaced through the pain.

Behind them, the patrol cops arrived. 'We've got a man down,' said Denise. 'Call for Emergency Medical Support.'

'Scrub that,' said Jack. 'There's no one down and no need for a medic yet.'

They moved across to the garage. Harper sent the patrolmen around the back entrance.

'We've got to break this,' said Harper.

Denise ran back for the lug wrench. She smashed down repeatedly on the lock until the old wood shattered.

Harper kicked the door and the lock finally gave. They dragged it open. Denise ran to the trunk of the car and lowered her head to speak. 'Ruth, Jerry, can you hear me? It's okay, this is Dr Levene. If you're in there, let us know and we'll get you out. You're safe now.' She heard a kick from the car. 'It's the children!' she shouted. She ran over to the car and tried the trunk. Locked. She called, 'It's okay, you're safe. We're with the police.'

The kicking continued, frightened, irrational thumping of panic.

'Stay still, you'll hurt yourselves.'

Denise tried to force the lock with the wrench but it didn't budge. She passed it to Harper. He tried but also failed.

'I've got an idea,' said Harper. He ran to the back of the car, a knife in his hand. He pushed the blade under the rim and tried unsuccessfully to pop the trunk latch.

He looked around and had a second idea. He opened the back door and found the seat lever. He pulled out one seat and cut a hole through to the trunk. Denise stood at his shoulder. 'Be careful,' she said. Harper ripped back the material with his hand. They waited a moment.

Two small hands, like two petals of a flower, reached out and turned in the dark air.

PART FOUR

Chapter Seventy-Two

North Manhattan Homicide
March 13, 9.22 a.m.

Denise waited for Harper all morning at the station house. She hadn't seen him since they'd recovered the children the night before. She'd tried his apartment early but there was no one in and Harper's phone went direct to message. When he didn't show up in the investigation room, she asked Eddie Kasper where he might be.

'Only four places I've ever found him:investigation room, the park, his apartment or the Cathedral.'

'The Cathedral?'

'St Patrick's. He's deep, you know.'

'He disguises it well.'

Denise left the team. They were poring over the details of the previous evening's operation. The relief was palpable: the two children, Ruth and Jerry Glass, were in police custody and they wouldn't make the same mistake again. But the repercussions of the night in Borough Park would be felt for some years. The only good thing to come of it was that so many neo-Nazis had been caught and arrested, so there were fewer of these misguided minds on the streets. Jewish organizations were working together to find an appropriate way to make a statement and show solidarity with the victims.

Jack Carney was the name being passed around, not Tom Harper. Carney had got there before Harper. He'd seen the danger. He'd spotted the killer, and even Harper admitted that Carney's presence had meant that they had avoided the unthinkable.

Maybe that's what was bugging Tom Harper. A rival for the city's affection. A new hero.

Denise found him alone, in the quiet of St Patrick's. He was sitting hunched over the pew in front of him. Not exactly praying, but somewhere close. She walked over and placed her hand on his shoulder. 'How you feeling?'

Harper turned, surprised. 'You,' he said.

'Eddie said you might be here.'

'When I need some perspective.'

'A close call.'

Harper turned and his eyes bored into her. 'The 88 Killer had them. He had his hands on them. If he'd wanted to kill them there and then, he could have. It couldn't have been closer.'

'But he didn't. And if you and Jack hadn't thought as fast as you did, then it would've been worse.'

'But how the hell did we miss it?'

'You didn't. They were in protective custody.'

'Then we've severely underestimated this killer.'

'He knew they could ID him – he took a very big risk. We were seconds away from catching him. Harper, this is what happens. You get close and they panic. This is how you catch them. You scare them into doing things in a way they don't want to.'

Harper hit the pew in front of him. 'What did we do wrong?'

'Nothing.'

'He should be behind bars by now.'

'Stop it, Tom. Without the surveillance operation, you never would have suspected he was after the kids. We never would have shut down their attack in Borough Park.'

'It's true.'

'Then let's leave the self-pity for later. He's still out there.'

'It's not self-pity, Denise. I'm grateful.'

'To whom?'

'Doesn't matter, it's just important that we're grateful. A few minutes later and we'd be searching for a child killer.'

'Don't think about it. We need you now. As I said, he knows

we're close and it's freaking him out. He's making poor decisions. We can flush him out, Tom.'

'Maybe,' said Harper.

Denise pressed both hands firmly on to his shoulders. 'There is a lot of detail to take in and process.'

'Yeah, I've been going through it. There's something we're missing.' He turned to Denise and saw her eyes searching his. He felt a jolt of emotion that caught him off-guard. 'He's going to do something big,' he said. 'If he knows the kids saw him, he realizes his time is short. He's not going to go out without a big finale.'

'You got any ideas?'

'Plenty, and I don't like any of them.'

'We need to work on his background,' she said. 'We need to understand him. It's still not coming together. He's acting the part of a Nazi, but I don't know why.'

'You're right about that,' said Harper. 'I can't get it straight in my head. Either I'm going mad or there's something here that just doesn't fit. You know what I think? I think our killer knows what we're up to. I need to work this through.'

'Just tell me if you're going mad,' said Denise, 'and I'll get you put in a nice ward, no question.'

'Appreciate it.' Harper let a half-smile curve his lips. 'Let's get back to the station house. I'm done with praying for now.'

Eddie Kasper appeared at the front entrance 'You okay, Harps?'

'I'm okay. How's things?'

'Still no sightings of Heming?'

'He's pretty good at evading us. Whenever our guys show up, he seems to have already left. Like he knows. Like he's getting information.'

'You think he listens to the police frequency?'

'I'd be a whole lot surer if I had him in the cell,' said Harper. 'Heming escaped last night, but it was a close call. This thing has wheels within wheels.'

'I got the photographs of Heming's place for you.'

'I visited last night after we got the kids back. Anything new?'

'They emailed it through. Take a look.'

Harper opened his email and glanced through the pictures. Heming's life was a sad little affair. But he was a serious Nazi. He liked swastikas, Nazi memorabilia and Nazi combat knives. Harper looked up. 'He's your all-American loser with a power fetish and a perverted intellectual grasp of history and politics.'

'Just about sums him up,' said Eddie.

'I want Denise to see it. She's still not convinced that Heming matches the profile of the 88 Killer. Will you show her?'

'Sure,' said Eddie.

Up in the investigation room, Harper flicked through the reports that had started to come in from the house searches on all the Nazi rioters. They had photographs from over twenty homes. It was all the same. Little hidden bedrooms and garages set up like film sets of the Third Reich. There were flags, insignia, Nazi literature, swastikas everywhere and framed photographs of mass murderers from the Nazi regime.

The poverty of the lives they were leading was unsettling. This was America. Brooklyn. One of the most diverse and vibrant places on the planet, and yet these resistant little cells continued, feeding on scraps that they could interpret as reason to hate. It wasn't life they were leading, they were in a spiritual and moral vacuum, unaware that every day, they were destroying themselves.

'Did they get anything I don't know about?' called Harper.

'They were thorough,' said Eddie. 'Every part of these apartments was tagged, boxed and removed. But it'll take weeks to go through all the computer files. We've cracked a big organization, Harper.'

'But left the lead psycho roaming the streets.' Harper looked up. He could see that the hate model that Denise had outlined would work with a man like Heming – personal slight, perceived slight, a build-up of violence and highs from the kills – but was this guy the same man who tortured Capske, killed Becky, Marisa and Esther, who was holding Abby?

Lafayette came down and patted Harper on the shoulder. 'Good work, Harper.'

'It's not over.'

'Not yet. But we got to hope, right?'

'Right.'

'Listen up,' said Lafayette. 'We just got a request from the Jewish community. They feel it's important to respond to last night's attack.'

'It sure is.'

'They want to show solidarity with the victims and give New Yorkers the chance to come together to show positive support for the Jewish community.'

'What do they say at Headquarters?'

'The Mayor is behind it, so we're behind it.'

'Could be a security risk. What are they planning?' asked Harper.

'There's going to be a major vigil for the murder victims and a celebration of the Jewish community. They want to use Union Park. Thousands will show up.'

'That's not good news – it could just be another target for him.'

'If you can't stop the killer then you sure as hell can't stop them mourning and joining together, Harper.'

'It's dangerous, that's all I'm saying.'

'That's why I'm here. Leave will be canceled. You need to put together your team. It'll be policed so heavily nothing could happen, but I want your eyes and ears down on the ground.'

Chapter Seventy-Three

He knew everything, past and present. He knew pain and the absence of pain. He knew success and he knew failure. He had failed. They were so fucking close. He had to think. He had to do something. Something that changed the game for good. He faced the wall in full uniform. He felt the pain again. Failure.

He took Abby Goldenberg, Prisoner 144002, out of the tiny closet that had been her cell for the past few weeks, and felt the rush of pain. He pulled her into the center of the room.

'Reject your Jewry or you die now.' The gun rose, pressed hard against her temple. She trembled but did not speak. He had failed. Again. His superiors would be unhappy with him. Again.

'It is a new game I have to play now, 144002. I have to hurt them. They have children who could identify me. I need to do something that will be remembered for all time. And you are going to pay too, unless you choose differently. What have you got to say?'

'I need food,' said Abby.

The killer snarled. 'No more food.'

'Please,' she begged.

'My boots are dirty.' The killer twisted the barrel of the gun tighter to her temple. 'Every day, my father made me clean his boots. And if they were not clean, he threw them into the cellar. I had to go down into the dark to fetch them. There were no lights in the cellar. It was damp and cold and so dark. I can't tell you how dark it was. When I was in the cellar, he would shut the door and lock it. I was in the cellar for hours. When he let me out, he would inspect his boots again. But in the dark, I could not clean them well. He would throw them down those stone steps again. Again and again, until his boots shone.'

'Your father was unkind,' said Abby.

'Cruel and unkind. Yes. Now open your shirt,' he ordered. Abby remained still. 'It is an order.'

Abby trembled and fumbled with her buttons. He dragged her shirt open and pushed it over her shoulder. 'You are scared to die, Abby?' He pulled a knife from his belt and held it to her chest. She shook and swayed but refused to cry out.

'144002,' he said. 'Now you must choose.'

'No,' she said.

'You repent now, 144002. Reject your religion. I am here to save you. You will be one of the saved. One of the 144,000. I have to help them. It is the final time, the moment, and we must be ready. Your time has come.'

She was crying. He rested the barrel on the top of her head. 'Can you feel how close death is?'

'Yes.'

'Do you reject your Jewry, Abby? Will you be one of our number? Reject it, as I have done. Abby? Will you?'

She looked up. She shook her head. 'No, I will not.'

He pushed her hard and in anger. She flew across the ground. 'You think you are better than me? I make them all reject their Jewry. You will too, when the pain is too great. I promise you, you will scream to give up your Jewry.'

Chapter Seventy-Four

North Manhattan Homicide
March 13, 11.05 a.m.

Erin Nash was standing at the entrance of the station house. She'd given up the subtle approach and was trying to stalk Harper into submission. He had studiously ignored her calls since the operation.

The NYPD had failed to capture Martin Heming. In fact, they'd let him slip through their fingers. Nash wanted the scoop. She knew from sources within the NYPD that Harper and Carney had nearly come face to face with the killer, and that Harper could give her an exclusive.

Erin had started digging into Heming's background. He was your standard little guy with a big chip on his shoulder and some dangerous ideology to help hone and focus all his negative energy.

From reading his websites, she guessed that Heming was acting out of personal anger and perceived slight, and out of the ideological bigotry he'd absorbed through ten years of neo-Nazi meetings and ultra-right-wing conferences.

Nash also found something more interesting. He seemed to be acting out of a long-lasting resentment of his own wife and hatred for her new Jewish husband. Was it that simple? He was just some failed, cowardly impotent, looking for a target to hit out at. There was nothing extraordinary about this man who had killed all those innocent people. Nothing extraordinary at all. In fact, he was banal.

Erin spotted Detective Harper and Levene walking across the

street to the station house. Harper looked bad. She jumped out and blocked his path.

'How's my hero?'

'I'm not a hero.'

'They say if you try hard enough, everyone gives in.'

'It's probably true, but how many years have you got?'

'Come on, Harper, I just want an interview. Your story. The cop who came face to face with the 88 Killer. You got to be heard, for the sake of those people who lost their lives.'

'I didn't see him.'

'They said you did.'

'Not me,' said Harper. 'Wish I had, but I was second to this one.'

'Who got there first?'

'Detective Jack Carney of Hate Crime Unit.'

'I don't know him. Should I be speaking to him?'

'He didn't see him either.'

'Sad, isn't it. You're having to play Buzz Aldrin to his Neil Armstrong.'

'This isn't moon walking, Erin. This is serious.'

'I know that, Harper.' She turned to Denise. 'Denise Levene. You're back at work? I didn't know you were on the case. The A Team is back in business, is that right?'

'No,' said Tom. 'Denise is not officially on this case.'

'Never mind,' said Erin. 'You're obviously quite special, Dr Levene. Tom Harper doesn't share his thoughts with many people.'

'Cut it out,' said Tom.

'Come on, something happened last night, didn't it, Detective? You had the killer in your sights, so how the hell did he get away?'

'He just did. We were a few minutes too late.'

'How did he get the location of the kids?'

'You heard the press conference, we are looking into it.'

'You fired shots in the alley. I hear your gun's been taken, right?'

'Standard procedure. We tried to take the killer down but the killer evaded us. He shot at me. I shot back.'

Harper made his way up the steps and pulled open the big brown door.

'I'm going to keep at it, Detective. I'm going to stick to this story until I get an angle. I always do, you know.'

Harper waved without turning and closed the door. He didn't doubt her.

Chapter Seventy-Five

Borough Park, Brooklyn
March 13, 11.17 a.m.

The killer straightened the front of his coat, flicked a thread from one of the shining black buttons, pressed his hair against his head and replaced the low cap that covered his face. His facial muscles creased and flexed as if he were trying to straighten out his expression. He had been standing across from the synagogue for two hours now and the soles of his feet ached. He felt that the world was spiraling away from him. He needed to concentrate all that pain on to one object. One detested type of person. He looked up at the sky. It was an uneven color. A line of dark gray growing across the horizon to a heavy ominous stormcloud just out in the Atlantic.

He checked his watch, moved his head from side to side to stretch his neck muscles, then shifted his weight from foot to foot. He had read most of the newspapers that morning and got a thrill out of the thrashing anger of the media. He liked it in the way an animal enjoys the resistance of its prey when it struggles in its jaws. They were angry, the Jews were outraged and the police were full of confident rhetoric. They were all pleased with themselves. But he was unconcerned. It was not him they should be hunting down, but the Jews conspiring against America.

He knew now what he had to do, though. He had to continue like he had been doing, keep the pressure on himself and keep watching. There were two security guards outside the synagogue, there to protect the Jews. He smiled at the thought and walked across. The synagogue was situated twenty feet back from the street, with a raised plaza in front with four benches.

The first security guard moved over to stop him. 'Can I help you, sir?' he said in a thick foreign accent.

'Terrible thing, last night, wasn't it?'

'Very bad thing,' said the guard.

'I want to help. Is there something planned?'

'You'll hear later today,' said the guard. 'They want to plan a vigil in Union Square.'

The killer nodded. 'A good idea. It will attract all their supporters. A very positive step.'

'It will be big,' said the guard. 'You can be sure of that.'

The man knew that the doors would soon open, the Jews would come out and he needed to disappear. 'Good luck,' he said. 'Hope it goes well. Hope nobody does anything stupid and ruins it.'

The guard looked on. 'Thank you.'

The door to the synagogue opened, and the men and women started to appear. They had been planning the event. A big event right in the heart of Manhattan. The killer lowered his head and walked away.

Chapter Seventy-Six

The late morning light streamed into the small room off the investigation room that Denise was using as an office. The Sturbe profile had been going backwards and forwards between her and Aaron Goldenberg. They were starting to piece together a picture of Josef Sturbe.

Harper walked along the corridor, the next phase of the investigation clicking through his mind. He pushed open the door. Denise looked up.

'I've been going through the profile again,' she told him.

'You need more time?'

'You left me less than an hour ago.'

'So did you get anything in that hour?'

Denise smiled and sniffed the air. 'You could do with a new set of clothes, big guy. You smell like a night in a cell.'

He couldn't say the same of her. Not at all. 'Less of the advice, just talk me through this Sturbe profile.'

'Initially, we thought Sturbe was chosen because he was a vicious Nazi who took the law into his own hands and murdered in his own way, in his own time. We thought this gave our killer validation as a model and an identity so that he didn't have to think of himself as doing these things. But now we don't think that's what the killer is seeing. We think that Sturbe means something personal to him.'

Harper crossed to the window. 'Is this going to be difficult?' he said. 'I haven't eaten or slept, and my brain's getting all dysfunctional on me.'

'Be quiet and listen,' said Denise. 'You can sleep later. The killer is a neo-Nazi who executes people with a point-blank gunshot to the head. He has this neo-Nazi agenda, this Sturbe identity, but he is psychologically and emotionally motivated, not ideologically motivated.'

'I understand, Denise, I'm not an idiot.'

'Sometimes it's difficult to tell.'

Harper gave her a look. Denise ignored it and continued. 'We've been hunting for the political elements of the killing and missing some key details.'

'Which are?'

'The Sturbe link isn't just political, Tom. This killer is acting out some ritual and the level of overkill is frightening. Sturbe isn't one of your well-known Nazis. He's been chosen for a reason. I don't believe things are chosen randomly, and if it's not random then the killer has some personal reason for taking Sturbe as his model. We're trying to find where the profile of the killer and Sturbe meet. In simple terms, Sturbe is hard to research – so where did our killer come into contact with him?'

'I understand,' said Harper. 'Well, soon as you've got something, let me know.'

Denise stopped. 'You heard anything from the team with the children?' she asked.

'I talked to the head psych.' Harper grimaced. 'He was less than impressed.'

'What did he say?'

'Would it help catch the guy? I said no. He asked me in what universe was it a good fucking idea to show these children a photograph of Martin Heming, their mother's killer?'

'And what did you answer?'

'The NYPD. It's that kind of universe.'

'He didn't laugh?'

Harper shook his head.

Lafayette appeared just as Harper was about to leave. 'How are you, Harper?' He paused but Harper remained silent. 'Okay, an easier question. What did Forensics find at the safe house?'

Harper rubbed his face. The whole team had been on the go all night trying to track the killer, but every lead had turned cold. 'Look, crazy as it sounds, they've not been able to find a single piece of material evidence.'

'What about the car?'

'Nothing there either.'

'This guy's invisible. You sure they got nothing?'

'They got all kinds of stuff, but it all belongs to the safe-house team, cops or the children. He must've tried real hard to keep things that clean.'

'What about the leak? Someone gave the killer the location of the safe house.'

Harper looked out across at his team. They were a hive of activity even though nothing was opening up. He turned to Lafayette. 'I've had all night to think about it. There's not many cops who knew the whereabouts of those kids, but one of them, for some reason, let that information leak. I'm not saying it was deliberate.'

'You got any ideas about this accident?'

Harper nodded. 'The killer didn't just know where the kids were, he knew that the second officer wasn't there.'

'You think it's the second officer?'

'I talked to him. He made a mistake. He knew he wasn't going to make it on time so he radioed Candy Simons. He gave the street name and said he wouldn't get there until midnight. All the killer would need was a scanner.'

Captain Lafayette shook his head. 'Shit. I can't believe that. You got a name? I've got to report this.'

'I already told him to own up. Better it comes from him.'

'Another fucking casualty of this thing,' said Lafayette, and walked off down the corridor with heavy steps.

Chapter Seventy-Seven

Apartment, New York
March 13, 12.14 p.m.

The killer lay on his bed holding a small fob with two keys in his hand and twisting them in the light. He smoked a cigarette and watched the smoke twirl above him. He was thinking about his next steps. His eyes flicked to the right. There was a map of New York City on the wall. He had marked each kill with a dot. Around his tour of duty was a thick black line. He knew what had to be done, but it wasn't enough. He put the two keys into his top pocket.

This was what it felt like, at the end of things. He knew the end was coming, but it needed to be on his terms, not theirs. He sat up and poured himself another drink. He took a sip, swilled it around his gums, then swallowed. Things had changed now, people were getting close. The children were still alive. That was a mistake. He didn't like leaving traces and the children could identify him. It cut deep, making mistakes like that. It was unacceptable.

The problem was Harper. Since he'd taken over the investigations, things had blown up all over town. The news was full of the shootings. The cops were all over his area and the Jews were walking in twos and avoiding going out alone at night. Harper was good. Harper had pieced together the attack on the children. Somehow, he had known about it. How was that?

Harper made links and connections that other cops didn't. Other cops were dumb and mindless. Harper had clarity, he looked sideways, he knew how to think. Harper was dangerous. The killer dragged hard on his cigarette and blew the smoke out fast. A haze of blue in front of his eyes. He needed a paradigm shift. He needed to change the nature of the attacks. Patterns were what cops looked for.

The Capske shooting had thrown them off the scent and given him time. It had allowed him to tour undisturbed, to kill again, to feel their subservient hands on his feet. Glass and Cohen lying in water or flat on cold ground, a ribbon of blood from the neat wounds. An execution or a re-enactment? He blew out smoke again. He couldn't afford another attack in the street. He needed something more substantial.

He thought about the vigil. It would be a cut right at the heart of things. But how? How to do it and how to humiliate Harper? He just had to work out a plan. The sunlight broke through a cloud and shot through his dirty window. He saw the dense blue smoke drifting in thin waves across the room, watched them for a moment – then suddenly the idea was there, in the room with him. He felt a sense of calm, as if he had finally found the door out of a prison.

The river was only half-crossed but there was no going back. His hands were thick with blood, but the species still lived on. He moved quickly to the window and looked out through the dirt and grime. He wanted the world purified, simplified, made clean. Just like the forest glade, a cut of green earth and a future for himself and others like him. Perhaps he was too confident, too clear-minded. Sometimes, it was necessary to cloud people's minds with fear. Maybe it was necessary to kill to feel nearer to God.

He thought about the other girl again. The girl he had loved who had ripped up the future. He saw her face in his mind's eye. Let the emotion at her memory run over his tongue. Was it love or hate he felt? He wanted to see her. He wanted to love her. He wanted to hurt her. He had to go out. He had to clean up. You couldn't kill them fast enough. There were just too many. He needed a way to kill more, to kill effectively, to get through them all.

Chapter Seventy-Eight

North Manhattan Homicide
March 13, 1.12 p.m.

Harper took some time to gather his thoughts, then brought the team back together. He looked exhausted from his sleepless night. 'This has got to get going, now,' he told them. 'We've got four unsolved murders with a link between them and a kidnapped girl. We've got less certainty than ever. Let's try to keep this organized.'

Denise looked across at Harper, indicating that she wanted to speak now. She wanted the team to understand the nature of the killer. Standing in front of them, leaning on the old table, she waited while he said to them, 'Clear your heads. We have four crime scenes that all need re-investigating. Dr Levene is going to give us the heads-up on this killer, then we're going to go back to basics. We're missing something here.' Harper raised his hand towards Denise. 'Thank you, Doctor.'

Denise cleared her throat, pushed her hair back and took a breath. 'The man we are searching for is not like you or me. He is a sociopathic murderer. He's not concerned with his personal safety. He is solely concerned with carrying out his project. As I understand it, his project has a racial element. He uses original Nazi bullets, he makes his victims clean his boots and then shoots them in the head as they do so. He enjoys their submission, but his crimes have not, up to now, had an explicitly sexual element. That is not to say that they are not sexually motivated.'

Denise paused for a moment. 'I happen to think that they do have a sexual element and by that, let me be clear, I mean that his control over his subjects gives him some kind of physical gratification. It may be that he is trying to stop his desires. These are crimes of hate to some degree, but they are not only crimes of hate. They are personal crimes that come from a powerful sense of inferiority that it is impossible for our killer to acknowledge. Our unknown subject believes he is hunting after Jews, after any Jew, but his victims are not just any Jews. I've thought more closely about the victims recently and they tell us something. Apart from David Capske, they follow a similar pattern. The women belong to a similar type. Look at this.'

Denise pointed at the women on the board. They all had different hair color, different faces. No one could see the connection. 'I don't get it,' said Garcia. 'They're all different.'

'Yes, they seem so, don't they?' Denise walked across to the boards and put the crime-scene photographs of each woman side by side. 'Do you see it now?' she asked.

The team stared at the three women. Esther, Becky and Marisa.

'They're all thin with long hair,' said Mary.

'Yes,' said Denise. 'That's right, they're all thin. He's not just after Jews. He's after a type. This is not just political, it's personal.'

'What about Capske?'

Harper replied. 'I think that's what the investigation has to ask itself. Why Capske?'

'I think I might know why,' said Denise. 'Did you ever interview Lucy Steller? I've been feeling I've been missing something and it suddenly came to me. Abby Goldenberg was the type, but so was Lucy Steller. Thin, with long hair. Maybe he wasn't after Capske, after all. Maybe he couldn't get the girl he wanted, so he took it out on Capske. Maybe Lucy was his target. He's full of desire and hatred for himself.'

'What do you think, Eddie?' said Harper. 'You spoke to Lucy.'

'It's interesting. Lucy certainly fits the type. He was watching them both. Lucy said that. She was sure about that.'

'Yeah, but Capske took her all the way home. He didn't have a chance,' said Harper.

'So, instead, he followed Capske. Maybe frustrated with not being able to get to his target.'

The team seemed buoyed by the idea. They hadn't had a lead for days and the new information seemed to open some doors.

'I call it a psychological fingerprint,' said Denise. 'He's leaving his ID all over these kills, we just can't read it yet. But we're getting closer.'

'Let's check it out,' said Harper. 'We've got to go back to Lucy. He could've been stalking her for a while and if so, then she might have seen him.'

'And if she was a target . . .' said Denise. She stopped. All eyes were on her. She wasn't sure whether she should say it or not. She looked at the floor and then back up. 'If she was a target, then she still is – and that means she's possibly still in danger.'

'We're already on it,' said Harper, pointing at three members of his team. 'Let's move!'

Chapter Seventy-Nine

Apartment, Upper East Side
March 13, 1.53 p.m.

Lucy Steller sat alone in her flat. She had been too scared to go out ever since the morning after David's murder. She couldn't forgive herself for falling asleep as he was being tortured.

She had slept in a warm bed, safe and comfortable as the man she loved was being tortured and murdered. She hated herself so much, she couldn't bear to see or speak to anyone.

She took the razor, looked coldly down on to her own arm and steeled herself. The razor lightly touched her arm, a delicate but unmistakable sting. Not pain, but painful. She pulled the razor across her arm, watching the trail appear – a red tail to a steel mouse. The stinging deepened and intensified. She raised her hand. It was a cycle. She would cut, then the white fear would come and she'd feel depressed, scared and lost. Then she would have to cut until the fear stopped. Hurt made sense. The line of blood collected into a glistening red ball on her wrist. The tipping point was reached and the ball of blood rolled down her arm. Seeing herself bleed, she relaxed a little, a physical relief from her emotional pain.

Her hand moved down to the cut; she drew a second line across the first line, forming a red cross. The pain from the second line mingled with the dying pain from the first. Emotional pain was layered too. Layers and layers of harmonic pain, shouting, screaming, grieving, crying.

Blood was dripping off both sides of her arm. She cut again as the pain dulled. Each time, the dulling came more quickly, until Lucy was slicing herself every few seconds. She continued for minutes. A hundred bloody cuts, a hundred red lines spreading out in every direction like marks on a butcher's chopping block.

Then it stopped. The tension and anger vanished and she was left sitting on the small couch, staring ahead, her pale face gaunt and drawn from a lack of food and sleep and iron.

Chapter Eighty

Apartment, Upper East Side
March 13, 1.58 p.m.

Outside in the street, the man looked up. He knew she lived on the fifth floor and counted until he imagined where she was sitting right now. He walked up the stone stoop and took out the key. He had had the key ever since he'd taken Capske out. The cops hadn't noticed that one of the keys on his fob was missing. Subtlety was lacking in their investigation. He pushed it into the lock and turned it. The lock was on some kind of electronic catch and the bolt buzzed and released. He entered the lobby.

The building was old and crumbling, with post-boxes half-torn off or covered with graffiti. It smelled of mold and damp. The panels to the basement door were smashed out and the lower-ground laundry odors mixed with the heat from the apartments and the whiff of old carpets.

He didn't like the dirt or the idea that he was breathing in spores. He moved toward the stairs and started to climb. The key to the apartment remained in his hand as he ascended to the fifth floor. He took a look over his shoulder and felt the excitement rising through his body, lifting him up with the sensation of flying.

In his coat pocket was his World War Two German Luger. A fine piece of engineering and beautiful to hold, the semi-automatic Pistole Parabellum 1908, to give it its correct name. He pulled the Luger out of his pocket as he reached the floor, took out an 8-round magazine and pushed it into the grip. Taking the toggle-joint between his thumb and forefinger, he pulled it back, then let the breechblock snap back into place, with a metallic clunk. A new cartridge was now waiting in the chamber. Lucy's bullet was primed.

Chapter Eighty-One

Apartment, Upper East Side
March 13, 2.09 p.m.

The street Lucy Steller lived on was quiet and tree-lined. There was a row of shops and that afternoon people were peaceably walking along either side of the street. A moment later, a distant squawk of sirens could be heard getting closer and closer. Soon, the sound was screeching and a few people on the street turned to look.

Eight police cars turned into the street and drove hard down towards them. The first car braked and skidded, then the other seven cars followed suit. Down the street, in a car, a man observed them closely. He checked his watch.

The people in the grocery store watched as every car door opened and several plain-clothed detectives got out. Three of the cars were squad cars and uniformed officers started to form a boundary.

The men and women hurried across to a building and in a moment they'd all disappeared. Only two uniformed officers stood on the street, telling the public that they ought to stand back.

Harper was first at Lucy Steller's door. He knocked, lightly at first. Then harder and finally, he was shouting her name. There was no response. 'Okay, break the door,' he said.

Two cops moved in with the battering ram. They hit the door once and the door jamb split. Harper pushed it open. He walked in.

'Lucy!' he called. There was no reply, but there was a smashed cup on the floor and an overturned table with a broken leg lying by the couch.

Harper knelt and touched the cup with his palm. 'It's still warm,' he said.

'Signs of a struggle,' said Eddie. 'We're too late.'

Harper led the cops through the rooms. 'Just look around. Anything you can find that might tell us something.'

Denise looked at the bookshelves. There was a row of diaries going back for several years, but two were missing. She ran her finger over the year on each diary. 'Harper, two of the last three years are missing.'

'Is that significant?'

'They might be somewhere, but if the killer is targeting her, maybe he thought she'd have information. He's getting very worked up, Harper. He's trying to close down anyone with knowledge of him. She might have seen him stalking her.'

Harper moved to the desk. 'The PC, take a look at this,' he said. 'There's no hard drive – another place that she might leave evidence.'

Harper then glanced at the small hook by the door. He walked across. 'How do you think he got in?'

Denise raised her head. 'Either he just rang the buzzer or he had a key. Point is, what's he going to do next?'

Chapter Eighty-Two

North Manhattan Homicide
March 13, 3.51 p.m.

Harper and the team left Crime Scene at Lucy Steller's apartment. Harper called Blue Team together.

'The coffee cup on Lucy Steller's floor was still warm, which means that the killer was only a few minutes ahead of us,' said Harper. 'He's coming out of the shadows. We should have protected this woman. She's in real danger now.'

'We didn't see it coming. It's a form of escalation,' said Denise. 'He's trying to cover his tracks and he's likely to try something more dramatic, something that gives him a bigger thrill than the kills.'

'It's hard to think what,' said Greco.

'We need to get going. We've got the vigil at Union Square to help with. The killer risked himself with Lucy, just like with the children. That means Lucy holds a clue to his identity, right?' The cops nodded. 'I'm going to leave Denise and Ratten here to go through everything from Lucy's apartment. My guess, based on the stolen diaries and hard drive, is that she either knew who he was or met him in the last two years. So we need to know when it was, who he was and how they met.'

Denise nodded.

Harper then pulled up the map of Union Square. Eddie looked at it. 'How the hell are they going to police that place?'

'It's going to be hard, that's all we know,' said Harper. 'But it's going to be peaceful. We're there with Hate Crime Unit, just to keep an eye out. We don't know that he'll try anything, but he may enjoy turning up, so we're videoing every entrance and exit. We've got face recognition software, and Heming's face plus every face that Hate Crime has on record is now in the database.'

'How does it work?' asked Garcia.

'Mathematics,' replied Ratten. 'Although you're pretty, your face can be reduced to a number of measurements and ratios. The software calculates those measurements for every face it sees and if it matches anything in the databank, it'll flag up.'

'So if Heming or any known neo-Nazi turns up, they'll be flagged and arrested.'

The team were just taking in the information when Captain Lafayette flew through the door. He was red-faced and full of excitement. 'Listen up, the press have just had another communication from the 88 Killer. A new email.' He held up a piece of paper. 'He emailed all the newspapers again. The boys downstairs have traced it, it's no fake. This comes from the same account.'

'So, what the hell does he say this time?'

Lafayette eyed the room. 'You're not going to like this, not one bit.' He drew the email in front of his eyes. '*Police Press Notice: March 14, Union Square Park. During the night-time vigil in Union Square Park to remember those killed in the recent spate of attacks on the Jewish community, NYPD detectives discovered the dead bodies of five Jewish citizens. As the vigil went on, the suspect known as the 88 Killer executed five people. Senior police officials are at a loss to explain how the killer managed to fool the NYPD and kill in such a high-security operation. In the words of one bystander: "The government and the police stood by watching, while someone walked in and killed five innocent people."*'

'How seriously are we going to take this?' said Lafayette. 'Every news station in America is going to be down in Union Square after they receive this. He's just set his stage.'

'Can he do it?' said Denise. 'I mean, is it possible?'

'Can we evacuate?' asked Harper.

'It's too late and the Mayor thinks it will be a PR disaster to pull the plug on this.'

'Then what?'

'We'll have police on every square inch of the place,' said Lafayette.

'And what if it's a bomb?' said Kasper. 'Then what do we do?'

The team looked at each other. 'Then we've got to hope that the sniffer dogs will find it. We're going to have to scramble everyone – Counter-Terrorism, the army, the Feds – on this. This is going to be big.'

Harper took the piece of paper. He read the email and passed it to Denise. 'It's a challenge,' he said. 'I don't like it. He's already three steps ahead.'

Lafayette looked at Harper. 'Can he do it?'

'Anything can be done,' said Harper.

'Not with the whole of the NYPD on his case.'

Harper shook his head. 'You've just had a message from a killer saying he's going to make fools of the whole government as we all pay our respects to the dead. You think we can police this? There's going to be thousands and thousands of people out there and we've got to find one determined and clever individual. He can do anything. We don't have a chance. Captain, you need to speak to the Commissioner and tell him that if he's not going to stop it, then he needs to prepare for the worst.'

Chapter Eighty-Three

Auto-parts Yard, Brooklyn
March 13, 4.18 p.m.

Karl Leer had sourced the vehicle two weeks earlier. He had found a decommissioned Auxiliary Support Unit Police Truck that was lying unwanted and unloved in a scrapyard.

As requested, Leer had checked out the engine and cleaned it, making sure that the paintwork was neat and without too many obvious scratches. Then he had left the truck outside the garage behind his workshop.

And now the killer was standing next to the big, dark blue truck. He walked around it and looked inside. He opened the back doors: it seemed to be the right size and would suit his plan. He checked over the outside. Because it was one of the NYPD Auxiliary Unit's trucks, rather than one of the official NYPD trucks, it still had its markings. That was essential. It had to look like the real thing and it would because it *was* the real thing.

The killer jumped inside and started to pull everything out. He wanted space to hold people. He had a plan and the plan was to make a fool of the NYPD and to try to kill more Jews than he had been able to so far. Shooting people one by one would take too long, but it was more than that. It was affecting him. He wanted more dead. He wanted a bigger impact. The hunger was in him again and he couldn't control it.

Nor could he afford to let failure happen again. Once the truck was emptied, he got in the back with a tube of sealant. He sealed up any and every joint and hole with silicon. Then he

342

added rubber all around the two back doors in order to create an airtight unit.

He walked back to the lock-up and found a long piece of hose. He measured the length of the truck from the bottom to the top and then halfway across the roof. He cut a length of hose and then found a ladder. He climbed on to the roof and for the next half-hour welded all the air vents shut apart from one. On to the last vent he welded a short metal nozzle. Then he attached the hose to the nozzle and tied it firmly in place with wire. He ran the hose across the roof, taping it down, then ran it down the side of the van.

Finally, he took the other end of the hose and, using another nozzle, attached it to the exhaust. He spent a few more minutes ensuring that each end of the hose was in place, and then painted the hose blue so that it was not so conspicuous. The whole operation lasted under three hours. He stood back and declared himself pleased. Then he went to the engine and switched it on. He let the engine rumble on and he climbed into the back of the van, leaving the door wide open.

Soon enough, exhaust fumes started to fill the space and he began to cough. He jumped out of the truck. This was the way forward. This was much more efficient.

Chapter Eighty-Four

North Manhattan Homicide
March 13, 9.56 p.m.

Denise Levene sat at her desk. There was something more to the killings than she had been able to understand in the last few hours that she'd been researching. She was reading through the remaining diaries and looking through the photographs. Gerry Ratten was trying to find Lucy Steller's online details. Although the killer had taken her PC, many people posted photographs online, kept blogs online, even stored their whole PC backup online. He just needed a breakthrough, but at the moment, there was nothing.

Harper was already out at Union Square Park with half the police in the city. Every time Denise called, he seemed more wired and angry. She called him again. 'How is it?' she asked.

'We've got a few thousand people in the square. The face recognition has picked up half a dozen known offenders, but no Heming. It seems smaller than we imagined it would be. We've got hundreds of men on the ground and no traffic coming in from any direction, so we've done what we can. We just have to hope that he was lying or that we get lucky. What else have you got on Lucy?'

'Nothing yet,' said Denise. 'But I'm going to call Lucy's friends. They might know something.'

'Anything more on Sturbe?'

'I've been in touch with Dr Goldenberg. He's sourced two possible ways forward. The first is a news report from fifteen years ago. A man called Edward Sturgeon was accused of being Sturbe. He lived in Boston. It may be that our killer had some Boston connection, but I can't find anything linking Heming and Boston.'

'What's the other way forward?'

'There was a book written about Sturbe. It had a very small circulation – in fact, it only went to specialist libraries, or libraries in Jewish areas. Dr Goldenberg has found a copy and guess what?'

'I don't want to guess.'

'This killer is copying his approach almost to the letter. The barbed wire was something Sturbe started in Warsaw. He captured Jews in the ghetto then allowed them to escape through barbed wire or get shot. They dragged themselves through the barbed wire until they got so caught up, they died there. He drowned others. And there's the rings. He cut victims' fingers off to get their gold. Our killer seems to have read this book.'

'Any way of finding a link?'

'Heming has lived his whole life in Brooklyn. This biography of Sturbe was held in fifteen libraries in the country. The Brooklyn Library had two copies. They had a special Jewish History section.'

'Is there any record of who took out the book?'

'We're going to check.'

'Anything else?' asked Harper.

'I'll keep you updated,' she said. 'I'm not sure how useful this information is.'

'Well, keep going. If he's copying this Nazi, then there might be something that leads us to him. For example, what kind of crimes hasn't he committed yet?'

Chapter Eighty-Five

Union Square Park
March 13, 11.41 p.m.

The vigil was almost entirely peaceful. The NYPD Command Truck was parked across the entrance to the square on the south side. Harper and Eddie Kasper arrived back from their seventh tour around the square and went inside.

'Update?' called Harper to Lafayette.

Lafayette was sitting at one of the seats with headphones around his neck. 'All are negatives. Nothing but complaints of infringements on human rights.'

'How many searches have they done?'

'Not got the numbers. Thousands, though.'

'No calls or emails?'

'Nothing. What's the mood like?'

'Peaceful,' said Harper. 'Everyone just wants to remember the dead. The park's ablaze with candlelight. It's moving. Really moving.'

There were four other men in the Command Truck monitoring their teams and liaising with the huge media operation. Harper stood at the door and stared across at their compound.

'If the killer doesn't show,' he said, 'they're going to have a lot of footage about the vigil.'

'Let's hope that's all they've got,' said Lafayette. 'We could do without another horror story.'

'I hear you,' said Eddie. 'The city's had enough tragedy.'

Harper nodded and made his way outside again. 'Another tour, Eddie?'

'Damn,' said Eddie. 'I thought you'd never ask.'

The two cops moved back out into the darkness. The police compound took up the whole of the southern end of the park. Hundreds of police vehicles stretched out. Cops everywhere, sitting around, patrolling, and catching a bite to eat.

Harper and Eddie moved back into the park. The choppers that circled overhead were useless. This was a one-man operation. The most difficult kind of perp to catch: a man who no longer cared for his own safety. It could have been any one of the thousands of men in the park.

They walked up past the media center. The reporters were wrapped up warm, sitting on the steps of AV trucks sipping coffee from paper cups. Everyone was waiting for something to happen, but no one wanted it to. A strange mood of uncertainty pervaded the press pack. They weren't their usual eager selves. Placards declared the need for peace and remembrance. Written messages told of someone's deep love for a person they had lost. Flowers and tributes grew throughout the evening.

The police operation was vast, but once in the park itself it was almost invisible. There were patrol cops everywhere, but many more non-uniformed officers from the NYPD, Counter-Terrorism and the FBI. There were units at every entrance with sniffer dogs and Geiger counters, doing checks and searches. They wanted to prevent any atrocities, and individual searches were the only way.

So far, they'd confiscated drugs and nothing much else. All around the park, sitting in tight groups in the semi-darkness, were several Rapid Response Units from all parties. Counter-Terrorism's Hercules Teams sat in blacked-out sedans at each corner of the park, waiting for orders. The NYPD's ESU SWAT teams were stationed in big black armored Bearcats, tooled up and ready.

As they walked through the crowds of people who were singing, talking, praying and crying, it looked like whatever it was, it wasn't going to happen.

Chapter Eighty-Six

Union Square Park
March 13, 11.56 p.m.

Crowds were still filtering in, some finding it hard to move through the streets towards the vigil. The killer stopped at the roadside and watched the people lining up and walking along with candles lit for the dead.

The crowds were different now. They were not the earlier enthusiasts or the serious mourners; these were groups of people coming out of bars and restaurants. They were probably a little drunk and looking for more excitement. And as they wandered the streets, they got caught up in the sound and mood of the all-night vigil.

The killer observed them with a sense of disgust. Revelers, unconcerned about what was happening to his city, to the country. They were mourning the loss of people who didn't deserve to be alive, people who were part of the problem. The killer took a cigarette from a pack on the seat and lit up. His anger had lessened since he'd snatched Lucy. She was his now and he felt good about that. It gave him a strong feeling of calm to know that she was his and his alone.

He sat in his truck and watched the groups move past. He needed to find the right group. He needed to choose the right profile. It amused him to think of all the effort being expended by the cops in trying to write his profile. He could write it in two words. *Pissed off.*

A small group stopped by the side of his truck just after

midnight. Jews with white and blue Israeli flags, chanting something he didn't understand.

He watched their hesitation as they stared down the street.

'It's quicker this way,' said one of them, a man.

'I think they've closed the south entrance,' said one of the girls.

'You have to wait in line for a bag search. You need to be getting home.'

'But it's important,' said the girl.

He had had enough. The killer shouted down from the cab: 'You guys want to get a ride right to the heart of this thing? Ever been in a police truck?'

They looked up. The driver was a bright-eyed cop. He was smoking too – a lit cigarette hung from his lips. This was not like some of the hard-faced cops they'd met; this guy seemed different.

'Where to?' one of them asked.

'I'm going to the police compound.'

'I'd like a lift,' said one of the girls.

'I got an empty truck here and I'm going through the crowds and down to the compound. You want to get a VIP seat to the vigil?'

This group felt invulnerable, in the middle of a huge police operation. In the middle of their people. Why would a group of five fear a single cop? It was all about gaining trust.

'I'm going now, anyway, make your minds up,' said the killer.

'I think we should do it,' said one of the guys. 'We should take the time to do this.'

'Okay, that's final,' said the killer. He jumped down from the cab, opened the back of the van and let them pile in, then he shut and locked the door. There was a light in the back to prevent them from getting scared, but the moment he started to drive he would switch it off. That way, they wouldn't be able to see where the gas was coming from and wouldn't be able to cover the vent.

'Ready to go?' he shouted from the front cab. He could hear their cheers as he started the engine, drove away from the curb and into the traffic.

He had read from the Nazi reports of the use of gas vans that screaming was a problem. They had tried to stop this distraction by gagging the victims prior to putting them in the vans, but that just wasn't possible in this case. The killer couldn't gag them, so he had another plan.

Inside the back of the van, the group lurched left, then right, but they were laughing as they fell across each other. After a minute of driving, the smell in the back of the truck was noticeable. They sniffed and stopped laughing, and someone started to cough.

The killer heard a bang on the side of the van. 'Stop the truck,' a man's voice called. 'We've got exhaust fumes in here.'

In the cab, the killer leaned forward and flicked off the light. In the back of the van, darkness fell.

As the killer turned up 2nd Avenue, he could hear them screaming. He knew it would take ten to fifteen minutes for the gas to kill them. He couldn't risk others hearing them, so he switched on the sirens and continued to drive; the loud wailing of a police truck was all that he or anyone else could hear.

Chapter Eighty-Seven

Union Square Park
March 14, 4.12 a.m.

The night had come and gone. No dead bodies, no explosions. The first lights of dawn were arriving and most of the crowd had dissipated. There were a few left in small huddles, wanting to ride it out until morning.

Harper had been forty-eight hours without sleep but was still standing, while Eddie sat down, his head low in the collar of his Puffa jacket. 'When do we get to go home?' said Eddie. 'He's not showing up. He's probably tucked up in bed, laughing at us.'

'We go when they all go,' said Harper, as his phone rang.

Denise had called throughout the night, with sharp, disturbing updates. There was no tiredness in her voice. She had spent the night going over reports about Sturbe with Abby Goldenberg's father and hunting any link between Lucy Steller and the killer.

'What have you got?' said Harper, his eyes still scanning a park now scattered with litter.

'Get this. Sturbe had an 88 tattooed on his chest. I have no doubt that our killer would copy this. And about future kills, he was involved in the destruction of the Great Synagogue.'

'Meaning?'

'I think he could try to destroy something big. He's copying this guy's ghetto history, and if he is, he's got a lot more kills to get through. Sturbe's own notes indicated he killed over forty people.'

'Anything you got that might help us track him down?'

'We found something on the Lucy front. We're close. We think there might have been a boyfriend.'

'A boyfriend?' Harper struggled with the thought.

'Yeah, her friends said she went out with a slightly older guy. I asked if it was Heming, they looked at the pictures in the papers and said it wasn't.'

'Maybe it's not the link then,' said Harper. 'Keep at it, Denise. We'll find something.'

'As far as I can see, Tom, it's all a grand delusion. Section 88 are finished, but this guy is carrying on. He fed his delusion through this assumed identity of Josef Sturbe and I'm worried about what he's going to try next.'

'We all are,' said Harper.

Dawn became morning. Harper watched from the surveillance truck as the rest of the crowds left, followed by the media trucks, all empty-handed.

The police operation started to pack up and leave. Harper was the last to go. He jumped off the Command Truck and waited as it pulled off. By 7.30 a.m., there was nobody left.

Harper stood with Eddie, cold, hungry and tired. They looked around the empty lot. Harper saw a single police truck standing in the street and moved towards it.

'What is it?' called Eddie.

'Auxiliary Support Truck,' said Harper.

Eddie shook his head. 'Auxiliary Support. Amateurs, Harper. They went home and left their truck!'

Harper walked across. There was no one in the cab. 'The keys are still in the ignition,' he said.

'Some part-time nobody went home,' said Eddie. 'He's going to wake up soon and think he's missing something.'

Harper walked around it. It was on his second round that he spotted the tube running up the side of the van. It was painted the same color as the vehicle. He raised his eyes. The tube went right up to the roof. Harper put his foot on the big back wheel and jumped up. His hands caught the top of the truck and he pulled himself up.

'What you doing?' said Eddie.

Harper didn't reply. He peered over the top of the truck. The tube ran right across the roof, to where there were three air vents. Harper looked at each. Two had been sealed up. The third one had a small metal nozzle sticking up from it. The tube crossed the roof and joined to the nozzle.

Harper dropped down from the truck and crouched beside it. He pulled out his flashlight and shone it under the chassis. The tube ran right under the truck and connected to the exhaust pipe.

Harper stared, the horrific truth coming to him in a flash. He stood up. Eddie moved across. 'What is it?'

Harper let the flashlight do the talking. He ran the beam over the tube, all the way from the exhaust pipe to the roof. Eddie watched the light. 'Jesus Christ.' He crossed himself.

'Evil,' said Harper. 'This is what it looks like.'

Harper put on a glove. 'Don't touch a thing,' he warned Eddie as he pulled the keys out of the ignition and walked round to the rear of the truck. 'I don't want to open it,' he said.

'You think you should?'

'What if someone's unconscious in there?'

Eddie nodded and Harper pushed the smaller key into the lock. It turned easily. He twisted the handle and pulled open the truck doors.

Both men reared back as the exhaust fumes that saturated the inside of the van billowed out into the glossy night lights still burning in Union Square Park.

The blackened insides of the truck were dark like a cave. Harper held his arm across his mouth and nestled his nose and lips into the curve of his elbow. He raised his flashlight and pointed the beam through the smoke. The widening beam of light caught bright pink flesh. Harper's light moved laterally. One, two, three, four, five. Their faces and hands glowed garishly from the carbon-monoxide poisoning; the skin was pricked and dimpled. Their bodies clung to each other, the whole image like some terrible vision of hell.

PART FIVE

Chapter Eighty-Eight

Lock-Up, Bedford-Stuyvesant
March 14, 6.12 a.m.

The killer stared out through the glass shield. His hands were coated in thick protective gloves and he could feel the heat from the metal below. He hadn't slept. He couldn't any more.

He pushed his arms forward. The fierce shriek of the angle grinder as it bit into the steel rod bellowed throughout the garage. Sparks sheeted out in every direction. The metal scaffolding poles had been picked up here and there. He had known they would be useful one day. His big idea was pinned to the far wall, sketched in pencil on to a roll of paper.

He cut the pole right through and it fell to the concrete floor with a clatter. There were several of these on the floor now, all the same length. He rolled the last one into the pile and then counted them again. His shoulder was aching and the heat in the small garage with the low iron roof was bad. He was streaming with sweat, wearing a shirt to protect his skin from the sharp fragments of steel and the red sparks.

The diagram on the wall was repeated in actual size on the floor. Two chalk lines extended from the back wall into the room. A third line connected them, forming a square. There was a wooden board on the floor, two pallets of bricks, and bags of sand and cement.

Having finished cutting his steel poles, which were going to be perfect tubes, he removed his shirt and undershirt. He took a spade from the side of the room and ripped open the cement bag. He poured it on to the board, and then added a shovel of sand. In the heat he went over to the hose and doused himself liberally first, before filling a bucket with water.

He used the spade to form a cavity in the sand and cement mix, then threw in water from the bucket, folding it in with the spade.

When he was happy with the consistency, he took a trowel and started to lay a thin line of mortar between the chalk lines. He then took the point of his trowel and formed a V in the mortar. From the block of twelve bricks he took the first one, laid it flat side down on the mortar and pressed it firmly into place with a slight twisting motion. He laid the second brick along from the first, filling in the joint between them, then placed his spirit level on top to check that they were flat. He continued until the walls were nearly all built.

The killer could see that the evolution of the species only worked if people destroyed what was weak. If not, humanity would continue to be diluted by impure genes. He lifted another brick and placed it on top of the mortar. He was still depressed about missing the children, but now he had Lucy. Second attempts were good enough.

He thought about Section 88. They were amateurs. Fools, most of them. They had been useful, but they hadn't understood him. Not at all. If there was one thing he knew better than anything else, it was how to keep a fire burning. It had burned through the last twenty-five years, it had grown through any slight, any injustice, and become a raging, tormenting anger.

The truth – if there was such a thing as truth – was that he now felt bad if he didn't kill. He felt cowardly, and as though he, too, was weak. Once you started to kill, the need was impossible to stop. It was mechanical and vast. It consumed him.

The killer heard a bark, then a whole series of barks. Someone was outside. He stood and reached for his gun.

A moment later, a knock rapped on the door. He unlocked the door and opened it.

'I got what you asked for, Sturbe,' said Martin Heming.

Chapter Eighty-Nine

Harper slept three hours then walked back to the station house, his head full of dark images. The news media had just picked up the story and the panic and rage were building.

There were no reporters outside the precinct and the investigation room was nearly empty. It would take Forensics another day to get anything from the Auxiliary Truck, but Harper already knew that there would be nothing. The killer was too good, and the purpose of the attack was unmistakable – it wasn't just to kill, it was to prove his superiority to the police.

Denise Levene sat in the circle of light from a low desk lamp in the corner of the room. She looked asleep. Harper moved across, his feet making no sound on the old carpet. Denise turned quickly as he approached. 'Tom! Are you okay?'

'I've never seen anything as bad as what I saw in that truck, Denise. We've got to find this guy. He's escalating beyond anything I could've imagined. Five kids gassed in a police van.' Harper threw himself into a seat. 'Anything coming together here?'

'I've got nothing new. We've been working all night.'

'No leads on Lucy?'

'We haven't found anything. He's cleaned all traces.' Denise stared up at Harper. 'It's always darkest just before dawn,' she said.

Harper smiled in response and stared down at the book that Denise was looking at. 'What is it? Your high-school scrapbook?'

'It's my casebook. I keep a close eye on the Abby case. I keep every detail, every article.'

'You really feel for her, don't you?'

'Sure, don't we all?'

Harper picked up the casebook. He held it as he crossed to the coffee pot and poured out a fresh cup of coffee. 'Interesting,' he said.

'What is?'

'Looking back over the life of a case.' Harper sat and started to flick through the images. He saw outrage, hope, despair, page after page. The turns and dead ends of a fruitless investigation. At the end, the presumption of death.

'They look alike, don't they?' said Harper, staring at a picture of Abby Goldenberg smiling in a high-school shot and the photos of the murder victims on the wall.

Denise stood up and stretched. 'Yeah. There's definitely a type he goes for. No question.'

'No, I mean Abby and Lucy.'

'They do,' said Denise.

'I don't understand how Lucy could be a target,' said Harper. 'Why?'

'She's not Jewish, is she? He must've been going for Capske, but then why come back for Lucy?'

'Because she saw something the night he was taken, something that would lead us to him.'

'Yes. I thought of that,' said Harper, 'but if she was only taken because of some accident, then it's damn strange that she's a dead ringer for Abby. I don't get how this fits together.'

'I don't get it either, but Lucy had something he wanted to keep from us.'

'Another thing, if we're working on the assumption that the killer is Heming, then why does it matter if Lucy saw him? It makes no sense. We know it's Heming, don't we?'

'No, but he's all we've got.'

'He's smart, right? Smart enough to find a police safe house and kidnap two kids, smart enough to leave no evidence. You met

Lucy. She's not a difficult target. She seemed kind of lost in her own head. Why did he feel the need to take her?'

'Could be part of the escalation,' said Denise. 'He's not thinking straight.'

'You read about Heming and his wife. She went off with a Jew. You don't think that's what's happened here, do you? Lucy was going out with Heming, maybe after the marriage broke up. Maybe lightning struck twice for him. She was dating him and then left him for a Jewish boy.'

'Could be,' said Denise. 'But they don't seem to be a good match.'

'No, and again, I can understand him wanting to punish her, if that's his psychosis, but why take the hard drive and the diaries?'

Harper flicked through Denise's casebook and stopped at a picture of Abby standing next to some boyfriend from her past. He turned to Denise. 'Our killer knows the children can ID him, right?'

'Right.'

'So he's confident he's got alibis and he's confident that there's no physical evidence to link himself to the crime. We didn't even get a strand of hair from the Becky Glass murder. He didn't rape her either, even though it looks like he wanted to. Perhaps he's afraid of leaving his DNA. I mean, maybe he's on file so he's got to keep the scenes clean. He certainly knows how to clean a crime scene. If it was Heming, the children could ID him from a photograph.'

'If the psych team allowed us.'

'He doesn't know that.'

'What are you saying?'

'The only thing that can put our killer at the scene is the children. And the only other person who is linked to the case and to him is Lucy Steller. Fuck!'

'What?'

'He killed Capske out of spite, because he was jealous, because he was in love with Lucy Steller. He let himself make that mistake. That's why he called the press. He knew he had to try to put us off the scent. The other kills are random, perhaps linked to Section 88 and hate attacks, but David Capske was never attacked by Section 88. David isn't his victim type. David was an error, a personal vendetta. That's why he's taken Lucy. Our killer knew her. And she knew him.'

'Where are you going with this?' said Denise.

Harper stood up and took his coat. 'It's the only thing that makes sense. Lucy is the key to his identity. Lucy is personal. And that means you need to work harder than ever to find out who she went out with.'

'Okay, we can do it,' said Denise.

'It also means something else,' said Harper. 'It means that we've been searching for the wrong man.'

'What do you mean?'

'It's not Martin Heming. It makes no sense to take Lucy or to try to take the children if the killer is Heming. Our killer's identity is locked up in those three, but Sturbe is not Heming.'

'The profile never matched,' said Denise. 'We've been chasing the wrong guy.'

Chapter Ninety

Lock-Up, Bedford-Stuyvesant
March 14, 10.40 a.m.

He'd been working on the structure for hours and it was nearing completion. The two Flemish bond brick walls came out from the back of the workshop, forming a three-sided space. The walls turned into the fourth side at full height, stopped for a door and continued with a two-foot wall and space for a window. The operation at the vigil had given him all the confidence that he needed, but he wanted to see them die. He didn't want them to die in the dark. He needed to see the pain on their faces.

The fourth wall was fitted with a door that had special seals to ensure that no air could get in or out. The final piece of the fourth wall was about to be completed. Glass would have been perfect but it was too heavy and too expensive. He'd bought a single eight-foot by six-foot piece of clear Plexiglass and fitted it into the large window space. On the inner side, he had cemented security bars between the two walls. The Plexiglass was sealed into place, and then he added a further layer of bricks on the sides and bottom to add strength.

He stood back, looked at his creation and was pleased. He opened the door and walked in. The door shut into a wide jamb and was sealed on the outside by an old-fashioned set of bolts. Inside, the space was ten feet by ten feet. It was large enough to make a cell for a number of people. He looked up at the ceiling. The small inner room was still open to the roof.

He levered four strips of corrugated iron into place across two supports made of simple wooden planks. He drilled the iron into the wood and then bolted it together to form the roof.

He climbed up the ladder and on to the roof carrying a thick latex sealant and coated all the joints and bolts.

It had taken all morning and he sat with a take-out staring at his construction. He finally picked up his tubes. He would have two feeder tubes running from the roof of the inner building. He cut two holes in the roof and fixed-shower heads into the corrugated roof, then sealed the join and a joining piece to his tubes and ran them both across the roof, down each side of the building and around to a central unit made of an old plastic bin with a sealed lid.

He welded the tubes together, ensuring that they were fixed. Finally he joined both to the large plastic bin.

He inspected his finished cell. It was perfect. He had a chair, throne-like, positioned opposite the Plexiglass wall.

He took a red flare, lit it and placed it inside the room and locked the door. The room filled with thick red smoke and for a while all the smoke was contained within the room, but soon, several wisps started to escape through the joins in the brickwork. He walked around, carefully marking each leak with a spray can. When he had marked each space, he started to plaster each one with more sealant or mortar. As he sealed, the red smoke reduced until no more was escaping. His cell was airtight. That was vitally important.

He watched for thirty minutes and then, satisfied, opened the door to let the smoke dissipate. He walked outside into the yard, pulled his balaclava back on, opened the trunk of his car and looked down at Lucy.

Chapter Ninety-One

Apartment, Upper East Side
March 14, 11.18 a.m.

Harper had re-sent CSU to look for what they could at Lucy's apartment. If the killer had been a past boyfriend, then there might be other evidence. He now paced around her apartment, looking and desperately trying to work it out. Then there was a call from the hallway.

Harper found the CSU team dusting the linoleum just inside the door and taking pictures. 'What have you got?'

'We've found a print of a boot. The bastard tried to clean it, but rubber can't just be dusted off. It's left one or two marks.'

'Is it anything you can work on?' Harper asked.

'Sure it is,' said the Crime Scene detective. 'Look at this.' He crouched and shone his flashlight at the boot-print. 'See these marks of the sole? There's lots of small tears in the rubber. It's unusual. It would identify the boot, for sure. It's as good as a fingerprint.'

Harper stared at the small marks. 'I think I know what they are,' he said. 'Tears from barbed wire. The killer was rolling David Capske with his foot. Shit, he hasn't even changed his boots. That's how confident this guy is. It's nothing if we don't find the owner of that boot. How the hell do we do that?'

'It might not help you find him, but it'll help you *nail* him, Detective.'

'I just worked out why the killer called the networks,' said Harper. 'David Capske was personal. He realized he'd made a mistake. Jesus, we should've seen it. That's what felt so wrong about the whole political angle. It was fake, but it worked. We were sidelined – and he knew that we would be.'

Harper's cell buzzed. He picked it up.

'I've got good news,' said Denise.

'What is it? I need some good news.'

'We followed your suggestion and looked into Lucy's past. We found something.'

'A name?'

'No.'

'A picture?'

'No.'

'Then what?'

'Get back over here and we'll show you.'

Harper rushed into the investigation room. Denise and Gerry Ratten were hunched over a computer screen.

'What have you got for me?'

'Ratten has found something. Postings on the Internet by a girl called Lucy S.'

'Is this Lucy Steller?'

'These are posts from fourteen months ago. And our suspect wouldn't have known anything about them.'

'Why not?'

'She wrote them on a women's forum, a help group for victims of domestic violence. A place to talk, to get up the courage to report the bastards.'

'What makes you think it's her?'

'She says she's writing a book. Her name is Lucy S.'

'It's not enough,' said Harper.

'And she says there's a grocer's which she can see from her apartment window.'

'It wouldn't wash in court.'

'We've got evidence,' said Gerry Ratten.

'How the hell did you find it?'

'You got to know where to look,' said Gerry. 'I just got a warrant and got her ISP to release her IP address and browsing history.'

'They give you the websites?'

'Yeah. We saw where she'd visited. We tracked a lot of them. I got two interesting things. One, that she was seeing a man that she called X. Two, that he was beating on her. Three, that he was racist and four, that about a couple of weeks earlier, they'd gone on a road trip to Yellowstone Park together.'

'Why did she call him X?'

'It's a domestic violence forum,' said Denise. 'You're not allowed to name the bastards. That would be against the law.'

'Seriously?'

'Yeah, seriously. She made over four hundred posts over an eight-month period. Read some of the highlights.'

I am in an abusive relationship. My boyfriend does not let me go out or look at other men. He tries to make me admit that I have had an affair. He interrogates me for hours until I admit it, then he beats me.

X hit me twice today. Both times in the back. I don't know what to do.

He drinks and he rapes me sometimes, but I kid myself it's not rape, right?

X accused me of liking Jews too much and Blacks. It's only because I'm supposed to be going to a party tomorrow. He said I'm trying to undermine him. He says I'm a slut. I said that I wasn't. He gave me a black eye so I couldn't go to the party.

I'm a good girl today. Will I get high fives all round? I finally broke up with X. It wasn't as bad as I'd expected. He wasn't happy, but he didn't shout or scream. He just stared at me. Just stared and stared and didn't say a thing. Not a word. Not one single word.

I got home today. X was standing outside the building again. He looked okay, but he'd obviously been drinking. I can always tell. Then he ran at me and put his hands all over me. It was only when I got inside the door that I realized that I was smeared all over with blood. I don't even know where it came from.

Midnight. I woke up, he was at my bed. He was in my room, at my bedside. I screamed in terror. He pleaded with me to take him back. I would die if he came back. I can't take it. He tells me that if I report him, he'll make my life a living hell. It already is. Not one day goes by without phone calls or visits or one of his reports.

Harper read what he could. 'No names.'

'We can probably glean information, but it'll take time.'

'You mentioned Yellowstone,' said Harper.

'It's the one date-posted message that tells us where our killer was for a week last year.'

'That's worth following up. Okay,' said Harper. 'We've got to go through Lucy's whole electronic history. There'll be a connection. We find she uses a credit card in some hotel, then we check every other receipt. He's got to be there. He was with her for eight months, he can't hide that well.'

Chapter Ninety-Two

Lock-Up, Bedford-Stuyvesant
March 14, 12.43 p.m.

The food left out in front of the shed had attracted enough of the local homeless. Not people, but stray dogs. He sat on a high pallet overlooking them. They were frail and needy. He saw the one he wanted. A little beige-brown mutt, about two foot high with a white underbelly and a nice clean snout. It was probably a hybrid of a hybrid, not a pure gene in it.

He climbed down from the pallet, took a biscuit out of his pocket and threw it to the one he wanted. The little dog looked up with big brown eyes, full of expectation and gratefulness. He threw it another biscuit.

As he walked away, the little beige dog followed him. It wasn't fast or eager, it moved with a tentative stride. He took a third biscuit out of his pocket and held it out; this time, the dog walked across and took it from his hand.

He went inside the lock-up. The little dog followed. He shut the door. He heard Abby move in the small room behind the door. She would get her chance soon enough. The dog stopped and seemed to be aware that somehow it was no longer free. It looked at the door, at the man – and then another biscuit was thrown in its path and it forgot its instincts.

The dog looked up. A line of biscuits ran all the way across the room. It ate and moved and ate and moved, and before long, the small beige mutt was inside the room that the man had built.

The man closed the heavy acoustic door and bolted it. He

moved to the Plexiglass window and looked in. The mutt had eaten the rest of its biscuits and was looking up at the window.

The man watched for a minute; there was something appealing in the dog, in its lack of knowledge. He turned, put on large yellow gloves, and opened a big round can using an old-fashioned can-opener. He poured the blue pellets into the plastic bin and then sealed the lid.

He crossed eagerly to the window. The gas was odorless and colorless. He watched for a moment, but nothing seemed to happen. He waited and watched. The dog sat, wagged its tail and barked once.

He moved closer to the window. Then the dog's muzzle sniffed. The gas must have reached the ground level where the animal was.

The scene was unpleasant to watch, if one watched it emotionally. But if one used the scientific side of one's nature and observed the effect of the gas, rather than reacting to the perceived pain of the dog, it was fine. Lucy was tied in the chair staring at the window. She was not detached, but then again, she was not supposed to be. He wanted to see the fear in her eyes.

The dog barked, scratched, ran a small circle and jumped up at the window. It was in agonizing pain and showed every sign of terror. But within seven minutes, it was lying on its side, almost dead.

The man raised his hand and pressed his palm to the Plexiglass. The little beige-brown mutt was still and lifeless. A harsh lesson in trusting strangers, he thought, but his experiment had worked.

Chapter Ninety-Three

In the precinct, they reopened the cases: the brown, scratched case-files, the box-files of accumulated evidence, the database that Harper insisted on that hooked up every detail, to find links and matches. They looked back through each case slowly, letting their minds wander over the detail, trying to see what they'd overlooked. They had Lucy Steller's phone records, Internet records, credit-card statements, bank statements and everything else besides.

On the board in front of them they had a large eight-month calendar. Every call, receipt, purchase or interaction was noted by each date. They were piecing together her life story from Internet forums, relatives, friends and the accumulated electronic data.

After just a few hours, the eight-month period was beginning to fill out. Harper stared at the board. Every time he spotted a date where Lucy was with Mr X, he had his team cross-check each receipt.

Harper had the team bring in every person who knew Lucy Steller. The interview rooms were all full and the corridors outside were lined with people. Someone had to have seen Lucy with this man, but they'd been at it for hours already and not a soul had seen him.

Denise walked up to Harper. He was staring at the cases. He had put the picture of Abby side-by-side with Lucy. He could see something. A pattern. He looked from Abby to Lucy to Capske. There was something there. What was it that was nagging away in his head? Something connected them. He looked across at the kidnapping of the children. All the unanswered questions came at once. What was the blue eagle the kids saw on the killer? How did the killer sit for hours with Capske with no one bothering him? How did he know about the safe house?

Harper's mind clicked once, then twice. He saw a picture in his mind. He saw another. Some route through all these threads seemed to be forming, but he just couldn't quite catch it.

'The boot-print,' he called to Swanson. 'What did CSU say?'

'Nothing at all. It's just a boot-print. No matches on record.'

'Jesus Christ,' said Harper. 'Come on, something must break here. Eddie, anything from the interviews?'

'Nothing yet,' shouted Eddie, 'but we're trying.'

Everyone was silent, working the case, poring over and over every detail.

Denise raised her head. 'I've found nothing in any of Lucy's old journals, not one reference to his name or appearance.'

'Then we've really got nothing,' said Harper. He looked up and saw Heming's face staring out from one of the boards.

'Where did you disappear to, Heming?' said Harper. He stared at the pictures of Lucy and Abby. They might be both alive, somewhere out there, with a man intent on torturing and killing them. Harper looked up again at the board. Something was speaking to him, he just couldn't quite hear it.

Back at the start of it all, they still hadn't worked out how the killer had enticed David Capske to East Harlem. Maybe there was something in it. They'd made so many small discoveries – the whole Nazi story – but none of it led to the killer. They knew so much, but so little. Then something emerged. He hit the desk.

Denise looked across. 'What is it?'

'Your profile, Denise. Listen, I've had this feeling all along. This terrible feeling that he's always ahead of us, always in the know.'

'What are you saying?' said Denise.

Harper pulled out his shield and looked at it. 'Remember the bird of prey that Ruth Glass chose? A blue eagle. We thought it was the Eagle of the Third Reich, didn't we? We fell into that trap.

Listen, Denise, the killer took a big risk in taking those kids. I think they hold the key.'

'But they won't let us near them. You've no idea where they are.'

'Maybe they've already given us the answer,' said Harper.

'What do you mean?'

'The cop who came out of Lukanov's apartment. He fooled the detectives, right? And you know what else? I even think that's how he got away with staying so long at the bodies.'

'I don't follow,' said Denise.

'How the hell did he drive the Auxiliary truck to the heart of a police operation without impersonating a cop?'

'I still don't see what you're driving at.'

'I've got an idea.' He looked at Denise. 'Come with me.'

Chapter Ninety-Four

Lock-Up, Bedford-Stuyvesant
March 14, 4.43 p.m.

Lucy looked all around her. She was in a brick room with a barred window. She looked up at the ceiling. Four shower heads.

She knew enough about history to know that this was no shower. She looked out of the Plexiglass and saw the metal tubes leading to the bin. She had smelled the strange smell from inside the van. Almond.

Outside, in his antechamber, a man was sitting on a chair staring into the window. It was him. Someone she had known. Someone she had made a mistake about. An evil man. He was concentrating. He clenched his fists hard in their leather gloves.

He walked through to the next room. He didn't appear to want to look at her. He returned with a metal can and walked over to the plastic bucket. Lucy watched him, terror in her eyes. She placed both hands on the Plexiglass and hit hard.

He would not look at her. He took the new can and opened it. Poured the whole tube of Zyklon B pellets into the plastic bucket. Then he turned and stared at Lucy. All he had to do was open the channel.

She tried to recall events, but her mind wasn't functioning. He must have drugged her. She couldn't remember things in the right order. Lots of the last few hours were blank. She could remember further back. She was his girlfriend, the love of his life, his black-and-white happy ending, his meaning, his everything. Not someone else's.

He walked across to the cell and stared inside.

'You're going to die,' he said, and smiled. 'Once upon a time, you made me sane. Just the warm curl of your skin and the smell of your neck – that's all it took, and the hatred was a world away. You gave me redemption, Lucy, then you took it away.'

She stared up at him, the tape around her mouth preventing her from speaking, preventing her from pleading.

'You were more than my lover. You never understood that you were my antidote. You were my hope and you left me.'

He pressed his face against the Plexiglass. 'I have so much hate and anger inside me now, Lucy, that I can't get rid of it. I have killed because of you. Then I realized why you hated me. Because you want a Jew for your bed.' He reached out his hand. 'I still want you, but I hate myself for it. You excite and repulse me. I found someone who looked like you,' he said, through the Plexiglass, 'but she wasn't enough. She didn't feel like you, Lucy. She didn't have what you have. Her name is Abby. She was bigger than you, Lucy. I had to starve her just so I could feel her ribs like I could always feel yours.'

Lucy stared out, shocked and silent. She was going to die. She knew it with horrible certainty.

Chapter Ninety-Five

Central Park
March 14, 5.15 p.m.

Harper drove down the side of Central Park with Eddie and Denise in the car.

'Where are we going?' Denise asked.

'To test a theory.'

'What theory?'

'Just keep your mind open and try to think of what kind of person this could be.'

Harper turned off and parked in East Drive surrounded by trees. He got out of the car. 'Hear that?'

'No,' said Eddie.

Denise got out of the car too. 'Nice to hear some wildlife,' she said. 'It's been an intense few days.'

'So many birds in this little park. Makes you think.'

'About what?' said Eddie.

'Life,' said Harper. 'Makes you think about life.'

'What the hell is he on about?' said Eddie. 'We came to hear a theory.'

Harper took out his NYPD shield and opened it up. 'I needed to tell you this somewhere private. Away from the rest of the team. Away from all the cops we know and love.'

'What is it?'

'Look at my shield. What do you see?'

'A police number,' said Eddie.

'A gold emblem,' said Denise.

'And what's in the emblem?'

'An eagle,' said Denise. Her voice dropped. The sound of birdsong rose high above them.

They stopped. Denise and Kasper suddenly saw where Harper was going.

'When did it click?' said Denise.

'A few hours ago. I've just been turning every angle in my head, trying to see if I'm thinking straight.'

'And are you?'

'Yes. I'm sure of it. Think about it. It clicked for me with the children. I couldn't make it work out. How the hell did this killer lure Capske into East Harlem? How did he lure Becky Glass off a street into an alley? How the hell did he dare to sit with Capske all that time? He's a cop.'

'You can't be serious,' said Eddie. 'How the hell could this happen?'

'It's the only thing that pulls this all together. He knew the safe house, right? He knew how many people would be there. Christ, he even knew the weak point between shifts. He knows so much, it's the only possible answer.'

'You might be right,' said Denise.

'I've been thinking about Denise's psychological fingerprint all day. We've got a killer who is fixated on Lucy Steller, a non-Jewish girl. She throws him off. She gets together with a Jew. And this guy's got levels of anti-Semitic hatred so deep he's never really acknowledged them, and this is the trigger. She leaves him and he kills someone who looks like her. A Jew. Esther Haeber. Then he abducts a girl who looks very like her. Maybe to try to replace her. But he can't deal with the lover, David Capske. So he kills him, then tries to disguise it. And now he's in love with his own power.'

'Damn right,' said Denise. 'Lucy's the trigger. He starts to stalk her after she ends it, then he starts to hassle Jews, and blame them, then he kills one. He starts to let this fantasy grow.'

'Then, he joins Section 88,' said Harper. 'But never as a member like the rest. Why conceal his identity even then? Because it would show up. Because he knew, even then, back at the start of this. He's known all along. How to kill in different precincts, how to stage, how to keep Abby from being fully investigated.'

'How comes he used the same bullet and shit?' said Eddie.

'Some things he can't help,' said Denise. 'He's a narcissist. He believes he's ultimately powerful. The rituals he can't change. He wants to be known, they are part of this identity, a uniform so that he can express this self.'

Harper looked up to the sky. 'He needed a name that allowed him to hide his identity but also to display what he was.'

'Sturbe,' said Denise. 'A Nazi serial killer.'

'Exactly. He wears the name like a confession.'

'Meaning?' said Eddie.

'Meaning, people want to show what they've done, so he's wearing the badge – the serial-killer name. Like some sick joke.'

'It's unbelievable.'

They stared at each other, a horrible truth dawning. Harper looked from Denise to Eddie. 'Tell this to no one. Not another soul. If our killer is a cop, then we've got to stay one step ahead of him – and that means keeping our communication tight.'

'How do we find him?' asked Denise.

Harper smiled.

'What you got, Tom, what you thinking?'

'If it's a cop, then he's listening in. He's got access to case information. You know what we do?'

'No.'

'We use the same lure on him that he's used on others.'

'What's that?'

'The lure of authority.'

'How?'

Harper sat down on the hood of his car. 'We've got to frighten him into believing we do know his face or are about to. I guess that's what he did with Capske. I guess he had something to sell. I guess he told Capske that he wanted to put things in the past with Lucy. We do the same. We lure him to us.'

'What's the plan, big man?' said Eddie.

'We go back in. We claim we've found something. A roll of film

– that's it. A roll of film from Lucy Steller's apartment, dated according to her journal on some trip and labeled *Yellowstone*. It might be enough of the truth to get him interested.'

'Yeah,' said Eddie. 'She was a good photographer. Used 35mm film. She had lots of photographs of animals from that trip. No reason why there wasn't another film.'

Harper nodded. 'We make all this known, we send the film to the photographic lab, then we lie in wait. And then he'll come to us.'

Chapter Ninety-Six

North Manhattan Homicide
March 14, 8.33 p.m.

The plan had been set. They didn't even tell Lafayette the truth. They only wanted the three of them to know. Any more added extra layers of doubt. A single offhand word, the smallest indication that it was a fraud and they were dead in the water. And that meant Lucy and Abby were also dead.

The evidence was sealed in a brown paper evidence bag. Harper brought it into North Manhattan Homicide after a further visit to Lucy Steller's apartment.

He threw it down on the table and called to Denise, 'Hey, we've found something that might give up the clue to this boyfriend.'

'What have you got?' said Denise. The team listened in.

'We've got a roll of film. Lucy used an old 35mm camera. She liked to take shots. This is dated the last week of May last year – anything in the journals?'

Denise nodded and moved towards her desk. The other members of Blue Team started to draw in.

'What is it?' asked Garcia.

'Film from Lucy Steller's place. Dated. Could have shots of the killer,' said Harper.

'Jesus Christ,' said Garcia, 'and it's just been sitting there all this time.'

'Exactly.'

Denise rushed back over with an open journal. 'That's fantastic,' she said. 'Lucy spent the whole week with this guy in Yellowstone. This is dynamite.'

Harper banged the table. 'We might just have him. Let's get this down to the photographic lab, see if they can get us something.'

Harper made sure that the team spoke about the new evidence via email, radio and phone. He had no idea who the killer was or how and when he was listening, but things were getting increasingly tense so he presumed the killer had some direct line.

Harper, Kasper and Levene made their way down to the Forensic Unit's photography labs. They checked in the evidence and walked through the corridors.

'We need to stick with the evidence,' said Harper. 'If he comes, it has to be tonight. Tomorrow would be too late if we had the film.'

'What about me?' said Denise.

'I want you to sit in the parking lot, keep an eye on who's coming and going. Try to give us some warning.'

The three of them walked to the photographic lab and looked into the room. 'That's the in-tray over there,' said Harper. 'In thirty minutes that's where our lure will be sitting.'

Chapter Ninety-Seven

The killer threw open the door of the lock-up and went inside. Several dogs were around his feet. He stared into the cell where Lucy was lying and snarled, 'You hid things from me!'

Lucy turned and shivered. 'I didn't do anything on purpose,' she cried out.

The dogs ran into the room and darted up to the Plexiglass and the door of the cell. They could smell the new intruder and sense their master's anger. The killer crossed to the cell and smashed the Plexiglass with his fist. 'Think, Lucy, or I'll cut your veins and let these dogs in.'

'Think about what?'

'*Me*, Lucy – images, pictures, videos of *me*.'

'I . . . there weren't . . . you made me destroy them.'

'I thought I did, but you lied – you had more.'

'No.'

'Think, Lucy. You have three minutes to let me know what was on that film.'

'What film?'

'Yellowstone. Our trip. What was on that film.'

'I . . .'

'Three minutes.'

The killer left and the dogs continued to circle and bark and jump up against her cell.

A moment later, he returned with a large package. He heaved it into the corner. It was a white powder. A chemical with a big hazard sign emblazoned on the side.

'This is going to end badly, Lucy,' he shouted. 'They think they've got me cornered, but I've got something in store for them.'

'What is it?'

'Ammonium nitrate, Lucy.'

'What for?'

'You'll find out one way or another.'

The killer left again and returned with another sack of the same white granules. He hauled it across to the corner. Lucy was staring, petrified. He left again and returned with two bags of nails and threw them on the ground next to the sacks.

'I didn't take any pictures of you. You didn't allow me.'

'Secret pictures, Lucy. Did you take any secret pictures?'

'Only pictures of the park, and the marmoset and the moose. Not you. I promise.'

'Not good enough. One minute and they'll eat you alive.'

The killer brought in two three-foot pipes that had been sawn down. He threw them to the side, then shut the door.

'Things are changing quickly, Lucy. The world is changing quickly too. It's not enough to live, you have to make a difference, leave a legacy. I could've gone on for years, but things change. They want this to end badly? Well, that's what it's going to do.'

'I can't help,' she said.

The killer marched across to the door and grabbed a large German Shepherd by the scruff of its neck.

'Let's see how honest you're being.' He opened the bolt and entered the cell. The dog saw Lucy. She was weeping and crying and shaking. The German Shepherd barked and bared its teeth.

The killer kicked the door shut and moved across, holding the dog firmly. 'Now, Lucy, what was on that film?'

He moved the dog's snapping jaw close to Lucy's face. The teeth flashed and the bark was high and persistent. She shook and held her hands to her ears.

'You!' she shouted. 'A picture of you!'

The killer moved back. 'You were always a liar and a coward.

What faith did you ever show me? None. I loved you so much and you gave me nothing, and now this. You betray me to the cops.'

'I didn't do anything on purpose. I really don't know. I really don't.'

'It's over now,' he said. 'It's all going to change. It's going to be big. It's going to change the world for good.'

Chapter Ninety-Eight

Photography Labs, Manhattan
March 15, 2.15 a.m.

The CSU photography lab was built of slabs of cinder block which were painted black. Rows of computers ranged one wall, while the rest of the room was lined with different lenses, enlargers and projectors. To the right, a room with a red light held the developing lab.

The majority of photographic work undertaken by the team was digital. Fewer and fewer jobs involved film, and when they did, the team soon uploaded the pictures on to a screen to enlarge and manipulate.

Still, most cops liked big glossy prints and the unit processed hundreds of prints each day, collecting the vast array of disturbing images from crime scenes across the city and sending out prints for the files.

The analysis work was complicated too. Working out locations from the merest details or the time of day from the detail of a single shadow. It was a busy, round-the-clock office except for now.

The last of the team had clocked off at 11 p.m., leaving Harper and Kasper alone. As agreed, Denise was stationed outside in a car.

Inside the building, the corridors went quiet. The night lights flickered on, providing just enough light to allow the security guards to walk the long tour of duty through the facility. The security guards were still patrolling, but tonight they had been told to leave any lone intruder to Harper and Kasper.

Harper had placed the package on the counter by the far wall.

He figured that the killer would see it from the corridor, through the big plate-glass window. But to put his hands on it, he would have to walk into the lab and past the three-tier shelving units.

Behind the first unit, Harper was sitting with his gun on the shelf. He had moved the boxes and books to give him a vantage point. Kasper was on the opposite side of the room. They could just about see each other to signal.

They waited, sitting on uncomfortable boxes, listening out and wondering if their plan would work.

Harper hunkered down, his eyes peering out through the shelves, his phone on vibrate.

He called Denise.

'How's it looking out there?'

'It's all dead quiet. There's a beautiful moon in the sky.'

'I've got a view of a dim corridor, want to swap?'

'No, I've never much liked waiting for serial killers.'

'It never improves,' said Harper.

'How's Eddie?'

'He's fallen asleep twice.'

'Nice to know he's relaxed.'

'He would sleep on Death Row.'

Denise stopped. She turned her head. 'I can hear something.'

'What is it?'

Denise listened. There was a faint sound. A car somewhere in the distance. Perhaps it was rolling towards her, perhaps it was a street further along. Then in the distance, she spotted headlights.

'We've got a car heading our way.'

'Type?'

'Difficult to tell. Going slowly. Engine's hardly audible.'

'Okay, slip out of sight, we don't want him to spot you.'

'I'm way off the lot, so we should be fine,' said Denise. She looked out at the car. 'The car's stopped quite a way up the drive.'

'Can you make the car out or the plate?'

'Can't see any detail.'

Harper checked his gun automatically and called across to Eddie: 'We've got a visitor.'

Denise watched closely. The car was parked along the dark driveway. She saw the door open and someone get out. They went around to the back of the car, opened the trunk and took something out.

'What's going on?' said Harper.

'One guy. He's taken something from the trunk. He's not coming my way. He's walking across the lawn to the side of the building.'

'He's probably going for the back entrance,' said Harper. 'Let us know if you see anything else.'

Denise agreed and hung up. She stared out. The car was still, the lights out, and the figure disappeared around the side of the building.

Chapter Ninety-Nine

Forty minutes of silence. Lucy counted it by the minute. She had heard the door shut and the dogs yap around him, but she waited forty minutes until she dared stand up.

Her legs felt tired as she stood. She looked out through the Plexiglass at a small garage. She stared open-mouthed at the sight that met her eyes. A large Nazi flag against the wall and a desk with a typewriter and Nazi memorabilia all around. A map of Manhattan had been stuck to the wall. The madman had drawn thick lines around the Jewish areas as if creating his own twenty-first-century ghetto.

Lucy tried to think back to the man she'd met. He'd seemed so normal, so kind at the start. But it hadn't lasted. He started to get possessive almost within the first week. Just the smallest sign, here and there. Not aggressive at that point, but he was just too interested in what she did when she wasn't with him.

It took two months for it to flourish into an all-out obsession. He said he loved her and wanted to understand her. He was obsessed by Jews from the start, as if they possessed something he never could. What was it? Belonging? That's why he wanted to possess her, body, mind and soul. Possess her and control her.

She stared at the tubes leading from the roof of the homemade cell to a structure on the other side of the room. She didn't want to think about it any more. He had lost his mind. He had turned crazy when she rejected him. But she didn't know what else to do. He had wanted her to never go out. He had wanted her to submit herself entirely to him. He had wanted her to clean his boots to prove her subservience.

She said no. And then he stalked her. She had been scared but thought it would just pass. Lucy's eyes moved around the room. It hadn't passed. His obsession had deepened. She wondered if he had been indulging in these fascist fantasies the whole time they were together. She thought back, remembered things they'd done. Her body convulsed with horror and disgust, as she began to realize that she had always been some puppet with which he was playing games of lust and disgust. To which he was as repulsed as he was attracted.

Lucy understood the Nazi images. The powerful confident black and red insignia was a way of controlling and dominating human fear and resentment, and trying to make the revulsion and attraction – the full neurosis – into something meaningful and ordered.

Her eyes moved across to another door. It was the door to a closet. Lucy remembered what he had said about a girl called Abby. She had read about the missing girl. She'd been missing for days already. Lucy's eyes widened. It seemed so much worse to her that another human being was caught and imprisoned. Her heart welled up and her hand moved instinctively over her mouth. Abby might be there, a few yards away. Abby might already be dead.

Lucy moved as close as she could to the door; she scraped her mouth and teeth against the wall until the duct tape pulled away, then she called out, 'Abby.' And she kept calling over and over again, terrified by the silence that came from the closed door.

Chapter One Hundred

Photography Labs, Manhattan
March 15, 3.55 a.m.

For nearly two hours, Harper and Kasper had been sitting tense and ready, but no one came. Harper called Denise to ask for an update. 'We've got nothing down here,' he whispered. 'Anything happening?'

'No one's come in or gone out.'

'Maybe he's waiting for the security guard's shift to change.'

'I don't know,' said Denise.

Eddie suddenly signaled across the counter. Harper looked across. Eddie's gun pointed into the corridor. Harper turned. A single flashlight streaked across the hallway.

'He's here,' whispered Harper. He lifted his gun to shoulder height. The beam flickered across the corridor from the ceiling to the floor. Someone was walking towards the room.

The plan was simple. *Catch the killer and don't kill him.* If they killed him, it would mean they might never find Lucy and Abby. And if they felt it wasn't safe to arrest him, they had to wound him.

Inside the room, they couldn't hear footsteps from the corridor, but the beam of light grew until it stopped at the glass door to the photography lab. The light turned towards them and hovered over the shelves. Harper held his breath. The light moved slowly around the room, then disappeared and the sound of the handle turning seemed to slow time.

The door opened with a low squeak and the light beam returned. Harper stared across at Eddie.

The figure moved towards the counter, paused and scanned his flashlight across the room.

Chapter One Hundred and One

Lock-Up, Bedford-Stuyvesant
March 15, 4.18 a.m.

Abby opened her eyes. She had been in the tiny cell for so long, fighting in her mind, but the starvation was sapping her will. She was feeling so weak that her head felt too heavy to lift, but something had pulled her back from her dreams. The food had stopped altogether, along with the water. Every few hours, she fell into some deep sleep; perhaps it was even unconsciousness. Her dreams raged and tormented her. The silver-blue lines of ocean waves were infested with snakes; her tongue seemed to swell so large in her mouth that she couldn't breathe or swallow.

'Abby!' She heard it again. It was a soft voice. A woman's voice, but not like a real voice, probably a voice from her dreams, hidden somewhere within her subconscious. But her eyes were open. She scratched her leg and the pain felt real. Her eyes lifted and there on the wall were the marks that she'd made with her restraints. If she was awake, then the voice wasn't imagined.

'Abby!'

Abby tried to speak, but her throat was dry. A low croak stretched her mouth and her lips cracked. She tasted blood on the tip of her tongue and started to suck on it. She tried again to speak, but only a low whisper came out. She felt herself start to heave with frustration and cry in dry, waterless sobs.

She heard her voice called out again and turned to her right. Her knee rapped hard against the door. She twisted herself again and again, the sound reverberating. Outside, the voice stopped as she continued to knock against the door with her knee. Then she stopped knocking and waited. It had been days and days since she had communicated with anything or anyone. Only a monster.

'I can hear you,' said the voice. 'Maybe you can't speak. Maybe he has gagged you. I'm Lucy. I'm in another cell, only a few yards from your door. I hope you're okay. You're Abby, aren't you? The high-school girl? Your mom and dad are still hoping. I saw them on the news. They're holding up okay.'

Inside the cell, Abby listened, and though they were only words, she felt as if she was being given a long drink. She wanted to speak out, but at first her words came out light and airy like feathers, so at each pause she knocked and when the voice stopped, she knocked and knocked and knocked until the voice started to speak again.

Finally, Abby pushed herself upright. She breathed deeply and called out, 'I'm here. I'm Abby.'

'God bless you,' said Lucy. 'You okay?'

'Yes, but need water.'

'Is there any way we can get out of here?'

'I don't think so,' said Abby. 'I really don't think so.'

Chapter One Hundred and Two

Photography Labs, Manhattan
March 15, 4.23 a.m.

The figure at the bench stopped and started to turn. There was no time left. Harper was already two paces across the room, his body charging towards the bench. Kasper jumped to his feet from the side. The figure turned to Eddie Kasper and as he did, the full weight of Harper's charge landed heavily on his side, throwing him to the ground.

Harper fell on top of him and they tumbled twice across the floor. The suspect shouted something, but Harper's arm was already around his neck pulling hard and Eddie Kasper already had the suspect's gun.

As Harper's arm jammed hard into the suspect's neck, the figure stopped fighting and lay still. Eddie Kasper flicked on the lights.

He looked down at the red face of the man on the ground. 'Fuck you!' the man shouted. Eddie looked away. Harper pushed the figure off him and stood up.

'We fucking cleared this with security,' said Harper. 'No one comes this way tonight.'

'You fucking animals,' said the guard, standing and brushing himself down. 'Animals.'

'What the hell happened?' demanded Harper. 'We could've killed you.'

'I got told to come here, do a sweep.'

'This is bad news,' said Harper. 'Who told you?'

'One of your guys.'

'What do you mean, one of our guys?'

'Cop. He had a badge. Said he was on the stake-out.'

'What did he look like?'

'Like a cop – big, arrogant, impatient and ugly.'

'Where?'

'He came by the security door.'

Harper and Eddie looked at each other.

'How long ago?'

'I don't know, ten minutes?'

Harper looked around. He spoke quietly: 'The killer knows we're here now, but he's still going to want those prints.'

'How the hell did he know we were on a stake-out?'

'He's not just a cop, is he? He's a fucking smart cop.'

A second later, the lights flickered and then died. Harper pulled Eddie to one side. 'He's going to try to take them – get out of the line of fire.'

In the darkness, they heard a key in the door to the room. 'He's locking us in,' shouted Harper. 'Do you have a key?'

'Sure,' said the security guard, but there wasn't any time. Something smashed the window of the door and a lighted bottle flew in the room. It shattered over the floor and the contents exploded into flame. Harper and Eddie jumped.

'What the fuck do we do?'

'Is there a sprinkler system?' said Harper.

'Sure, in the corridor, but not in the photography lab.'

Harper ran towards the door as the flames spread and caught the wood of the benches and the books and files.

The security guard moved to the door and tried his key. 'Shit, he's broken his key in the lock.'

Harper's flashlight picked out the jagged edges of the door windows. It was too small to get through. Eddie moved across, holding his mouth as the thick black smoke started to rise and fill the room. He stumbled against the broken glass, his hand sliced across. 'I'm cut, Harper.'

'We got to get out of here,' said Harper. 'Get you some help.'

The smoke was filling the room. Harper took his Glock and pumped three bullets into the lock mechanism, then kicked the door open. He rolled into the corridor, his gun in one hand, his flashlight in the other. 'All clear,' he shouted.

The security guard led them as quickly as they could through the dark corridors. He pressed the alarm on the wall and the sprinkler system kicked in. Somewhere down the corridors, they could hear a door slamming. The killer was ahead, but not far.

'Is there a quicker way out of here?' asked Harper.

'Not unless you just burst out through the windows.'

'Which windows?' said Harper.

The security guard moved across to a door and opened it. The room was illuminated by the faint moonlight from outside. 'Gotcha,' said Harper. 'Get an ambulance, Eddie.'

'I got to come with you,' said Eddie.

'You'll slow me down,' said Harper, then he ran at the window, shot once and watched the plate-glass shatter and fall. He leaped on to the bench and out of the window.

A figure was moving quickly across the ground, towards a car. Harper sighted him and shot twice. The shots missed and Harper sprinted towards the car. The figure jumped in and the car's engine rumbled to life. Harper shot again and hit a side window. The car didn't make a U-turn as expected, it turned to the right and Harper heard the sound of its undercarriage screech and scrape on the concrete edge of the lawn. The headlights rose across the ground and Harper was suddenly illuminated in a wide patch of grass with no hiding place.

The car started to gain speed, the bumps in the ground making it lift and lurch left to right. It was a hundred yards away and gaining fast. Harper had no time to run; he stood firm and put his gun hand out, steadying it with the other. Shooting someone dead through the windshield of a car that was traveling at speed was hard enough; with the tension and the darkness it was ten times more difficult.

He waited as the car approached. He had one chance and had

to leave it as late as possible. Harper counted down. At two seconds he would shoot to the right side of the driver and jump to his left.

His finger pressed. Three seconds. He was blinded now by the headlights, by the roar of the engine. Two seconds. He shot twice and threw himself to the left. The car veered right and clipped Harper's feet as he was moving through the air.

Harper turned, his gun pointing as the car drove on a few more seconds, then stopped. Harper exhaled. He'd hit him. The killer was down.

Harper scrambled to his feet and moved cautiously towards the car. He peered into the darkness, but through the shattered windshield he couldn't see a thing. He moved round to the driver's side. There was a body leaning against the door. He could just make out the trickle of blood from a wound on the side of the head. Harper pulled open the door. Then a gunshot rang out from inside the car. Harper was thrown backwards and the dead driver was pushed out on top of him.

A masked face glanced across. The killer moved across to the driver's seat and drove the car away.

'Two of them,' said Harper. 'There were two of them.' He shoved the dead weight off him, stood up and turned over the body at his feet.

Martin Heming's grimace and wide eyes stared back at him.

Chapter One Hundred and Three

Photography Labs, Manhattan
March 15, 4.53 a.m.

Harper ran across the open ground and reached Denise in the car. He was breathing deeply. 'We got to follow that car.'

'Yes – are you all right?'

'I'm okay. What the hell happened?' said Tom.

'I don't know,' said Denise. 'They must have dropped one guy off earlier. One guy came out, then the second guy came out a couple of minutes later – the one you shot at.'

'Let's follow,' said Harper. 'We've got to get this killer.'

'Where's Eddie?'

'He got hurt.'

'Bad?'

'I hope not. He's okay, I think.'

Denise drove off.

'Did you get the plates?' Harper asked.

'Sure, here.' Denise tossed him a notebook. They could see the tail lights up ahead. Harper called base and put out an APB on the license-plate.

'It was Martin Heming,' said Harper.

'Heming?'

'The guy on the grass. He's dead. I don't fully understand his involvement yet. We got a lot of working out to do. He wasn't involved in the killings. There was only one guy at the Capske scene and the Glass scene. Heming might have been helping him. Or maybe the killer was blackmailing him, who knows?'

They drove in silence, Harper trying to keep focused on the tail lights ahead. 'He's heading into Brooklyn,' he said.

'Abby and Lucy are in danger,' said Denise. 'If he's panicking, he could do anything. We can't lose him.'

'That's right,' said Harper. 'So put your foot down.'

They drove over the bridge and into Brooklyn. The car they were following headed into the area called Bedford-Stuyvesant. Harper watched the car slow ahead. Then it turned.

'I think we've found his lair,' said Harper.

'You think we should call for backup?'

'Yes, but we can't wait for it. We've got to get Lucy and Abby out of there now.'

They turned the final corner and saw a long alley. The car had vanished. They drove on, then turned and circled, but the car was nowhere to be seen.

'What now?' said Denise.

'Now,' said Harper, 'we try to find him again. We've lost him. I'll call Patrol, get this area saturated.' Harper shook his head. 'Shit. How the hell did he slip away? We almost had the bastard.'

Chapter One Hundred and Four

The killer entered the lock-up and slammed the door. He was sweating; it had been a very close call. Too close. They had nearly caught him. Time was short now. There was nothing else to do. His final plan had to be actioned. Ahead of him, Lucy stared out of her Plexiglass and brick prison. His shirt was covered with pieces of glass and his face was bright red.

He stood for a moment, shaking, unable to move; his rage was burning him up inside. He moved across to his desk and violently swept everything aside. The typewriter and papers and Nazi medals cascaded to the floor. Then he turned. He stared at Lucy. She was the origin. He picked up the typewriter and threw it across the room. It hit the Plexiglass and rebounded on to the floor.

He turned away, running his fingers through his hair. Across the room, he had written the eighty-eight words that once upon a time had meant so much.

There was nothing else left now. There was no need to wait, no need to hide, no need to keep Lucy or Abby alive. They were closing in on him. He felt the noose tightening. He had to destroy them, pack up, and then make his final point.

Heming was dead but it didn't matter. The man was expendable. He had come across Heming when he needed help, when he had needed Section 88 to help hurt and destroy.

He had big plans now and he'd have to carry them out alone. Karl Leer had got him another old truck. It was an orange Dodge and it was waiting outside.

It would be just like it was in the book about Sturbe. The book that he had devoured, that had incited him and made him feel that he also had the power to turn all that feeling of being bullied and broken into revenge – not against his attackers, but against those that they attacked too.

Sturbe had come alive in his mind. He was like a father to him. A guiding light. When the Jews tried to resist, in the Warsaw Ghetto, German troops destroyed the synagogue. A final symbolic gesture. He would do the same.

He turned to Lucy. The time had come. They all had to die. He had to die too. No question, no question at all. It was only a matter of when.

He opened the door to Abby's closet, pulled her out forcibly and dragged her to her feet.

She was weak but she screamed her lungs out in a hoarse voice. The killer held her neck and squeezed, watching the pain cross her face. Lucy banged frantically on the Plexiglass. She howled at him to stop.

He stared at Abby with grim satisfaction before pulling open the door of his gas chamber and throwing her inside as Lucy raced at him, trying to reach the door before he slammed it shut and bolted it.

He stood staring at them, breathing deeply. He wasn't sure any more if it was real or a game. He felt the emotion welling up in his chest. He had to be strong to the end.

He moved across to the canister of Zyklon B and saw the reaction in the gas chamber, as blind panic spread over the faces of Abby and Lucy and they began screaming and hitting the Plexiglass. He would not kill them yet, he decided. They would be last. First, he had to make sure of something. Everything was a battle and this one he wanted to win.

Chapter One Hundred and Five

The Brooklyn Library
March 15, 7.05 a.m.

'Lafayette, it's Harper. We lost the killer. We chased him to Bed-Stuy and he disappeared. Eddie's in the hospital – he'll tell you everything.'

Lafayette was pacing his room. 'Shootings at the Forensic Unit, Harper? An operation I knew nothing about? Is this right what I'm hearing? I'm telling you, get back here now.'

'I can't. He's going to do something. He's taking big risks. He's feeling the pressure. You've got to let me do what I can to try to find him.'

'The Chief of Detectives has called me in, Harper. You know what he's saying? I've fucked up. I can't lead my men. And you, Harper, you've let this case run away with you.'

'I'd like to listen to the lecture, Captain, but I'm running out of time.'

'Don't you dare hang up. I'll have you on a charge, Harper.'

'Then I can't come in until this is finished, you understand.' Harper hung up and turned to Denise. 'This has to work. We've got to find out who this killer is.'

'No one knows if it will or won't help, but Aaron has been working through the library stacks. He thinks it's the only link.'

'What's he got?'

'Just like we said – the book on Sturbe was in very few libraries.

He know our killer is local, so we can presume his local library was in Brooklyn. Only one Brooklyn library held his book.'

'And this is it?' said Harper, looking up at the dark Gothic façade.

'Dr Goldenberg's already inside. We had to get the librarian to come in and open specially for us.'

'I'll leave you here,' said Harper. 'I'm going to see Eddie and then I'm going to see if those patrol cops got any leads in Bed-Stuy. If there's nothing, I'll be talking to the agents selling Nazi memorabilia, see if they got me anything. Call me.'

Aaron Goldenberg brushed a thick layer of dust off an old volume. His face was growing more drawn each day. Denise put her hand out and touched his arm. 'She'll be okay.'

'She's been missing so long. Be honest with me, Denise, what are her chances?'

'We got to keep trying, got to keep believing that she's still alive.'

'I will try,' he said. He looked around the room. 'I spend a lot of time here.'

'Studying?'

'Now, yes, but as a kid I didn't study much. Like Abby. She's lazy too.'

'Didn't think of you as the rebel type.'

He took out his reading glasses and put them on, then he walked along the stacks, saying, 'Come on, let's be quick. Abby's out there, right? The answer's in here, yes?'

Denise saw a long line of old filing cabinets. 'Yes, Aaron. In here. We just got to find it. You go that way, I'll see if they've got a catalog.'

'Sure,' he said, 'but it won't necessarily lead you to the book.'

'It doesn't need to, does it?'

'Guess not.' Aaron Goldenberg moved slowly down each aisle, moving his eyes up and down the rows. He knew the numbering system. 'They never moved to Dewey. They never liked Dewey.'

'And why's that?'

'Stupid system.'

'Really?'

'No. Dewey set up a club. It excluded Jews. Hard to swallow.'

'The truth often is,' said Denise. She located the catalog. 'These aren't in title or author order. What do I look for?'

'Depends.'

'On what?'

'On the judgment of the librarian. Sturbe's story could come under a number of headings. Biography, Military History, Holocaust, Infamous Jews, Criminal Minds.'

'Great.'

'You just have to use your instinct. If it was here, it'll be in the catalog. I never knew the book. Not my thing as a boy.'

'What was your thing? Rabbinical texts? Kabbalah?'

'You have me down as an academic, Dr Levene.'

'You are, aren't you?'

'I am now. Back then, no. Back then I liked Harold Robbins.'

'Seriously?'

Aaron nodded. 'I hid his books in Rabbinical texts.' His face creased. Every few minutes she could see the horrible thoughts crossing his mind. He was trying to keep himself together, but it wasn't easy. He was tortured by the imaginings that he couldn't keep from appearing

Denise felt his pain. She knelt by the side of the first filing cabinet and pulled out the old metal drawers. The whiff of mold and mildew mixed with the puff of fungus dust. She leaned back. 'I'll start with Biography.'

'Please do,' said Aaron.

Silence fell in the room. Aaron's slow footsteps continued to move along each shelf, and Denise's search was punctuated by the squeal of old runners. She flicked through the old cards, her eyes looking for the single word. *Sturbe*. He wasn't in Biography, or under Criminal Minds, or under Holocaust. Denise shut the drawer. 'There's only a dozen entries under Holocaust.'

Aaron stopped and looked up. 'Holocaust. Yes. Specifically

titles addressing the generic topic. Anything else will be under a more specific title.'

Denise looked down the letters on the front of the cabinets.

She thought about Tom Harper and looked at her watch. He'd be wanting a call by now.

Her eyes stopped on the 'W'. She opened the drawer and flicked the files forward. She stopped at *Warsaw*.

'Aaron,' she called out. 'She filed it under the Warsaw Ghetto.'

Aaron moved quickly towards her, with his face full of expectation. 'You found it! Come on, Denise. We've got to be quick.'

Denise held up the card. *Sturbe: The Story of a Jew* by Malachai Jiresh. The writing was on a pink card that had faded all along the top edge. The typing was old and in two colors, half blue, half red with some letters light on the page. She handed it to Aaron.

'I didn't think we'd find it,' he said. Tears would've come, but he shook his head. He let the feelings turn hard and tried to focus his mind. He looked at the number.

'H.831.33.2,' he repeated.

Denise and Aaron ran back up the stairs. 'You don't want to find the book?' she asked.

'I want the bastard's name, not the book,' he panted.

'I understand,' said Denise.

They rose up the wooden stairs and into the light.

Denise approached the desk. The library wasn't open but she saw the bright-eyed woman who'd helped get them access to the archives. 'We found the reference.'

'Well, then,' said the woman, 'if you've got the book number, I'll see what I can get you.'

The woman disappeared. Thirty minutes later she came back. 'It's not good, I'm afraid. I'm sorry.'

'What? It's not there?' said Aaron.

'No, please, come this way.'

Denise and Aaron followed her down a long corridor. 'I had hoped that the records would have been put in some order.' She opened the door marked *Archive* to reveal shelves of old ledgers.

'Even for her day, the librarian was an old-fashioned woman, but fastidious. Once you have the reader, you can look through the reader cards and find the whole of his or her reader history. But without a name . . .'

'Can we set ourselves up in here?' Denise asked.

'Sure, please do. I'm sorry it's not any easier.'

The door closed. Denise and Aaron stared at the rows of books. Aaron pulled one out. He opened it. 'All handwritten. There's a lot of borrowing. We're never going to be able to find him.'

'We will. Let's just try to narrow it down to some dates.'

'How?'

'A ten-year slot. He's in his thirties. He might have started this as a teenager. So, let's say he's thirty-five. Twenty years ago he's fifteen. About the right age, give or take a couple of years. We can go five years either side of thirty-five. So let's start in 1990. You go five years forward, I'll go five years back.'

'I don't understand your logic, Denise, but it's a plan.'

Chapter One Hundred and Six

Lock-Up, Bedford Stuyvesant
March 15, 7.35 a.m.

Abby pulled herself up slowly and stared out. 'We can't sit here like victims. We've got to do something.'

'No.'

'You've got to help, Lucy,' said Abby, straining with each word. 'You know him. What makes him tick?'

'He doesn't like women.'

'Or Jews. He wants me to reject my Jewishness. Why should that matter to him?'

Lucy pushed herself against the brick wall. 'He's Jewish, Abby.'

'No,' she said. 'He can't be. That's . . . Come on, Lucy, help me. I need something. I feel so weak. Please.'

'He's a cop. Did you know that?'

'Then he'll kill us.' Abby felt her legs aching and she stumbled against the wall and fell to the ground. Since getting out of her tiny cell, she wanted to walk, to feel her limbs again, but she couldn't. She didn't have the strength. She looked up at the shower heads.

'He's made a gas chamber. He's Jewish? I can't understand it.'

'He was adopted. His mother was Jewish, I think, and he was adopted by a Christian family. I think his mother was a prostitute, but I don't know. I don't know if he knows. He wanted to find her as a kid, as he was growing up, as he was feeling different, but he couldn't trace her. He was adopted when he was five. He loved her, you know. Guess she didn't love him back.'

'Did they mistreat him?'

'I guess they did. Not like you'd call social services,' said Lucy. 'They just weren't kind to him.'

'That's it?'

'I don't know.'

'What about his father and the shoes in the cellar?'

'He didn't have a cellar. I don't think it's his story.'

'Then what's his problem?'

'He's sensitive, I don't think he was ever loved. I don't think he could belong. Other kids knew he was Jewish – he was bullied and all that – but he wouldn't talk about it. He won't talk about anything that makes him feel weak.'

'He hurt you?' said Abby.

'To some men, Abby, a woman constantly makes them feel weak. He needed me and hated it. He hated my existence. Look – I'm not a psychiatrist.'

'He joined the cops because he wanted to exert power,' said Abby.

'Probably,' said Lucy.

'Is there anything that you can remember? Anything that might help us?'

Lucy stared blankly ahead.

Abby waited but nothing came. She walked around the walls, pushing at every brick, looking for a weak point. 'I'm not going to die like this, Lucy. You got to fucking think.' She looked at Lucy, who was crying. Abby stood over her. 'Quit it!' she rasped. 'Just fucking quit it.'

Lucy looked up, surprised and upset.

'I want you to *think*, Lucy. We need something to get this bastard to think twice, or to pull back. What does he want, Lucy? What does he really want?'

Lucy closed her eyes. 'He always said he wanted to find his mom. He imagined that she'd be proud of him. A cop. A detective. Big and strong.'

407

'Well, she's not going to be proud of this fucking get-up, is she? Nazi crap. He's like a child, playing games. I don't know if it's real. You look at his eyes and they're empty.'

'I'll try to think of something,' said Lucy.

Abby paused. She stared out at the Nazi flag. He had become the worst thing he could become. 'You don't need to think of something,' she said. 'I think you already did.'

Chapter One Hundred and Seven

Brooklyn
March 15, 9.05 a.m.

Harper stood outside the home of Martin Heming and stared at the street. What had they missed? He had nothing from the research on the memorabilia. He walked down the rundown street, looking for a clue as to why these people formed their sick little hate groups. As he reached the subway, he got a call from the Hate Crime Unit.

'It's Jack here. How are you, Harper?'

'I'm out on a limb, Jack. I guess you heard about the operation.'

'I'm down with Heming's body now. I heard all right. We're hoping there's something on him.'

'Been there already, I got nothing. Shit, Jack, I went out without authorization last night.'

'You got to do what you got to do.'

'That's okay if it works,' said Harper. 'But if it doesn't?'

'You got Heming, that's got to weaken the killer's position.'

'That's true.'

'No right-hand man to help him out.'

'No.'

'Did you see the other guy? See anything at all?'

'No,' said Harper. 'I got nothing.'

Carney's voice lowered slightly. 'Listen, Harper, don't get all fucked up. You tried to find something on Heming. After you left, they did get something. He had a cell phone without a SIM card, right?'

'That's right.'

'We found the SIM card.'

'Where was it?'

'In his right sock.'

'Shit, does it tell you anything?'

'I think we might have something here, yes.'

'What have you got?'

'Heming is the key to finding the killer,' said Carney.

'And Lucy and Abby,' said Harper.

'Well, Heming must've been with the killer, with him in his lair, right?'

'Right.'

'With the SIM we can see who he called. We can even get a location on the phone's position. We can locate where he was when he made the calls.'

'That's fucking great, Jack. What have you got?'

'We've got several locations, but the most promising is a set of garages. I'm heading over now to do a drive-by and a little surveillance. You in?'

'We should get Blue Team and SWAT.'

'You *are* Blue Team, Harper. We've got the Hate Crime Unit, so we're not alone. But we can't be sure he was with the killer, so let's take a look at this before we call in the cavalry. You don't want another botch-up, do you? And I certainly don't.'

'What's the address?'

Carney gave him the street name. 'There is no number for the garages. It's just a row of dilapidated real estate. There's a garage on the corner, we're going to meet up there and see how the land lies.'

'I'll be there,' said Harper.

Chapter One Hundred and Eight

The Brooklyn Library
March 15, 9.09 a.m.

Denise and Aaron Goldenberg sat side by side at two large oak tables. Each of them had the handwritten ledgers for a five-year period. They were flicking through at a pace, their fingers sliding down the pages. All they needed to find was the name of someone who had borrowed the book on Josef Sturbe and this could lead them to Abby, to saving Abby. It wouldn't be conclusive, but it might give the investigation something.

Denise saw the name *Josef Sturbe* on the page. She felt herself tingle. 'I've got one here,' she called out.

'Who is it?' said Aaron Goldenberg.

'Her name's Hannah Sternberg.'

'Age?'

'I need to check her reading card.' Denise crossed to the large files and searched for Hannah Sternberg. She took it out. 'She's about fifty-two now.'

'Not our killer.'

'Maybe not, but she's interested in the Nazis – look at this record.'

Aaron pulled Hannah Sternberg's reading record. There were several books on Nazis and the ghettos and the Holocaust.

'She might have been trying to find something,' said Aaron. His face contorted in pain. 'But it's not her, is it? We're not going to find my Abby. Never, never, never.'

'Don't give up now,' said Denise.

'I can't stand it. I miss her like . . . You could never understand.'

'No, I couldn't,' said Denise. 'But this is all we've got, so let's keep searching.'

Aaron calmed himself. 'Yes, for Abby. Because we must always have hope.' He clenched each fist slowly and continued to search.

Denise's phone rang a few minutes later. It was Tom Harper. 'How are things in the archives?'

'It's okay, we're getting through quite fast. Not many people read this book. One so far, a fifty-two-year-old woman.'

'Keep going,' said Harper. 'I've got a lead. Set of garages on 118th in Bed-Stuy that we think Heming used when he was in hiding. It just might be the place.'

'Be safe,' said Denise. 'You want help?'

'I don't want Aaron around if his daughter's there. Keep in touch.'

'Okay,' said Denise.

'Call me if you need me.'

'I will,' said Denise.

They continued to search. Aaron raised his hand in the air fifteen minutes later. 'I found another name. A man called Albert Moile.'

'Go check his file,' said Denise.

Aaron looked through and found the library record card for Albert Moile. He looked across. 'If he's still alive, he's ninety-five,' said Aaron.

A moment later Denise's finger ran down the page and stopped. She saw the name *Josef Sturbe* again and moved her finger across the ledger to the borrower's name. She looked down at it and felt her body chill. 'I've got a name,' she said, with a tremble in her voice. 'It's the killer. I know who it is.'

Chapter One Hundred and Nine

Harper arrived at the garage on the corner and Jack Carney was already there, waiting.

'We've got a vague location point for the lock-up along this row,' said Carney. 'Let's go.'

Harper and Jack Carney ran up the street searching for some sign as to where the killer was. They did two sweeps of the road but couldn't see anything.

'Where the hell are these garages?' said Harper.

'They must be somewhere around here,' said Carney.

Then Harper spotted a broken wire fence and walked over. He looked at the edge. 'Jack, check this. The wire's been bent recently. The scratches on the wall are recent too.'

Harper pushed through the fence, quickly followed by Carney. They walked across the wasteland, their eyes scanning every building, before fastening on an old abandoned lock-up. Then Harper stopped. 'Listen.'

Carney listened. 'Banging.'

'And voices,' said Harper. They moved quickly towards the sound. Harper saw the garage. He looked at the bolts. 'New bolts in a derelict area.'

'This must be it,' said Carney.

The banging became more intense and frightened. They could

hear two women crying out for help and looked at each other. Carney stood by the door as Harper moved all around the building. He reappeared at the other side and shook his head.

'No windows.'

They looked at the door. 'You kick it in,' said Carney quietly.

'Let's hope to God that they're okay,' said Harper. He motioned for Carney to move to the side, raised his gun and indicated the handle. Carney put his hand on it.

'Let's take a look,' said Harper.

Carney depressed the handle and Harper pulled the trigger. The padlock split open and Carney pushed open the door. 'NYPD. Put your hands in the air.' Harper raised his gun and moved in. 'What is that smell?' he whispered.

'Cyanide,' said Jack Carney.

Harper scanned the room with his gun. He saw the two women directly ahead in a strange prison. He saw the pipes running across the length of the room and to the roof of the cell. Just like the gas van.

Inside the cell, the two women were screaming and shaking. They were pointing towards the back of the garage. Harper swiveled round and suddenly felt something hard against his skull.

Jack Carney's gun was pressed tight to his head. 'Drop your gun, Harper, or I kill you right now.'

Chapter One Hundred and Ten

Harper stared into Jack Carney's eyes. A hundred tiny inconsistencies and questions suddenly fell into place. He felt sickness in the pit of his stomach. Disgust so sudden and violent that he couldn't speak.

'The gun, Harper, or I kill you.' Carney eased the trigger back.

Harper heard the click of the breech and he dropped his gun to the ground. His hands formed into large, heavy fists, and hatred and anger burned in his eyes.

'Tom Harper, I thought you were better than this,' said Carney.

Harper held his gaze and looked directly into the eyes of the ruthless killer.

'It's hard to believe,' said Carney. 'Move over to the cell.'

Harper edged backwards. 'You're dead, you fucking animal,' he shouted. 'You know that? There's no fucking way out. You're trapped, Carney, you sick fuck.'

'Anger and hatred, Harper. You feeling it?' Carney smiled. 'This is the killer's Luger. You were the only one who could work this out,' he said. 'I knew you were close but I'm not ready to give in.'

'They all know,' said Harper. 'It's over. Let these two go.'

'I don't think so,' said Carney. 'Now they're going to have a big problem on their hands. You went off on your own last night. The story is going to go like this – the killer lured you here and you heroically tried to save the girls. But oh, how close you must've come.'

Carney moved across to the canister of Zyklon B. 'I add these pellets in here, they react with the air and Lucy and Abby will die. You will try to open the door and the killer will shoot you.'

'It's a good plan, but people know.'

'Who?'

'Everyone.'

'You sure about that, Harper? Don't bluff the master.' Carney chuckled.

'You got to give yourself up,' shouted Harper. 'You need help.'

'I've got a mission, Harper. A mission.'

'Open the cell,' Harper commanded, but Carney moved across to the cyanide.

'Lucy,' called Harper into the cell. 'Is there any way out of here?'

She shook her head.

Harper turned and looked at the drained and emaciated figure of Abby in the cell behind him. He smashed his fist against the Plexiglass but it was too thick. It wouldn't break. He turned and stared at Carney. 'You can't do this, you've got to stop. You're a cop.'

Carney took the can across to the small tub. 'This is the Zyklon B. Everything had to be authentic.' He smiled. 'It causes a slow and painful death.'

'Why are you doing this?'

'The heart has reasons that reason knows not of,' said Carney. He turned to Harper and moved close to the Plexiglass. 'And because I hate them. All of them. Jews, her, you, everyone.' He opened the canister, pulled back the lid of the plastic bucket.

'How long will it take them to die?'

'Ten minutes, a little more,' said Carney.

They heard the sound of the first pellets hitting the base of the bucket. Harper moved across to the door and barged at it with his full weight. He tried again.

'You won't rescue them,' said Carney. 'That's not the story I've planned.'

Abby Goldenberg pulled herself to her feet with her last reserves of strength and moved up to the front of the cell. 'I know what you are!' she called out.

'Do you?' shouted Carney. 'Well, I'm Josef Sturbe and you're dead.'

'Your mother was in touch with Lucy. Did you know that? You think you know everything. You couldn't find her yourself, but Lucy found her. Lucy told her about the beatings, about the man you'd become. She was disgusted.'

Carney stopped and stared across to the cell. He replaced the lid on the pellets. 'Fuck you, you're lying. She's dead. Fucking dead.'

Lucy was crouched in a corner. 'She's not dead, Jack. She's alive. I met her.'

Jack Carney moved across to the cell. 'Have you been telling secrets? Did you find my mother?'

Abby's voice was barely a whisper. 'She's the only one who knows where your mother lives. You kill her and you'll never find her.'

Abby was a smart kid, Harper thought. She was buying time. He looked around. What could he do? The gas ran through hastily welded scaffolding pipes, across and then above him.

'Where is she?' said Carney. 'I want her dead. I want you all dead. Fuck her. It's too late. It's too fucking late.'

'It's not too late,' said Abby, drawing breath slowly at each sentence. 'She's been living right here in Brooklyn all that time. Knew who you were. She's been keeping clippings of you, your whole life.'

'Is this true, Lucy? Speak or you die.'

Lucy nodded.

'Tell me where she is. She'll be the next one to die.' Then Carney looked at them and laughed. 'You're both lying. You'll regret that.'

Carney turned and headed back to the Zyklon B. Harper jumped and grabbed on to the scaffolding pole with both hands. It snapped under his weight. Carney turned and shot. It hit the Plexiglass. Harper swung hard and low. He didn't want to miss.

The pole hit Carney's legs and he fell. Harper moved to him, but Carney was good. The Luger pointed directly at him. 'Go on, make another move, Harper.'

Harper stopped. 'You're not going to gas them, you fucking freak. You can shoot us all, but your sick little experiment isn't going to work.'

Carney pulled himself up from the floor. 'I don't care a damn for her! Lucy, you understand? Fuck you all. Fuck her. I'll show you. I'll show her too. I'm going to be written about for years.' He pointed the gun at Harper's face.

Then at the door, he heard a shout. 'Drop your weapon.' They turned and saw Denise Levene step in the door. She raised her gun. 'Move away from the bucket, victim,' she shouted.

Carney let out a laugh. 'You too.' His hand started to turn.

'Don't try it, victim!' she told him.

Carney saw her fear and smiled. 'You wouldn't dare – that's your problem, isn't it?'

'Try me,' she said. Denise remembered everything Mac had told her. She wasn't afraid; she was the hunter – not him. She fired, two quick rounds, into the wall. Carney's hand stopped moving. 'Drop the weapon.'

'You don't want to kill your beloved detective, do you, Dr Levene?' sneered Carney. 'You shoot me and I'll put a bullet through his head.'

'It doesn't matter,' said Denise. 'It's over now. We know – Blue Team knows. They're on their way. We found you, Jack. We traced the book on Sturbe, traced your lending record. It's all there. Jack Carney's self-hatred. The Jew who couldn't stand to be a Jew.'

'Fuck you,' said Carney.

'And you know what, Carney? We understand how it happened.'

'What do you understand?'

'You were searching for your mommy, weren't you? That lovely Jewish woman who abandoned you. The one who gave you your Jewish blood then dumped you on a group of Gentiles. Confusing for a kid, wasn't it? It's not unusual, Jack, to become obsessed, to identify with your attackers, to try to destroy the part of yourself you think they hate. You're not a special case, you're just a boy who didn't grow up properly – not emotionally. You learned to hate yourself.'

'So clever and so wrong.'

'Really? We found your mother, Jack. She borrowed the same books as you. Every book you read, she read a week later. She was looking out for you all that time. Must've been watching you. Desperate to contact you, but scared. Her name was Hannah Sternberg.'

'Sternberg?'

'She left you when you were five. I guess what happened was that you only vaguely remembered her name. There weren't any adoption records. That's partly why your parents hated your Jewishness. What they did was illegal: take a child off a twenty-year-old Jewish girl with no other options. So you searched for your mother, didn't you? For a name you could only half-remember. Sterne, Sterne-be. Sturbe. You came across this Nazi, and he made sense to you, right? You thought it was some incredible truth about you. And you devoured it and replaced all that loss and pain with this monster.'

Jack looked shaken. He stepped backwards. He was finding it hard to take in. 'Is she alive?'

'She wants to see you, Jack.'

Carney lowered his head. 'It's too late,' he spat. 'It's way too late for that Jewish whore to save you, any of you. I'm going to make you all pay for this. I'm going to finish this for good. I must complete the transformation. I have it all planned. There is nothing else to do.' He fired suddenly without lifting his head. The bullet hit the door. Denise threw herself against the wall. It was enough. Carney rose quickly, pushed past her and darted out of the lock-up.

Chapter One Hundred and Eleven

Crown Heights, Brooklyn
March 15, 10.33 a.m.

The orange truck was heavy over the potholes, the back end lifting and heaving on the old springs. Carney tapped impatiently on the steering wheel. He turned too quickly into 82nd Street. The van lurched high on its suspension and sat flat with a jolt.

'Damn roads. City's run by fucking monkeys.'

Still, that didn't matter now, did it? He felt the walls moving in. Harper had survived. They all knew. Everyone would now be chasing Jack Carney. It had to be now. Nothing mattered any more. Not anyone, either. Friends, colleagues. Screw the lot of them. All except one.

There were still things he wanted to say to Lucy. Their separation had never made sense to him. All that talk about his behavior and her need for freedom. All that he had understood when she ended things was that she had rejected him because he was a Jew. And then she had started dating Capske – a Jew. The insult was unbearable, so much so that he could hardly let himself think about it. The implication was clear – it wasn't his Jewishness that offended her, it was just him. Carney felt the anger rise again; he still nurtured the wounds as if they were fresh cuts.

He felt the weight of thirty years of being oppressed by the filth who now ran this country. He felt their betrayal as a stream of invective. The Nazi slogans and racist bile jumbled in his mind.

He hit the steering wheel hard with the heel of his hand. 'Shit alive, I hate this fucking world.' He drove on with a determined expression. Past an NYPD Charger with two asshole cops eating in the front seats. One Hispanic and one black.

'Take a fucking look at that, Josef, that's who we answer to now. The fucking parasites are leading the beasts.'

Carney patted his antique Luger pistol, pressed hard against his hip, raised his hand towards the officers and formed a gun with his fingers. They didn't bat an eyelid as they watched the bright orange truck trundle by.

He turned into the street and pulled to a halt halfway down. He looked over at the big mansion on the corner. The location had been carefully chosen. The synagogue lay at the eastern end, but it would be empty today. The Museum of Tolerance to the west, however, would be full of Jew-lovers. It was the perfect target. He reached for a pair of binoculars and brought the façade into sharp focus. It was a nice building. Gothic. It looked like a French château. Another example of the fakery ruining the western world.

To the left and right, the leafless trees had green buds beginning to emerge. It gave him an uninterrupted view. He checked his watch. The doors to the Museum of Tolerance would open soon enough, the crowds would enter and then he would start his work.

Carney thought of himself as a security expert. He told people willing to listen that he was an ex-Marine. In truth, he'd never made the Marines and ended up as a cop. He had become a good cop too, keeping his leanings hidden and his need for power in check, satisfied by seeing the destruction of others through his work with Hate Crime.

Maybe the assholes who were running this investigation would get to him, but he didn't think so. He'd outsmarted them before, but not on this scale. This would give the truth about the Jewish conspiracy the maximum chance to get proper billing. Every story needed a picture and this would be it, a shattered street and a screaming line of hostages. He would make them recite the eighty-eight words into the camera, standing tied up in a bomb-shattered street. That was how it had gone in his mind, over and over again.

Carney took out his gun and held it as he watched the people start to gather at the Museum of Tolerance on the corner. It was a crisp spring morning, still below zero. He chewed on a piece of gum and watched as cars and people bustled by. All the time, Carney was counting the visitors entering the museum.

He drove the truck another hundred yards and parked right outside the museum next to an old beige bus, as close as he could so that the truck wasn't visible from afar.

He got out quickly before anyone had the chance to question him, went into the back of the truck to set things up, then emerged carrying two metal crutches. He locked up and moved away. He limped towards the museum.

Chapter One Hundred and Twelve

Brooklyn
March 15, 10.45 a.m.

Harper had seen the truck leaving and caught two numbers on the license-plate. It was an orange Dodge, but he didn't catch its tail. By the time he was out on to the street where Denise's car was parked, the orange truck had disappeared.

Harper and Denise called backup, but it was already in the street. They heard the sirens getting closer. Harper pulled back the bolts and moved across to Lucy.

Denise rushed to the exhausted body of Abby Goldenberg. She knelt at Abby's side, stroked her face and looked down at her. 'You okay?'

Abby managed to nod, but the last few minutes had left her reeling, her eyes closed.

Harper helped Lucy to her feet and walked her out of the brick cell. He looked across to Denise. 'You want to get her out?' he said.

'We need a gurney, Tom, she's very weak.'

'We got to get on Carney's tail, Denise. Soon as backup gets here we go, right?'

'Okay,' she said. Denise looked at Abby's eyes. She was still the girl in the photographs, the beautiful, bright teenager, but the experience had left her gray and gaunt. 'You're going to be just fine,' said Denise. 'If I can do it, Abby, and I'm half as willful as you seem to be, then you'll be back on your feet in no time.'

Abby's eyes flickered open. 'Where's my daddy?'

Denise held her hand. 'We'll get him for you, dear. He's fine. He never gave up. He's been helping all this time, helping the cops find you.'

'I knew he wouldn't let anything happen,' said Abby. 'I felt him here the whole time.' Then the girl's face contorted and Denise tried to calm her. The noise of the squad cars and ambulances broke in from behind.

Denise turned as the uniformed cops entered with two para-medics. 'Let's get you to hospital, Abby. You need a little attention first.'

Denise let the paramedics take the girl. 'You ready?' she said to Harper. She steeled herself. It wasn't over, not yet. The predator had ousted the victim once and for all, but the prey wasn't down.

Harper ran for the exit, Denise followed. They jumped into a squad car and Harper started to drive.

'Where we going?' said Denise.

'Carney's got nowhere to go. He's going to do something bad. We just have to try to get to him first. Every cop in New York will know about him by now.' Harper called Lafayette as he drove. 'What have you got set up?'

'We've got all the bridges in Manhattan covered. Ditto all routes in and out of New York. He's circled, Harper. An orange truck won't go unnoticed. We got hundreds of men out there. It's going to show up. It's just a matter of time.'

'He's going to do something,' said Harper. 'You alerted Counter-Terrorism?'

'All Hercules squads are live and active. If we get one sniff of him, he's ours.'

'That's good,' said Harper. 'I'm worried about it, though. He's known this day is coming for a while now.'

'I know,' said Lafayette. 'We're doing what we can.'

'Parkways and expressways covered?'

'Yep, like I said, we've got patrols on all major routes in and out.'

'I don't think he's leaving. I think Carney knows this is over.'

'He's a dead man walking,' said Lafayette.

'No,' said Harper, 'he's a ticking bomb.'

Harper hung up and continued to drive. He felt the frustration of being unable to do a goddamn thing. Denise had been trying to make calls on her cell phone.

'How was Abby?' he asked.

'She's pretty messed up, but the light's still in her eyes,' said Denise. 'I guess she'll be okay. I tried to call Aaron. He's not at home and his cell went straight to message. He's going to scream.'

'He's a lucky man. Down to you, Denise. You did good. Real good.'

'*We* did good. What did Lafayette say?'

'Nothing seen or heard yet, but roads are covered everywhere.' Harper cast his eye down another side street. 'I need something on Carney,' he said. 'What's he going to do?'

'You want my analysis?'

'Yes. You got anything?'

'He's going to make a final gesture,' said Denise. 'He's a cornered animal now, there's no way out.'

'I know, but what's it going to be?'

'Josef Sturbe was there on the last day of the ghetto.'

'And what happened on the last day?' said Harper.

'The Nazis blew up the Great Synagogue of Warsaw.'

Harper's mind raced. 'God help us, if that's what he has in mind.'

Denise nodded to herself. 'He might. It's symbolic – a final action. I remember reading the reports by one SS officer. He said: "What a wonderful sight!" when looking at the burning synagogue.'

Harper called Lafayette immediately. 'He might be going for a synagogue. Send the word out, get the patrols to every single one.'

Chapter One Hundred and Thirteen

Museum of Tolerance, Brooklyn
March 15, 10.48 a.m.

Inside the lobby of the Museum of Tolerance, Carney stopped and took out a handkerchief. He wiped his brow and leaned down to feel his leg with a grimace. He tried to move on his metal crutches. The two security men stared across. One of them said something to the other. Carney's training told him two things about getting through security – get noticed and then get the guards themselves noticed. Guards don't like to be embarrassed.

Carney acknowledged their look and started over to them. His right leg slipped from under him and he sprawled to the floor, his leg lying straight as if injured. Carney yelled in pain. He tried to push himself to his feet but he couldn't get up. One of the beefcakes moved slowly across.

'Help me!' Carney shouted.

The guard looked awkward as he crossed the marble floor.

'Sorry, man, this is real embarrassing,' said Carney. 'I can't get this attached without a seat.'

'No problem, sir. I'll fix you up.' The guy put his hands under Carney's arms, picked him up and helped him across to a bench seat.

'God, I hate these injuries. Humiliate the life out of me at every moment,' said Carney.

'How'd you hurt the leg?'

'Afghanistan,' said Carney.

'You in the service?' asked the security guard.

'Yeah, until the IED blast. You're a soldier too, right?' said Carney.

The security guard showed his tattoo. A Marine. Carney nodded.

'Those bastards bombed the fuck out of us and what did our government do? They withdrew troops.'

'It's too bad.'

Carney shook his head. He felt close to tears. Sincere tears. He pushed down his jeans and stood up.

'I gotta thank you, fella.'

'Not a problem. Good to help a soldier.'

Carney stood up and, with the aid of his crutches, hopped towards the gate with the security guard. 'I hope I didn't embarrass you.'

'Not at all. War wound is something to be proud of.'

'You're a real gent.' Carney pointed at the metal detector. 'You don't want me to hop through there without these babies, do you? I'll be flat on the floor again if you do.'

'No, man, that's cool, just walk through.'

Carney walked through. The machine beeped. He stopped and turned.

'Am I all right to go on?'

'Sure, man, take it easy.'

Carney walked slowly down the corridor away from the gate. He could feel the sweat soaking his shirt and his hands shaking, but he was smiling now, not that they could see it. He found the elevator, pressed the button and waited.

The problem was that Lucy was about the only person he'd ever felt safe with. Why was it? Why was he so complicated? A Jew who was not a Jew, who hated Jews, who was betrayed by a Jew. He had felt safe with hatred. Hatred silenced all his self-loathing.

Carney walked into the bathroom on the second floor. He felt warm and flushed. He threw water over his face. She'd remember him after today, wouldn't she? In the mirror, a worn-out man stared back at him. Older than his years. He was tired, red and looked mad as hell. In his head, he'd felt like a hero. He turned his face away quickly.

He took out a folded piece of paper from his coat pocket and opened it up. On it, the words looked small and hazy. He couldn't focus, even in the bright fluorescent lights of the toilet. He recited the words. One powerful paragraph. Only eighty-eight words.

Chapter One Hundred and Fourteen

Crown Heights, Brooklyn
March 15, 11.02 a.m.

Harper made a judgment. Crown Heights had the largest number of synagogues in the area. He picked up Denise from the hospital. He needed someone with knowledge of Brooklyn. They drove towards the first on his list. He stopped and got out of his car, stretched his neck to get a good look up and down the street. Denise got out beside him.

'Anything?' she asked.

'No,' said Harper. 'Let's try the next.'

Harper saw a huge flock of starlings rise in a single movement from the rooftops. He looked up. It was a moment, that was all. He didn't have time to wonder. A second later, a massive explosion ripped through the morning air with a horrifying shriek of violence. In a heartbeat, the world had changed once again.

At the shock of the explosion, Harper dived. His knees bent, and almost instantly as the first soundwave rushed by, he darted towards Denise with an outstretched arm, using his body to shield her. His mind was still taking in the noise, his body in adrenalin production, as he held Denise close to his chest. Time slowed. The blast lasted under a second, but the soundwave continued, lessening, widening like a gunshot disappearing over a plain, ricocheting off tall buildings.

A second after the blast, the treetops rushed with sudden air. Then the air was still.

And for a fragment of a second, it was so quiet. Maybe it was longer. It seemed longer. The silence seemed to hang in the air. Then someone took off the pause button and the scene burst to life with the shriek of car alarms and children crying.

Harper and Denise stood up. The blast had been close. Close enough for them to feel the shockwaves. Close enough for them to hear the raw burst of force and pressure. Maybe half a mile away, or less.

They watched a plume of black and gray smoke rise above the rooftops.

Harper's ears rang and he saw the people all around dash into huddled groups. Taking Denise by the hand, Harper raced back to his car. 'Get in,' he shouted. They pulled away, turned and drove towards the center of the explosion.

Chapter One Hundred and Fifteen

Crown Heights, Brooklyn
March 15, 11.18 a.m.

Harper and Denise abandoned their car a street away. The traffic was too bad. Hundreds of cars packed tight. They got out and ran hard towards the scene. There was no telling what the bomb had done or how many were injured. The priority for the team was to get the injured out of there and to secure the scene. His priority had to be to stop Jack Carney.

Harper moved through the crowds at the end of the street. He slowed as he came across the scene. A gray New York street spread out from the center-point of chaos. Scattered, twisted, smoking metal. The wasted hulk of an exhumed truck, quietly breathing gray-black smoke. The spread of debris. Dazed victims, some staggering at the edges of the blast, some moving on the ground, others still. The whole front wall of the museum blasted to pieces. Carney hadn't targeted the empty synagogue but a museum full of people. What's more, like some final insult, he'd chosen Aaron Goldenberg's workplace. Harper's mind raced.

He stared at the devastation in a civilian street. Blood on concrete. Torn clothes. Papers and shoes. Body parts against fast-food wraps. The pressure wave had been enough to crush the closer victims. Their bodies were hit by an impenetrable wall of high pressure and had been thrown against the buildings. Further out, the shrapnel had caused carnage. The mix of bright red blood and black soot was smudged across the entire frontage of the museum.

Harper made for the makeshift Incident Command. He scanned the scene quickly.

There was no one in the bomb zone except the essential medical services and the Bomb Squad. There were two Bomb Squad detectives in big green EOD 8 Bomb Suits, fifty layers of Kevlar shielding them from any potential explosion. Thank God that they'd put the city on red alert. Every team had been up and mobile. The response time was astonishing and it meant that lives were being saved. The bomb crew were on all fours looking under cars along the street with a mirror.

A great phalanx of injured bodies lay at the entrance of the Museum of Tolerance. It was the epicenter.

'There's too many. Far too many bodies,' said Harper.

Denise was in shock. She turned. 'What?'

'Something's wrong. A street scene at this time wouldn't have been this busy.'

Harper watched for a moment as the paramedics continued the pre-hospital triage – a hell of a thing to be doing in a New York street: tagging each of the wounded red, amber or green depending on how long they'd live. The red-tags were already being moved to the ambulances. Amber and greens would have to wait in the street in horrible agony.

As soon as Harper and Levene entered Incident Command, they spotted Sergeant Luce Colhoon, who called them across.

'Just got here,' Harper said. 'You have anything on the bomber?'

'Listen, we've got emergency services taking care of the wounded. Three dead already in ambulances. We got the utilities on it – there's a burst gas main somewhere down the street, but they've closed off the gas already. I've got no idea about the bomber. What we got to know, Detective, is this: what the hell happened?'

'You speak to any witnesses?'

'Nobody who can hear me. They're all deaf.'

Harper went back to the street. He looked again at the mass of bodies outside the museum, and then across the street. Debris, smashed car glass. Walls full of shot. Dazed and wounded people sitting where they could, receiving treatment. The ground scattered with nails. A sickeningly barbaric device aimed at maiming the maximum number of people.

But there were too many dead and wounded. That's what he saw again. Normally at this time, the street would've maybe had a dozen or so people on the sidewalks, but this looked like someone had let off a bomb in a crowd.

Harper edged forward, mentally totting up the numbers. He put his hand on the shoulder of a cop trying to clear a path for the paramedics.

'You get anything from any witnesses?'

'I don't know. There was a guy on the second floor of the building opposite the museum who said he was watching the street. Saw a crowd streaming out of the museum – and then the blast shot his window out. He's in one of the ambulances. Maybe he's gone already.'

'They were coming *out* of the museum before the bomb went off?'

'That's what the man said.'

Harper thought for a moment and looked up at the museum. There was a window out on the second floor. Not unusual given the scene, but it was the only one out. Maybe there had been a smaller blast first. Maybe it was just a coincidence. Maybe someone had set off an alarm.

Harper pulled Denise across to the entrance and in through the shattered glass doors. Two security officers were helping set up a temporary hospital area in the foyer.

'We got to find out what happened,' Harper told Denise. 'Talk to people.'

'This is where Aaron Goldenberg works. I need to find him. He might be hurt.'

'Okay, try to locate him,' said Harper. He went up to a security guard. 'Detective Harper. I need some information fast.'

'Okay, sir, I'll tell you what I can, but you gotta speak up.' The guard tapped his ears by way of an explanation.

'Okay. Listen, did something happen prior to the blast, anything you see from in here?'

'Yeah, something, but I don't know what it was. The fire alarm went off and people began to walk towards the exits, then this crowd started down the stairs from the upper floors, in a panic, caused everyone to stampede. We couldn't stop them. They got out of the doors and then, BAM! The device went off.'

'The alarm went off first? You sure? Sometimes it can get confusing.'

'It went off first. That's why the blast hit so many. Like they were running right into it.'

'Can you show me where the alarm was set off?'

'We didn't get a chance to look. The control is in the back office. I'll take you.'

The security guard took Harper inside the main office and through a back corridor to the security unit. It was empty. The security officer stood in front of a bank of lights. 'It's flashing in Area 8B, I got to look it up, give me a second.' Harper gazed at the TV screens as the guard looked up the code. Two screens were blank, but the two screens on the outside of the building were still working.

'8B is up on the second floor in the exhibition room.'

'And these two cameras that are out?'

'Shit, I didn't see. Okay. Maybe something happened. They're both from the exhibition room. Shit. That's bad news. You don't think someone's set off something to . . .'

'To what?'

'To create a diversion and steal the artefacts?'

'If that's what's going on, it's the most fucked-up theft I ever heard of.' Harper was already out the door, his Glock 19 firmly in his hand as he leaped up the stairs to the second floor. The security guard followed.

The second floor was quiet. Harper stopped. The big wooden doors at the end of the corridor were closed. He waited until the security guard caught up.

'They should be open, right?'

'Yeah.'

'Okay, let's take this nice and slow. We don't know what's going on.'

'Nice and slow.'

Harper made his way down the marble corridor, his reflection perfect in the freshly polished floor. At the door, he stopped and sank to his knees. He put his eye to the large old-fashioned keyhole and stared for a moment. It was enough. He turned and pulled out his radio.

'Sergeant Colhoon, it's Detective Harper,' he whispered. 'I'm in the museum up on the second floor.'

'So what have you got for me, Detective?'

'This is worse than we thought. The first blast happened up here. We've got several casualties on the second floor. And you're going to need to call a SWAT team. Maybe two. The bomber is in the building. And he's got hostages.'

Chapter One Hundred and Sixteen

Museum of Tolerance, Brooklyn
March 15, 11.32 a.m.

The truck had been packed with explosives. Nothing ornate or fancy. Ammonium nitrate sitting loose in a flat box. Three bangers stuck in there and a can of fuel. All according to the instructions he'd been given. Carney had also thrown in a few bags of old nails he had no more use for.

The truck bomb had worked better than he'd expected. The fuse must've been just right. He'd had exactly the right amount of time to walk up to the second floor, set off a small incendiary device, start screaming, 'Fire!' all over the place, and then watch as the chaos ensued. All of them running as if to freedom, only to feel the heat of a bomb blast and a barrage of red-hot nails flaying their skin.

In the chaos, he shot out the two cameras on the second floor and then he shut the door to the exhibition room behind him. Those who hadn't managed to escape stood there in front of him. Mindless sheep, unable to think or realize what was happening. He blocked the doorway. The crowd stopped.

'What are you doing, man?'

'There's a fire in the stairwell. Smoke's real bad. It'll kill you.'

'What do we do?'

'There's another stairway. Follow me.'

There were about twelve of them. Men, women, children. They turned from the exit and followed Carney down a corridor and into another exhibition room. When they were all in the room, Carney shut the door and pulled out Josef.

'What are you doing?'

'Making a point that needs making. Now all of you, sit the fuck down.'

The twelve hostages started to scream and panic. Carney shouted but the panic had set in. He pulled a man out of the crowd of wailing, crying people and pushed his Luger hard into the man's cheek.

'Shut the fuck up.'

Carney shot one round into the floor, then returned the gun to the man's face.

'What's your name, Jew?'

'Jeb Rosenbaum,' the man said. Slowly, the group fell silent.

'I'll kill the children first, if you scream again.'

Jeb held his head in his hands. He was crying. Carney turned to him. 'What are you crying for, Jeb? You're the lucky one.'

He took Jeb by the elbow and pushed him against the opposite wall.

'Why are you doing this? What do you want?'

'I want people to know.'

'What?'

'Kneel.'

'Please don't kill me. I've got three children.'

'It's the breeders that are the worst. Fucking kneel!' shouted Carney.

Jeb knelt and Carney took out a knife from his boot leg. He stood in front of him and stared.

'You know what a scapegoat is, don't you?'

'I don't know what you mean . . .'

'Yes, you do. It's the innocent goat sent away bearing the sins of its people.'

'I don't understand you.'

'You will. Don't you worry about that.' Carney produced a roll of barbed wire from his backpack. He threw it down. 'I'm going to wire you up, Jeb.'

The twelve stopped and stared. Carney stared back. He stepped up to the man and held up his gun. 'You are not human. You are no longer human, you understand?'

Carney moved in with the barbed wire. He took Jeb and wrapped the wire three times around his neck.

Chapter One Hundred and Seventeen

Museum of Tolerance, Brooklyn
March 15, 11.37 a.m.

Harper sat with his back against the wooden door to the exhibition room. Inside, he'd seen Jack Carney clutching a Luger and pointing it at a group of hostages. He counted twelve: one of them was half-wrapped in barbed wire.

Harper looked through the big keyhole again. Carney was armed. His face and clothes were coated in a film of soot from the incendiary device. Harper watched in silence as Carney taped an explosive device around one of the hostages. Harper felt his breath shorten as he listened to the hostages pleading. They were terrified. Carney would be in no mood for negotiation. Harper could sense the tension in his voice. It was a bad sign. Carney clearly had a plan and he was going to stick to it.

Harper spoke low into his shortwave. 'How long till SWAT get here?'

'Three to four minutes. Keep it nice and quiet up there.'

'I don't think this guy intends to live. That makes him very dangerous.'

'I'll pass it on, Harper. Just sit tight.'

Harper tried to breathe deeply. Three to four minutes to get to the location. A minute to get out of the SWAT truck and a minute to get up to the second floor. Inside, a couple of the younger hostages were sobbing. In the background, further off, was the sound of crying and shouting. A scuffle, then silence. There was too much silence.

Harper looked again. Right in front of him was a man. He was about forty years old; three sticks of dynamite were now taped around his waist beside the detonation device. His face was blank. He had goose bumps all over his body.

Harper heard the killer walk up and down the room.

'I just want the world to see you as you are. Rich bastard, aren't you? I want you to crawl out of this place. I want to hear you bleat like a goat.'

Then what? Harper considered the plan. He looked at his watch. Time was too tight to call. If he waited for the SWAT team to get there, something might have happened, but if the killer was planning on getting his hostage to crawl out of the museum, he'd have a chance. Harper heard Carney's voice barking commands.

'Okay, all of you now get down on all fours.'

Harper leaned in and watched the killer orchestrating his delusions. Then he called into Command.

'We've got a situation developing. He's wiring the main hostage with explosive devices.'

'They want to know the exact layout of the rooms, you got that information?'

'Sure. But how long till we got some backup here?'

'They're caught in the fucking chaos. They've left the truck but they'll be maybe another five minutes.'

'I could take a shot.'

'This is an order, Detective. Do not, I repeat, *do not* attempt a rescue.'

'Okay. I'll hold off.'

Inside the room, the terrified hostages were on their hands and knees. When the device blew, the explosion would savage them all.

Harper watched Carney stand back.

'Look at you go. Terrified to die, my little goats?' Carney wiped his mouth. Spit was forming on his lips. He looked tired. The adrenalin must have hit him in fits and starts – rising up and then falling like a wave.

Carney approached Jeb Rosenbaum.

'You want to know what's going to happen? You're going to crawl out into the street.'

Carney laughed.

Jeb dared not look up. Carney took out a small black device that looked like a cell phone. He held it up.

'You know what? I'm going to see how far you all get to. I shall let you go, just so long as you don't squeal. But if they touch you, I press this number; it dials, connects to the little receiver next to that dynamite and what it will do, Jeb, what it will do . . . is explode.'

Jeb started to shake.

'The idea is that it will rip your head clean off. Your head will go flying into the crowds. It's up to you. You keep them off you, you'll live. For a time. I want the TV crews to see you Jews as you should be seen.'

Harper listened and turned to the security guard. 'If he gets that hostage into the street, that fucks up the whole idea of a rescue. Any other way into that room?'

The security guard pointed to the stairs. 'You can get into it from the other side.'

Harper nodded. 'Keep watching through the keyhole. Soon as you see me on the far side, knock three times on the door. He'll look up and I'll . . . well, I'll do something.' Harper stood and shot up the stairs.

The security guard waited in terrified silence. He didn't hear someone coming up the stairs until she was right there. He turned and saw a blond-haired woman. 'Who are you?'

'Denise Levene. I'm with Harper. Where's Dr Goldenberg?'

The security guard shook his head. 'I don't know. Harper's gone round the other side.'

'What's his plan?' asked Denise.

'I don't think he has one.'

Inside the foyer of the museum, Aaron Goldenberg stared down at the dead and injured. The cops had taken the worst to the ambulances. He saw one of his security guards lying on his back, a bloody bandage pressed to his shoulder. He approached the man and knelt at his side.

'What happened, Bill?' he said.

'Dr Goldenberg. God, Dr Goldenberg. A bomb, that's what happened.'

'I know there was a bomb. The alarm went off in here. Why?'

'They think he's in here, the 88 Killer. The cops just went up. I'd like to go up with them. Some lady is looking for you, too. I sent her up to the exhibition room.'

'The 88 Killer?' said Dr Goldenberg.

'Detective took the other guard. They went upstairs. Exhibition Room.'

Aaron Goldenberg let the pain emerge. He could think of just one thing. He reached down to the security guard's side and opened the plastic holster.

'What are you doing, sir?'

'Shh,' said Aaron. 'He's got my daughter.' He pulled the gun out and held it in his hand. He looked at it. 'How do I work it?'

'You can't do it, Dr Goldenberg. You got to leave it to the police.'

'I have – for seventeen days. Now I've got to do something. He's here. Where's the safety?'

The guard nodded to the side of the gun. Aaron pushed down the small button. 'This ready now?'

'Yes, sir,' said the guard.

Aaron touched his cheek. 'I took it without your knowledge. And thank you, Bill.'

Aaron Goldenberg stood, held the handgun by his side and walked across to the stairs.

Two floors up, Carney circled his hostages and continued to speak in a slow drawl. 'The problem with you guys is that you think you have a right to own the fucking world. Everyone's got to feel sorry for you. Who feels sorry for guys like me? Guys who want the world back, guys getting destroyed by your conspiracies.'

'I don't understand what that has to do with me.'

Carney looked up. 'It's because . . .'

Carney stopped a moment, the little black phone in his hand. His mind seemed to miss a beat, as if the usual connection wasn't available and he didn't know what else to say.

The hostage went on: 'You know no one's to blame here. We're all just trying to make a living like you.'

The words dragged Carney back to life.

'Like me? You don't fucking know what being like me *is*. You people . . . you've bled us fucking dry. This is America.'

'I'm American.'

'That right? You can be American when it suits but you only care about your own kind.'

Aaron Goldenberg walked up the stairs through broken glass. His heart had been walking through broken glass for days.

The 88 Killer. The man who had his daughter, Abby – who had her imprisoned somewhere – was in his building. He reached the first floor and then started up to the second. He wanted his daughter. He wanted revenge. The purpose focused him.

'Abby,' he said to himself. 'Abby, Abby, Abby.' In his heart, he felt she was dead. That was all he'd learned to expect, that there was only worse to come – a broken, beaten corpse, his daughter's magnificent life reduced to nothing. Tears were streaming down his face, a burning agony in his chest. He had never known feelings like these. Suicides and murders hadn't ever come within his world, but now his purpose was clear. He could not live without his daughter. He *would* not live without her. Not another day.

He would not walk alone on earth without love. And the killer would not walk on the earth another day either. Let this be the end.

He knew what he had to do.

Inside the exhibition room, Carney stood up. 'They're here. Time to take you all for a walk.'

He took the cell phone and brought up the number of the receiver hanging around Jeb's neck.

'Time to go, goat-boy. Crawl forward.'

Carney moved to the door and pulled it wide open.

The security guard and Denise Levene stared in horror at the hostages on their hands and knees.

'Who the fuck are you?' Carney demanded.

'Security.'

Carney laughed. 'Fuck you.' He pulled out his gun and shot the security guard without a thought. The gunshot reverberated throughout the building. Denise felt a wave of shock and nausea. She stepped backwards.

Carney stood at the entrance to the exhibition room. 'Ah, Dr Levene – you made it.'

'I understand you, Jack,' she said, trying to hide the tremble in her voice. 'You need help. We can get you help. This isn't the end of the line. There's a way out here.'

'What do you mean? This is it. The media is all run by Jews. No one tells the truth, that's why I've got to splash the truth all over the front page.'

'Is that why you're doing this, for attention?'

'American soldiers die every day, we report that, but every day, Americans here in America are being destroyed by the Jews running the country.'

'How?'

Carney walked across to the stairwell and leaned over. There was a solitary man walking up the stairs, but Carney could see all the way down into the foyer.

'I represent true American interests,' he shouted. Down in the foyer, horrified people stared up at the killer, paralyzed with fear. 'I am fighting to free America from the insidious influence of the Jew and his kind. These here are the Jewish scapegoats. These poor Jews are going to die for the sins of their brothers and sisters. They are going to be sacrificed.'

He turned to Denise. 'In my hand here, you can see the detonator. One move and I blow them, and the rest of us, sky-high. If my thumb presses dial, this little goat will erupt, splattering his offal all over you. So back right off, Dr Levene, and watch the show.'

Carney pulled back. 'Keep walking, goats,' he commanded.

Jeb and the other eleven hostages started crawling towards the stairs.

Harper was at the far door of the exhibition room when he heard Carney talking and shouting. He then heard a woman's voice and realized that it was Denise. He could see the poor hostages, all stripped and tied with wire. Carney had lost his mind. He was going to go out in a blaze of hatred. There was no time to wait.

Harper saw the detonator in Carney's hand. Any trigger and Carney could blow them all to pieces. The security guard raised the thumb on his fist and raised his eyebrow. It was enough. Harper got it. The explosion was a single movement of his thumb.

Down below, on the marble floor, Harper could hear the sound of boots. Lots of boots. The cops were coming up the stairs. At this point, that was bad news. Carney would blow them all up.

Harper pushed off his shoes and started to move across the floor of the exhibition room, his Glock held out ready to take a headshot. Denise saw him move. She understood. 'Hey, Carney, you know what Lucy said in the ambulance?'

Carney turned. 'What did she say?'

'She said she thinks you're right.'

'What?'

'She doesn't understand why you took her. She's not a Jew.'

'Because she knows I am,' he said. 'I made that mistake in school, I made that mistake with Lucy. You tell someone you're a Jew and they shit all over you.'

'Damn right, they do,' said Denise.

Harper was five feet from Carney. His gun was aimed at his head. Carney caught one of the hostages glancing behind him and Harper saw him tense. A boxer knows muscles – and Harper had boxed for years. He knew what muscles did when they sensed danger, when they were about to move. And Harper saw Carney's right arm and shoulder flinch ever so slightly. The hand crease, the finger move.

Carney had just about begun to turn his head. Harper had the start on him and lowered his gun. He had to get the cell phone, but couldn't afford a struggle. In a struggle, everyone was dead. Even with a headshot, the thumb could press the button.

Harper moved in tight and pulled the trigger. The nozzle of his Glock was thirty centimeters from Carney's elbow and the bullet ripped the joint to pieces. Carney's body froze. Enough time for Harper's right hand to grab Carney and pull his thumb from the detonator.

The two of them slumped to the floor. Harper's left hand reached out towards Carney's right hand. Carney's arm was limp but his hand was still hard-gripped around the cell phone.

Denise Levene watched in stunned awe. She didn't move. Her mouth just opened wide.

The room went silent. They were all waiting for the blast. Harper's right hand was firmly around Carney's thumb. Harper's left hand slowly prized the cell phone, finger by finger, from Carney's grip.

Harper suddenly realized he needed to breathe. He'd been holding his breath the whole time he'd walked across the room. Maybe two whole minutes. He breathed in deeply, took Carney's other hand and crushed it with his boot until the Luger dropped. Harper grabbed it and rolled away from Carney with the gun. He held up the cell phone.

He looked at Jeb. 'It's okay. Keep calm. I got it. Denise, untie these people.'

Harper checked Carney and cuffed him. They could deal with him later. Denise and Harper moved across to the hostages. Behind them, Aaron Goldenberg reached the top of the stairs. He could see Jack Carney lying on the ground. All he could feel was anger and pain. He wanted this man dead. He stopped and stood over Carney. 'You know who I am?'

'Yes,' said Carney.

'Where's my daughter?'

'She's dead. You're all dead.'

Aaron pointed the gun at Jack Carney's head. 'Then I'm going to kill you.'

'Then do it, Jew.'

Denise turned and saw the gun rise and tremble. She called out, 'Aaron, stop, don't do it! Don't ruin this now!'

'After what he's done,' said Aaron, 'why shouldn't I kill him?'

Aaron's hand was shaking. His finger tightened around the trigger.

Denise was next to him now. 'Aaron – we got Abby. She's alive. Abby's alive. Don't throw it away now. She's okay. I mean it – I've seen her.'

Aaron Goldenberg seemed not to hear. Then his head turned. He looked at Denise. 'Where is she?'

'Brooklyn Memorial.'

Aaron Goldenberg dropped the gun and ran towards the stairs.

Epilogue

Crown Heights, Brooklyn
March 15, 2.29 p.m.

Harper rested on a bench next to a paramedic. There wasn't anything wrong with him physically, but he was shaken. All those dead and dying bomb victims, and then the killer's capacity for more. It was only beginning to sink in. He stared around him and tried to remember what he had felt as he watched the cops hustle Carney into a police truck and slam the door.

He felt good. That was it.

He looked at Denise. He was holding her hand as they sat in silence and stared at the scene.

Denise was still pumping from the adrenalin rush. 'We got him,' she said. 'We nailed him. This feels good.'

'You are something else,' Harper said. 'I don't know how you do it, but you do it. You nailed him, Denise. You.'

'*We* nailed him, Tom. We're a team, right?'

'The best,' said Harper. 'How did Aaron sound?'

'Like a man waking up from a nightmare into paradise. They're both going to be okay.'

'He saw her?'

'Yeah, he saw her. He's dancing on air. He said they just hugged for the first hour. Just hugged and cried.' Denise paused. 'She wasn't . . . the doctor told him that Carney hadn't touched her. It's good to know. It'll make the recovery easier. Abby's mother is on the way over now.'

'He was attracted to her, right? That's why he took her, isn't it?'

'Partly. She was similar to Lucy, but yeah, he desired her and he wanted to control it. Actually, he wanted to destroy it, as if he could destroy his lust by destroying the object of his lust. It's a crazy case.'

'People try to destroy love, right, because love makes them feel weak. It's similar, isn't it?'

Denise looked across the street, the carnage still in evidence everywhere. 'I think you're right. He loved Lucy in some way, but I guess whatever she did, he'd never felt loved, so the brutality and control started up.'

'How did he keep it hidden for so long?'

'Working Hate Crime, I suppose. Finding a job where he was meeting sickos like himself every day and seeing punishment every day. Maybe that's what kept him straight for so long.'

'You think he might've been doing this a lot longer if he wasn't a cop?'

'I think he might have cracked earlier, yeah,' said Denise.

'We got some details from his lock-up. I've just been on to Garcia. They found his boots. He didn't ditch them. All cut up with wire. They also got some information on his case-files.'

'What did they find?' asked Denise.

'He had been letting Section 88 off the hook for years, allowing them to terrorize the community while offering up half-baked investigations. He liked to meet the victims. To see the aftermath, the Jewish community in tears, in fear. Section 88 were like his own attack hounds. He let them run the streets of Brooklyn and walked after them, free of any suspicion, looking at the pain they caused.'

'And the killings?' asked Denise.

'Section 88 weren't killers. He did it all himself. He even set up that lowlife doing time for Esther Haeber's murder. That's going to have to be looked at again.'

'What about Heming?'

'Heming owed Carney, I guess, for letting his team roam the streets. Carney used him to get him barbed wire and trucks. He must've always figured that if we started to link the killings, then Section 88 would be the prime suspect.'

'They were for a time. He read it all like a pro.'

'He was trained to be a pro, that's what kept him in the game.'

Eddie Kasper came over to them. 'My favorite pair,' he said. 'I got to congratulate you two. How you feeling?'

'Good, Eddie,' said Harper.

'You going to wash some time soon?' asked Eddie.

'Some time soon.'

'That's good. I like my heroes clean, Detective Harper. Nice and clean.'

'Why did he do it, that's what I'd like to understand?' said Harper. 'We all grow up with problems and we learn to fight them, right?'

'The absence of love, Tom, that's the breeding ground. Hated and abandoned at an early age. It makes self-hatred turn into something deeply damaged and vicious. And yeah, he's also an alpha male, isn't he? So he's got all that capacity to be something but inside, he feels like a loser, a man who'll never fit in. Such men turn to Nazism because it's such a strong image. They need that cloak to cover up all the pain and anger. For a while, the hate makes them feel normal, like all that anger has a purpose. Self-hatred needs a hell of a lot of power and glory and murder to convince it that it's worthwhile.'

A hand appeared on Harper's left shoulder.

'Sorry, Detective, sorry, ma'am, we need to talk to you both.'

Harper and Levene looked up.

'You need to talk to us *now*?' said Denise.

Harper blinked into the sunlight. Two guys stared down on him, both over six foot, both wearing shades and dark blue suits.

'Come on,' said Harper. 'They want the paperwork.'

Harper checked his annoyance. It was no good getting riled. He'd done his fighting. He had, Denise had, and they'd both come up good. Not Jack Carney, though. He'd been fighting something else. Some deep, dark inheritance. His own personality, the abuse he had suffered – his own failures, of course, but it was something bigger than that: the state-sanctioned evil that he'd inherited from reading about it in the past.

The attraction of evil had caught Jack Carney; it had caught and tangled up all the hatred he felt for himself and forced all that hatred on to another target. His life was over, but the forces that animated him were not dead. Harper looked at the blackened walls of the buildings along the street. The battles were still out there to be fought and won.

Harper stood, feeling the downside of the adrenalin kick, and let himself be led away from the chaos, still holding Denise's hand.

He saw Captain Frank Lafayette running across, his face red and heaving. Harper smiled. 'I got to debrief,' he said. 'Can the disciplinary hearing wait?'

'Fuck that, Tom. I just wanted to . . . I just wanted to see my best cop. You did us proud.'

'You're welcome,' said Harper. 'Can you believe it?'

'Which part?' said Lafayette.

'A cop – that part, the part that destroys the faith in the system.'

'Cop or anything else, this isn't about his day job. This is about a sick man who sought out the job to allow him to hunt as he worked. You don't get much more cynical than that.'

'You think he thought about it from the start?'

'Yeah, I do. He abused the system, sure. He got through, sure. He'll provoke a whole barrage of "it must never happen again" thoughts and articles. There will be outrage, disgust and pain. From the Jewish community especially. A cop who's meant to protect, who does the opposite. The powerful using their position to abuse and murder.'

Harper glanced at Denise. 'It'll take decades to undo this kind of betrayal of trust. You'd think this would be a stark message to all those racists and extremists, but a few years down the line, it will happen again. We always say we'll never forget and we always fucking do.'

'Not everyone forgets,' said Denise. 'Not you. Not me. Not the vast majority.'

'The vast majority aren't going to bring up Becky Glass's two kids,' said Harper.

'No, but they pay to keep cops like you on the streets so that degenerates like Carney get taken down.'

'I hope they're okay, that's all,' said Harper. 'Ruth, Jerry and Abby. I just hope they can get through this. You got to have hope, right?'

'You've given them more than hope, Tom. You've given them an ending.'

'I'm hoping I've given them something else as well,' he said as he turned to her.

'And what's that?' asked Denise.

'A new beginning,' said Harper as he smiled.

Acknowledgements

Thank you to everyone out there who has read my books. I'm grateful for all your reviews and comments which always make me want to write more and try out new ideas. I hope you enjoy them.

Thank you to my wife. For everything – from just putting up with me to continuing to inspire the best in me, and of course for reading draft after draft and for all the great suggestions and necessary corrections. Thanks to my children. You're just the best. I feel very lucky to be able to write surrounded by such support. Thanks also to Laura, my American adviser, for all her help. A huge thanks to my whole family who continue to forgive me for neglecting them!

Thank you to my agent, Andrew Gordon, for his continued enthusiasm, good sense and clear guidance. His knowledge of what's right and what works has helped to make this book as good as it possibly can be. Thank you to the whole team at David Higham Associates who have helped get this book to print.

Thanks to the brilliant team at Headline, who manage to make everything about book publication feel personal and important. Thank you to all those in Marketing, Publicity and Sales who have done such a brilliant job in getting this book out there. I am most indebted, of course, to my editor, Vicki Mellor. Vicki has incredibly good judgement and her intuition and guidance have helped shape and form this book and me, as a writer. Thanks, Vicki.

Every book involves a struggle, but this one has also been a thrill to write. I hope you enjoy it. All of us had great fun in the creation but we're having even more fun now it's done.